Fou
Four
Mills & Boon is thrilled to p

A

Royal

WEDDING

Four brand-new, irresistible romances
from beloved authors

TRISH MOREY, CAITLIN CREWS,
NINA HARRINGTON & RAYE MORGAN

Dear Readers,

At the end of 2009 when we were thinking about the books we wanted to publish in 2011, we had no idea that there would be a real royal wedding in April. But how exciting and how lovely!

We wish Prince William and his beautiful bride every happiness.

We hope that you will all be entertained by the four very different novellas in this perfectly timed super collection.

Also, to celebrate this historic event, Mills & Boon have created a special ebook collection: Royal Weddings... through the ages. Read about the future king's ancestors and the people who helped bring their special days together. Seven couples, seven marriages, seven stories for you to enjoy! Visit www.millsandboon.co.uk.

Enjoy!

The Editors

A *Royal* WEDDING

TRISH
MOREY

CAITLIN
CREWS

NINA
HARRINGTON

RAYE
MORGAN

MILLS & BOON

DID YOU PURCHASE THIS BOOK WITHOUT A COVER?

If you did, you should be aware it is **stolen property** as it was reported *unsold and destroyed* by a retailer. Neither the author nor the publisher has received any payment for this book.

All the characters in this book have no existence outside the imagination of the author, and have no relation whatsoever to anyone bearing the same name or names. They are not even distantly inspired by any individual known or unknown to the author, and all the incidents are pure invention.

All Rights Reserved including the right of reproduction in whole or in part in any form. This edition is published by arrangement with Harlequin Enterprises II B.V./S.à.r.l. The text of this publication or any part thereof may not be reproduced or transmitted in any form or by any means, electronic or mechanical, including photocopying, recording, storage in an information retrieval system, or otherwise, without the written permission of the publisher.

This book is sold subject to the condition that it shall not, by way of trade or otherwise, be lent, resold, hired out or otherwise circulated without the prior consent of the publisher in any form of binding or cover other than that in which it is published and without a similar condition including this condition being imposed on the subsequent purchaser.

® and ™ are trademarks owned and used by the trademark owner and/or its licensee. Trademarks marked with ® are registered with the United Kingdom Patent Office and/or the Office for Harmonisation in the Internal Market and in other countries.

Mills & Boon, an imprint of Harlequin (UK) Limited,
Eton House, 18-24 Paradise Road, Richmond, Surrey TW9 1SR

A ROYAL WEDDING © Harlequin Enterprises II B.V./S.à.r.l 2011

The Storm Within © Trish Morey 2011
The Reluctant Queen © Caitlin Crews 2011
The Ordinary King © Nina Harrington 2011
The Prince's Forbidden Love © Helen Conrad 2011

ISBN: 978 0 263 88957 4

012-0511

Harlequin (UK) policy is to use papers that are natural, renewable and recyclable products and made from wood grown in sustainable forests. The logging and manufacturing processes conform to the legal environmental regulations of the country of origin.

Printed in the UK
by CPI Mackays, Chatham, ME5 8TD

The Storm Within

TRISH MOREY

Trish Morey is an Australian who's also spent time living and working in New Zealand and England. Now she's settled with her husband and four young daughters in a special part of South Australia, surrounded by orchards and bushland, and visited by the occasional koala and kangaroo. With a lifelong love of reading, she penned her first book at the age of eleven, after which life, career, and a growing family kept her busy until once again she could indulge her desire to create characters and stories—this time in romance. Having her work published is a dream come true. Visit Trish at her website, www.trishmorey.com.

Look for *The Heir from Nowhere*, Trish Morey's most recent novel from Mills & Boon® Modern™.

Dear Reader,

There's something about a craggy Mediterranean island topped with a looming castle that really appeals to me as a setting. The combination of remote with imposing might well be a mirror to the hero, who is as unapproachable and intimidating as the island setting itself.

Count Alessandro Volta is as unapproachable and intimidating as they come. Scarred both physically and mentally from a tragedy that left him the only survivor, Alessandro shuns society and the media and takes to self-imposed exile on his storm-ridden island home. Until a discovery is made in the secret tunnels beneath his castle, the lost pages from an ancient book of healing.

The woman who comes to evaluate the find is not the crusty academic he was expecting and suddenly Alessandro finds his escape from the world challenged by Dr Grace Hunter, a passionate scientist whose unwelcome presence threatens to break down the dark shields around him and thrust him once again into the light.

But can the fabled book of healing live up to its reputation and heal a heart so savagely broken? And will this unlikely couple ever earn their summer royal wedding?

I hope you enjoy finding out.

With very best wishes,

Trish

x

With grateful thanks to the real Archival Survival
team, Angela Henrickson and Geoff McIntyre,
and especially to Annie for all her help with
a project that was so totally left field.

I'm not sure if this is what you envisioned Annie,
when I first put the premise of this story to you, but
thank you so much for your advice and assistance
and for your sheer enthusiasm! Any mistakes or
omissions are purely author error.

Thank you Annie!

CHAPTER ONE

SHE was coming. From his office overlooking the sea, Count Alessandro Alonso Leopold Volta watched the launch approach the island that was home to Castello di Volta and the seat of the Volta family for more than five hundred years.

The boat hadn't even docked and already the bitter taste of bile hovered menacingly at the back of his throat.

He growled. He hated visitors, hated the way they brought the smell of the outside world with them, as if clinging to their very clothes. He hated their wide-eyed stares and their looks of horror when they first saw his scars, horror that bleached their faces white and sent their eyes skidding away to the floor or to the nearest work of art. Anywhere, it seemed, that wasn't his face.

But most of all he hated their pity, for the horror always gave way to pity.

He preferred the horror.

His hands curled into fists at his side. He didn't want anyone's pity.

He didn't want anyone. *Period.*

The launch slowed, rocking sideways on the bumpy water as it neared the dock and its wash caught up with it. He ground his teeth together and turned away, knowing that this time he had no choice. The package found tucked away in the caves deep beneath the castle had seen to that.

Why here? he asked himself again. Why, of all the places in the world, of all the places that would welcome the attention such a discovery would bring, why had what could be the lost pages from the fabled *Salus Totus*, the legendary *Book of Wholeness*, had to turn up here? When had fate taken to wearing a clown's mask?

He grunted his displeasure and dropped into the chair behind his desk. One week Professor Rousseau had promised him the job would take. No longer than one week to examine and document the pages, to determine whether they were genuine, and if so to stabilise their condition until they could be taken away and prepared for display. One short yet no doubt interminable week, with a stranger clattering around the castle, asking questions and expecting answers, and probably expecting him to be civil in the process.

He looked down at the file he'd been reviewing before the onshore wind had carried with it the thumping beat of an approaching engine, but his skin pulled achingly tight over his jaw and the words before him danced and spun and could have been printed in a different language for all the sense they made.

It could be worse, he rationalised, clamping down on the rising black cloud of his resentment, forcing himself to focus on the résumé in his hands. He flipped the page, turning to the photograph of the woman he was expecting. Reputedly one of the best conservators in the business, Professor Rousseau boasted more than forty years' experience in the industry. And with short grey hair cut helmet-style around features that looked as if they'd been sculpted from parchment rather than skin, she looked the kind of person who enjoyed books more than people. If he had to put up with a visitor to his island, he could do much worse than this shrivelled-up scientist.

Maybe. And yet still this heavy sense of foreboding persisted in his gut; still the jagged line of his scar burned and stung, as if someone had dragged their nails down his face and chest and sliced open his wound.

One week, he thought, touching fingers to his burning cheek, half surprised when they didn't come away wet and sticky with blood. One week with a stranger poking around his castle, asking questions, getting under his feet. And whoever she was, and however she looked, it would be one week too long.

CHAPTER TWO

DR GRACE HUNTER TOOK a gulp of sea air and did her best to ignore the butterflies that had seized control of her stomach and were right now threatening to carry it away. Excitement, she told herself. Anticipation. Maybe a little bit of motion sickness too, given the way the launch bounced and lurched over the chop.

But excitement. Definitely there was excitement.

The *Salus Totus* was the Holy Grail, the Troy of the conservatorial world, and the plum job of examining the pages discovered had fallen right into her lap. If the pages were authentic, and indeed the fabled long-lost pages, if she could prove they were no hoax, her studies of it and the papers she produced on it could make her career.

She *should* feel excited.

And yet there was something else beneath the thrill of the chase. Something else lurking below the anticipation of holding a page written hundreds of years ago, of feeling that connection between writer and reader that transcended the centuries and rendered time meaningless. And that something else twisted in her gut until the butterflies turned into a serpent that coiled and squirmed in her belly.

Difficult, Professor Rousseau had described Count Alessandro Volta, during her unexpected and rapid-fire phone call from the hospital yesterday, and when Grace had asked what she meant there'd been a distinct hesitation on the line, before other muffled voices had intruded, and she'd added a rushed, 'I have to go. You'll be fine.'

Sure. She'd be fine. She gulped in air as the boat ploughed resolutely through the chop and headed for the relative safety of the shore. *Relative*, because nothing about the rocky island and the imposing castle set upon it looked remotely welcoming. Not the rocky shore or the towering cliffs or the clouds that seemed to hover ominously above the brooding castle in an otherwise clear sky.

She frowned up at them. Lucky she was a scientist, really, and not some paranoid panic merchant who saw portents of doom in every swirling cloud or flutter of apprehension. She was here to do a job after all.

The skipper cut the engines, letting the wash carry the boat into the dock, while the other crew member secured a line, taming the motion before starting to offload cargo onto the dock, her duffel bag amongst it. She gathered her things, her leather backpack and her briefcase containing the Professor's letter of introduction, along with her specialist tools, glancing up at the castle that sprawled so arrogantly across the clifftop. From sea level the sheer scale of the place was daunting. Up close it must be intimidating, with its high walls punctuated at intervals by perimeter towers topped with crenellated battlements, a central tower rising high above it all, almost sending out a challenge—*enter if you dare.*

Welcoming? Definitely not. A movement startled her and she jumped as a figure unexpectedly stepped from the shadows thrown by the rocky escarpment into the bright sunlight. Through grizzled eyes in a leathery face the man looked her over as one might consider an unwelcome stray dog found whimpering on the doorstep, before he grabbed her duffel in one dinner-plate sized hand and flung it in the back of a rusty Jeep. He made a lunge for the briefcase in her hand and she pulled her arm away. There was no way she was letting Mr Sensitive loose on her tools.

'Thank you, but I'm good with this one.'

He grunted. 'You are not who we were expecting,' he said in gravelly English, his accent as thick as his ham-hock biceps, before he muttered a few words in Italian to the skipper and hauled himself into the driver's seat.

'No. Professor Rousseau sends her apologies. Her mother—'

'The Count will not be pleased.'

She had no comeback to that, other than to swing herself onto the withered and cracked upholstery of the passenger seat before he could drive away without her.

The Jeep lurched into life and she clutched her briefcase tighter in her lap as the vehicle tore up the narrow road. If you could call it a road, Grace thought, as it narrowed to little more than a one-lane track, zig-zagging up the cliff-face. She made the mistake of looking out of the car as he took another impossibly tight bend, and saw stones spraying over the edge of the cliff, spilling towards the boat now shrinking below. She squeezed her eyes shut.

'Do you think maybe you could drive a little slower?'

He shook his head gravely, muttered something under his breath.

'Only I would like to get to look at the discovery before I die.'

'The Count,' he almost grunted, ignoring her attempt at humour, 'he is expecting the Professor.'

'Yes, you said. I tried to explain—'

'He will not be pleased.'

Conversation was clearly not his forte. She tried to concentrate on the spectacular view across the expanse of Mediterranean to where the coastline of Italy was just visible in the distance, while trying not to think about the height of the cliff they were scaling that made such a magnificent view possible. But it was the subject of her driver's concern who stole her concentration and reminded her that the real reason for this coiling uneasiness in her gut was not down to anticipation at working on an ancient text, or motion sickness, or even the brooding castle, but dread.

Therese Rousseau had warned her. She'd said he was difficult and the driver's words did nothing to suggest the Professor had been unfair in her description. In fact, if anything, maybe she'd been a trifle flattering.

What exactly happened when the Count was not pleased? What was it that she had to look forward to?

At least the Jeep had managed to scale the cliff. The track was widening and now bordered in rocks she could tell had once been painted white, though now they were chipped and faded, their paint worn from exposure to the salt-laden air.

She shivered—the air was noticeably cooler at this height— and looked up in time to see the sun disappear behind the darkening clouds. And despite knowing in her brain that it meant nothing, that it was purely a meteorological phenomenon she was witnessing and not some kind of omen, even though she fought it with all she knew about the world, still she felt an unwanted and illogical sliver of fear slip down her spine.

The massive iron gates clanging shut behind them as they entered the castle grounds did nothing to assuage her unease. Now tension had her tightly wound, but she kept her breathing light as her driver crunched the gears while circling a tiered fountain featuring water nymphs and dolphins—a fountain that was as dry and neglected as the border of leggy, unkempt rosemary bushes that surrounded it.

Everywhere, it seemed, was shrouded in neglect, as if nothing had been touched for years.

And she wondered how anything as fragile as a book had survived in this place for the centuries it was reputed to have.

A miracle?

Or a curse?

This time the tremor seemed to chill her very bones. Great, she thought, doing her utmost to shake off the irrational sense of impending danger. So much for priding herself on being a logical scientist.

The Jeep jerked to a halt and the driver jumped out. 'Come,' he instructed, not bothering with her duffel this time, but leaving it to her to retrieve as he pushed open giant timber doors that stretched at least twelve feet high and yet still looked minuscule when compared to the mountainous castle walls that dwarfed them.

And then they were inside and the temperature dropped again. Her footsteps over the massive flagstones echoed in the vast, empty entry hall. Or maybe that was just her heartbeat racing fast and loud…

For a thickset man, her guide moved fast, his short legs carrying him surprisingly quickly up a flight of stairs that looked as if they'd come straight from Sleeping Beauty's castle. 'Where are you taking me?' she asked from the bottom of the stairs, but he gave no answer, and she didn't need it to know there was no hope of him taking her directly to the documents she'd come to examine.

The Count, she knew. The same Count who she'd been warned repeatedly would not be pleased. She sighed and started up the stairs behind him, lugging both her briefcase and her duffel. Might as well get the unpleasantries over and done with in that case. Maybe then she could get to work.

She followed him along a long passageway. The walls were dressed with rich burgundy drapes, between which hung portraits of, she assumed, counts long gone. Superiority shone from their steely eyes, along with a sense of entitlement for the world and all its riches. The Counts of Volta, she surmised, were not of modest, unassuming stock. But then why should they be modest, with potent looks that were as masculinely beautiful as they were darkly dangerous?

Slight differences distinguished one from another—a slight tilt of nose, an angle of jaw—and yet all of them in that long, seemingly endless row bore the same dark eyes and brows, topped by the same distinct hairline that intruded onto their temples in sharp points, almost like a shadow cast from… She stopped herself, refusing the link she'd made in her mind. They so did *not* resemble horns! She was being ridiculous even thinking it.

Besides, she'd researched the latest Count Volta late last night, after the Professor had called with her news, when both the excitement of the task ahead and the cryptic 'You'll be fine' had banished any thoughts of sleep. And she'd remembered then why his name had seemed vaguely familiar, remembered hearing around her eighteenth birthday news reports of the party boat explosion off the Costa Smerelda. Last night she'd read again of the shocking death toll and of the miracle survivor who'd lost his fiancée and his friends that night and who, scarred and bereft, had walked away and turned his back on both a promising career as a concert pianist and society.

The media had pursued him for a while, she'd read, seeking exclusives and exposés, before apparently tiring of the fruitless chase and moving on to juicier, more obliging celebrity prey. And so, entrenched in his self-imposed exile on his island home, he'd slipped into obscurity.

Who could blame him for cutting himself off from the world after an accident like that? Maybe it was no surprise he was 'difficult'. But it said something for the man that he hadn't kept the discovery of the documents secret. He would have known the potential for the discovery to once again focus the world's attention squarely on him. No wonder he'd insisted on only one specialist, and for the job to be completed inside a week.

Which was fine with her. She didn't want to hang around a crotchety old hermit and his crumbling castle a moment longer than necessary. She wouldn't get in his way and hopefully he'd stay out of hers.

Her guide came to an abrupt halt, rapping briefly on a pair of doors before poking his head inside one of them, leaving her no choice but to cool her heels behind him. 'She's here but it's not the Professor,' she heard him say. 'I've told the boat not to leave until you're ready.' And then he swept back past her without a glance, as if fleeing in case he was blamed for collecting the wrong baggage.

So that was why he hadn't brought her bag in and she'd had to lug it herself—because he thought she wasn't staying.

If she'd needed anything to dispel any remaining shred of apprehension, her introduction as some kind of afterthought fitted the bill perfectly. She pushed open the door he'd left ajar.

'My name is Grace Hunter and I have a letter of introduction from Professor...' Her words shrivelled up in a throat suddenly drier than the fountain outside, and it might very well have been clogged with stranded sea nymphs and beached dolphins.

Where was the crotchety old hermit she'd been expecting? The modern-day Robinson Crusoe complete with beard and tattered clothes? Someone who matched the air of neglect that shrouded the rest of this barren island and its crumbling castle? But there was nothing tattered about the man who stood looking out of the window across the room from her now, nothing neglected.

'...Rousseau.'

The name fell heavily into the empty space between them. He stood still as a statue, his hands clasped behind his stiff back, clad in a suit tailored so superbly to his tall, lean body it almost looked part of him.

But it was his profile that captured her attention, and the clear similarities to his forebears lining the portrait gallery. His strong nose and resolute jaw, and the unmistakable mark of the Counts of Volta, the clearly defined dark hairline that intruded in sharp points at his temples. And he was every bit as powerfully beautiful as those who had gone before. Which made no sense at all...

She swallowed. 'Count Volta?'

CHAPTER THREE

ACROSS the room she saw the flare of his nostrils. She heard his intake of air. She was even convinced she saw the grind of his jaw as he stared seemingly fixedly through the window. And then he turned, and the truth of his scars, the horror of his injuries, confronted her full-on.

A jagged line ripped down one side of his face from the corner of his eye through his jaw and down his neck, where it thankfully disappeared under the high collar of his jacket.

She gasped. She'd seen scars before. She'd witnessed the results of man's inhumanity to man during a year where youthful idealism had sent her to one of the world's hellholes and spat her out at the end, cynical and dispirited. She'd thought she'd seen it all. And she'd seen worse. Much worse. And yet the sheer inequality of this man's scars—that one side of his face would be so utterly perfect and the other so tragically scored by scars—it seemed so wrong.

His eyes narrowed, glinting like water on marble. 'Didn't anyone ever tell you it's rude to stare?'

Chastened, she blinked and scrabbled for the pocket of

her briefcase and the letter from the Professor she'd come armed with. 'Of course. Count Volta, Professor Rousseau apparently tried several times to contact you last night to tell you that she couldn't make it.' She pulled the envelope free and crossed the floor to hand it to him.

He looked down at the letter in her hand as if it was a poisoned chalice. 'You were not invited here.'

'Professor Rousseau's letter will, I'm sure, explain everything.'

'You are not welcome.' He turned back to the window, putting his back to her. 'Bruno will arrange for your immediate return to the mainland.'

His decision was so abrupt—so unjust!—that for a moment she felt the wind knocked out of her sails. He was dismissing her? Sending her away? Denying her the opportunity of working on the most important discovery since the Dead Sea Scrolls for no reason?

No way! 'I'm not going anywhere.' The words burst from her lips before she'd had a chance to think, a chance to stop them. 'I am here to do a job and I will not leave until it is done.'

He spun round and once again she was confronted with the two sides of him—each side of his face so different, each side compelling viewing, the masculinely perfect and the dreadfully scarred. Beauty and the beast, it occurred to her, co-existing under the one skin.

'Did you hear me? I said Bruno will arrange for your return.'

It was all she could do not to stamp her foot. 'And I said I'm not leaving!'

One arm swept in a wide arc. 'I have no dealings with you. My arrangement was with Professor Rousseau.'

'No. According to the documents, your arrangement was with her business, Archival Survival. When the Professor was unable to come, she contracted me.'

He grunted, no way about to concede the point. 'So what is her excuse for being unable to fulfil her contractual obligations herself?'

'If you'd read this letter you'd know. Her mother is in hospital after suffering a major stroke and she's rushed to be with her while she clings to life. Admittedly, as excuses go, that's pretty thin. Clearly it's more about inconveniencing *you*.'

If his eyes were lasers, she figured, with the heated glare he gave her she'd be wearing holes right now, and she wondered if she'd overstepped the mark. She'd grown up in a family that prided itself on being straight-talking. Over the years she'd learned to curb that trait while in civilised company. The Count, she'd already decided, for all his flash clothes and a portrait gallery full of titled ancestors, didn't qualify.

'I expected an expert. I do not intend spending a week babysitting someone's apprentice.'

She sucked in air, hating the fact it was tinged with a hint of sandalwood and spice, with undertones of something else altogether more musky, hating the possibility that it might come from him, hating the possibility that there might be something about him she approved of when the rest of him was so damned objectionable.

But that was still okay, she figured, because finding something she might possibly like only made her more resentful towards him. 'Seeing you refuse to read this letter, where all the facts are set out in black and white, perhaps I should spell it out for you? I have a Masters in Fine Arts from Melbourne University and a PhD in Antiquities from Oxford, where my thesis was on the preservation and conservation of ancient texts and the challenge of discerning fraud where it was perpetrated centuries ago. So if there's an apprentice on this island right now, I don't think it's me. Does that make you feel more comfortable?'

He arched one critical eyebrow high. 'You look barely out of high school.'

'I'm twenty-eight years old. But don't take my word for it. Perhaps you'd like to check my passport?'

Dust motes danced on the slanted sunlit air between them, oblivious of the tension—dust motes that disappeared with those slanting rays as the sun was swallowed up by a cloud and the room darkened. She resisted the urge to shiver, resisted that damned illogical brain cell that suggested there was some connection between the Count's dark looks and the weather. And instead she decided that his momentary silence meant assent.

'And so right now I'd like to get to work. After all, I believe you want this text taken off your hands as soon as possible, and we've already wasted enough time, don't you agree? Perhaps you could arrange someone to show me to the documents so I might get started?'

He scowled as he took the letter from her hands then, scanning its contents, finding everything was as she said and finding nothing to arm him with the ammunition to demand she leave.

He wanted her gone.

He didn't want women around the place. Not young women, and definitely not halfway to pretty. He had his fix of women once a month, when the launch brought across a local village woman. He never asked her name; she never offered it. Each time she would just wait for him naked in the guest-suite bed, then throw back the covers and close her eyes...

And afterwards the launch would take her back to her village, considerably better off than before she had made the crossing.

No, Alessandro had no need for women.

He shrugged and tossed the letter down on his wide desk. What did it matter what the letter said or didn't say? 'I said you are not welcome here, Ms Hunter.'

She stiffened to stone right where she stood, her mouth pursing. '*Dr* Hunter, actually. And I will ensure my stay is as brief as possible. I have no desire to stay any longer than necessary where I am not welcome, I can assure you.'

He sniffed at the correction as he regarded her solemnly. She looked like a woman who had no desires, period. Sure, she was younger than the dried-up Professor, but with her scraped-back hair and that pursed mouth, and in khaki pants and T-shirt, it wasn't as if she was anything like the women who had once graced his arm and his bed.

God knew, another twenty years or so of staring into her desiccated papers and she'd probably be as dried up and crusty as the Professor. Maybe he had nothing to worry about.

And she was right about one thing: he did want the find off his hands as quickly as possible. If the Professor proved unable to do it personally because of her ailing mother someone else would have to be found, all of it spelling delay after delay.

He ground his teeth together. The longer he waited, the more likely news of the discovery would filter out. The last thing he wanted was the media sniffing around again, turning the place into some kind of fish tank.

'Then make your assessment as brief as possible and make us all happy by leaving.' He turned back to gaze out of the window again, knowing she would do exactly that. People always ran from him. And then he frowned, remembering the way her big blue eyes had stared at him...

Yes, she'd been shocked. But where was the revulsion? Where was the pity? Instead she'd examined him as one might regard some kind of science project.

And the snarling beast inside him didn't like that notion any better.

'I'd like to see the book now.'

He turned back, surprised she hadn't changed her mind and taken the opportunity to flee while his back was turned. She was surprisingly feisty, this one, holding her ground when many men twice her age and size would have gone running for the hills. Did she want the opportunity of examining and documenting this discovery so much that she had somehow summoned the will to fight for it? Or was she always this feisty?

Her eyes held his, bright and blue and cold as ice. Once women had looked at him with lust and desire. But that was long ago. There was no lust in Ms Hunter's eyes, no desire— or at least not for him. But there was something else he read in them. The yearning to become famous? Probably. This discovery, if it proved authentic, would probably make a young conservator's career.

'It's not all it's cracked up to be,' he said.

She blinked—a fan of black lashes against her peaches and cream complexion. And it occurred to him that it was almost a shame to condemn such translucent skin to the Professor's wrinkled fate. 'Pardon?'

A rap on the door and the reappearance of Bruno curtailed any response. 'The boat wishes to leave,' he grunted. 'Are you finished with the girl?'

And with the question came Alessandro's first smile of the day. In one way he was—though not the way his valet was clearly expecting. He'd agreed she could stay, and this meeting was now over. He'd planned to have Bruno take her to the book. He'd need to have little more to do with her. But *was* he finished with her?

Maybe not.

What would it take to make her run? What would it take to shake up those frosty blue eyes and strip off that sterile scientific cladding she wrapped herself so tightly in and see what really lay beneath? Besides, if he admitted the truth, he could do with a little entertainment. The woman might provide some mild amusement. She was only here for a few days. What possible harm could it do?

'No, I'm not finished with our charming guest, Bruno.' And this time he directed his words at her. 'In fact, I do believe I've scarcely begun. Come, *Dr* Hunter, and I'll show you to your precious documents.'

She left her luggage and briefcase where he directed, following him through a tangle of passageways, down wooden stairs that shifted and creaked under their footfall, and then down again—stone steps this time, that were worn into hollows by the feet of generations gone before—until she was sure they must be well below ground level, and the walls were lined with rock. And finally he stopped before a door that seemed carved from the stone itself.

He tugged on an iron ring set into the stone. 'Are you scared of the dark, Dr Hunter?' he asked over his shoulder, and she got the distinct impression he would love it if she were.

'No. That's never been a particular phobia of mine.'

'How fortunate,' he said, sounding as if he thought it was anything but. Then the door shifted open and she got a hint of what was to come—a low, dark passageway that sloped down through the rock. When he turned to her the crooked smile she'd seen in his office was back. 'Every castle should have at least one secret tunnel, don't you think?'

'I would have to say it's practically *de rigueur*, Count Volta.'

His smile slipped a little, she noted with satisfaction, almost as if she hadn't answered the way he'd expected. Tough. The fact was she *was* here, and with any luck she was on her way to the missing pages of the *Salus Totus*. Although what they were doing all the way down here…

A slow drip came from somewhere around her, echoing in the space, and while she wished she'd at least grabbed a jacket before descending into the stone world beneath the castle, it was the book she was more worried about now.

'You are taking me to the book?'

'Of course.'

'But what is it doing down here?'

'It was found down here.'

'And you left it here?'

His regarded her coldly, as if surprised she would question his decision. 'The caves have guarded their treasure for centuries. Why would I move it and risk damaging such a potentially precious thing?'

Plenty of reasons, she thought. Like the drip that echoed

around the chamber, speaking of moisture that could ruin ancient texts with mould and damp. Something so ancient, even if it proved to be a forgery, should be kept where the temperature and humidity could be regulated and it would be safe from things that scuttled and foraged in the night. She didn't expect the Count to necessarily know that, but she would have expected him to have had the sense to move the find somewhere safe.

Inside the chamber there was just enough light to see with the door open. She blinked, waiting for her eyes to adjust, but then he pulled the door closed behind them with a crunch and the light was swallowed up in inky blackness and there was nothing for her eyes to adjust to.

Afraid of the dark? No, she wasn't, but neither did she like being holed up in it. Not with him. She could hear his breathing, she could damn well smell that evocative masculine scent of his, and she dared not move for fear she might brush against him in the dark. She heard the scratch of something rough, caught a hint of phosphorus and saw a spark that burst into flame atop a torch he held. The shifting yellow light threw crazy shadows against the walls, illuminating a cable running overhead with light bulbs hanging sporadically.

'You couldn't have just turned on the lights, I suppose?'

'A storm last night knocked out the cable from the mainland, which is no doubt why your Professor could not contact me. Power is back on in the castle, but the caves will take longer. Don't you like the torchlight, Ms Hunter. I find it so much more—*atmospheric*.'

He had just enough accent to curl around the word, transforming it in a way that turned it somehow darkly sensual—something that put a peculiar shiver down her spine. Peculiar, because instead of the chill she'd expected it warmed her in places she didn't like to think about. Not around him. Shadows danced on the walls of the tunnel, light flickered against the unscarred side of his face, highlighting cheekbone and forehead and that sharply defined hairline, throwing his eyes into a band of black from which only a glint of amusement escaped.

And she could tell he was laughing at her.

Damn him.

'It's fine, I guess, if you're interested in atmosphere. Right now I'm more interested in getting a look at those pages.'

He gave a mock bow in the shadowed darkness. 'As you command,' he said, and led the way down the tunnel. Deeper and deeper through the winding channel through the rock they walked, footsteps echoing on the dusty floor, the yellow flame of the torch flickering in the cool air, lighting the way, but never far enough to see more than a few feet at a time. They passed other tunnels that dived away, left and right, and she wondered how you would ever find your way out if the light went out and you were alone down here. She paused to look over her shoulder at one such intersection, trying to get a glimpse of the path behind, but the darkness had swallowed up the view, along with her sense of direction, and she realised that she'd never find her way out alone.

Great. So she had no choice but to trust a man who didn't want her here and seemed to delight in making her uncomfortable—a man who was leading her through a maze of tunnels a Minotaur would be happy to call home with nothing but a lighted torch to find their way.

Bad call. Did she really want to think about Minotaurs and labyrinths now, when she was down here with a man whose broad shoulders filled the width of the tunnel? Especially when she thought about what had happened to the seven youths and seven maidens from Athens who'd been thrown into the labyrinth to their doom as a tribute to the Minoan king.

Maybe she should have brought a ball of string…

Something clapped down hard on her shoulder—his hand—and she panicked, every instinct telling her to flee. It was only its weight that kept her anchored to the ground.

'You don't want to get lost in here,' whispered a deep voice in her ear, his breath fanning her hair, warm in the cool tunnel air. 'We might never find you again.'

She turned slowly, hoping to calm her face and her rapid breathing before he could see just how much he'd frightened her, but she was fighting a losing battle on slowing her heart-rate, given what his proximity was doing to her nervous system and his scent was doing to her defences. 'You startled me,' she admitted, licking her lips as she looked up at him in the torchlight, struck again by the difference between one side of his face and the other—one side all strong, masculine lines and sharply defined places, the other so monstrously scarred.

His left eye had thankfully escaped the worst, she was close enough to see, and his strong nose and wide mouth were blessedly untouched. It was as if the skin of his cheek and neck had been torn apart and rejoined in a thick, jagged line that snaked up his throat and cheek and tapered to the corner of one eye.

Both those dark eyes narrowed as they looked down at her now. 'Come,' he said gruffly, dropping his hand from her shoulder and turning away.

Her shoulder felt inexplicably bereft—*cold*—the warmth from his long fingers replaced with a bone-deep chill, and she hugged her shoulders as she trailed behind him through the maze of tunnels, trying not to think of the weight of rock above their heads. The tunnels had clearly been here for a long time—surely the ceiling could hold just a little longer? Especially when they must be getting close to their goal.

A surge of adrenaline washed through her. Could the pages truly be from the lost copy of the *Salus Totus*? How complete would they be? Could she really be close to solving the mystery of generations? The mystery of the contents of those lost pages?

'Watch your step,' he said, then asked her to wait as he descended a short steep flight of stairs cut into the rock. At the bottom he turned, holding the torch above him so she could see her way down the narrow steps, but it was the hand he offered to her that looked the more threatening. A large hand, she noted. Tapered fingers. Would it be churlish to refuse? But there was nothing to be afraid of—she'd survived the last time he'd touched her, hadn't she?

And so she slipped her hand into his, felt his long fingers wrap around her own, and tried not to think too much about how warm they felt against her skin. How strong his grip. How secure.

'Thank you,' she said, lifting her eyes to his as she negotiated the last step, wondering at the suddenness with which he turned his face away, only to be distracted by the sudden space around them here, as the tunnel widened into a wide, low room. There were tables set around, and shelves built into the walls containing racks of bottles—dozens and dozens of bottles. 'What is this place?' she asked, stepping around him.

'Welcome to my wine cellar. Here you'll find every vintage of Vino de Volta going back to 1797.'

'Hell of a place for a wine cellar,' she mused, strolling

past the racks of bottles, pausing to peer at a label here and there, the lover of ancient and even not-so-ancient treasures inside her completely fascinated.

'There's more,' he said, 'through here.' He dipped his head under a low doorway leading to another room, this one more like a cavern, its walls similarly stacked.

She followed him in, made a wide circle as she took it all in. It was the perfect place for a wine cellar, the air cool and dry, with no telltale dripping. And a spark of excitement flashed through her. Because if it was the perfect place to store wine...

'Are they here?' she asked, unable to keep the excitement from her voice. 'Is this where the pages were found?'

Her enthusiasm lit up the cavern more effectively than any amount of torchlight. She was like a child, excited about a present she'd asked Santa for and for which she'd promised to be good, her eyes bright with expectation, a dancing flame alive on their surfaces.

And he felt a sudden twist in his gut that made him wheel away, for she was so vibrant and alive and everything that Adele had once been—everything that he no longer was.

Blackness surged up and threatened to swallow him whole; not the black of the caves but the blackness that came from within, the blackness that had been his constant companion since that night. He'd thought he'd learned to control it, but it was there, lurking in the scars that lined his face and body, lurking on the very edges of his sanity, waiting to seize control, and he cursed himself for giving in to the urge to amuse himself with her. Cursed himself for putting a hand to her slim shoulder. Cursed himself for wanting more and for then finding an excuse to take her fragile hand in his own.

It had been a long time since he'd touched a woman he hadn't had to pay.

Such a long time…

He dragged in one breath and then another, forcing the blackness back down, refusing to give in to its power, determined not to succumb. Not here. Not now. 'This way,' he managed to grind out, through a jaw that ached with the effort of those two simple words.

Behind him she blinked, letting go a breath she hadn't realised she'd been holding. What had just happened? For a while she'd imagined he was loosening up a bit around the edges, losing some of his antagonism and resentment towards her. She'd even sensed he was getting some kind of sick pleasure from his teasing about secret passageways and the atmospherics of torchlight.

And then suddenly he'd changed. In the blink of an eye his entire body had set rigid, his skin pulling tight over a face in which his eyes had turned harder than the stone walls that enclosed them. As he'd turned from her she'd witnessed the tortured expression that strained his features and in the shadow-laden light had turned the scarred side of his face into the mask of a monster. A legend, she told herself, her heart thumping as she was reminded again of the story of the Minotaur. *Just a legend*.

But she must have gasped, she must have made some small sound, for he turned back, studying her face, his eyes strangely satisfied with what he saw as he leaned closer to her. 'What's wrong, Dr Hunter? Do I frighten you at last?'

'No,' she said shakily, praying for composure, trying to block out thoughts of monsters and Minotaurs and the twisted maze of passageways that lay between her and freedom, wondering if he would chase her if she ran. *Wondering what he might do if do if he caught her.* 'No.' This time she said it with more certainty, even though her heart was still pumping furiously and her breathing too shallow. Once again she sought to regain control. 'I'm not afraid of you, Count Volta.'

He drew back momentarily on an intake of air, his lips curling to bare his teeth, before he exhaled in a rush as he came closer again. 'Then you should be, Dr Hunter. You should be.'

He was too close. She could feel the heat from his face and his breath against her skin. But, while her heart was thumping loudly, she realised it wasn't fear that was making her blood pound and her heart race.

It was the man himself.

And in spite of herself, in spite of his implicit threat, she felt herself drawn towards him, her skin prickling with awareness, her breasts strangely, *achingly* full.

And from somewhere deep inside her, some dark, dangerous place she hadn't known existed, she managed to summon a smile. 'If you want to frighten me, you'll have to do better than that.'

The torchlight flickered gold in his dark eyes, until she could almost imagine it dancing with the devil within—the devil that made him grind his teeth together as if he was battling with himself even as he leaned still closer. So close that his face was scant millimetres from hers. So close that his lips were a mere breath away...

CHAPTER FOUR

SHE heard his growl of frustration as he swung away, leaving her with only heated air scented by his musky scent and wondering shakily why she was trying to bait him, what she was trying to achieve. What was happening to her?

'Do you want to see these papers or not?' he said, already heading deeper into the secret cellar, and she thanked her lucky stars that one of them was thinking straight. For what had she been thinking? That he was going to kiss her? A man she'd met barely an hour ago? A man who had made it plain she was not welcome here, who had objected to her presence and then set out to make her uncomfortable in his?

Difficult? The description didn't come close. The sooner she was finished with her assessment and away from the Isola de Volta, and its scarred Count, the better.

Tentatively she followed him into a smaller cavern, the doorway rammed firm with beams the size of tree trunks. The room was sparsely furnished, with an old table and two chairs. There was a well-thumbed pack of cards in one corner, and what looked like a bunch of old ledgers on a shelf nearby.

'Over there,' he said, indicating towards the shelf. 'Do you see it?'

Her hopes took a dive. Surely she hadn't been brought all the way out here—surely she wasn't being subjected to all this—for a bunch of mouldy old records? But then to one side she saw something else—what looked like some kind of cleft in the rock-face, almost invisible except for the shadow cast by the torch he'd shoved into a ring set into the wall. Intrigued, she took a step closer. Could that be what he meant?

He was already there—impatient to be rid of her, she guessed—his hand seemingly disappearing into the rock-face before it re-emerged, this time holding a flat parcel.

In the flicker and spit of torchlight she held her breath, excitement fizzing in her veins as he brought the package to the table, depositing it more gently there than she could imagine someone his size doing anything. And then he stood abruptly. 'This is what you want so desperately to see?'

He was angry with her, but right now his bad mood rolled off her. Her eyes, her senses, her full attention were all focused on the parcel on the table. She licked her lips, her mouth dry with anticipation, her eyes assessing. A quick estimation told her the size was about right for something containing the long-lost pages, but that didn't mean this was it.

She took a step closer, and then another, the man beside the table and his disturbing presence all but forgotten now as her eyes drank in the details of the worn pouch that looked as if it was made from some kind of animal skin, of the rough clasp that had been fashioned to keep the parcel together.

A pin of ivory, she guessed, stained yellow by the passage of time.

'May I?' she said, with no more than a glance in his direction, unwilling to take her eyes from this precious discovery for more than a second lest it disappear in a puff of smoke. She should wait until they'd brought the package back to the castle and she had the right lighting and the right conditions. She should wait until she had her tools by her side.

She should wait.

Except that she couldn't.

Adrenaline coursed through her. She had to look. She had to see. So she slipped her arms from her backpack and pulled a new pair of gloves from the pocket where she kept them and drew them on, fingers almost shaking with excitement. *Calm down.* She heard the Professor's voice in her head, heeded it, and willed herself to slow down. To breathe.

She knew what she was looking for. She'd studied what little remained of the *Salus Totus*. She knew the language and the artwork. She knew what inks the artists had used and how they'd been sourced, and she knew what animal's skin had gone to make the parchment. And nothing on this earth—*nothing*—was more important to her than the thrill of seeing what could be those missing pages and seeing them *now*.

With gloved hands she gently prised the clasp open and pulled back the leather wrapping, folded like an envelope around the treasure within.

A blank page met her hungry eyes, but the bubble of disappointment was happily pricked in the knowledge that, whatever their purpose, whoever had taken these pages had realised they needed some form of protection.

She took a steadying breath. A big one. Gingerly, she lifted the cover sheet and moved it to one side.

And what little breath she had left was knocked clear out of her lungs.

Colour leapt from the page—vivid reds, intense blues, yellows that ranged from freshly picked corn to burnished gold. And even in the flicker of torchlight the quill strokes of another age stood out clear and bold, the Latin text as fresh as the day it had been written, although it was clear the parchment itself was old, despite being in amazing condition.

Her eyes drank in the details. The similarities to the remnants of the *Salus Totus* were unmistakable. And tears sprang to her eyes. Whether authentic or a cleverly crafted fraud, it was a thing of beauty.

'Well? Do you think it's what you're looking for?'

She jumped and swiped at her eyes, suddenly embarrassed at the unexpected display of emotion. She'd been so absorbed she'd forgotten completely there was anyone else present.

And the last thing she wanted was for this man to see her shed tears. So she turned away and delved through her backpack again, pulling out one of the acid-free boxes she'd packed, thankful for the excuse to have something to do so that she didn't have to look at him.

'I don't know. I have to get it back to the castle. Do you have somewhere I can use as a study?' Reluctantly she replaced the protective cover over the page and refolded the bundle before slipping it into the slim box. She had to get it back before she was tempted to look at the next page, and then the next. She could prove nothing down here but her insatiable curiosity.

When finally she did look up, wondering why he hadn't

responded, his features looked strained, a flicker of inner torment paining his eyes. But then he merely nodded and said through gritted teeth, 'I'll take you there now.'

He said nothing as he led the way back to the castle along the twisted passages and for that she was grateful. Her blood was alive and sparking with possibilities. Her mind was already processing the little she'd seen and working through the steps she'd take once she got the package back somewhere with decent lighting and her tools.

And as for her other senses? They seemed one hundred percent preoccupied with the Count. That damned evocative scent teased her at every turn, the fluid movement of his limbs was like a magnet for her eyes, and then there was his shadow, looming menacingly against the wall...

She swallowed. He was so big he dwarfed her. He was powerful and dangerous and he was angry, and he'd made it clear he didn't want her here. He should frighten her. That would make sense. But instead she felt something no less primal and every bit more confusing.

Because he excited her on a level so deep she'd never known it existed. He caused a quickening of her heart and an ache in her breasts and made her wonder what he'd have tasted like if he'd kissed her back there...

Madness, she decided. He'd done the right thing in turning away. She didn't want to kiss him. She was here to do a job. She didn't need the complications.

Yet still she wondered...

Soon they were back in the castle, past the stone door and making their way up the winding stairs. There was space here, and light, though gloomy and thin. The sound of the wind was growing louder. She wondered if things might be different now they were above ground, not so strained and tense between them. And then a shutter banged somewhere and curtains fluttered on unseen draughts.

'A storm is building,' he told her over his shoulder. Unnecessarily, she thought. Given the setting and her dark companion, she would have been more surprised if a storm *wasn't* building.

Then he did surprise her, by showing her into the room that was to be her office. It was remarkably well thought out. No external windows to let in draughts or damp. A large desk to spread her things out with lamps for extra lighting. A heater in one corner. A dehumidifier in another. She circled the room, stopped before the desk and nodded her appreciation as she took it all in.

'Did the Professor give you a shopping list?'

She turned and took a step back and gasped, so surprised to find him within a metre of her that she took another involuntary step backwards against the desk, one hand reaching down to steady her, the other over her pounding heart, willing it to slow. So much for his impact being less intense above the ground. An aura surrounded him, a mantle of power and presence, and a scent that wove its way into her senses like a drug. So how exactly was she supposed to calm her racing heart?

His eyes glinted, his lips curving into the slightest smile, as if he was relishing her reaction. 'You really think I would take chances with something potentially so precious?' He nodded knowingly before she could reply. 'But of course, you do. You thought I was irresponsible to leave it in the caves, didn't you? In the place that had harboured it safely for perhaps hundreds of years.'

She licked her lips, regretting the gesture immediately

when his scent turned to taste on her lips. Regretting it more when she saw his eyes follow the sweep of her tongue.

'I'll admit it,' she said, trying to get a foothold on the conversation and justify her position. Because she *had* thought exactly that. Until she'd felt the air down there and realised it was probably the reason why the pages were in such good condition. 'It did seem a trifle reckless, at least—'

'*Reckless?*' he repeated, jumping on the word, his eyes gleaming, refusing to let hers go. 'I take it you're not a fan of being reckless, Ms Hunter?'

'No, but—'

'But you make exceptions?'

'No! That wasn't what I was going to say at all.'

His eyes gleamed, searching hers with a heated intensity that left her breathless, until with a blink they cooled and flicked towards his wristwatch and then at the door, as if he had somewhere he had to be. 'No. You really don't seem the type. And now I shall leave you. Anything else you need, Bruno will see to it for you.'

Right now she could uncharacteristically do with a stiff drink, though she'd quite happily settle for tea. She was still strangely stinging from that 'you really don't seem the type', and she wasn't even sure why. She'd never been reckless in her entire life. She'd been too driven, so focused on what she wanted that even her friends at university had affectionately labelled her a nerd.

'How will I find Bruno?' she asked, surprising herself with how calm she sounded now that he'd eased away and given her space. 'If I need him?'

'Bruno will find you. He has a way of anticipating one's needs.'

A psychic henchman? But of course a count would need

one of those, along with his secret tunnels and his crumbling castle. It was just what she needed to improve her mood. 'Excellent,' she rejoined, with exaggerated enthusiasm and a smile designed to get right under his skin. 'Then it appears I'm all set. I'd better get to work.'

And with a glower and a nod he was gone and she could breathe again.

She slumped into the nearest chair. The pages, she thought, her fingers pressed to her temples. Think about the pages and all they mean to you. And she would, she promised herself, just as soon as she'd caught her breath. Being with the Count was like being caught in a whirlwind and spun in circles until she was spat out again, dizzy and confused.

Difficult? The man was turning out to be her worst nightmare.

A sharp rap on the door and she jumped, instantly alert, but it was only Bruno, bearing a tray.

'Something to eat,' he grunted, placing the tray on a side table.

Grace blinked and caught a whiff of something warm and savoury. Frittata, she realised as she approached, feeling suddenly hungry and remembering she hadn't eaten for hours. And, if she was not mistaken, a pot of tea. She lifted the lid and took a sniff. English breakfast. Maybe he really was psychic. 'How did you know I'd prefer tea to coffee?'

He shrugged. 'You're *inglese*, no?'

'Australian,' she corrected. And he shrugged again, as if it were the same thing, and disappeared.

Lucky guess, she figured, and poured herself a cup, enthusiasm once again building inside her. A quick meal and she could get to work. Strange, though, given how excited she'd been at getting this opportunity, that something could distract her to such an extent that at times she almost forgot the book completely.

Well, not something—*someone*. And maybe he was difficult and dangerous and tortured and gave her heated glances that made her squirm—still, it wasn't like her at all.

He paced his office, walking past windows rattling with the wind and splattered with raindrops from the first of the coming squalls. Clouds obliterated what was left of the sun until day turned almost to night.

He paced the room uncaring. He saw nothing but the expression on her face when she'd turned that cursed page. It had been bad enough when she'd thought they were close. She'd looked so alive with hope and anticipation. He hadn't thought it could get any worse, that she could look any more alive than she had in that moment.

And then she'd turned that cover page and her eyes had widened, her face had lit up and her whole body had damned near ignited.

He'd damned near combusted watching her. He'd been rock-hard with need and so hot it was a wonder he hadn't turned to a column of ash right there and then. And all he'd been able to wonder since then was if that was the way she looked when she was looking at some piece of ancient parchment, how good might she look when she came apart in his arms?

He wanted to find out.

He burned to find out.

What was wrong with him? She was a scientist, with scraped-back hair and a passion for ancient relics, and he was lusting after her? Damn! What on earth had possessed him to let her stay?

Alessandro threw himself into his chair and then spun straight out of it, reaching for his phone. God, he didn't need this!

Bruno answered on the second ring.

'Fetch the woman from the village,' he growled.

There was hesitation at the end of the phone and he could almost hear Bruno's mind working out that it was not quite a month since her last visit. But instead he said, 'The boat will not come with the storm brewing.'

'Offer them double,' he ordered, and hung up.

Five minutes later Bruno called back. 'The captain says it's too rough. He will bring her tomorrow.'

'I don't want her tomorrow!' This time he slammed the phone down, turning his gaze out through the windows to where the waves were wearing white caps from which the wind whipped spray metres into the air. And then rain lashed the windows until they were running like a river and the sea beyond blurred to grey.

Curse the damned weather! How dared it confound him when he needed a woman?

But there was already a woman on the island.

He wheeled away, trying hard to lose that thought. He could see her even now, poring over her precious pages as if they were the Holy Grail. In that moment he'd seen inside her. He'd seen beyond the scientist who made out she had no desires. He'd seen the woman beneath—a woman born for passion.

And she was waiting for you to kiss her.

He strode down the passageway, raking hands through his hair, not knowing where he was going, refusing to give credence to the sly voice in his head that refused to shut up.

She baited you.

She didn't know what she was asking.

She wants you.

No. No. And *no*! She did not want him. She was a fool. She had no idea.

But you want her...

He found himself outside her room, the sliver of light under the door telling him she was still working, his hands clenching and unclenching at his sides.

Would she welcome his visit?

Would she welcome being spread over that wide desk, scattering her precious papers, while he buried himself in her depths? Would her eyes light up for him the way they had in the cave? Would her entire body shimmer with desire and explode with light?

Blood pounded in his ears. His fingers were on the doorknob.

Or would she close her eyes and turn away?

He could not bear it if she turned away...

Blackness, thick and viscous, oozed up from the depths. His fingers screwed into a ball as he forced it down.

Maybe she wouldn't. Maybe she was different. She didn't shy away from him. She didn't recoil in horror. She treated him as if he was almost normal—as if his scars didn't exist.

But you're not normal, the dark voices said. *You can never be normal again.*

The blackness welled up like a rolling wave. What had he been thinking? Why was he doing this to himself?

He should have made her leave when he'd had the chance!

He pushed away from the door, forced his feet to walk,

but he'd gone no more than a few paces when he heard the door open behind him.

'Count Volta?'

He dragged in air, turned and nodded stiffly. 'Dr Hunter.'

She had a hand on her chest, as if she'd been frightened of who or what she might find in the passageway. 'I was just about to go to bed. I thought I heard a noise. Did you want something?'

God, yes.

'No. I'm sorry if I disturbed you.' He didn't want to think about Dr Hunter and bed. And then, because he should be interested, 'How does your investigation progress?'

Her eyes lit up that way they did until he would swear they almost shimmered with excitement. 'The pages are wonderful. Do you want to have a look before I put them away?'

On that same desk, when all he wanted was to spread her limbs and plunge into her slick depths and feel her incandescent exhilaration explode around him?

'No!' he said, so forcefully that she took a small step backwards and he had to suck in air to regain his composure. 'Maybe tomorrow,' he added more gently. 'It's getting late. Goodnight, Dr Hunter. Sleep well.'

He wouldn't sleep, he knew, as he descended the wide stairs leading to the ground floor. Not now, not after seeing her again. Instead he would read in the library and listen to the storm continue to build outside. He would take comfort in the savagery of the elements and the pounding violence of the sea. He would be at one with its endless torment.

And perhaps in the morning he might have Bruno fetch the

woman from the village after all. God knew, books weren't going to cut it tonight. He would need something.

In the gloom of light he passed the doorway to the ball-room, a flash of lightning illuminating the empty space. Empty but for the grand piano sitting bereft in the far corner of the room.

He paused and gazed at the imprint the lightning had left behind and felt a pang for something long gone. Across the marble tiles, under the rumble of thunder, he approached the instrument like a one-time friend whose friendship had been soured by time. Cautiously. Mistrustfully.

Once he'd known her intimately. Known her highs and her lows and how to wring every piece of emotion from her. She'd been a thing of beauty when the world had been all about beauty.

Before life had soured and turned ugly.

Yet still she sat there, black and sleek, totally shameless. And even now she beckoned, luring him like the memories of a mistress he hadn't quite finished with before they'd parted company.

And what surprised him more than anything was that he was tempted. He lifted the lid, ran his fingers along the keys, hit a solitary note that rang out in the empty ballroom and felt something twist inside him.

He could have put the lid down then. He could have walked away. But the way his fingers rested on the keys, familiar yet foreign, wouldn't let him go. Outside the waves crashed; the thunder boomed until the windows rattled. Inside his fingers reacquainted themselves with the cool ivory. He let them find their own way. He let them remember. Let them give voice to his damaged heart.

* * *

She woke with a start, her breath coming fast, her heart thumping, not knowing what had woken her, just grateful to escape from her dreams. She reached over to snap on her bedside light but the switch just clicked uselessly from side to side. Great. The storm must have taken out the power again.

The wind howled past the windows, searching for a way in. The sea boomed below, the waves pounding at the very foundations of the island.

What had woken her? Maybe it had been nothing. Certainly nothing she could do anything about now. She settled back down, willing her breathing to calm, not sure if she wanted to head straight back into the heated confusion of her dreams. She ran her hands thought her hair. No way did she want to go back there.

Often when she was working on a piece she would dream of her work, her mind busy even in sleep, imagining the artists and scribes who had produced whatever artefact she was studying. Often her mind would work at solving the puzzles of who and what and why, even when those answers had been lost in time.

But not tonight. Tonight her dreams had been full of one man. A scarred count. Menacing and intense. Unwelcoming to the point of rudeness and beyond, and yet at the same time strangely magnetic. Strangely compelling.

He'd been watching her in her dream, she remembered with a shudder. Not just looking at her—she knew the difference—but *watching* her, his black-as-night eyes wild and filled with dark desires and untold heat. And even now she could remember the feel of that penetrating gaze caress her skin like the sizzling touch of a lover's hand. Even now her skin goose-bumped and her breasts firmed and her nipples strained to peaks.

She shook her head, trying to clear the pictures from her mind; she punched her pillow as if that was the culprit, putting them there when she knew it probably had more to do with the storm. The lightning and thunder were messing with her brainwaves, she told herself. All that electrical energy was messing with the connections in her mind. It was madness to consider any other option. Madness.

She didn't even like the man!

She was just snuggling back down into the pillow-soft comfort of her bed, determined to think about the pages and the translations she would commence, when she heard it—what sounded like a solitary note ringing out into the night. But the sound was whisked away by the howling wind before she could get make sense of it.

She'd almost forgotten about it when there came another, hanging mournful and lonely in the cold night air. She blinked in the inky darkness, her ears straining for sounds that had no place in the storm.

And then, in a brief lull in the wind, she heard what sounded like a chord this time, an achingly beautiful series of notes that seemed to echo the pain of the raging storm. Curious, she stretched out one hand, reaching for her watch, groping for the button to illuminate the display and groaning when she saw what time it was. Three-forty-five.

She had to be imagining things. Lightning flashed outside, turning her room to bright daylight for a moment before it plunged back into darkness. A boom of thunder followed, shaking the floor and windows and sending a burst of rain pelting against the windows.

She pulled back her arm and buried herself deeper under the thick eiderdown. She had to be dreaming. That or she really was going mad.

CHAPTER FIVE

MORNING brought surprisingly clear skies with little trace of the storm that had threatened to rend the night apart. Grace blinked as she drew open the curtains and gazed out over the view. Every surface sparkled with its recent wash, the sapphire sea calm now but for a breeze playfully tickling at its surface. Not a cloud in the sky as far as she could see. She looked up and promptly revised her weather report. Not a cloud in the sky—except for the wispy white one hovering over the castle. She smiled, feeling brighter despite the night-time's interruptions. Like the tunnels underneath the castle, it would almost be disappointing if the cloud weren't there.

She wasn't left to wonder about the arrangements for breakfast. True to the Count's prediction, Grace had no sooner bathed and dressed than Bruno appeared with a breakfast tray. She didn't mind if she was being snubbed by being made to take her meals alone; the arrangement suited her. Less chance of running into anyone, she figured. At least less chance of running into the Count. She wasn't sure she was ready for another encounter so soon after last night's discomfiting dreams.

And even though she had some questions about the pages, like how he thought they might have come to be in the caves below the castle and who might have left them there, they could wait until he came looking for her. He was sure to come and check how long she thought she would be here.

She was back in her makeshift office across the hall before eight. She'd photographed each of the pages yesterday, taking her time to get detailed photographs of every page and then more detailed shots of the cut edges where they'd been sliced from the book.

The rest of the day she'd spent making meticulous notes on the condition of each of the pages. For something reputed to be upwards of six hundred years old, they were remarkably well preserved, a fact that at first had her doubting they could possibly be authentic and wondering if they were nothing more than a clever forgery. After all, nobody really knew what had been in the missing pages, only that the book and its prayers had been famous for their healing words.

And yet the more she'd examined the pages, the more she'd been convinced they were the genuine article. It couldn't be confirmed until samples were matched with what little remained of the *Salus Totus*, but she almost didn't need that confirmation right now to be sure. And the longer she examined the pages, the more certain she was that this had the potential to be the very biggest discovery of the twenty-first century.

And she was at the heart of it.

Her heart raced with the potential. People worked thankless long decades in this industry, re-examining texts already long known, searching for an angle, a point of difference with which to elevate their careers out of obscurity. Seldom did people have an opportunity like this, the chance to examine a new discovery practically thrust upon them.

It was really happening.

And now, because the pages were in such amazingly good condition and she didn't have to spend time stabilising what was left, she could get to work on the translation. Some time this morning the power had been restored and gratefully she snapped on the lamps she'd arranged around the desk.

She'd recognised just an odd word or two as she'd performed yesterday's tasks and it had been tempting to stop and decipher more. Now she had the luxury of time to study them more closely. So it was with a heart bursting with possibilities that she retrieved the package from the box in which she'd stored it and gently placed the first page in front of her.

It was hours later before she happened to glance at her watch. Excited about her work so far, she knew she had to move, so she stood and did a few stretches before heading to her room across the hall and the jug of water she had left there.

She poured herself a glass and took a long drink, gazing out of the window, musing over the pages, before her eyes caught on a movement below the castle. A boat was nearing the dock—it looked like the same boat that had brought her over yesterday, although she'd got the impression from the way the men spoke that the provisions runs happened no more than once or twice a week. She glanced down and saw Bruno standing ready to meet it. Curious, she waited for it to dock, wondering what they were bringing this time.

Make that who, she amended, as a raven-haired woman was handed by a smiling skipper to the shore. A striking woman too, in a peasant top and skirt that showed off a tiny waist and generous curves. With a laugh and a wave to the skipper, she pulled a scarf around her shoulders and climbed into the Jeep alongside Bruno. Grace lost sight of them as they started up the cliff track.

Who was she? Grace had got the impression visitors weren't exactly welcome here. She shrugged and drained the rest of the glass. Maybe someone who worked at the castle. And with any luck a cook, given how hungry she suddenly felt.

Barely ten minutes later she was back at work when Bruno appeared, a very welcome tray in his hands. Whatever was on it, it smelled wonderful. She smiled and thanked him as he put it down on a table set a safe distance away from the desk and her work, even though she knew her words wouldn't make a dent in his grizzled visage.

'You're busy today,' she said. He merely grunted in response, peering at her from under tangled brows that looked like something that had been washed up in a storm. 'I saw you down at the dock. Who's the woman? Does she work here?'

He threw her a dark look. 'The woman is not your concern.'

'No, of course not. I just thought it might be nice to say hello—'

'Forget the woman!' he said, marching back to the door. 'She is not here for your benefit.'

The door closed behind him with a bang. Okay, maybe his message was none too subtle, but he was right. She should just get on with the job. At least then she could finish up here and leave. God knew, the prospect was tempting.

* * *

She was waiting for him. He let himself into the darkened room, the ache in his loins more insistent than ever after a night spent torturing himself thinking about that damned Dr Hunter. He refused to let himself think of her as anything else. He needed to think of her as a cold-blooded scientist and not as a woman.

Which made no sense when all he had wanted last night was have that woman bucking beneath him.

Why was she doing this to him? And how?

He dragged in air. Damn her. He was hard as a rock, his loins aching with need and another woman waiting naked in bed for him. Why was he even thinking about her?

He growled and approached the bed, shucking off his robe and tossing it to the floor, already half dizzy with the heady anticipation of release. His erection rocked free, heavy and hard. He steadied it with one hand to don protection and felt his searing, throbbing heat against his palm. *Dio*, he needed this.

He pulled back the covers and stared down at her in the dim light. She was smiling knowingly, even though her eyes were dreamily closed, her head tipped back as if she was already in ecstasy, her hands busy at her breasts, tugging at her nipples, making them hard for him. Usually he'd spend some time with those breasts, but today his need was too great.

'Open your legs,' he commanded, and if she wondered at his brusque manner she didn't show it in the way she acquiesced without a murmur. And why shouldn't she do what he asked she when she was going home with the equivalent of a month's wages in her pocket? She'd do anything he asked and more.

He gazed down at her, took in the glossy hair splayed

over the pillow, her olive skin with its satin-like sheen in the half-light, her breasts plump and peaked. He was rock-hard and wanting and he wondered why the hell he was hesitating and not already inside her.

Until he realised that there was somewhere else he'd rather be.

With a cry of frustration he snapped on the light. 'Get dressed,' he ordered. 'Bruno will take you to the boat.'

'Did I do something wro—?'

He was reaching for his robe and tugging it on, but not before she'd opened her eyes to plead, no doubt worried she would not be paid. He caught the exact moment of change, when her eyes moved from protest to revulsion, and she pulled the covers back over herself as if to protect herself from his hideousness.

With a roar he ripped the covers straight back off. 'Just go!'

He could wallow in them if he wanted. He could let those black waves rise up and swallow him whole, sucking him back to that dark time and those dark nights when there was no respite, no relief.

Or he could deal with the problem, get rid of the source of his aggravation, and be able to breathe in his own space again.

He would not be sucked back.

He would deal with the problem.

Because everything had been fine until *she* had come along. She would just have to leave.

Now.

He headed to her office to tell her exactly that. After all, it wasn't as if the pages were in terrible condition and too fragile to be shifted. They looked fine as far as he was concerned. And besides, the longer she was here, the more chance someone would talk, someone would stumble on the news of the discovery, and the sharks and parasites of the media world would descend *en masse*. The story could break somewhere else—anywhere else; he didn't care—and then the media attention would be someone else's problem.

So he would tell her. And then she would go.

Nothing could be simpler.

The door to her office was slightly ajar. He pushed it open, still rehearsing his speech. It wouldn't be a long one. *Pack your things and be ready for the next boat*, was about the size of it. Still, knowing Dr Hunter and how she liked an argument, he was mentally preparing for a fight.

He was also preparing himself to win.

She was sitting at the desk, so intent on one of the pages she was studying and on the notes she was typing in the notebook computer alongside that she didn't hear him enter. She looked younger today, even with the frown puckering her brow, or maybe she just looked fresher. She'd dispensed with the ponytail and instead had twisted her hair behind her head so the blonde tips feathered out, and she'd swapped the khaki shirt for a white tank with straps so thin he wondered how they covered her bra straps.

Assuming she was wearing one...

Breath whooshed from his lungs. His blood rushed south. She muttered something, still oblivious to his presence, and jumped out of her chair, wheeling around to the briefcase on the credenza beside her, rummaging through its contents. It would be rude to interrupt now, he thought, when she was so intensely involved in her work. Besides, the view from the back was no hardship to endure either. A well-worn denim skirt lovingly hugged her bottom and made his hands itch to do the same. But it was the length of the skirt he approved of most, or rather the lack of it, showcasing the surprisingly long legs beneath.

He sucked in air, desperate to replace what he had lost. She was nothing like the woman from the village. That woman was olive-skinned and dark-eyed, lush with curves and sultry good-looks. Whereas this one was blonde and petite, blue-eyed and more than slightly bookish. It made no sense.

Except for one more difference that made all the sense in the world.

This woman he wanted.

She pulled something from the briefcase then, a sheaf of papers, and looked up, blinking warily when she saw him standing in the doorway. 'Count Volta. I wasn't expecting you.'

He nodded. 'Dr Hunter,' he acknowledged, moving closer, searching his mind, certain that he'd been intending to say something but knowing only that he needed to get closer— maybe then it would come to him. And maybe he might even find an answer to his earlier question. But before he could latch onto his reason for coming, or work out whether there were telltale lines under her singlet after all, her face broke into one of those electric smiles. He felt the charge all the way to his toes, felt the jolt in his aching length.

'You picked the best time to drop by. Come and see.'

'What is it?'

'I translated the first of the pages. It's a prayer, a midnight prayer, beseeching the coming of dawn and an end to the darkness of night.'

He looked at the page and then at the translation she had up on her screen. 'And that's important because…?'

'Don't you see? The *Salus Totus* was revered—no, more than that, almost worshipped in its own right—as a book of healing. But little of the book remains to explain why. Remnants talk of eating and drinking in moderation, of taking fresh air, and while that is good advice, scholars have always felt there must have been more to warrant such a reputation for miracle cures and saved lives. Speculation has existed for centuries as to what might be in the missing pages and why they were removed.'

He didn't understand what she was getting at. He couldn't honestly say he cared. But her face was so animated with whatever she'd discovered that he could not help but join in the game. He shrugged. 'Because the pages offended someone they had to be destroyed?'

She shook her head. 'That's the most common theory, I agree, but I don't think it's right. Not now. I think they were sliced from the book not to destroy them but to save them.'

'Why?'

'Because they're secular. They're prayers of life and living that talk about the earth as mother of all. Nothing offensive to us now, in these times, but for all their gentle truths and wisdom they would have been seen as blasphemy then. The only reason we have what remains of the *Salus Totus* is because these pages were removed from inside its covers. With them gone there was no risk of offending anyone and the book could live on in more than memories. If they had stayed, the *Salus Totus* would surely have been thrown into the fires. So you see, by removing them from the book someone was trying to preserve them. Someone was trying to ensure their survival.'

Colour was high in her cheeks. Her blue eyes were so bright they had a luminous quality. He didn't know anything about ancient texts or book-burning, but he knew *he* was burning and if he didn't do something soon he would self-combust. His hand found its way to her shoulder, scooped around to her nape, his fingers threading into the upward sweep of her hair. She blinked up at him, questions in her clear eyes to which he had no answers.

Except that he wanted her.

CHAPTER SIX

SHE trembled slightly as he dipped his mouth and brought her close, but it was not fear he sensed under his hand but an answering tremor of need. And then his lips touched hers and she sighed into his mouth. It was all he could do not to crush her to him. It was all he could do to remember to breathe. And when he did it was filled with the tantalising fresh perfume of her set amidst the coiling scent of desire.

He drew her closer, her lips soft under his own, pliant, her body close enough that they touched, chest to chest, her nipples hard against him. *No bra*, he registered with that small part of his brain still functioning, aching to fill his hands with her sweetness. Aching to fill her. Aching...

His hand cupped her behind, angling her back towards the desk, deepening the kiss as he lifted her.

She should not be doing this. She should have told him no. She had felt his warm hand slide around her neck, seen his mouth descend and known she should stop him.

Except she hadn't.

Just one taste, she'd foolishly thought, before she'd insist they stop. One taste of a man who could turn her inside out with just one heated glance. One taste of a man who made her feel more acutely aware of her gender and her innate femininity than she'd ever felt before.

And now, with his lips on hers, coaxing, bewitching, one taste wasn't enough. One taste led to a hunger for more. He was addictive. Compelling. Impossible to deny.

Her body was his accomplice. Her skin rejoiced at his touch. Her mouth revelled in his mastery and his mystery.

Even when his hand slid to her behind, squeezed her and caused every muscle inside her to contract and then bloom, even when she felt a moment of panic and knew this was dangerous and foolhardy and reckless and so many of those things she had never been, she could not stop herself. For whatever he was awakening in her, whatever madness he was unleashing, she wanted more.

She gasped into his mouth and found no respite, for he claimed her lips in a savage kiss that fuelled her desires and quenched her now wafer-thin resistance. And, whatever he was doing, she knew it was well worth the price. For his kiss was a drug, pulling at her sensibilities, his touch on her flesh a sizzling brand.

Divorced from reality, she was his for the taking—almost. For when she felt his hands beneath her, lifting her, when she felt herself settled somewhere he could so deliciously insinuate his legs between hers, there came the tiniest glimmer of doubt—almost as if she'd lost hold of something she should remember in the firestorm of their mutual desire.

But no rational thought could find a way through this forbidden haze of primal need, and she gave herself up to the wanton pleasure of his hot mouth at her breast.

Until she reached back to steady herself against his pressing weight and felt her hand brush something aside—something featherlight that fluttered from the table.

She wrenched her mouth away from his, turned her head to see the centuries-old page flutter to the floor. With a mighty shove born of panic she pushed him away. 'What the hell are you thinking?'

The words were directed as much as to herself as to him. She was madder with herself, because she should have known better. What a fool! She swiped a glove from the box on her desk, pulling it on as she knelt down. If her actions had compromised the page's condition she might as well give up her job now. She would never forgive herself. Maybe she should give it up anyway, given she'd so easily disregarded her first responsibility. A paper that had survived for centuries only to be destroyed by a thoughtless couple behaving on top of it like hormone-driven teenagers—and one of them the person charged with ensuring its preservation. That would look good in her report. If she wanted to make a name for herself in this industry, a name nobody would ever forget, there would be no faster or surer way.

What the hell had she been thinking?

That was an easy one. Clearly she hadn't been thinking— not beyond her own carnal desires.

'It looks fine.'

Maybe to him. Nothing looked fine from her angle. Everything was off-kilter. Everything was wrong. She swiped sudden tears from her eyes, not sure if they stemmed from what had just so nearly happened on the desk or from relief that the page appeared to have survived its ordeal intact. But she was not about to risk dripping salty tears all over the page and add insult to injury. 'Just go, will you?'

She slid a folio beneath the page, lifting it gently back

to the desk, using the opportunity to take a few more steps and put the desk between them at the same time. She would have to check the page for materials and fibres picked up from the rug, but pulling out her tweezers and microscope would have to wait until the Count had gone and her hands had stopped shaking.

'Dr Hunter…'

'Haven't you done enough? I asked you to go.'

His jaw firmed, his eyes grew hard edged. 'You're blaming me?'

'I certainly didn't kiss *you*!'

'No? I distinctly remember there were two of us there. And I sure as hell don't remember anyone complaining.'

She squeezed her eyes shut, remembering only too well her lack of resistance. 'I think we both made a mistake. And now, if you don't mind, I have work to do.' She curled her hands into fists, willing the shaking to stop, trying to make sense of this unfamiliar recklessness and get her scientific self back together while he loomed there, her very own dark cloud.

'Have dinner with me tonight.'

Her breath caught. Dinner—*and what else?* Why the sudden hospitality? Unless he was looking to finish what he'd started?

'I'm not sure that's such a good idea.'

'You have to eat.'

'I'm very good at eating alone. Luckily, as it happens.'

'If that's a dig at the way you've been treated here—'

'Take it how you like. But I live alone. I'm good with it.'

He regarded her coolly from under hooded lids. 'You're afraid.'

'I'm not afraid of you. It's just that I don't see the point. Every time we're together we end up arguing or—'

His chin lifted, a spark glinted in his eyes. 'You are afraid we will not argue?'

'Should I be?'

'I think whether or not we argue is something that is as much up to you as it is to me.'

And that was *exactly* what she was afraid of. One kiss and she'd forgotten who she even was. How could something as mechanical as the meeting of two mouths do that? She'd had lovers before, and neither of them had come close to making her feel anything like this man did. Okay, so maybe her first time had been more clinical than exciting, and borne of desperation that she would be the sole virgin in her university graduating class, and the second time had been grief sex with a colleague after a child she'd nursed for days in the refugee hospital had died in her arms. It had been bitter and sweet and life-affirming and exactly what she'd needed at the time, but it had been nothing to rival the impact of even this man's kiss.

Dared she dine with him? If he kissed her again, how would she resist? And with what? She had no defences against such an onslaught. If she even wanted to stop it. She hadn't before, and if that paper hadn't fallen to the floor what would they be doing now? She shuddered and squeezed her eyes shut, but it didn't stop the images dancing in her mind's eye. Right there, *on the desk*.

'You can tell me more of your theories,' he prompted, clearly sensing her waver, 'and perhaps I can share mine about why the pages might have ended up here under the castle.'

He had a theory? She looked up. She wanted to hear that.

She just wasn't certain about the *you-show-me-yours-and-I'll-show-you-mine* subtext. 'Or,' she countered, 'you could just tell me now.'

'But you have work to do, my dear Dr Hunter. And I have already disturbed you enough.'

True, but he would continue to disturb her whether or not he was here—now more than ever. 'Look,' she said, shaking her head, knowing it would be crazy to expect they could dine together and pretend that kiss had never happened. She gestured down at her casual singlet and skirt. 'I didn't expect to be entertained. I brought nothing—'

'On the contrary,' he interjected, 'you look charming. But if it pleases you I'm sure we can find you something you will be more comfortable in.'

She sighed, knowing she was fighting a losing battle. Of course he was sure to have an entire women's wardrobe at his disposal. Or maybe Bruno was also a fine seamstress. 'Fine,' she said in resignation, just wanting more than ever to get back to her work. There was an outside chance she could finish up the translations today, and if she did that, given the excellent condition of the pages, there was no reason why she couldn't leave early and finish the rest of her report elsewhere. She had contacts in any number of universities across Europe that had the right facilities and who would be delighted to play host to such a famous text. And he wanted her gone. Surely she could survive just one meal together? 'Fine. In that case I'd be delighted to join you for dinner.'

His eyes glinted with victory. 'It is a long time since I had the pleasure of a beautiful woman as my dinner companion.'

'You don't have to resort to flattery, Count Volta. I have already said I'd come.'

'Alessandro,' he said, with a nod and a smile at her

acquiescence. 'And I shall call you Grace. I think we can drop the formalities, don't you?' He bowed his head and finally headed for the door. 'Until dinner, then.'

She nodded absently, turning back to her work, knowing she should be concentrating on that rather than replaying the sound of his name in her head.

Alessandro.

Oh, no. She didn't like that. She didn't want to give him a name. She didn't want to think of him as Alessandro. She preferred to think of him as the Count. It made him sound remote. A little unreal.

Whereas Alessandro made him sound almost human. It made him sound like a man.

And she didn't want to think of him as a man.

'Oh, and Grace?'

She blinked and looked around. 'Yes?'

'That wasn't flattery.'

He had her. He strode back to his office, knowing that tonight she would grace both his table and his bed. She was as good as his. And tonight, and for all the nights that she remained here, he would have her. Nothing surer.

He almost growled in anticipation. He didn't understand this need, this compulsion to have her. He hated strangers. And yet he wanted her more than he had ever wanted anything before in his life.

Did it matter why?

Wasn't it enough to know that he wanted her and that she was his for the taking? And by the time she left he would have rid himself of whatever spell this was that she had cast over him—rid himself of this compulsion to bed her and to watch the sparks in her eyes, to feel the electricity inside her as she came apart around him.

He could hardly wait.

CHAPTER SEVEN

GRACE rubbed her eyes and leaned back in her chair, a bubble of excitement glowing pearlescent and pretty as her raw theory took shape and substance—a bubble only slightly tainted by a niggling concern that she had missed something.

She couldn't quite put her finger on it. Her supposition that the pages had been removed to protect them rather than to destroy them wasn't just a rash idea now; the pages she had translated since then only lent weight to her theory.

One page had been in praise of mothers and motherhood and the sacred mother-child bond. Another had been a celebration of spring and renewal in all things spiritual and physical. Another an endorsement of acting kindly to friends and strangers alike. All of them fabulous. All of them a revelation into thoughts based more on humanitarian principles rather than the dictates of any particular religion. That would have been crime enough to have them destroyed.

But it was the last page that gave the most credence to her theory.

It was probably the most spectacular of all the pages.

The inks were fresh and clear, the colours almost leaping from the page, bold and beautiful. It was the message that disturbed her on some deep, uncomfortable level.

It warned of an affliction with no cure. An odd subject, Grace had thought, in a so-called book of healing, assuming it must contain a description of a disease beyond the range of a physician's treatment. Cancer, or any number of things that would have been similarly incurable back then.

The affliction was random, the scribe warned, regardless of wealth or station. It was ruthless and devastating in its impact.

It must be something like cancer, she'd mused as she'd made notes before continuing. But, reading on, she'd realised she'd been wrong.

It made your chest thump and left you breathless and weak. It turned your mind to a porridge filled with poems and songs and other, darker, carnal longings. And should you fall you were doomed, and no god in heaven or on earth could save you. Yet if you succumbed you were the most blessed soul alive.

Love, Grace had realised with a smile, working through the translation. Love was the scribe's fatal affliction, its victims both doomed and blessed. She'd heard plenty of modern ballads with similar themes. It never ceased to amaze her how some things transcended not only the generations but the centuries.

Still, something bothered her. She checked her notes, unable to dispel the glimmer of uneasiness. But there was nothing untoward that she could see, and anyway it was time to pack up and get dressed for dinner.

She gathered her things, sending up silent thanks to who-ever it was who had removed the pages from the book for safekeeping all those centuries ago. Soon, if all went well and her findings were corroborated, the pages and the book would be reunited.

And tomorrow she could leave. Her heart gave a little lurch she interpreted as relief. Already she felt better about dinner, more in control. The doctor was back in charge, her earlier recklessness put aside. Dinner would be fine, she told herself. She'd tell him what she'd found and ask him about why he thought the pages had ended up here. She'd tell him she was leaving and ask him to arrange transport. What could possibly happen when she was leaving tomorrow?

She returned to her bedroom. Gloomy light was filtering into the room courtesy of the dark clouds hiding the sun. Wind rattled at the windows. Another rough night, she presumed, the scientist in her firmly back in control. There was nothing sinister about it. Stormy nights were just the way things were here.

But the weather faded to insignificance when she turned on the light and saw what was waiting for her on the bed.

It was a gown of liquid silk, a waterfall of blue and green rippling over the coverlet, and it was the most glorious thing she had ever seen. She held it up against herself and realised it was new, its store tag swinging free. A store she'd never been game enough to walk into in her life. It must have cost a fortune. How on earth had he found it?

Ten minutes later, showered and fresh, she slipped it on. It floated over her skin, setting it alight like a lover's caress, reminding her of the sensation when Alessandro's big hands had skimmed over her. She shivered with the memories, turning this way and that in the mirror, trying to focus on what she saw and put out of her mind what she remembered. The one-shouldered design fitted perfectly, its silk feeling magical against her skin. She loved what she saw. Spinning around in front of the mirror, her inner girl delighted. She never wore pretty things. It was usually jeans or a denim skirt for work, and practical suits for presentations to libraries or at conferences. She owned one whole cocktail dress. Black, of course. Never in her life had she worn something so utterly—*feminine*.

She coiled her hair—nothing special, with loose tendrils refusing to behave and escaping, but it would have to do. She applied what little make-up she'd bothered to bring and stepped into the silver sandals left with the dress and made one final check in the mirror.

Would he approve? She hoped so. And immediately wondered why it even mattered what he thought. She was leaving tomorrow. Still, she thought, with a flutter in her tummy as she headed for the dining room, he always looked so regal in his high-collared suits. It would be nice to appear for once in something less casual. And it would be gratifying if he at least approved.

He had the hard-on from hell. One look at the vision that had just entered the room and it was a wonder it hadn't bodily dragged him across the room. God, but he wanted her!

He forced his hungry mouth into a smile as he poured her a glass of champagne. 'You look—ravishing.'

She actually blushed, and stumbled delightfully over something she'd been going to say, ratcheting up his hunger tenfold. Was she so unused to compliments? She was a goddess in that dress, needing no jewellery when her blue eyes sparkled like sapphires. And if she was a goddess in it, he couldn't wait to see her out of it.

Soon, he assured the ravenous beast bucking for release. *Soon*.

'The dress is lovely, thank you.' She headed uncertainly towards him, taking the circuitous way round as if interested in the photographs lining the mantelpiece in the grand high-ceilinged room. She had to watch what she said. When he'd told her she looked ravishing she'd almost said, *So do you*.

But it was true. In another of those high-collared jackets, that fitted him like a second skin and showed off the tapering of shoulders to hip to magnificent effect, he looked like royalty.

He *was* royalty, she reminded herself. A count. With connections that went back for ever. Which reminded her of much safer territory than how good he looked right now...

'Did you want to tell me about that theory of yours? About how the pages might have ended up in the caves below your castle?'

He handed her a glass of sparkling gold-tinged liquid and their fingers brushed, causing an electric jolt to her senses and her heart. The silver shoes, she figured, preferring to blame static electricity than take heed of the niggling worm of doubt lurking in the back of her mind.

He smiled down at her, as if he'd sensed her sudden discomfiture, and she was forced to meet his eyes and pretend unconcern, closing her lips before she could tell him he smelt ravishing as well, clean and masculine and all too addictive.

'Pirates,' he said simply.

She blinked up at him, lost in his scent, trying to regain hold of the conversation. 'Why would pirates care about a few random pages cut from a book? Wouldn't they be more interested in treasure and looting?'

'Perhaps they didn't care about the pages themselves, but the money they were paid to hide them. They would know where to secrete them to keep them safe from prying eyes. The caves beneath this castle were used by pirates for centuries, even while the first Counts were in residence. Perhaps someone paid them to find somewhere safe—somewhere the authorities would never find them. Somewhere they didn't know the location of themselves.'

'So they could never give it away if anyone asked...' Her mind was working through the possibilities. 'They must have known they could be lost and might never be found.'

'It was no doubt a better option than to be burned outright. Little would have existed of the *Salus Totus* then.'

She looked up at him. 'You sound like you care—like the *Salus Totus* really matters to you. Why do you care about these pages? You could have left them there and not told anyone. Nobody would have been any the wiser.'

Before he could answer the door swung open on Bruno pushing a trolley.

'Ah, dinner is served,' the Count said with a smile. 'Please be seated.'

He put a hand to the small of her back to direct her, and she felt warmth and heat and an instant connection. It was utterly innocent, she was sure, and the fabric of her dress was separating them, and yet she had never felt anything quite so shockingly intimate. Did he have any idea what that low touch did to her? How it stirred her in secret places and moved her to remember a kiss that had near wrenched her soul as well as her defences away?

She swallowed, some of her earlier confidence trickling away. She was leaving tomorrow but that still left tonight. Why had she thought it would be such a breeze? What if he'd planned dinner to be one long assault to her senses? The brush of his fingers when he'd handed her the glass, the touch of his fingers to her back—was it all part of a long, sweet seduction?

He leaned over her as she was seated and she felt his warm breath stir the ends of her hair and brush her ear. She shuddered, suddenly breathless and flushed and trying to ignore the thrum of blood in her veins.

She was reminded of that line of the translation…

'It makes your chest thump and leaves you breathless.'

Where had that come from?

No. That was laughable. Ridiculous. Although her brain must certainly be turning to porridge if she entertained any such thoughts!

'It is random, regardless of wealth or station.'

That proved nothing. She was tired, overwrought after a long couple of days, and the lines were fresh in her mind.

'It turns your mind to a porridge filled with poems and songs and other, darker, carnal longings.'

There! Not once had she felt inclined to burst into song or break out a sonnet. And she wasn't the type to have dark, carnal longings. Even if just a tiny fraction of her wondered about his hard body and how it would feel to have him inside her. If that paper hadn't fallen, if they hadn't stopped…

Her body hummed with unfamiliar awareness. A pulse she'd never known existed made itself known and almost ached…

'Is something wrong?'

The room came back into focus. She noticed the delicate porcelain bowl in front of her and the scent of wild mushroom and herbs from the soup someone had ladled into it. And she noticed him, watching her. Somewhere along the line her appetite for food had disappeared, been replaced with an appetite for something else entirely.

Lust, she thought. She hadn't had much personal experience but she guessed that could be a chronic affliction too. But not necessarily fatal. Definitely temporary. She'd start feeling better as soon as she'd left the island.

'It's been a long day,' she offered. 'I'm sorry. I'm probably not very good company tonight.'

'Did you have trouble with your work today?'

'No. On the contrary, I managed to cover a lot more than I expected. In fact, I was going to talk to you about that. I've got enough done that I don't need to trouble you any more. I'm hoping the boat can pick me up tomorrow morning.'

The atmosphere flat-lined between them.

'Tomorrow.'

It wasn't a question. More an accusation.

'Yes. Will it be a problem to get the boat, do you think? Only the pages are in such good condition they are more than safe for transportation, and I can continue my studies and complete my report elsewhere before the discovery goes public.'

'You're going to leave?'

She blinked. 'Isn't that what you want? For me to be gone as soon as possible?'

Yes!

But not this way. Not this soon. Not now! 'How can you be sure there's nothing more to learn here? What is the point of rushing elsewhere?'

Escape.

'I'll just have to take that risk.' There would be more to learn, she knew it. She would love to investigate the tunnels beneath the castle some more, to learn more of their shadowy past, but there was no way she'd trust herself down there with him again. 'I'll make my report. Others might want to fill in more details and undertake a research trip later.'

'I don't want *others* here!'

'That's not my problem!'

A flash of lightning rent the skies and shook the very foundations. A boom of thunder followed hot on its heels, along with a burst of rain splattering against the windows.

'Is it always stormy at night here?' she asked him, when the rolling boom had finally died away, breathless with the shock of the onslaught.

'Not always.' He was leaning back in his chair, his jaw set, his eyes as hard as the rock this castle was constructed with. He picked up his spoon. 'Sometimes it's stormy during the day too.'

Lovely. Clearly she'd visited the castle in the high season. She followed his lead, only to toy with her spoon, barely tasting the soup. She'd known they would either argue or end up in each other's arms and more. Clearly it would not be the latter tonight.

Which was a good thing, wasn't it?

She had no intention of ending up in his bed. Even if she was leaving tomorrow and the idea of a one-night affair came with a frisson of the forbidden. One night with a dark count with a savage heart. One night of passion unleashed.

Utter recklessness, she told herself, shifting a little in her chair. Of course she didn't want that.

Bruno grunted when he made to clear away her plate. 'Not finished?'

'Thank you, it was lovely. I'm not really that hungry.' She smiled up at him, wondering if he ever smiled. 'Does Bruno do the cooking too?' she asked as he disappeared with their plates, looking for a safer topic to discuss.

'Of course not.' Alessandro almost snapped the words, seemed to think twice and made another effort. 'Of course I have a cook.'

'Oh, I think I saw her. A pretty dark-haired girl?'

'You saw her?'

'I happened to see the boat come in earlier today. She was on it. I thought she must work at the castle.'

A muscle in his jaw twitched. 'My cook is named Pietro. There are no women who work at the castle.'

'Oh.'

He didn't volunteer who the woman was and she wasn't about to ask. Maybe she should have picked another topic. An antique mantel clock rang out the hour and then fell silent again. She studied her hands, busy tying themselves into knots in her lap, while outside the rain continued to come down. It would clear tomorrow, she reassured herself, just like it had cleared today.

Right now the boat couldn't come soon enough.

Somehow, stiffly, they made it through the rest of the courses, and Grace was never more grateful than when coffee was served. Conversation had been stilted and terse and limited to little more than the likes of, 'How is your duck?' and, 'Lovely, thank you.'

It had been an ordeal rather than a meal. She knew he was angry with her, but what she couldn't work out was why. He'd been the one to make her feel unwelcome from the start. He'd been the one who'd insisted she leave as soon as she was finished. And now he was acting as if she was cutting and running. And now he was the one who glowered at her with those dark eyes until she shivered with the intensity of it all.

What was his problem?

'It's late,' she said. 'I should get my things packed.'

'Of course,' he said, standing as she rose. 'You will forgive me, Dr Hunter, if I do not see you off in the morning. Bruno will collect your things and take you to the boat.'

Something lurched inside her—something beyond the unexpected hurt of him dropping the Grace and resuming use of her title. So this would be the last time she'd see him? How strange that felt, when she'd been expecting relief.

'Thank you, Count Volta. Both for your hospitality and for returning the lost pages of the *Salus Totus* to the world. I will be sure to accord your contribution due recognition in my report.'

He gave a slight bow, formal and brief. 'Goodnight, Dr Hunter.'

She was halfway to the door when he called her, and she turned uncertainly, unable to prevent or understand the tiny bubble of hope that came with his call. 'Yes?'

'Take the dress when you go,' he said. 'I have no use for it.'

She knew she shouldn't be disappointed. He'd made it clear he was angry with her. But she would take the dress. She doubted she would ever have cause to wear it, but she would treasure it for ever. 'Thank you. I meant to ask—wherever did it come from?'

His eyes looked back at her, bleak and soulless. 'It was my fiancée's.'

She was leaving. He sat at the empty table, a hint of her perfume the only remaining trace of her.

She was leaving.

Somehow he'd made it through the dinner, forcing food into a body already shutting down.

She was leaving. And, beyond locking her in a turret room or throwing her into the caves below the castle, he had no choice but to let her go.

He'd always intended to let her go.

She did not belong here.

She did not belong to him.

But, God, he had not planned on losing her so soon.

The blackness was there, lurking in the fringes of his mind, bubbling away like boiling mud and fouling the air with stinking gases. It was there and mocking him for letting her go, ready to claim him again. He'd thought there was a chance of...

He searched helplessly to latch onto what he was looking for. He didn't know.

Only that he had come to recognise she offered a chance of something—a chance to reclaim what he'd once had, a chance to reconnect to a world of light instead of dark. He wanted to at least taste that light.

And after a decade of burying himself away in the dark he'd seen that light in her expression and lusted after it for himself.

Just a taste.

Was that too much to ask?

Clearly too much. And so he'd pulled back before she could further cut him loose. He'd withdrawn into his dark state to preserve what little of himself there was left.

He'd hurt her in the process.

He'd seen her stricken face when he'd told her about the

dress. He'd sensed the trembling under her pale skin before she'd fled in a flurry of blue silk on a wavering goodnight.

Why had he told her that?

Payback? Because she'd teased him with the taste of something he'd long given up on, only to deprive him of it when he'd been lured under her spell? Because she'd reminded him of his failure with the village woman he'd sent packing because he wanted her instead?

Or maybe just because he'd finally become that monster he'd always been made out to be?

Because that dress had been made to be worn, and even if Adele had ever deigned to select it from her extensive wardrobe it would never have looked half as good as it had tonight on Dr Grace Hunter.

Why hadn't he told her that instead?

He knew why.

Because she was leaving tomorrow.

CHAPTER EIGHT

SHE should have thought to bring something to wrap around herself. She was almost frozen by the time she returned to her room. And it wasn't just the storm outside and the wind that wailed a mournful song outside that turned her skin to goosebumps. It was the dreadfulness of dinner and the anticlimax of it all. She was chilled from the inside out.

She was leaving tomorrow. She should feel relieved.

And yet instead she felt this massive let-down.

Hormones, she told herself, or the sudden lack of them. The post-adrenaline rush. Nothing more scientific than that.

But still…

She unzipped the dress and let it slide from her body, letting it pool on the floor at her feet.

His fiancée's dress.

She shivered anew. God, what that had done to her. A dress chosen by the woman he had loved. The woman who had died that night along with so many others all those years long ago. Why had he wanted her to wear it?

She collapsed onto the bed and buried her face in her hands while the wind outside howled her distress.

She took a deep breath to steady herself. It was okay. She was leaving in the morning. Everything would be fine in the morning.

Like an automaton she packed her belongings to the sounds of a storm that mirrored her mood perfectly—every clap of thunder cheered, every burst of rain celebrated. The packing took nowhere near long enough for the storm. Her tools she'd already cleaned and packed. The pages were secure in acid-free packaging, padded to protect them from bumps during transit. There was nothing for it but to sleep and pray the storm had blown itself out by morning.

And the dress? She left it on a hanger in the dressing room before she slipped between the covers and settled her head into the pillows. It was a beautiful gown, there was no doubt—more exotic, more expensive than anything she had ever seen before or could ever afford—and she'd felt a million dollars inside its silken drapes. But it wasn't hers.

It would never be truly hers.

It was dark when she awoke, disorientated and confused after another fitful sleep and wondering again what had roused her. At first she thought it must be just that the wind had dropped and the rain had ceased, the lull leaving everything suddenly almost unnaturally quiet.

Until she heard it. The sound wound almost hauntingly through the night air until it was carried away with the next gust of wind.

She sat up. Definitely notes from a piano. Maybe she hadn't imagined it last night after all.

Between gusts of wind she caught more snatches, the

notes melancholy and slightly off-beat, increasing in parts. Bewitching.

She snapped on her light, relieved the power was still on, saw that it was two in the morning and listened, wondering where it was coming from. The music had moved to a more comforting melody, undulating and lyrical, soft and warm, except there were gaps and she hated that she kept missing bits—hated that they were carried away on the wind. Then rain splattered against her windows, drowning out the sound entirely.

Intrigued, she slid from between the covers, drawing on her robe. If she opened her door just a little she might hear more over the weather.

The door snicked open and light spilled into the shadow-filled passageway. She listened. It was coming from somewhere downstairs. The rain intensified, thunder rumbled overhead and the poignant notes were lost again. She took a step towards the stairs, and then another, barefoot and silent in the darkened hallway.

She reached the top of the stairs and peered down into the inky depths. The music was hauntingly beautiful and yet so utterly, utterly wretched. And she felt compelled to hear more.

She looked around the darkened empty hall, nervous and excited at the same time. Nobody would see her, and if they did surely there was no crime in listening? Still, she took the steps gingerly, the haunting notes luring her further and further down. It was coming from the ballroom that, from the impression she'd gained in her brief time here, seemed to take up one half of the massive frontage of the castle.

With no light to guide her, with the music leading her feet, she silently descended the stairway, hesitating on that final step as the rich emotion of the piece washed over her. It was building now, in time with the storm outside, a rising of passion that left her gasping at its intensity. She took one tentative step closer to the wide French doors leading into the ballroom, and then another, until she could see inside.

She didn't need light to know it was him. Even through the night-filled room, even across the yawning space between them, there was no mistaking the dark shadow at the piano, no mistaking it was pain he was feeling as he poured himself into the piece. She felt it too—felt that pain, felt that loss and his constant struggle.

And she fought with herself as she felt her own heart go out to this man. He had clearly lost so much.

He could be cruel, she reminded herself, remembering the dress and the cold way he'd told her it was his fiancée's. He was autocratic. Imperious. Cold.

He'd wanted her gone and then he'd frozen her out when she'd told him she would be.

And that was after he'd practically forced himself upon her.

Except that he hadn't...

He'd kissed her and she'd responded in the only way she'd been able—by responding in kind, by kissing him back. Because, so help her, she'd wanted him then and it hadn't even occurred to her to stop him. And she wouldn't have if it hadn't been for that paper. She would have opened her legs and welcomed him.

She swallowed, her mouth suddenly dry, aching in that hollow space between her thighs. How could she judge him?

The notes rang out, fighting the storm raging outside for supremacy, frenetic as the passion burst into a climax of such frenzied intensity that tears sprang unbidden to her eyes. A flash of lightning lit the room and displayed him in all his tragic beauty, his pain and torment clear in every stark feature and the scarred plane of his cheek.

The room went dark as the music crashed so suddenly down to earth that she held her breath and nearly turned and ran lest he discover her there, watching him.

Except that before her feet would move the notes resumed, almost from nowhere, soft and melodic. She recognised the earlier tune, only sweeter this time, and more poignant if that were possible. The notes tumbled like a stream, light and magical and so evocative that tears spilled down her cheeks.

She watched him as much as the storm-ridden night allowed as he coaxed honeyed sweetness from the instrument so that it almost bent to his will, compliant as a new lover willing to please—until he changed direction and willed it to insanity once again, urging it higher and wilder until the notes meshed one final time with the storm outside, only to collapse and shudder to a dramatic conclusion.

She heard the piano lid bang closed. She heard breathing, loud and close, and froze, panicked, only to realise it was her own ragged breaths she was hearing. She cursed herself for the time she had lost in making her escape.

She'd wheeled around, trying to make sense of the dark shadows before her, when light flooded the room—a chandelier of one thousand tiny globes above turning night to day.

'Was there something you wanted, Dr Hunter?'

Adrenaline flushed through her veins. Her heart pounded frantically in her chest as she surveyed the stairs. Escape was right there, brilliantly and starkly illuminated, and yet her feet remained frozen to the floor. She dragged in air and pulled her robe tighter around her before she was game to turn around, trembling with panic and guilt at being caught out, knowing he would not welcome her intrusion.

'I heard music, Count Volta. I was curious.'

He was standing near the doorway, wearing the same suit he'd worn at their disastrous dinner, as formal and regal as ever, though his eyes seemed darker and even more tortured if that were possible. 'I hope I did not disturb your sleep.'

No more than usual. 'No. Really, I was…' She swiped at a wayward tear on her cheek. 'I was just getting up for a glass of—' His dark eyes narrowed and she forgot what she had been going to say as he came closer, his eyes missing nothing as he took in the robe and the tightly cinched belt.

'But you have been crying.'

'The music,' she said. 'It was so beautiful. I'm sorry. I'll…'

But he was already wiping away the moisture with the pad of his thumb—so tenderly, so at odds with the dark, tortured eyes that raked her face, that more tears squeezed free. There was a tightness to his features. His face was set almost like a mask. It was a tightness that spoke of anger and resentment and some barely controlled agony.

A tightness that frightened her and yet excited her on some primeval level, just as his touch set her skin alight. 'It is late,' he said tightly, his fingers resting lightly on her cheek. 'You should be in bed if you are leaving tomorrow.'

'I'll go now,' she whispered, wondering if he might stop her. Half wanting him to.

'I'll see you to your room.'

'I'll be fine.' She had to get away. She couldn't stand the tension of having him walk alongside her, wondering all the way, back to her room. She couldn't stand the disappointment if he merely left her at the door and walked away. 'I know the way.'

She turned back, her feet programmed now to flee, only for the storm to unleash one more act of savagery. The boom crashed overhead and reverberated through the floor and walls. For a split second the room was still lit with the light from the chandelier, only to plunge the next instant into blackness so thick it was like a wall.

Panicked, she plunged into it, only to trip against the first step—would have fallen if he hadn't been there first to gather her into his arms.

Air was knocked from her lungs, and when she breathed again the air came full of the heady scent of him. His arms were like iron bars around her, powerful and strong, as slowly he righted her until her feet touched the ground. Her knees buckled and his arms tightened, pulling her against the hard wall of his chest.

She heard his ragged breathing, she could feel the pounding of his heart in his chest, and she didn't need light to tell her he was looking at her. She knew by the intoxicating fan of his breath against her face and by the sheer intensity of his stillness. She knew by the sudden fullness of her breasts and the aching tightness of her nipples.

'You are leaving tomorrow,' he said, sounding almost as if he was reminding himself, trying to convince himself.

'Yes.' Her word was no more than a whispered breath, and she sensed rather than saw the shake of his head.

'You should not have come downstairs.' His voice was choked and thick, and a shudder rippled deep and evocative through her. 'You should not have come.'

His words were warm and rich and scented with the

unmistakable essence of him and she drank him in, tasting him. 'I had no choice,' she admitted, her lips hungry and searching the darkness. 'You gave me no choice.'

He made a sound, strangled and thick, as her drew her closer, her head cradled in his hands. 'I am giving you a choice now. Tell me, before I give way to the monster inside me and decide for you, what do you want?'

Her heart lurched. Her senses lurched. His hands were hot on her face and in her hair as he waited for her answer. Her skin was alive with the touch of him, her body alight with need, and right now there was only one answer. Lust, she told herself, feeling herself falling further from reality and the safe world she had always known, the safe person she had always been. But she was leaving in the morning. Was one stolen night too much to ask?

And she put her hands over his, lacing their fingers together. 'I want you.'

Lightning flashed. Thunder boomed. And the room was suddenly so bright she was surprised she couldn't see her need splashed right across the ceiling.

But she could see him. Saw the flames flare in his eyes as his mouth crashed down on hers. And she knew she was lost. His kiss was wrenching at her very soul just like the music had done, reaching inside her to unleash emotions she'd never known existed. His mouth was setting her alight, his touch sending her skin aflame.

And then, still kissing her, she was in his arms as he mounted the stairs two at a time, with a speed that she would normally consider reckless but which now felt strangely necessary. Because she wanted him. Burned for him.

She didn't know where he was taking her in the dark. She didn't care whose bed it was he laid her down upon.

She only cared that soon he would soon quench this aching need. This burning desire.

Her fingers scrabbled with his jacket, protesting at the barrier, and without leaving her mouth he ripped it off and let it fall to the floor. He tugged loose her robe while her hands clawed at his shoulders, wanting him back, wanting to feel him against her. She forgave him when she felt his palms sliding from her thighs to her breasts, drawing her nightgown upwards with it. She lifted her head to let it go while his fingers trailed back down her body.

'Beautiful,' he growled, leaning over her, rolling one tight nipple under his thumb and making her back arch into the bed. 'Do you know how much I want you?'

'Please,' she implored, desperate now. Nobody had ever called her beautiful. Nobody had ever told her they wanted her. And now his words fuelled a body already screaming for release. Her hands were at his waist and then below, until she gasped into his mouth as she discovered exactly how much he wanted her, her fingers marvelling, tracing his rigid length.

He groaned like an animal in distress and grabbed the offending wrist, pinning it to the bed while he freed himself with the other and ripped open protection with his teeth. *Surely now!*

But still she had to wait. 'Please!' she cried when his hand peeled away her panties, his fingers slipping between her folds and brushing that tiny nub that seemed the repository of every nerve-ending she'd ever possessed while his mouth suckled one peaked breast.

She bucked into the bed and cried out with the sheer ecstasy of it, cried out with the unfairness of it all when his fingers teased her cleft. It was something else she wanted, something else she needed.

She curled her fingers in his hair, dragged his head from her breast. *'Please!'*

And then she felt him there, at her entrance, felt his heated pressure and his power and wondered for just one second if she was dreaming and at any moment she was going to wake up alone in twisted sheets, feeling cheated and unsatisfied.

A bolt of lightning rent the skies above, turning night into day, and her body yearned with pleasure unbound. And he was there, poised above her. 'You're so beautiful,' he murmured in the storm-light, his voice so tight with longing that it hurt to hear the words—until he stilled and entered her on one long, deep thrust that stretched her, filling her so completely, so perfectly—*so magically*—that she cried out with the wonderment of it all.

He was inside her, part of her. Every cell in her body was aware of his presence, shimmering with sensation. And then he started to withdraw, and lights exploded behind her eyes.

He gasped at their joining, taking just a moment to savour the exquisite tightness around him. He could feel her pulse in the slick flesh that sheathed him, could feel her muscles stretching to accommodate him, and he feared he would not last. And then he moved inside her and felt her buck beneath him, her muscles tighten around him, and he *knew* he could not last.

Lightning flashed overhead, thunder rumbled, and he pounded into her as the hail pounded at the windows. His own storm was building, and the woman beneath him was like a cyclone herself, wild and unpredictable as she thrashed below, urging his storm to intensify with her slick heat and electric spasms, until with a booming cry he exploded into her.

The lightning captured the moment, and he saw her up-turned face alight with wonderment, her blue eyes bright like stars. And even when the room was plunged into blackness again he felt the force of that light all around him.

It would not last. It could not last. She would go and once again the blackness and the bleakness would return. But for now he would live in the light.

He collapsed on top of her until his breathing was less ragged, his pounding heart quieted. Then he peeled himself away. 'You cried out,' he said. 'Did I hurt you?' He slipped her supine form in between the covers.

'No,' she whispered. 'It was—amazing.'

And he could hear her face light up in her words. He leaned over and kissed her before ridding himself of his shoes and trousers and climbing in alongside her.

She snuggled into him when he joined her, sighing against his shoulder, her hand sliding over his shirt. 'Why did you leave your shirt on?'

'Because the lights will come on some time.'

'You don't want me to see you?'

He remembered the look of revulsion on the village woman's face. 'You don't want to see me.'

Her fingers made lazy circles on his chest. 'I see your face.'

He caught her hand then, squeezed it briefly and let it go. 'You do. But this is much worse.'

Her hand skimmed his chest, drinking in the width and hardness of him, running down the length of his arm. She wanted to know everything about him. She wanted to be able to remember it all when she was gone. So soon she would be gone.

So little time...

Unless the storm continued? But the rain was no more than a sprinkle now against the windows, and the wind had blown itself out. The clouds were clearing enough for thin moonlight to slant over the bed.

'What time will the boat come?'

Never, he wanted to say, wanting to keep her here for ever, to hold onto her light. But she had to go. She wanted to go and present the lost pages to the world. She wanted the fame the discovery and her theories would bring.

And he had no right to beauty.

'Early,' he said. Her trailing fingers were stirring him, making him hard, so he caught them and showed her, unaccustomedly delighted with her small mewl of pleasure and the tentative exploration of her fingers. 'We'd better not waste any more time.'

He took much longer this time, none of it wasted. He took longer to pleasure every part of her with his hands and his mouth and his tongue, bringing her apart until she screamed with release before he pulled her astride him and lowered her slowly down his aching length.

God, she felt good as she rode him. Moonlight slanted across her body, turning her pale skin silver, her high breasts tipped with pink. She was a goddess and he was a monster.

And she was leaving in the morning.

She cried out as he flipped her onto her back, still inside her. *She was leaving.* He powered into her, pouring his frustrations and anger and desolation into every lunge, and she met him blow for blow, bucking under him, urging him on, her hips angled higher to take him deeper, her teeth at his shoulder, her hands clawing into his back and tangled in his shirt as the storm inside her built again. With one final thrust he sent her screaming into the abyss. She contracted around him, sparking and sizzling with electricity, and he had choice but to follow her as he pumped his own release.

They collapsed together as the first thin grey of dawn peeked through the windows. Vaguely he was aware of the buttons that had been wrenched away. Vaguely he knew he should do something before he fell asleep. But his arms were so heavy, and she was so warm and soft in his embrace, and the air was thick with the musky scent of their lovemaking. He would do something in just a while.

CHAPTER NINE

SHE woke with a start, disorientated and wondering where she was, until she remembered she'd fallen asleep in his arms not that many hours ago. Bright light now poured through the windows—the kind of light, she reflected sadly, that heralded sunny skies and an absence of storms. The kind of day, she cursed, just perfect to take a boat ride.

She could hear his steady breathing behind her and eased herself over to look at him. Had they really done all the things she remembered? Oh, yes, they had, she realised, if the unfamiliar aches in her body were any indication.

And then she saw him.

He was lying on his back, the shirt she remembered tearing apart in the height of passion open, exposing his chest to her gaze. She'd got just a hint of his injuries last night when her fingertips had grazed a ridge or encountered an unexpected dip under his shirt.

Now the ridges and dips made sense. Whatever had sliced into his face had dug deep into his chest as well, and then something more terrible had happened. It looked as if the left side of his chest had been blown apart and roughly patched together in some kind of ugly puckered design, brutal and savage. It looked as if whatever had blown his life apart had blown his chest apart with the same brutal effect. It looked so damaged that she ached with knowing what it must have cost.

'I told you that you didn't want to see it.'

She looked at him. Saw him watching her from under hooded lids, his eyes guarded as if he was waiting for her, almost challenging her to look away as he made no attempt to cover himself up. 'What happened? I read that your boat exploded, but how did this happen?'

'This was metal flying through the air,' he said, indicating the long line from his face to his chest. 'And this mess came courtesy of burning oil.'

She shuddered, imagining the horror and the pain. Unable to come anywhere close. And then, because she could find no words that would express anything that would help, she dipped her head instead, and lightly pressed her lips to his scarred chest.

'What are you doing?' he said, recoiling from her touch. 'Can't you see how ugly it is?'

'It's horrible,' she agreed. 'But it's just skin.' She touched a hand to his scarred cheek. 'And it's still you.'

He pulled his cheek away, gave an anguished cry. 'Don't.'

'I won't if you don't want me to.'

He pulled the shirt around him and flung himself from the bed and into an adjoining room. She knew she'd made him angry. She gathered her nightgown and pulled it over her head while he was gone, suddenly embarrassed by her nakedness and sorry she'd said anything about his scars.

Sorry they were going to end things this way after such a night. But how else could it end? They'd had a one-night affair and now she was leaving. It wasn't as if there was anything to stay for. It wasn't as if she was in love with him.

She stumbled over the last thought. No. Impossible. She would miss his dark, tortured looks. She would dream of this night for ever. But that was all it could be.

He came back in, wearing a robe this time, looking anywhere but at her. 'I should get going,' she said.

'Yes.'

The word sounded as if it had been dragged from him, and if she'd needed any more reason to leave that was it. Clearly the Count wasn't looking to extend their liaison and why should he? Why should she even want him to? Except that it had been the best sex she'd ever experienced. Probably the best sex she ever would.

She slipped from the bed, balling her panties and pulling her robe around her, giving the tie an extra tug. She would become practical Dr Hunter again, and put away the wanton she had been for just one short night.

And then she heard it—the unmistakable thump of the boat engine drawing closer. 'I guess that's my cue. Thank you, Count Volta, for your hospitality.' She was almost at the door when he finally spoke.

'Stay.'

She blinked and turned around, her veins still sizzling, her heart afraid to beat for a moment at his unexpected request, and then resuming with a thump that challenged the sound of the approaching engine. 'What did you just say?'

He crossed the room in rapid strides until he stood before her. 'I said stay.'

'Why?'

'Because there is no reason to cut and run. People expect you to be here a week. Why do you need to go before you have finished your research?'

He managed to smile a little then, as he touched his fingertips to her forehead and traced down the line of her hair. 'You enjoyed our night together?'

She blushed so hard there was no need to answer. She leaned her face into his touch. 'I thought you were angry with me.'

His fingers stilled at her cheek, his smile vanquished. 'Nobody has ever touched my scars by choice. Yet you put your lips to them. I was—' He looked down at her and she could see both the anguish and the confusion in his eyes. 'Don't you understand? I was shocked.'

She smiled uncertainly up at him, touched by his simple declaration. 'It's not something I generally do, I admit.'

'Then why this time?'

'I don't know. It just seemed the right thing to do.'

'So stay,' he urged, winding his fingers in her hair, pulling her closer. 'That is also the right thing to do. I know it.'

'But the boat…'

He kissed her forehead, then rested his head against hers. 'The boat will return when you need to go. Stay for now and do your work, and when you are finished the boat will come back and you can leave.'

But will I want to?

If she was having trouble leaving now, if she was tempted to stay now, what would it be like in two or three or however many days' time? How could she just board a boat and sail away, knowing she would never see him again?

His hands trailed down her back, tracing the curve of her behind and warming her, firing up desires she'd thought well quenched during the night but which were clearly all too ready to be reignited. What would cool, calm Dr Hunter do? she wondered as he pulled her closer until she could feel the press of his erection against her belly. The wanton in her knew the decision she would make. It made sense to continue her study here, where the documents had been found, and she could do her work during the day and enjoy the pleasures of the night.

It made perfect sense.

Just a few days, she told herself as his mouth dropped to hers, coaxing her lips open with a kiss that promised paradise. She knew it didn't. She knew she was kidding herself. But after all, she rationalised, she had to work *somewhere*.

Three more days she stayed, working on her report during the days, making love with the Count late into the nights. Three more days that took her closer and closer to the time she knew she would have to leave.

Neither of them spoke of her departure, and she wondered if he'd even noticed—whereas she was counting down the hours, her inevitable departure like a dark cloud growing ever more heavy over her. A dark cloud to replace those that had graced her first two nights here. For now the weather steadily improved, the storms almost forgotten as they made love on crisp moonlit sheets.

But she would have to leave. Her report was almost complete. She was already spinning out the topics, taking more time to check and double-check every word, every reference, avoiding the page on the fatal affliction as much as she dared. Its message was still unsettling.

There was no real reason she should stay.

Except that she could not bring herself to leave.

For with every passing day she knew it would almost kill her to leave—just to walk away and never see Alessandro again, never to feel his strong arms around her, never again to feel the thrust of his hard length. And so she put aside concerns about how long she was taking and how much she wasn't doing and revelled in what he could give her. That was the now. And she had no intention of leaving before she had to.

They were in the bath, breathless and replete, when the phone call came—an urgent call for Dr Hunter from Professor Rousseau, otherwise Bruno would never have bothered them, he assured the Count.

She wrapped herself in a thick robe to take the call, still shuddering from her latest climax and guilty with it, as if the Professor might know, just by talking with her, what she'd so recently been doing.

'Professor,' she said. 'How is your mother?'

'No better, sadly, but no worse. But, tell me, what have you found?'

Grace summarised her findings, unable to keep the excitement from her voice.

'Excellent,' the Professor said. 'Because I have yet another favour to ask you...'

She listened to her colleague's request, one part of her alive to the opportunity she had just been offered, another part so heavy she thought her heart might fall clean out of her chest. But in the end, despite the warring inside her, she knew she had no choice. This was what she had wanted, what she had worked and hoped for.

'Of course, Professor. Of course I will do it.'

'What did she want?' Alessandro asked when he joined her from the bathroom.

'Her mother is still gravely ill. But she has a speaking engagement in London tomorrow evening and there is no way she will make it. She wants me to take her lecture, to use the chance to announce the discovery of the lost pages.'

'And you said yes?'

'Of course I said yes. What else was I supposed to say?' And immediately she felt contrite, because she hadn't wavered, and she'd made it sound as if she couldn't wait to get away. But it hadn't been like that.

'Alessandro,' she reasoned, when he turned away to his dressing room, 'I was always going to leave soon. We both know that.'

'Yes,' he said, glancing back over his shoulder. 'And it's the opportunity you wanted when you took this job. You will be famous the world over, Dr Hunter. People will fill auditoriums and hang onto your every word and credit you for bringing to light an unknown chapter in the development of human society. That's what you wanted all along, isn't it?'

Yes, but why did he have to make it sound as if there was something wrong with that? And why the sudden 'Dr Hunter'? How long had it been since he'd called her that?

'You know what this means to me,' she argued. 'It's my career.'

'Then go,' he flung over his shoulder. 'As you say, we knew you would leave. I'm not stopping you.'

His rapid change of face did not deter her. He'd been disappointed with the news of her imminent departure, she was sure. Or at least unhappy with the news.

'Come with me,' she said on impulse, following him. That way she could have her career and not lose Alessandro. And suddenly not losing Alessandro was more important than she could fathom. 'This is your discovery as much as mine. People will want to know everything they can about the pages.'

'And what could I tell anyone beyond the fact they were found in the caves below my castle? You do not need me there for that.'

'Then come anyway. Come and keep me company. It will do you good to get away from here for a while.'

'My place is here!'

'Why? So you can bury yourself on this island while your castle crumbles around you? Until you end up as dried and broken-down as that fountain outside?'

'You do not know what it is like.'

'Because you're scarred? No, I don't know what it's like to be scarred. I don't know what it's like to have people turn from me in horror. But I do know you can't let your scars define you. You are more than that. And I know I couldn't live that way, burying myself away where nobody might see me.'

'How do you know? You do not know the first thing about me! You have no concept of what it is to like be the only survivor of a party of eighteen. All of them dead. *Dead*! All of them. Apart from me. How do you think that feels? Special? No, Dr Hunter, it does not. Instead it makes me feel damned. Cursed. And the scars are a constant reminder. The scars never let me forget it.'

She felt his pain in the wave of anguish that rolled off him. 'I'm sorry for what happened. I'm sorry for what you suffered—'

He rounded on her. 'You have no concept of what I suffered!'

She recoiled from his outburst. Recoiled and then reloaded,

knowing she had to let him know she understood. That she cared. 'I know you lost your fiancée and your friends.'

'I lost much more than that. I lost hope that night. I lost trust.'

Her heart went out to him. 'I understand how that could happen after an accident like that.'

'Do you? I doubt it.' His mouth pulled into a snarl. 'I doubt that you have any idea of the kind of woman my fiancée was—the kind of woman who was so in love with the media fantasy that we were the "It" couple that she would have done anything to maintain it, even when it was already over.

'She threatened to leave me that night, for another of my friends she said wanted her. She would go with him if I did not marry her immediately and fulfil the destiny she had planned. But our relationship was already soured, and her attempt to make me jealous was her last-ditch effort to save our floundering relationship. I told her it was over. And that instead of having a blazing row in a nightclub we would break amicably and put out a joint press release the following day. That night, on our way back to the castle, the accident happened.'

He dragged in air, as if struggling with the memories. 'Someone there overheard us talking and reported it to the police, and so when they came to the hospital, while I was barely recovering from injuries so horrific they expected me to die, it was to inform me that I was the suspect in a mass murder case.'

Ice-cold water sluiced through her veins. She took a step closer. His pain was so clear on his face she could read his story there, etched in his scars. That anyone had suffered so much pain, that *he* had suffered so much, destroyed her. His pain became hers, and she wanted to do anything she could to make things right. Knowing she never could, no matter what she felt for him, knowing now she'd had a right to be scared of staying.

'Alessandro…'

'Can you blame me for burying myself here and hiding away from the media's macabre pursuit, Dr Hunter? Can you begin to understand?'

'It doesn't have to be like that,' she offered softly, but knew it could indeed be like that. 'It never has to be like that again.'

'No. Not if I stay here.'

And she knew she had to play her final card—the final truth she had taken this long to admit. 'And if I told you that I loved you?'

He looked at her then, savagery mixed with tragedy. 'Then I would say you are the most cursed of all.'

CHAPTER TEN

THE applause rang out loud and long in the Washington auditorium, and Dr Grace Hunter smiled in her sensible suit and bowed one final time to the audience, finally able to withdraw to the quiet of the room generously labelled her dressing room—little more than a closet to store her things, really, but at least it provided her with a bolthole.

The lecture in London three months ago had been such a resounding success that she'd been booked almost solid ever since. City after city wanted to hear the story of the lost pages, wanted to see her presentation and hear the lost messages from the fabled book of healing.

She felt a fraud every time—tonight more than ever. How could it be a book of healing, she wondered, when she felt so heartsick every minute of every day? And yet she had the fame she had sought. She had the respect of her peers and her colleagues. She had a book deal and offers of chairs at universities all around the world. Even, in her latest coup, a last-minute slot on a prime time chat show.

How was it possible, with all that success, to feel so wretched?

Or had Alessandro been right? Was she the most cursed of all, loving a man who could not return her love?

She peeled the jacket from her shoulders and pulled the court shoes from her feet, remembering another outfit—a waterfall of silk atop silver sandals that shimmered with every step. His fiancée's dress. Had he realised how much he'd hurt her when she'd heard that? Or hadn't he cared because in his mind she'd already ceased being his fiancée before she had died? Whatever, she supposed she should be thankful that at least he'd taken the trouble to find her something that had never been worn. And it had been a beautiful dress.

She sighed, picking up her programme folder to remind herself of where she would be next. There was no point focusing on the past. She must look to the future. She had career decisions to make and continents to decide between.

There was a knock on the door and she pushed herself from her chair reluctantly, remembering the drinks organised for after her presentation. No doubt a reminder call. She was probably already late.

She pulled open the door, ready to make her excuses, but the words dried up in her throat, incinerated by the lightning bolt that coursed through her. She blinked up at him, her eyes moving past his beauty and his horror to drink in the man himself.

'I heard your lecture,' he told her, when he clearly realised she was incapable of speech. 'You were amazing.'

She swallowed. 'You heard it?'

'I wouldn't have missed it for the world.' And then, perhaps because he sensed she was incapable of rational thought, 'Perhaps you might invite me in?'

And she shook her head to scatter her woolly thoughts and remembered her manners. 'Please, Count Volta.'

'Alessandro,' he corrected, and her stunned heart—not yet ready to hope—warmed just a little.

There was barely room for the two of them. He refused to sit, his wide frame shrinking what little space there was. 'What's happened?' she asked, knowing what it must have cost him to leave the castle—knowing what it must have cost him in the stares and whispers of strangers, in the camera flashes of the paparazzi. 'Why are you here? Someone will have seen you.'

His tortured eyes confirmed it, but he shook his head, as if dispensing with that mentality. 'You once said to me that I should not define myself by my scars—'

'No—please. I had no right. I had no idea of what had really happened.'

'Grace,' he said, taking one of her hands in his own, 'you had every right. You were right.' He took a breath, and then another, and she could see how much it was costing him to tell her this. 'Don't you see? I became my scars. I hid behind them because it was easier to live in the dark. Because it was easier than facing the light.'

'It's okay,' she said, wanting to spare him any more pain, knowing what it must have cost him in media attention to get here, suspecting there was a pack of photographers waiting outside right now to see him. 'You don't have to explain it to me.'

'But I do. Don't you see, Grace?' He took hold of her other hands, held them both up in his. 'You brought me back the light. You were the one who chased the darkness away. You made me see it was all right to live again.'

Her heart skipped a beat, and then another, because

she didn't want to believe what it might possibly mean. 'I did?'

He smiled. 'You did. You turned up in my dark world and showed me what life could be like with your enthusiasm, with your joy of discovery. At first, I admit, I hated you for it, because you reminded me of all the things I had lost and of all the things I would never know again. But bit by bit I wanted to be part of it. I wanted to share your light. I wanted to share your joy.'

She thought back to the disastrous dinner and his cruel comment about the dress. 'You were protecting yourself.'

'I couldn't let myself crumble. It took me years to recover after the accident. I couldn't let anything like that happen again, even if it meant losing the best thing that had ever happened to me. I was desperate to find some kind of outlet. I hadn't played the piano for ten years until you came. It was something I associated with *her*. It was part of my former life and I couldn't bring myself to touch the keyboard until wanting you drove me to it. Drove me back to something I loved. Just as you drove me back to life and living and I realised it didn't have to be the same.'

Tears leaked from her eyes. Her heart was pounding in her chest.

'You kissed my scars, Grace. I was shocked and I overreacted, but do you have any idea what was happening to me? You broke something free inside me, something dark and poisoned and toxic. And bit by bit you chased the blackness away.'

For the first time she noticed the moisture glazing his eyes too, as he brought her hands up to his mouth, closed his eyes and kissed them.

'I had to come,' he said at last. 'I knew it from the first

day you left. I knew I had missed an opportunity so golden that it might never come again. But still I couldn't do it. I told myself you were busy becoming famous, that you could not possibly have any place for me in your life. Fear bound me to the castle, just as you said. But as the days and weeks went on I had to know. I had to find out for myself, whatever it took.'

He hesitated then, as if searching the depths of his soul for words. 'Grace, you once told me you loved me. Is there any chance you might love me again? Love a man who was too blind to recognise his own love when it stared him in the face?'

Her heart swelled so large with his words she thought it might explode with happiness. She threw herself into his arms, drinking in his scent, relishing the hard plane of his chest. 'I will always love you, Alessandro. *Always.*'

And he sighed, almost with relief, as if there had ever been any doubt, and drew her closer into his embrace. 'You do not know how I have longed to hear those words again— if only for the opportunity to tell you that I love you with everything this scarred heart can offer. You have it all. But I know you have your career, and that must come first—'

Alarm bells sounded. 'What do you mean that must come first? Before what?'

'We can work it out. You will prefer to continue working, of course. You will not want to be tied down…'

'Alessandro, what are you saying? Maybe you should spell it out first.'

His dark eyes were troubled and uncertain, and she had never seen him so vulnerable. He had risked everything for her today, she realised. Everything. And she would love him for what that had cost him for ever.

'You have your work.'

'Tell me!'

'I hoped—I wondered—so long as it doesn't interfere with your work—' she glared at him '—I wondered if you might agree to become my wife?'

'Yes!' she cried, tears of joy springing to her eyes. 'Yes, I will marry you, Alessandro. Yes, I will become your wife.'

And his face lit up brighter than she had ever seen it, until both sides of his face were beautiful, both sides of him magically, wonderfully hers.

EPILOGUE

THE dock had been sanded and oiled till it gleamed in the sun, the rocks bordering the track freshly painted white. Flags fluttered gaily along the route, and the small harbour was filled with dozens of bobbing white pleasure craft.

It was to be a small affair, he'd promised her. No more than two or three hundred guests. And under the lure of a perfect summer's day they spilled out of the massive ballroom and filled the grounds around the castle, admiring the view across the sea to the Italian coast or having their pictures taken in front of the dolphin fountain, where the water played and splashed like jewels in the bright sunshine.

He looked magnificent, she thought as she caught a glimpse of him through the crowd, in one of his beautifully tailored suits that showed the long, lean line of his body to perfection. He looked magnificent and at ease with himself at last—as if he'd cast his demons from his shoulders, as if he'd come to terms with his past. He'd even wooed the inevitable media, so it was now fully behind him, and covering his wedding as if it was some kind of fairytale. And it *was* a fairytale, she knew.

But it was much more than that. *He* was much more than that. Right now he was talking to someone hidden by the crowd, his beautiful scarred face animated and alive.

He caught her eye across the space and held it, and she felt that now familiar slow burn of heat flare up inside her as he excused himself and headed her way, looking neither left nor right as he cut a swathe towards her. He was at her side a heartbeat later, sweeping her up in one arm and swinging her around.

'Have I told you how beautiful you look today, Countess Volta?'

She smiled. 'Maybe once or twice,' she said, though they both knew it was many, many more times than that. 'And have I told you how magnificent you look, my husband?'

'So many times,' he growled, nuzzling her ear, 'that I fear I may just start to believe it.'

'Believe it,' she said. 'You are the most handsome man here.'

'Grace—'

'No, it is true. You are smiling so much you are like a beacon. Everyone wants to talk to you. Why else has it taken this long to have a moment with you alone?'

'I was just talking to Professor Rousseau.'

Grace looked around, trying to find her through the crowd. 'Oh, I should have come over to you. She doesn't know many people here, Alessandro.'

'She's fine. I left her talking to my best man.'

'To Bruno? I wouldn't have thought they would have much in common.'

'On the contrary. It turns out they both have pirate ancestors.

Bruno has offered to show the Professor through the caves below the castle.'

'He has?' She scanned the crowd, which finally parted enough that she could see them both in deep conversation. As if aware he was being discussed, Bruno suddenly looked up and gave a bashful smile. 'He smiled at me,' she said. 'Bruno actually smiled.'

The man beside her laughed, and she found so much joy in the sound that she wondered... 'Do you think it's true, Alessandro—the legend of the *Salus Totus*? Do you think it really is a book of healing? Do you think it a coincidence that it was found here?'

He took her hands in his own. 'I think you are the healer here, Grace. You came to an island where a monster resided, where only darkness existed. You lit up that world and shook it until your light and your love chased the darkness and the monster away. And I will love you for it for ever.'

He kissed her as tears sprang to her eyes. Tears of love. Tears of joy. Tears for the wasted years, and tears for all the years that were yet to come.

Years they would spend together.

* * * * *

The Reluctant Queen

CAITLIN CREWS

Caitlin Crews discovered her first romance novel at the age of twelve. It involved swashbuckling pirates, grand adventures, a heroine with rustling skirts and a mind of her own, and a seriously mouthwatering and masterful hero. The book (the title of which remains lost in the mists of time) made a serious impression. Caitlin was immediately smitten with romances and romance heroes, to the detriment of her school social life. And so began her lifelong love affair with romance novels, many of which she insists on keeping near her at all times.

Caitlin has made her home in places as far-flung as York, England and Atlanta, Georgia. She was raised near New York City, and fell in love with London on her first visit when she was a teenager. She has back-packed in Zimbabwe, been on safari in Botswana, and visited tiny villages in Namibia. She has, while visiting the place in question, declared her intention to live in Prague, Dublin, Paris, Athens, Nice, the Greek Islands, Rome, Venice, and/or any of the Hawaiian islands. Writing about exotic places seems like the next best thing to moving there.

She currently lives in California, with her animator/comic book artist husband and their menagerie of ridiculous animals.

**Look for Caitlin Crews' latest exciting novel,
The Replacement Wife, available in July.**

Dear Reader,

I've always been fascinated by the idea of an ordinary woman, going about her ordinary life, only to look up and find herself face to face with her destiny.

If it involves far-off kingdoms, thrones, and a dangerously compelling hero, all the better.

That was my premise for *The Reluctant Queen*. I wondered what my heroine would feel when she found herself caught up in a fate she'd thought was little more than a childhood dream. And I wondered what her long-lost betrothed would be like, so determined to win back the only woman who'd ever captured his heart—and who he must convince to marry him if he is to take the throne that was always meant to be his.

I hope you enjoy travelling to their distant kingdom, Alakkul, and falling in love with Lara and Adel. I loved telling their story!

Happy reading!

Caitlin

CHAPTER ONE

"HELLO, Princess."

It was a dark voice, low and deep, and echoed hard and deep in Lara Canon's bones—making them sing out in recognition. She turned without conscious thought, as if compelled, searching for the man responsible, though some part of her knew at once who he must be. Her gaze flicked across the parking lot of the unremarkable supermarket in her Denver, Colorado, neighborhood, scanning out from the side of her car where she'd stopped still.

She found him at once, unerringly, as if he'd commanded it. Her heart began to beat wildly, even as her skin prickled.

He was even more compelling than his voice, tall and broad like a warrior, with jet-black hair and deep gray eyes above a hard, unsmiling mouth. He held himself with an ease she knew at once was deceptive—he was too watchful, too ready. He wore a black, tight shirt that strained against the tautly packed muscles of his broad chest and flat abdomen, and trousers in the same color that clung to powerful legs and lean hips. He was beautiful in the way that dangerous thunderstorms were beautiful, and Lara discovered that she was breathless.

He was the most gorgeous thing she'd ever seen, for all that he was the most arresting. And more than that, she recognized him. *She knew him.*

She had thought she'd never see him again. She felt her pulse pound beneath her skin.

"I did not expect that you would grow to favor your father," he said, those remote, storm-colored eyes seeming to see right through her, shocking her, looking straight into the past she'd long denied. The shopping bag in her arms slipped a few inches as her fingers lost feeling. As panic surged through her.

She realized two things, clutching at the brown paper bag before it fell to the asphalt at her feet. First, that he was not speaking English. And second, that she could understand the language he *was* speaking.

It made her think at once, of course, of Alakkul. Her father's tiny, oft-contested country in the Eurasian, sometime-Soviet mountains, where his family had ruled with iron fists and an inflated sense of their own consequence for generations.

The country she and her mother had escaped from, in the dark of night, when she was sixteen years old. The country that she had been running from, in one way or another, ever since. And the last place she had seen this man, when he had still been more of a boy. When he had been far less beautiful, far less dangerous, and had still managed to break her teenaged heart.

Her stomach clenched into a thick, tight knot. She told herself it was panic—that it could not be that old, familiar desire she'd been so overwhelmed by as a girl. They were in a busy parking lot, filled with people on this bright June evening. He was standing far enough away that she didn't think he could reach over and grab her—and anyway, she was twenty-eight years old. Her father could hardly attempt to regain custody *now*. There was no reason for him to be here. And therefore no reason for her to acknowledge their shared history.

"I'm sorry," she said. In English. She shrugged to indicate her lack of comprehension and, hopefully, polite disinterest. It had been so long. Maybe she was seeing ghosts. Maybe it wasn't him at all. "Can I help you with something?"

He smiled, and it was far more disturbing than his voice, or his hard, shocking beauty. It made his gray eyes warm slightly, with a flash of what looked like sympathy. It confused Lara even as it set off a tiny trail of flickering flames across her skin, licking up and down her limbs. Reminding her. Making her yearn for things she dared not name.

"You are the only one who can help me," he said, in his perfect, exotically accented English. His mouth crooked. "You must marry me. As you promised to do twelve years ago."

She laughed, of course. What else could she do? She laughed, even as old memories chased through her head— long-buried images of crystal-clear mountain lakes, snow-capped peaks jutting in the distance, the spires of an ancient castle hewn from the very rock of the steep hills. A lean, feral young man with dark gray eyes, looking down at her with a fierce expression while her heart beat too fast and the white-cloaked priests murmured archaic, improbable words through the haze of incense and ritual. His head bent close to hers to whisper secrets in the middle of a great festival dinner, making her shiver. His smile, his occasional laughter, that fire in his stormy eyes when he gazed at her...

How long had she told herself those images were part of a dream? That they could not be anything *but* a dream? Yet the man who stood before her was undeniably, inarguably real.

And worse, she knew him. Her body knew him—and was reacting exactly as it had then, when she had been so young. She'd spent a long time convincing herself that all that fire had been no more than a young girl's fantasy. That he could not possibly do these things to her. That she had embellished, exaggerated, as young girls did.

"Thank you for the offer," she said, as if she was placating him. As if she did not, in fact, remember him. "But I'm afraid I have a personal policy against marrying strange men who approach me in parking lots."

"I am Adel Qaderi," he said, in that calm yet implacable voice, his gray eyes on hers, that name sounding within her like a gong. Her breath tangled in her throat. "I am no stranger to you. I am your betrothed, as you know very well."

It was such an odd, old word. Lara concentrated on that— pushing away the fluttering of her pulse, the constriction in her throat. The onslaught of too many memories she'd thought forgotten long ago.

"I'm sorry," she said, dismissing him. If she didn't accept this was happening, it didn't have to happen, did it? "I'm late for a—"

"You are the Crown Princess of Alakkul," Adel said in that low, commanding voice, somehow making it impossible for Lara to turn and get into her car as she knew she should. "The last of an ancient bloodline, warriors and kings throughout history. The only child of the great King Azat, may he rest in peace."

She felt the blood drain from her face. Her knees wobbled beneath her.

"May he...?" she echoed. She shook her head, trying to clear it. What could this mean? How could it be true? Her father was the monster under her bed, the nightmare that lay in wait when she closed her eyes. Hadn't her mother always told her so? "He's...*dead*?"

"At least you do not deny your own father," Adel said, his expression stern. He moved closer to her but then stopped, as if he felt called to an action he chose not to take. Still, somehow, she knew he grieved for her father in all the ways she could not. It made a headache bloom to life in her temples. "Perhaps we can dispense with the rest of this game of pretend now."

"You approached me in a parking lot, like a vagrant," Lara hissed. Unwilling to face what he'd just told her. Unwilling to imagine what it might mean. "What did you think my reaction would be?"

"I did so deliberately." His gaze was cool. Assessing. *Dangerous.* "I assumed you would feel more at ease in a public place. After all, you have spent most of your life running away at the slightest hint of your homeland."

Lara shifted the bag in her arms, and wished her head would stop spinning. How was she supposed to act? Feel? She had not heard from her autocratic father directly in twelve years. She had not wanted to hear from him. If asked even five minutes before, she would have announced without a qualm that she hated the man.

But that did not mean she'd wanted him dead.

"I need to inform my mother..." she began, her temples pounding, wondering how fragile, prone-to-hysteria Marlena would be likely to take such news. Wondering, too, what her mother would center her life around now there was no more King Azat to hate and fear and blame. But perhaps that was unkind.

"Your mother is being notified even now," Adel replied coolly.

Lara found herself staring at the play of muscle in his strong arms, his hard abdomen. She felt her body's treacherous heat, its instant response to the very sight of him, despite her emotions.

"I am afraid your business is with me, Princess. I cannot allow you the necessary time to grieve." Was his tone ironic? Or did she only imagine his judgment? Was that guilt she felt, pooling inside of her? "We must wed immediately."

"You are insane," she told him, when she could speak. When the red haze of confusion and emotion receded slightly. When she could jerk her attention away from his warrior's body. "You cannot really believe I'll marry you!"

Adel smiled again, though this time, there was nothing particularly sympathetic about it. Where was that younger man she remembered, who had been so eager to see her smile?

"I understand that this is a shock," he said. "But let me be clear. You have only two possible choices before you, and while I am aware neither one is necessarily easy, you must choose one of them."

"Your attempt at compassion is insulting," Lara managed to say, her hands clenched tight into the bag she held. Part of her wanted to fling the sack at him as he stood near the trunk of her sensible sedan. And then run. Only the fact that he probably expected that reaction kept her from it.

"Nonetheless, it is real," he said. His storm-colored eyes moved to hers, and darkened. "It would never have been my choice to confront you in this way, with this news. I regret the necessity. But it does not change anything."

"I have no idea what you're talking about," Lara said after a moment, her temper kicking in—replacing the wild swirl of far trickier feelings. Anger was better. Anger *felt* better—more productive. "And more important? I don't care."

"Yet you must listen," he told her. So quiet. So sure. And she could only stare at him. And obey. "I am sorry for that, too, but so it is."

There was something about the way he looked at her then that…bothered her, in a way she couldn't quite categorize. As if he could see the buried truths she'd denied existed for years. The old dreams. The yearnings for a life, a family, the kind of things other girls took for granted while she trailed around after Marlena, cleaning up her messes. The way she'd felt about him all those years ago, the things she'd dreamed they'd do together—

Lara blinked, and steeled herself against him—and the surprising swell of something like grief that she would have sworn she'd never feel.

"What, then?" she asked, her voice too rough, as she fought back the unwieldy emotions that shifted and rolled within her. "What is it you think I need to hear?"

"You have a choice to make," he said again, and the worst part, Lara realized in a sort of horror, was that his voice was kind, his eyes the same. As if he understood exactly what she was going through—as if he *knew*.

And yet he was continuing anyway, wasn't he? He was an Alakkulian male. An Alakkulian king. Just like her father, he thought only of himself. That much was blatantly obvious, no matter how kind his eyes might seem. No matter her memories of his smile, of his tenderness.

"The only choice I will be making," she told him, enunciating clearly, deliberately, with razor-sharp precision, as if sounding tough would make her feel that way, too, "is to get in my car and drive away from here. From you. From this ridiculous conversation. I suggest you get out of the way, unless you'd like me to run you over."

"You did not merely promise to marry me, as any young girl might," Adel said in the same calm, commanding tone, as if she had not just threatened him. "You entered into a binding legal contract."

"I was a teenager," Lara retorted. "No court in the world would ever hold me to it. It's absurd you would think otherwise—this is not the Stone Age!"

"You overestimate the progressive nature of the world's courts, I think," he replied, something almost like humor flashing briefly across his face. But she did not want to think of him as human, as capable of humor as he'd been before, and ignored it. "But in any case, it does not matter. Your father signed for you when you were too young, as is the custom. When you came of age you did not withdraw your consent from the contract—which, according to the laws of Alakkul, means you thus agreed that you entered into the terms of the contract of your own free will."

"I will not marry you," she said. Her shoulders tightened, her chin rose like a fighter's. "I would rather die."

"There is no need for such theater," Adel replied in a faintly reproving tone. Yet his mouth curved slightly—as if he found her amusing. It made her temper kick in again. That, she told herself, was the feeling that pounded through her, shaking her. "You may break the contract, if that is your wish. But there is a price."

"Let me guess." Lara scraped her heavy curls back from

her face with an impatient jerk of her hand. "My honor will be smeared? My family name forever muddied? Isn't that how you people think?"

"By 'you people,'" he asked, his voice staying even though a cold fire blazed to life in his gaze, "am I to understand you mean your own people? Your countrymen?"

"I'll live with the dishonor," Lara told him, not wanting to admit the twist of shame she felt move through her. Much less the odd urge she had to reach over and touch him. "Quite happily."

"As you wish," Adel said with that great calm that, for some reason, infuriated her as surely as if he'd openly taunted her. It made her want to scratch at him, poke at him—made her want to see beneath the surface, rip off the mask she was sure he wore, see what lurked beneath. She just wanted to *touch* him.

She had no idea where that urge came from. Nor why it seemed to move through her like a scalding heat, rippling over her skin and pooling in places it shouldn't.

The city seemed to mute itself around them, the parking lot fading, the bright sky above and the slight breeze from the Rocky Mountains in the distance disappearing. There was only this dangerous, compelling warrior of a man in place of the boy she had once known, and too many emotions to name. She felt…pulled to him. Drawn. As if he'd cast a spell with that fascinating mouth and that commanding, resolute gaze of his, and she was helpless to resist, no matter how many reasons she had to avoid him and how little she wanted to hear what he might have to say.

But if there was one thing she refused to be, it was helpless.

"Wonderful," she said, pulling herself back from the

brink of disaster. Her tone was acerbic, as much to defend herself against this man as to convince herself he was not getting to her in so many odd, uncomfortable ways. "I'm glad you traveled across the world to tell me all of this. You can consider our absurd betrothal ended."

"As you wish," he said again. But he did not move. His gaze seemed to sharpen, as if he was some great predator and she nothing but prey. She fought off an involuntary shiver. "You need only pay me the bride price."

"The bride price?" she repeated, caught as much by the sudden ferocity in his dark gaze as by the words themselves.

"Your dowry was the throne of Alakkul, Princess," Adel said quietly, deliberately. "I am afraid that the sum my family paid for you was significant, give or take such things as the exchange rate, the rate of inflation, and so on."

He named a number that she could not possibly have heard right—a number so astronomically high that it, too, made her laugh. It was as patently absurd as him suddenly appearing in a parking lot and announcing he was going to marry her, just as she'd dreamed when she'd first left Alakkul—and as impossible.

"I have nothing even approaching that amount of money, and never will," she said flatly. "I am an accountant. I live an entirely normal and ordinary life. That amount of money is a fantasy."

"Not to the Queen of Alakkul," he said, and something flared between them, hot and bright, making her breath tangle in her throat, making her ache low in her belly. "Or to me."

"That is another fantasy, one I have no interest in."

"I am a compassionate man," Adel said after a moment,

though the expression he wore made her doubt it. "I will release you from your obligations to me, if that is your desire. You need only repay what your mother stole from the palace when she disappeared twelve years ago. It is not so much. A mere nine hundred thousand dollars, and some precious jewels."

"Nine hundred thousand dollars," Lara repeated in disbelief. "You must be joking. I don't have it—and if my mother took it, it is no more than she deserved, after what my father subjected her to!"

Adel merely inclined his head. "I will not argue with you about your mother," he said. "Nor will I debate your choices with you. They are simple. Marry me, or pay the price."

He held up an autocratic hand when she started to speak, and she knew deep in her bones that he was every inch a king as well as a warrior. She should hate that—him. And yet her treacherous body, instead of finding him repulsive, *yearned*.

"There is not much time, Princess," he said. "I regret the necessity, but you must make your decision. Now."

CHAPTER TWO

HE APPROVED of the woman she'd become, Adel thought, her fierceness and her attempts at fearlessness, and was not certain why that surprised him.

"Do you accept credit cards?" she asked icily after a moment, her silver-blue eyes glittering in the late-afternoon light, even as she held herself so rigidly, so determinedly still. "If so, I am certain we can work something out."

Adel only smiled, enjoying her, even under these circumstances. The girl he had never forgotten for a moment had become a woman he wanted to know better. "You are stalling."

"Of course I am." She shifted her weight and let the paper sack she carried fall to the ground at her feet. He heard the faint crunch of glass against the pavement, but she only glared at him. "It will take me more than thirty seconds to choose between marriage to a man I hardly know or a lifetime in debt I'll never pay off. The interest rates alone would kill me! You'll just have to wait."

He liked that, too. She was as much the child of the late

King Azat, his revered mentor, as she was of the faithless woman who was her mother. Brave. Vibrant. And she would be his wife. His queen, as had been decided so many years ago. The warrior in him appreciated the way she stood so straight, emotion darkening her eyes but not overtaking her, her body lean and supple and strong. The king in him imagined the future her blood assured, the children they would bear together, the way they would rule his beloved Alakkul. And the man in him wanted to taste the fullness of her mouth, and sink his fingers into the dark glossy waves of her long hair.

Just as he'd always wanted her, even back when they were both young.

He had wanted her even after her lying mother had spirited her away, taking her far from her home—far from Adel. He had wanted her in all the years in between, when the old King insisted they leave her to her new life and Adel had wondered when he could ever lay claim to the woman who had always been his. He wanted her as she denied him, as she fought with him, as she looked at him as if he was her enemy.

He had wanted her so long, it had become as much a part of him as his own name. It did not matter what she'd done in all the intervening years. It did not even matter if she'd forgotten him. He was here now, and she was his.

She was far too Western. She was dressed for summer in America—all bare skin and tight clothes that outlined curves his hands itched to touch. Her hair was untamed, uncovered, a silken black mass of curls spilling around her creamy shoulders. Her high, full breasts filled out the tight, V-necked shirt she wore to perfection, while her slim hips and long legs were encased in scandalously tight denim.

Her feet were bare to his sight, her polished pink toenails in thonged sandals.

These things should have displeased him. Perhaps even angered him. Yet they did not. She did not.

At all.

He was fascinated.

"Explain this to me," she said after a moment, her eyes meeting his and then falling, as if she could sense the direction of his thoughts. "My father signed me away to you? When I was twelve? And you are the sort of man who wants to honor that kind of archaic, misogynistic agreement?"

"Your father was the King of Alakkul," Adel said swiftly, not rising to the obvious bait. "And I am his chosen successor. You are his only daughter, and the last of your bloodline. It is fitting that you become my queen."

It was more than fitting—it was necessary, though he did not plan to share that with her. Not now. Not yet.

Her throat worked. Her eyes clouded over, though with temper or hurt, he could not tell. "How romantic," she managed to say.

"Surely you have always known this day would come, Princess," he replied, keeping his voice even, wondering why he felt the urge to comfort her. There was no point addressing that bitter note in her voice. "You have been permitted to live freely for years. But it was always on borrowed time."

"Interestingly, I was under the impression that I was simply living my life," she said, her gaze freezing into a glare. "I had no idea you were lying in wait!"

"You cannot tell me you do not remember me." He saw the tell-tale brush of color on her cheeks, heard the catch of her breath. He remembered the sweet taste of their first, stolen kiss. The music of her sigh of pleasure when he touched her. He could see she did, too. "I can see that you do."

"It might as well be a dream!" she said fiercely, though her flushed cheeks told a different tale. "That's what I thought it was!"

"Life is often unfair, Princess," he said, his voice low, his attention on the way she stood on the balls of her feet, as if she meant to run. Would she dare? "But that does not change the facts of things."

"There are your facts, and then there are my facts," she said in a low voice. She took a breath, and her silver-blue eyes turned to steel. He liked that, too. The warrior in him, who had fought and trained and gladly suffered to achieve all that he had done, sang his approval. "You can go ahead and sue me for your money. I won't pay it. And whatever the courts in your tiny little country might say, the court of public opinion will have only one word for a king who chases down a defenseless woman like this. *Bully*."

Adel smiled then, because she was so much more than he had dared imagine, when he'd thought of her growing up so far from her people, her traditions, him. She was not her mother's daughter at all, as he had feared, no matter how that worthless woman had tried to poison her against all that was hers.

"You will make a magnificent queen," he told her, though he doubted she wished to hear such things. "It is your birthright."

She shook her head, as if he'd insulted her, and turned her back on him. It was a deliberate dismissal. And yet he felt it like a caress, shooting through him, desire and admiration coursing through his veins. *Finally*, something in him whispered. *A woman who is worthy. A woman who is not afraid.*

"Find another queen," she threw back over her shoulder as she opened her car door. "I'm not interested in the job."

Adel moved closer, putting out his hand to hold the door of her car open as she went to get in. He did not crowd her—but he also did not step back when she whipped back around to face him. He stood there for a moment, waiting until her breath came faster, and her gaze dropped to his mouth. He could feel the tension wind between them, and longed to close the distance between them—longed to take her mouth with his and reintroduce himself in the best way he could.

"I spoke of facts, Princess," he said, when she dragged her gaze back to his. "Let me share a few with you. I have every intention of marrying you, as we both swore to do in our betrothal ceremony twelve years ago. That is a fact."

"Your intentions are your business," she replied calmly, though her eyes flashed blue steel. "They have nothing to do with me."

"If you do not honor your obligations," he continued as if she had not spoken, "I will not simply be forced to take measures to secure the bride price owed to me. I will also have no choice but to have your deceitful mother arrested and returned to Alakkul, where her theft of so much money and so many jewels—not to mention her kidnapping of the Crown Princess—will no doubt result in an extremely long and unpleasant jail term. If not death. As your husband and your king, of course, I would be willing to forgive such criminal acts on the part of your relative. But why would I extend such a courtesy to a stranger?"

"And again," she said after a long moment, her mouth

trembling slightly, as if he'd hurt her. "What words do you think come to mind when you say such things?"

"I cannot compromise," he said softly. Fiercely. "I will not."

"And that is what kind of man you've grown into," she replied in the same voice, as something like an ache, a need, swelled in the warm summer air between them. Adel wanted to touch it. Her. "So much for the boy who promised he would never hurt me, that he would lay down his life to avoid it."

He wanted to smile—did she not realize how much she revealed with that memory? How much room she gave him to hope? But he refrained.

"I wish I could place your feelings above all else," he said, inclining his head slightly. "But that is not who I am. I cannot pretend that I will not do anything and everything in my power to secure you. And thus the throne. I owe nothing less to the people of Alakkul." He moved slightly, closer, unable to keep his distance as he should. She was too much—too magnetic, too proud. Too…everything he'd dreamed. "*Your* people, Princess."

"You can call me *Princess* all you like," she said, strong emotion cracking across her face, in her voice. "That doesn't make it so. I left all of that behind. I have no interest in a foreign country I can hardly remember."

"What will spark your interest, I wonder?" he asked, hearing the danger in his own voice, even as he saw her awareness of it, of him, in her gaze. "Are you as cold-hearted as you would like me to believe? Are you prepared for the consequences of your refusal? Not just to your faithless mother," he said coldly when she began to speak, "but to the very people you claim to care nothing about. If you do not take the throne with me, I will have to fight for it. That is not a euphemism. I am talking about civil war."

She rocked back on her feet, and dragged in a deep, ragged breath. Her eyes were unreadable when they met his again, dark gray now instead of blue.

"Why ask me at all?" she demanded, her voice strained. "Why pretend that I have a choice to make if I do not?"

He wanted to trace the shape of her delicate cheekbones, the bold line of her nose, the full swell of her lips. He did not understand what he felt then—tenderness? Affection? Need? All of the above at once?

"Here is what I will promise you," he said abruptly, called somehow to fix the darkness of her expression. "I will honor you and respect you, a claim I do not make to many without cause, but one I made to you twelve years ago. I will not take lightly the sacrifice you are making today. I doubt I am an easy man, but I will try to be fair."

He saw tears at the back of her eyes, making them shine too bright. But she did not let them fall. He saw the panic, the uncertainty, the fear. But then she swallowed, and let her hands drop to her sides, and he knew it was as much a surrender as a challenge.

He could handle both. He'd been waiting for her for over a decade. For the whole of his life. He was amazed at how much, how deeply and how completely, he wanted to handle her. In every sense of the term.

"Congratulations," she said bitterly. "You've won yourself a completely unwilling queen."

Adel did not, could not care if she thought she hated him now. He would win her. He had won her years before—and she had already showed him she remembered more than she claimed she did. He would build on those memories, and he would win her all over again. And this time, in the way a man won a woman he meant to keep.

"I will take you any way I can get you," Adel said now, and extended his hand, keeping the hard, bright triumph that flared inside of him under tight control. She was his. Finally. "Come," he said. "Our future awaits."

He saw her pulse go wild in her throat, saw her remarkable eyes widen a fraction. He saw her waver. He saw her legs shake as if she fought against the urge to bolt. Still, he held out his hand, and waited.

She bit her lip, surrendered, and slid her hand into his.

She had no choice.

Everything seemed to burst into speed and color, exploding all around her.

There was the feel of his warm, strong palm, his skin against hers, arrowing deep into her, making her soften and yearn. *Just like before.* There was his strong, dangerous body too close to hers—so close she imagined she could *feel* his heat—and the way she wanted to lean into him even as her mind shrieked in denial of everything that was happening. Her body had already decided. Her body had chosen him years ago, and was now exultant at his return. It was her mind that reeled, that was desperate for an out.

But what was her alternative? Her mother jailed? *War*? How could she possibly live with any of that, knowing she'd had the power to prevent it and had refused?

And she did not doubt that Adel Qaderi was more than capable of the things he'd promised. She could feel his ruthlessness taking her over like an ache in the bones, making it impossible for her to breathe. It was his ruthlessness, she told herself firmly, and nothing more—certainly not that old, demanding heat that only he raised in her. Certainly not that.

Adel raised his hand, and they were suddenly surrounded— by a fleet of hard-mouthed, serious-looking men who spoke in staccato tones into earpieces and herded Lara into a limousine she had not seen idling nearby.

It was only when she was tucked inside the car and it was speeding away, while her head spun wildly, that her eyes fell on the pieces of luggage on the seat opposite her. She recognized them at once. She had last seen them in the hall closet of her apartment.

She stared at them for a moment, her brain refusing to make the obvious and only connection, and then whipped her head around to stare at the man who sat with such devastating confidence beside her.

He only raised his dark brow, and watched her.

He had known she would surrender.

He had planned it.

"Your belongings have been packed up and are being shipped," he said without the slightest hint of apology in his tone. But why should he apologize? He'd won. "But should you wish for anything else, it is yours."

"Except my freedom," she said with more bitterness than she'd intended. "My *life*."

"Except that," he agreed, his voice moving from that exotic steel to a softer velvet.

He shocked her then by reaching over and taking her hand in his far bigger one, holding it between his palms.

Lara jumped, a shudder working through her body, as she stared at the place they were connected, her fingers curling toward his. She felt herself blush, hard, the heat prickling over her and casting her in a hot, breathless red.

"Is it so terrible?" he asked softly, very nearly amused, his voice a caress in the stillness of the car's plush interior. "I am not a bad man."

"You'll understand if I choose to reserve judgment on that," she said in a voice that sounded so much stronger, so much crisper, than she felt—and yet she did not pull her hand away from his. "Given that you are currently blackmailing me into marrying you, as if we are in some gothic novel."

"You intrigue me, Princess," he said, his voice insinuating itself in places it should not have been able to reach. Heat moved between them, or she simply burned, and she could not pretend that she was not at least partly as motivated by that as she was by her concern for the rest of it. What did that make her?

"That sounds like a fantastic basis for a marriage," she managed to say. "You are intrigued, I am forced into it against my will, and the fate of my mother and all the citizens of Alakkul hangs in the balance. How delightful."

"Ah," he said in a voice that made her think of much darker delights, skin against skin, long, hot nights, all those things she'd long imagined with him but thought would never come to pass, "but will is a delicate thing, is it not?"

He lifted her hand to his mouth. Trapped, captivated— *appalled*, she told herself!—she only watched. As he turned her hand in his. As he brought her palm closer to the hard line of his full lips. As his thunderstorm eyes met hers, electric, demanding.

And as he kissed the center of her palm, sending a lightning bolt of impossible desire directly into her core.

CHAPTER THREE

LARA snatched her hand back, jumping in her seat as if he'd bitten her. And then she felt herself melt into a wild heat, imagining what it might be like if he did exactly that.

"What are you doing?" she demanded, horrified at herself, curling the palm he'd tasted into a fist and shoving it into her lap. Would she fall for him so easily, so quickly? After twelve years and far too much water under the bridge? "You can't—you can't *possibly*—"

"We are to be married," he said, leaning back in his seat, his gray eyes gleaming silver now, his hard mouth allowing the smallest curve. "What do you think I'm doing?"

She could not think at all—that was the problem! Her mind was a loud, buzzing blank, like static, and it was all too much to take. Adel's unexpected appearance in the parking lot. The threats, the compulsion. The news of her father, which she could still hardly bear to think about, could still barely bring herself to accept as real. Her own capitulation that had led to her presence in this car. And it was his fault! She could not seem to form a single coherent thought, save that. *He* had done this. Lara was perfectly clear about the fact that Adel Qaderi was capable of anything. It was just as her mother had always said—Alakkulian men could not be trusted.

Hadn't he just proved that? What decent, honorable man would behave as he had done, under these insane circumstances?

Her own pounding need, her own desire—Lara could not let herself consider.

"How can you possibly imagine that I would welcome your advances?" she hissed at him. "I will never—"

"Never is a very long time," he said, with a soft laugh, as if she delighted him. "Be careful how you use the word. It might come to haunt you."

Suddenly, the future she could not escape yawned open in front of her, a deep, black hole. It was one thing to offer to make a sacrifice, knowing it was the right thing—the only thing—to do. But how was she meant to survive *this*? The day-to-day, moment-to-moment reality of being in this man's possession? Being a wife? A queen? A *lover*, a voice inside whispered, and her stomach clenched again.

"Are you so delusional that you truly believe that a woman in my position would *ever* want you to touch her?" she asked, her voice rasping over everything she could not say, everything she feared—including her own reactions to this man. *Especially* her reactions. The heat between her legs. The ache in her too-heavy breasts. Her inability to draw a full breath. The car seemed too close around her. *He* was too close.

"I don't know about a woman in your position," he murmured, stretching his arm out along the back of the seat and in so doing, drawing her attention away from her own panic and bringing it to his electric physicality. "That is far too abstract for me. I can only tell you what is concrete." His hot gaze dropped from her eyes to her mouth. His voice lowered. "What I see, what I smell, what I know."

"That I can barely remember you?" she supplied in desperation, shifting to be sure she avoided even the faintest brush of contact with his arm. "That I want nothing to do with you?"

"That your body wants me, no matter what you might say to the contrary," he said, seemingly unperturbed by her acidity. He even smiled, as if he could see the way her breasts firmed, her thighs clenched. As if he knew her treacherous body better than she did. As if he understood the potent, wild combination of emotion and arousal that made Lara feel like a stranger to herself.

"You know nothing about me," she threw out, desperately. "We might as well be complete strangers!"

He leaned forward, and Lara had to force herself not to squeak like a mouse and shrink away from him. But pretending to be strong only left her far too close to him. Close enough to see the faint hint of his beard along his strong jaw. Close enough to find herself mesmerized by that hard mouth she now knew could be devastatingly soft, if he chose. Close enough to smell the faint hint of sandalwood that clung to him, and something else, something male and only his, beneath.

"We are not strangers," he said, his eyes gleaming pure silver now. "We never were. I am the man who will be your husband, your lover, the father of your children. These things will happen, Princess. Perhaps not today. Perhaps not even soon. But believe me, they will happen."

"I said I would marry you," she breathed, locked in his

uncompromising gaze, lost in the spell he cast around them. "I can't do anything else, can I?"

"No." His eyes seemed to warm, and to warm her, too. "You cannot do anything else."

"I never said anything about...the rest of it," she continued, deeply unnerved. She was aware of him—every part of him. The way he looked at her, the heat that seemed to emanate from his tautly muscled form, even the places his gaze touched as it swept over her. She had to force herself to breathe. And then again.

His smile deepened, as if she was precious to him somehow. As if she was more than merely a pawn in his game. But how could that be?

He reached down with the hand he'd laid against the back of their seat and traced a line along her jaw, from temple to lip, until he held her chin in his fingers.

She knew she should jerk away. She told herself hers was the fascination of the fly for the spider, the moth for the flame, and it would be suicidal to pay more attention to the unfamiliar heat and *want* that scorched her than to her own mind—

But she did not move.

She only watched him. Helpless. Caught. And unable, in that moment, to think of a single reason she should fight him.

"We will work it out, you and I," he said. Quiet command rang in his voice, through her. "It was foretold when we were children. Never doubt it now."

"Of course," she said, aware of his fingers like hot brands against her skin—aware, too, of the rich, wild heat that washed through her because of it. Of how much she had always wanted him, even when she'd believed him to be no more than a dream. "Because you say so. Does the world always align itself with your wishes, according to your commands?"

"Of course," he said, echoing her, that smile of his lighting up his eyes, broadcasting that calm confidence, that deceptively graceful strength of his. "I am the King."

The shockingly luxurious private jet hovered somewhere high in the night sky above the Atlantic Ocean, the world shrouded in black on all sides, but Lara could not sleep as she knew she should. She stared blindly out the window as the plane cut through the dark clouds, shivering slightly as reality sank into her like a great weight.

What had she done? How could she possibly have agreed to this?

She had spent her whole life avoiding exactly this—her return to Alakkul. Marlena had spoken of it as if it was the worst possible scenario, the ultimate pit of doom and despair. As if they would die should it happen—or, worse, wish to die. *"Azat will hunt us down and drag us back there,"* she had told the young Lara again and again. *"He will make you one more of his little puppets, who live only to serve him!"*

They had taken Marlena's mother's maiden name as their surname. No more Princess Lara. No more *Your Highness.* Marlena had moved them whenever she felt threatened, whenever she had reason to think the King's goons were drawing near. Always, King Azat was the boogeyman, the monster they sought to avoid. Lara wasn't sure when the crushing fear had started to recede—or why Marlena had finally permitted them to settle down in Denver. She only knew that once she'd finished college, Marlena had seemed far less worried than she'd been before, and far happier to make herself a home in nearby Aspen.

Lara wasn't sure when she'd first started to wonder if, perhaps, Marlena had simply been overreacting. Perhaps there had never been any goons—any escape. Perhaps Marlena had simply wanted a divorce. But thinking such things had always felt deeply disloyal to the only parent she had access to, and felt doubly so now. Lara pushed the thoughts away.

Adel sat not far away, frowning down at the documents before him, a soft reading light surrounding him in a warm halo. Lara could not help but watch him. He was so much more than the cascade of her teenage memories, her teenage feelings, and the simple fact of his commanding presence. He was everything she had been taught to fear about Alakkul—and Alakkulian men in particular. Autocratic bullies, Marlena had said—content to use their power to crush, maim, destroy.

Wasn't that what he'd done today? Wasn't that what she'd let him do? Emotion rose like bile in her throat, and she had to struggle to keep from crying out. She squeezed her eyes shut and tried to breathe.

She did not know this man. She had only the memories she'd held on to for years, and her own sense that she owed Marlena this—that she could not let her mother pay such a high price for their escape. That was all. And yet she had agreed to marry him? To be the queen of a country she hardly remembered—had gone out of her way, in fact, to forget? Lara shifted in her seat and wondered if she would wake up and find herself in her bed at home in Denver—if this was one more of those dreams she'd used to have, all desperate and yearning and dark until she woke, gasping for breath, her heart pounding in her chest.

But when she looked up, she was still on the plane. It was all too real. And Adel was watching her from his place across the cabin, as if he'd heard her very thoughts.

"You should rest," he said. His gray eyes were shadowed now, storm-colored and stern, not silver at all. She did not know why she should feel that as a loss—why she should want to change them back. "You will need your strength, I think, for what lies ahead."

"Thank you," she said past the dryness in her throat and the clutch of panic that still gripped her. "That is very comforting."

"Your father lies in state in the palace," Adel said, his voice giving her no quarter, his hard eyes allowing her no mercy. "He must be buried as his legacy and consequence demand. As his country demands."

Lara opened her mouth to make a wry comment on that— to mention, perhaps, what sort of legacy he'd always held in her mind—but swiftly thought better of it. Adel Qaderi, handpicked by King Azat to succeed him, always the son to her father that she could never be, was unlikely to find Marlena Canon's stories of the cruelties visited upon her particularly persuasive. Given the way he'd referred to her mother already, however offhandedly, Lara suspected Adel believed a deeply skewed version of reality. He was King Azat's chosen heir! She knew exactly what he believed: the story her father had told him.

But what if Marlena had made all of that up? a small voice asked. She swallowed. It didn't matter any longer. It couldn't. It was twelve years too late. She would have to go on believing what she'd always believed.

Something must have showed on her face, because his attention seemed to focus in on her then. Too intent. Too demanding. He exuded far too much raw power, even sitting there with his work in front of him, like some kind of common businessman.

Common, Lara thought, with a shaking deep within that she could not quite convince herself was panic, was something Adel Qaderi could never be.

"If you have negative things to say about King Azat, as I can see you do, I suggest you say them to me here," Adel said. His voice was harsh, his gaze frankly condemning. "You are unlikely to find a receptive ear in Alakkul, where he has long been considered a hero as well as a monarch."

"Perhaps," Lara said, conscious of the edge in her voice, her skin prickling with the urge to slap back at that disapproving note in his voice, to defend herself and her mother, "he was a better king than he was a father or a husband." She raised her brows in challenge. "For your country's sake, I certainly hope so."

"And you feel qualified to judge him as a man, as a father?" Lara did not mistake that silky tone for something soft—she could see the steel in his gaze. "You, who showed your daughterly devotion by pretending he did not exist for twelve long years? You, who were not even aware that he was ill, nor that he had died?"

"I do not need to justify myself or the intricacies of my family's dynamics to you," she snapped at him, surprised that his words pricked at her.

His eyes bored into her from across the cabin. Why should she want to squirm? Why should she feel something far too much like shame? "I witnessed, firsthand, what your abandonment wrought."

"I can imagine how it must have pained him to lose two

of his many interchangeable, nameless possessions," Lara said sarcastically.

"Azat will raise you to be nothing more than a pet," Marlena had told her. Repeatedly. *"Meek. Easy. Forever owned and operated at his command, at his disposal. Is that what you want? Is that any kind of life?"*

"Believe me, he knew your name," Adel replied in that low, furious tone. His mouth twisted, and his gaze chilled. "And your mother's."

"My mother is the only hero I'm aware of being related to," Lara threw at him, feeling a desperate, consuming need to defend Marlena. To avenge her. To fight for her, even now, even when she wasn't sure she believed her story. "But that's not something a man like you can understand, can you? The plight of a single mother on her own, forced to run from all she knew—"

"Forced?" Adel laughed, but it was a mirthless sound. "You must be joking. The only thing your mother was ever forced to do was face her own failings as a wife. But she could not handle that, and so she ran from the palace with you rather than deal with the consequences of her behavior." His gaze hardened. "And when I say 'consequences,' let me be clear. I am speaking of her admitted infidelity."

"Don't you dare speak of her!" Lara cried, rising from her chair without knowing she meant to move. Her hands moved of their own accord, out in front of her as if she meant to strike him. As if she dared. And oh, how she wished she dared! "You know nothing about her, or me! You have no idea what our life was like!"

"No," he said with a seething sort of impatience, and that hard gaze that seemed to arrow into her very core, "I know what your life *should* have been. I know what was stolen

from you. And from the King. And from your people."
He made an abortive gesture with one hand. "I know that
when the country needed you, you—*the Crown Princess of
Alakkul*—were toiling away in some pedestrian job, in some
life far beneath your station, acting as if you were nothing
more than a run-of-the-mill, anonymous nobody. Instead
of who you really are. The last Alakkulian princess. The
dawning of a new age for our people. How can you possibly
defend the woman who so dishonored you?"

There was a searing kind of silence. As if the whole
world hung there between them, changing even as she tried
to breathe. Lara could feel her pulse hit hard against her
neck, her ribs, her wrists. And between her legs. Just like
his voice.

"My mother *saved* me!" She could not take his words
in, could not let them register. She could only remember
the stories, so many stories, and the nights her mother had
wailed and screamed and cursed, and there had only been
Lara to comfort her. Had it all been lies? *All of it?*

"From what, exactly?" Adel demanded, incredulous,
sitting forward in his chair. "Your wealth? Your heritage?
Everything that should have been yours? *Me?* Are you certain
she is the hero of this story—and not its villain?"

"I know all about the life I might have led, had I languished
in that horrible place," Lara threw at him. She wanted to
hurt him back. To make him pay for saying these things to
her, and she did not want to think about why she blamed
him. "I thank God every day that my mother saved me from
that. From you—a fate worse than death!"

"Says someone who has never faced death," Adel said
smoothly, his voice a dark current that moved over her,
through her. That made her feel things she hated—that made

her hate herself. Things that made no sense. "Because had you done so, you would not make such naive statements. Did your mother fill your head with this foolishness? That *death* was preferable to your birthright? To a marriage that at sixteen you wanted desperately?"

"A birthright—a marriage—that would have been nothing but a prison term," Lara retorted, desperate to strike back at him, to make him as off-balance as she felt, somehow, as some kind of retaliation. Because she could remember, now, that desperate, dazzled yearning for him. Oh, how she had wanted him! It made her even angrier now. "A whole life shut away in a gilded cage—never allowed to think or dream or *live*. Trained from a girl to be nothing more than a biddable wife, a possession, a *thing*. The pawn or the prize for men like you. No, thank you."

"You say things you cannot possibly mean," Adel said, his voice growing softer, more dangerous. She was reminded, suddenly, that he was a warrior first, a king second. That he had all manner of weapons at his disposal. His head tilted slightly as he regarded her. "When I kissed you, you cried tears of joy. When I took your hands in mine, you trembled. You were sixteen and in love with me, and I remember the truth of what was between us even if you do not. She took that from you, too. And from me."

"No," Lara said, her hands in fists at her sides, afraid to let his words penetrate—to let herself remember the things he did. "I was a teenager. I was in love with the idea of love. You were incidental. My mother did us both a favor!"

"There are any number of words I could use to describe your mother, Princess," Adel said in a deadly tone. The hairs on Lara's neck stood at attention. "But I will refrain from using them in your presence because they are disrespectful."

His eyes flashed. "Not to her, about whom I could not care less. But to you, my future queen."

"Your mean your possession," Lara flashed at him. Her temper was a live thing, fusing with her panic, her fear, the memories of her sixteen-year-old heart. Making her too reckless, too thoughtless. But she couldn't stop—as if she was as desperate now as she had been then. "Your pawn. Your *object*."

"If that is how you see yourself, who am I to contradict you?" he asked, but she could see the temper he kept at bay. It was in the fire in his cold eyes, the set of his hard jaw. "Demean yourself as you see fit."

"You would love that, I'm sure," she seethed at him, drifting closer to his seat, so focused on her anger that she hardly noticed what she was doing. *Or maybe you just want to be close to him, as you always have,* a small voice whispered, daring her even closer. "Why don't I just bow down and give you all the power? Why don't you just treat me like one more mindless marionette who dances on a string for your pleasure?"

She did not like the way he stared at her, the way his hard mouth curved into an even harder smile, the way his gray eyes glittered. She did not understand the loud beating of her heart, much less the way she shook.

She did not *want* to understand.

"Ah, Princess," he said, his voice a low growl that seemed to reverberate through her like a drum. "You should not tease."

And then, with an economy of movement and a shattering male grace, he hauled her into his arms, across his lap, and took her mouth with his.

CHAPTER FOUR

LARA had no time to react.

His mouth was on hers, hard and demanding. One hand held her at the nape of her neck, the other at her hip, holding her fast against the granite expanse of his chest.

His kiss was possessive, angry, hot. Nothing like the sweet kisses they'd stolen so long ago—and yet so much more. Lara could do nothing but glory in it, even as her hands rose to his shoulders—whether to push him away or pull him closer she would never know.

Fire rolled through her, scorching her, making her forget everything except the power of his kiss, the dark mastery of it, the tight, lush angle of his mouth, his heat and his taste and the breathtakingly sensual way he held her.

As if he had all the time in the world to explore her mouth.

As if tasting her was a matter of critical importance.

As if he was already inside her, claiming her, taking her, making her his in every way.

She felt more than branded. More than stamped, somehow, as his.

She felt more than the molten, restless heat between her legs, more than the wild drumming of her heart, more than his hardness beneath her, against her.

He kissed her as if he knew her as well as he claimed he did. As if it had been only moments since the last time he'd kissed her, instead of years. As if they had always been destined to come together like this, mouth to mouth, body to body, passion to passion.

As if they were meant for each other. As if he was, finally, the home she'd spent her whole life searching for.

It was that last, impossible thought that had her rearing back, her head caught fast in his large hand, to look into his silver eyes.

She hardly knew herself, much less him. Their history was lost in the mists of time, a teenage fantasy at best. This was all too real. Too much.

"You can't…" she began, but she had no idea what to say. How could she tell him that kissing him made the world fall away? That she forgot who she was? That she wanted nothing more than to burrow into him, lose herself in him, and the very madness of that idea made her tremble with need?

Just like before.

"Kiss me," he urged her, as if he knew all the things she could not say.

It was not until he closed the gap between them again, that fascinating mouth so hot against her own, so right, that she realized he had stopped speaking English yet again. And more to the point—so had she.

She tasted sweet, just like he remembered. Like ripe summer berries and the kick of *woman* beneath it. She went to his head like wine.

Adel wanted her, this untutored, disrespectful princess of his, more than he could remember wanting another. More than he wanted almost anything else. Her lush little body curled into his, against his, as if she too could not get close enough. As if she felt the same rush of desire that surged through him, making him want to forget himself in her.

Just as it should be. Just as it had been.

He let his hands travel over the body he'd longed to possess totally for so many years. He tested the shape of her full breasts, traced the indentation of her waist, learned the intoxicating swell of her hips. She writhed against him, her lushness against his hardness, driving him ever closer to distraction. And still he kissed her, again and again, drinking from her, reveling in her, making her pant and shake against him.

Again, he felt triumph beat like a drum in him. She was his. She was *his*, and she was more than simply this lush body, this elemental passion. She was the dream of his family for generations. She was the throne of Alakkul. She was his destiny taking shape, finally, after so many years spent preparing for it.

She was the only woman he had ever loved. His queen. *His*.

Which meant he could wait a little bit longer before taking her, though he longed to do it now with every inch of his body, the want of her so fierce, so total, there was a long moment he was not at all certain he could let go of her.

She would be his queen.

She made a soft sound of distress when he tore his mouth from hers, and set her away from him. Her silver-blue eyes were wide and dark, her mouth damp and slightly swollen from his kisses. He felt a sharp surge of possessiveness, of desire. He let his hands rest on her shoulders for a moment, then dragged his thumb over her full lower lip, smiling when she shuddered her response.

"Not here," he said, though it was more difficult than it should have been. "Not now."

She blinked, and he could see when she understood him. Color flooded her face, staining her cheeks as she disentangled herself from him.

"You are getting ahead of yourself," she snapped at him, in what he imagined she intended to be quelling tones, and might have been, were she not still breathless.

His smile deepened, and he let his hand drop to her breasts, where her nipples stood out, proud and taut, against the tissue-thin fabric of her shirt. He traced one hard peak with the pad of his finger.

"Am I?" he asked lazily.

"You are a pig!" she hissed, rearing back from him, putting space between them and climbing to her feet.

Adel let her go. Temper made her coloring that much more dramatic, and in any case, he had tasted the sweet honey of her desire. He could see the way she trembled, the way her eyes kept returning to his mouth. He knew the truth. If she had to hate him, if she had to pretend—well, he knew what her body wanted, what it needed. It would betray her easily enough.

"Calm yourself," he suggested mildly.

She looked murderous for a moment. He heard her sharp intake of breath, and then, stiffly, she gathered herself, her flowing dark curls like a curtain around her slender shoulders. He watched her spine straighten. She stood near the line of windows, and looked away from him for a moment. Then another. Biting her tongue, he had no doubt.

"I will not rut with my future queen here," he told her when she turned toward him again, her gaze shuttered, as if she could hide from him. "On a plane, God knows where. You deserve greater respect from me than that."

"How interesting," she said, her voice sharp. "*Respect* seems an awful lot like *control*."

"I am sorry to disabuse you of your deep-held fantasies," he said softly, "but the truth is that I do not wish for you to be my puppet, dancing on a string or otherwise. I want you to be my wife. My queen." He smiled slightly. "The dancing is purely optional."

"And what about what I want?" Her voice was strained. Stark. He did not think this was defiance—he thought this was something else, perhaps even the thing that haunted her, making her eyes too big in her face, her skin too pale. Would she tell him what it was? Would she learn to trust him?

He wanted her to do so more than he wanted to admit.

"Tell me what you want," he said, his voice hushed, as he struggled with urges inside of him he could not entirely understand. "If I can give it to you, I will."

"Perhaps I wish to rut with you, right here and right now," she said, her eyes meeting his boldly. He could not help but harden even further at that—almost to the point of pain—as he imagined her astride him, beneath him, her lush mouth fastened to his, her softness spread out before him. "Why do you get to make the decisions? Am I to be your queen or your slave?"

He could think of several answers to that question, but chose to take the query seriously.

"We will rule together," he said. "As tradition requires."

"What does 'together' mean to an Alakkulian male, I wonder?" she mused, her eyes narrowed. "I somehow doubt it means the same thing to you as it does to me. What if we wish to rule differently? What if you are wrong? Who gets to decide?"

Their eyes met, held. The attraction that sizzled between them seemed to intensify, seemed to beat at him with hot, dangerous flames. Why did her anger, her restless intelligence, make him want her all the more?

"I suspect," he said after a moment, "that you already know the answer."

She made a scoffing noise, and folded her arms over her chest. "What a surprise," she said after a moment, in a bitter sort of tone.

And something in him tore free. He could not have said why. It was her defiance, perhaps, or—more curious—his surprising, continuing sympathy for her plight. He felt more for her than he had ever felt for another, even across these long years of separation. He wanted her as he had never wanted any other woman. And still she looked at him as if he was the enemy. As if she did not quite grasp who he was.

Perhaps it was time to tell her. To remind her.

He was on his feet before he knew he meant to move—a shocking deviation from the usual iron control he maintained over himself and anyone in his orbit. He stalked over to her, enjoying the way her expression changed, became far more wary, though she only squared her shoulders as he came closer. She did not cower. She did not run. She only waited, and he knew she was more his queen in that moment than she realized.

He moved closer, deliberately stepping into her space, so she was trapped against the wall of the plane and forced to look up at him. He placed a hand on the smooth surface of the bulkhead on either side of her head, framing her face, and leaned in.

"If you kiss me again," she told him fiercely, "I will bite you."

"You will not." But his attention moved to her mouth. "Unless I ask you to."

"Stop trying to intimidate me," she ordered him, but once again there was that tell-tale breathiness in the voice she'd clearly meant to sound stern. He smiled, and allowed himself to touch her hair—pulling one dark black curl between his fingers, running the thick silk over his lips, and inhaling the scent. Mint and honey. *His princess.*

"Stop it!" she whispered, her eyes wide. Wary.

Wanting, he thought, with no little satisfaction.

"Listen to me," he said. He let the curl drop from his hand, but he did not move back. Her hands moved, as if she went to push him away but thought better of touching him. "I am not one of your American men. I am not politically correct."

"Really?" Her tone was dry. Defiant. "I hadn't noticed."

He liked being so close to her. More, perhaps, than he should. He could smell her, almost taste her, feel the heat of her. But because indulging himself would lead precisely where he did not wish to go, not yet, he leaned away, still keeping his arms on either side of her, but removing his mouth from the temptation of hers.

"I am not modern." His voice was low. As if he offered her his confession, though the very thought was absurd. "I cannot pretend to be to save your feelings, or to coddle your Western sensibilities."

"Is that what's been happening so far?" she asked, her

brows arching. She shook her head. "The mind balks. What's next? The barbarian horde?"

"I was trained to be a soldier since I was a child," he told her, not certain why he'd started there. Not at all easy with the baffling urge to share himself with her, to let her see him, know him, as he'd thought she might long ago. Not sure he wanted to examine that urge more closely. "A barbarian by your measure, I suppose. My parents sent me to the palace when I was still a child, barely five years old. I was raised to be a weapon. A machine. One of the King's personal guard."

She only stared at him. "The *cadre*," she murmured. And he knew that she remembered the tight band of warriors who had shadowed her father's every movement, each one of them more dangerous than the next, whose honor and duty it was to accompany the King wherever he went. To lay down their lives for him at a moment's notice. To live in service to his whims. He had been the youngest ever inducted into the *cadre*'s elite ranks. Perhaps she remembered that, too.

"I was taught to sever all emotional ties," he continued, fighting the urge to touch her soft skin, to feel her heartbeat with his hands. "I learned to focus only on one goal—protecting and serving my king, my country. I did so, gladly. I wanted no greater glory than that. Until your father gave me you."

"I was not his to give," she said, but her voice was soft, as if she felt this same, strange tenderness. Her eyes moved over his face.

"And you wanted me, too," he reminded her. "Duty and desire, all at once. We were lucky, Princess."

Memory and desire shimmered between them, like need. Like heat.

"I remember you, Adel," she admitted in a stark whisper.

She swallowed, nerves and memories and something dark in her gaze. "I do. But that doesn't mean I can be who you want me to be. Maybe not ever."

"I will protect my country," he said, though he suspected that was not an answer she would like—that she might not even understand why he said it. Or the stark truth of it. "No matter the cost. Nothing means more to me than that."

"Not even the throne?" she asked, incisive yet again.

"There is nothing I would not do for Alakkul, nothing I would not sacrifice, and no one I would not betray in service to my country, if my duty to my country demanded it." His voice was so sure, coming from deep within him. Why did he want her to understand? Why did he want her this much—so all-consumingly? So overwhelmingly? She gazed up at him and there was an expression on her face that made something in him twist over on itself. "I cannot pause in this and make you easy with the role you must assume. I would not even know where to begin."

Something pulled taut between them, dark and glittering. She pulled in a breath, then another, her gaze unreadable.

"Don't worry," she said, her voice tense. Almost sad. "I told you—I remember. I know exactly who you are."

"No," he said, his voice harder than it should have been, though she did not flinch—and he admired her for it, almost grudgingly. "You don't. But you will, soon enough."

Lara woke slowly, aware that she was stiff and that her dreams had been wild pageants, complicated and emotional and much too heavy. It took long moments to dispel them, to remember where she was, and why.

And then she looked out the window and wondered if she'd woken up at all.

The great valley of Alakkul, mystical and secretive, spread out before her—ringed by the sharp, snow-capped mountains on all sides. Her half-remembered homeland sparkled in the morning light, white snow and deep green fields, the rich browns and greens of the forests, and the deep crystal blues of the clear mountain lakes. From high above, she could see the remotest villages and the farmer's fields, the bustling towns and the bigger, busier cities, tucked into the foothills and spreading across the valley floor.

She did not merely *see*, Lara thought in a mix of elation and despair—she *felt*. It was as if a great wall within her, one she hadn't known was there, began to crack into pieces, to fall. Her eyes drank in the bright red flowers that spread across the high mountain fields like a boisterous carpet in the summer sun, so cheerful against the deep greens of the grassy meadows and the smoky blues of the far mountains. All of it seemed to resonate within her, as if she had been hiding all her life and only in this moment had stepped into the light.

You are being fanciful, she cautioned herself, but the plane was dropping closer and closer to the earth, and she could not tell the difference between memory and reality—she could only feel. Too much. Much too much. The spires and steeples of the sacred city appeared before her, until they flew directly over the ancient palace itself, its turrets and towers arching gracefully toward the summer sky above.

Home, she thought, and felt that word ricochet through her, leaving marks.

Lara found she was holding her breath, but even that could not seem to stop the great swell of emotion inside of her, that seemed to rip her into pieces. She could not tear her eyes away, not even when the plane continued its inexorable descent and bumped gently down on the runway.

She could not breathe. She was afraid she might be sobbing and she couldn't even tell for sure, because her ears were ringing and she could not *think*—and the plane was taxiing to a stop and this was really happening. She was really, truly here, after twelve long years.

She rose in a daze, and followed the smiling air hostess out into the morning light. It was so blinding. So clear and pure. The high mountain air was so crisp. She walked down the stairs to the tarmac, and noticed almost distantly the way the people standing there reacted, bowing and crying out her name in their language. But her brain couldn't quite process what they said. What that meant. Her attention was on the view all around her—the mountains, the trees, the magical palace—all of it clearly Alakkul and nowhere else. She knew, suddenly, that she would know where she was if she was blind. She could smell it, sense it. Taste it. Feel it deep in her bones.

Home, that voice whispered inside of her again, ringing through her. It shook her to the core. Changed her, she thought irrationally. Changed her forever.

It was only then that she heard someone else come down the metal stairs behind her. She turned, and there was Adel, broad and dark against the summer morning. His attention was entirely focused on her, and she felt herself burst into a riot of flames as he drew closer. How could he do that, she wondered helplessly, even now, when she felt both more lost—and more found—than she ever had before?

He stopped before her, and reached over to take her hand. She should stop him, she thought. She had not yet processed any of the things that had happened, what had passed between them, and yet she did not pull her hand away. She couldn't seem to do it. She couldn't seem to *want* to do it. How could she feel safe with this man, when she knew all too well that was the one thing she was not? Once again, she was aware of the people standing at a respectful distance, all of them bowing again, some even sinking into deep curtseys. But Adel was beside her, his hand around hers, and she felt the panic inside of her ease. Just as it always had, even twelve years ago. As if he could make the world stop at his command. She remembered the feeling. She felt it now.

Adel raised her hand to his lips and then, impossibly, his dark eyes meeting hers for a searing moment, bowed his head over it.

"The King is dead," he said in ringing tones that carried across the tarmac, perhaps rebounding off the looming mountain guardians of her childhood to lodge in her soul.

His dark eyes connected with hers, silver and serious, and made her stomach twist inside of her.

"Long live the Queen!" he cried in the same voice, and turned, presenting her to the assembled throng. There were flashbulbs. Applause. More bowing, and some cheers.

"Adel..." But she didn't know what she meant to say.

"Welcome home, Princess," he murmured, his hand warm around hers, his eyes dark gray, his mouth that familiar unyielding line.

It made the hard knot of panic inside of her ease. She felt herself breathe in, felt her shoulders settle, as if he'd directed her to do so. As if he made it possible. Just as he'd done long ago, this not-quite-stranger. He bowed his head again, and that firm mouth curved slightly.

"My queen," he said.

And, somehow, made all of it both real, and all right.

CHAPTER FIVE

THE funeral was an ornate affair, with priests and dignitaries and far too many eyes turned in the direction of the new Queen of Alakkul.

Lara sat in the great cathedral in the position of honor, with Adel close to her side, both of them outfitted in the finest Alakkulian garments. The fabric of her severe black gown felt rich and sumptuous against her skin, despite the fact the occasion was so grim. But she could not let herself think about that, not even as the assembled masses rose to sing an ancient hymn of loss and mourning and faith in the afterlife. She could only bow her head and try to calm herself. Try to breathe—try to stay upright. Beside her, Adel shifted, and briefly squeezed her hand with his.

She dared not look at him directly, no matter how his touch moved her—how it seemed to trickle through her veins, warming and soothing her. A quick glance confirmed he looked too uncompromisingly handsome, too disturbing in his resplendent military regalia, as befitted the highest ranking member of the country, save, she supposed with the still-dazed part of her brain that was capable of thinking of these things, herself. She was afraid that she would stare at him too long and disgrace herself.

As, of course, no small part of her wanted to do. Anything to avoid the reality of her father's death. Of the fact that this was his funeral, and she had hardly known him. Would, now, never know him. She had hated the man passionately for almost as long as she could remember, she had gone out of her way to do so to better please and placate her mother, so why did she feel this strange hollowness now? Did she believe the things that Adel had said about Marlena? If not, then surely she should feel either some small measure of satisfaction or nothing at all?

The truth was, she did not have the slightest idea what she felt, much less what she *should* feel. How could she? She had been in this strange place, with its surprisingly fierce kicks of nostalgia and odd flashes of memories, for under forty-eight hours. She had been whisked from the airfield to the palace, her meager possessions placed carefully in a sumptuous suite she only vaguely recalled had once been her mother's—and soon augmented by the kinds of couture ensembles more appropriate to her brand-new, unwanted position. She had been waited upon by fleets of bowing, eager attendants, who were there to see to needs she was not even aware she ought to have. Her wardrobe. Her appointments. Her new, apparently deeply complicated life.

Her first official duty as the new Queen was this funeral. This sending off of a man who clearly inspired loyalty—devotion—from his people, and from the man who stood beside her now. Lara did not know how to reconcile the man they spoke of here, in hushed and reverent tones, with the monster her mother had conjured for her for so many years.

She did not know how to feel about the disparity. She did not want to believe Adel's story of her mother's infidelity—but could not seem to put it out of her head.

She did not know how to feel about anything.

Her orderly, comfortable life in Denver was gone as if it had never existed. The only constant was the man at her side, and the only thing she knew she felt about him was a deep and abiding confusion. Her body still longed for him, in deep, consuming ways that startled her. Her mind rebelled against everything he stood for and his own designs upon her. And yet her heart seemed to hurt inside her chest when she pictured him as a child, forced to play war games in the royal palace, torn from his own family when he'd been hardly more than a toddler. It seemed to beat faster when she remembered their first kiss, her very first kiss ever, so sweet and forbidden, in a hidden corner of the castle ballroom when she had been just sixteen.

She did not have to examine these things more closely to know that she was undeniably, and disastrously, consumed with the man who had an intolerable level of control over this new life of hers.

The question, she asked herself as the service ended and the procession began, and he was still the only thing that she could seem to focus on, was what, if anything, did she plan to do about it?

Much later, after King Azat had been interred in his final resting place beneath the stones of the ancient mausoleum and all the polite words had been spoken to all the correct people, Lara found herself still in her new, stiff black gown, standing awkwardly in one of the palace's smaller private salons.

Across from her, framed by the gilt and gold that graced every spare inch of the walls and floors and ceilings of this fairy-tale place, looking every inch the new King, Adel poured himself a drink. He did so with his customary masculine grace, and Lara could not understand why even something so simple, so mundane, as this man splashing amber-colored liquor into a crystal tumbler should cause her blood to heat. He turned to look at her as if he'd felt the weight of her gaze, his expression that same watchful, careful calmness that she knew all too well by now.

Knew, but could not quite read. Why should that make her heart speed up in her chest?

Lara felt as awkward and as stiff as the fussy room they stood in, as the elegant gown she still wore when she longed for something more casual, more comfortable. Her hands moved restlessly before her, plucking at the fabric of her long skirt. She could not seem to keep still. She wandered the edges of the small salon, stopping before the great windows that looked out over the ancient city, all the spires and rooftops gleaming white and blue as the sun dipped toward the western mountains. It looked indescribably foreign to her eyes, and yet some part of her thrilled to the sight, as if she was as much a part of the landscape as he was. As if it was in her blood.

"They cheered," she said, not knowing she meant to speak, not knowing her voice would sound so insubstantial. She swallowed, and reached a hand toward the window, the glass cool beneath her reaching fingers. "When we were in the car, heading back here. Why would they do that?"

"You are their princess, now their queen," Adel said, his even voice filling the small room, pressing against her ears, and burrowing beneath her skin. "The last of an ancient and revered bloodline, the daughter of a beloved ruler now lost to them. You were stolen away from them when you were just a girl. They celebrate your safe return to the place you belong." He paused for a moment. "Your home."

She looked over her shoulder at him, not knowing why she trembled, why his eyes seemed so sure, and yet managed to make her feel so raw inside. She wanted to speak—perhaps she wanted to scream—but nothing moved past her lips.

"They adore you," he said.

"Not me." She shook her head, swallowed. "Some idea of what I should be, perhaps, but not me."

He heard the dark, wild panic in her voice, and moved toward her, though he had promised himself he would not touch her again. A promise he had already broken repeatedly. In the cathedral. In the car. In the endless reception. He, who held his vows to be sacred. And still, he moved behind her, setting his untouched drink on a side table and letting his hands come to rest on her shoulders.

"It becomes easier," he murmured, close to the perfect shell of her ear, the tempting, elegant line of her neck.

"How do you stand it?" she asked, her eyes fixed on the city outside the windows, as if one of the most beautiful views in the kingdom disturbed her. "All that...expectation?"

She sounded torn. Terrified. And he wanted to soothe her. He wanted to kiss the panic from her body, make her forget herself and the demands of her station. But he could not afford that kind of misstep. Not now, when the King was buried and gone. When so much remained at stake.

"We will marry at the end of the week," he said gruffly. "There is no time to waste."

He felt the shock move through her body, like an electrical current.

"What is the hurry?" she asked, turning so she faced him, not seeming to notice that his hands remained on her, sliding down to hold her upper arms in his palms. "Surely what matters is that I am here. Must we force all of these changes into only a handful of days?"

Her voice caught slightly on the word *changes*. He hated himself for pushing her, but he had no choice. He had been bound over to his country so long ago now he no longer remembered any other way. There were far greater things than the hurt feelings of one woman to worry about, even if it was this one, and far more important things to consider than his abiding desire to comfort her. There was much more at stake than these quiet moments that he knew, somehow, he would never get back.

But he had never had any choice.

"The ceremony will be in the cathedral, as tradition demands," he said as if he had not heard her. She frowned up at him. He found himself frowning back at her, a surge of sudden, unreasonable anger moving through him, though he knew it was not her he was angry with. "Will you fight this, too, Princess? Will we see who wins this latest battle? I should let you know that I am unlikely to be as easy on you as I have been. My patience for these games of yours wears thin."

For a moment she looked as if he'd slapped her. Her face whitened, then blazed into color. She pressed her lips together for a moment, and then her silvery eyes seemed to look straight into him. Through him.

"What is this?" she asked, in a calm voice that sounded

eerily like his own. As if she'd learned it from him. "What are you not telling me?"

He did not know, in that moment, whether he wanted to strangle her or tumble her to the floor. He was appalled at the riot of emotion inside of him. He stepped back, forcing himself to let go of her. Making himself breathe and regain his own control.

He had always known he would marry this woman, that she was his. And he would make that happen, one way or another. The fact that he loved her, that he burned for her—that was incidental. It had to be.

"Many things," he answered finally. "Did you imagine it would be otherwise? Have you shared all your secrets with me?"

Her wide eyes searched his, then dropped. He saw her pull in a steadying breath, and wanted to touch her—but did not.

"It occurs to me that I am already the Queen," she said after a long moment, looking every inch of her heritage, her head held proudly, her inky black hair in that elegant twist. "While, if I am not mistaken, you must marry me to become king."

"You are correct," he said silkily, watching her closely, the warrior instinct stirring to life within his blood. Was that pride he felt? That she was a worthy opponent even today of all days? "Your ancestors have held the throne of Alakkul since the tenth century."

Her head tilted slightly to one side as she considered him. "And what is to prevent me choosing a different king?" she asked in that soft voice that he did not mistake for anything but a weapon. "One I prefer to you?"

He felt himself smile, not nicely. Far stronger men had

quailed before that smile, but Lara only watched him, her eyes blazing with a passion he did not entirely understand. But oh, how he longed to bathe in it.

Soon, he told himself. *Soon enough*.

"Theoretically," he said, "you can choose any king you wish."

She blinked, and then seized on the important part of what he'd just said. "But not in practice?" she asked.

"There is the matter of your vows and our betrothal," he said. "Honor matters more here, to those people who loved you enough to cheer you in the streets, than in your other world. Breaking your word and defying your late father's wishes would cause a deep and lasting scandal." He shrugged. "But you are American now, are you not? Perhaps you will not mind a scandal."

"I think I'll announce to the world at large that the new Queen of Alakkul is in need of a king," she said, her eyes bright, daring him. "Surely any number of suitors will present themselves. It can be like my own, personal reality show."

She expected him to react badly, he could tell. But he saw the way her pulse pounded in the tender crook of her neck, and smiled.

"By all means, Princess," he said. "Invite whoever you like to court you."

"You don't mind?" Her voice was ripe with disbelief. "You don't think you're the better choice?"

He laughed, enjoying the way the sound made her frown.

"There is no doubt at all that I am the better choice," he said. "But more than that, I am the only choice."

"According to you," she said, defiant and beautiful.

"No," he said softly. He reached across and traced a

simple line along the elegant length of her neck, smiling in satisfaction when she hissed in a breath and goose bumps rose. "According to you," he said, his own body reacting to her arousal. "You have loved me since you were but a girl. You will again. Your body is already there." He did not smile now—he met her gaze with his own, steady and sure. "You will not pick another king."

That bald statement seemed to hang between them, making the air hard to breathe. Lara's stomach hurt, and her hands balled into fists.

"Why must I marry anyone?" she asked, her voice low and intent, growing hoarse with the emotion she fought to conceal, even as her body rioted, proving his words to be true no matter how she longed to deny them. "Why can't I simply be queen on my own?"

But Adel only shook his head, in that infuriating manner of his that made her itch to explode into some kind of decisive action. But then again, perhaps touching him was not a good idea.

"Why should I trust anything you say?" she threw at him, angry beyond reason, dizzy with all she wanted and would not allow herself. "You've done nothing but lie to me from the start!"

"I will do whatever it takes to secure the throne and protect this country," he threw back at her. Did she imagine the hint of darker emotion in his voice? Flashing in his gray eyes? Or did she only *want* it to be there?

"You are exactly like him," she said, her voice a low, intense throb of all the pain she had not been able to admit she felt today. All the loss and the bewilderment, and her inability to understand why she should even care that King

Azat was dead. Why should it matter to her? Why should she be questioning her mother's motives? And why should she feel so betrayed that Adel was the same kind of man, when he had never pretended to be anything else? When he had as good as told her that he would do just what he had done? When he—like her father before him—cared only and entirely about the damned throne to this godforsaken place?

Hadn't her mother told her this would happen, years before? *"He picked another snake for you, Lara—just like himself!"* she'd hissed.

"If you mean your father," Adel said evenly, the suggestion of ice in his voice, "I will accept the compliment."

"He forced me into this years ago, on my sixteenth birthday," she said dully, wondering why her heart felt broken—why it should even be involved. "Didn't you know? That was when my mother knew we had to escape. She refused to let me—"

"Please spare me these fantasies." His voice was a hard whip of dismissal. Startled, she noticed his eyes had turned to flint. "Your mother left because her extramarital dalliances were discovered. She took you with her as insurance, because she knew that if she stayed here she would have been turned away from the palace in shame. Never deceive yourself on this point. She knew that as long as you were with her, your father would never cut off her funds. Just as she knew he was too concerned with a daughter's feelings for her mother to separate you."

"What?" She couldn't make sense of that. She literally could not process his words. "What are you—? We lived on the run for years! We had to hide from his goons!"

"There was never one moment of your life that the palace

did not know where you were," Adel said coolly, every word like a blow. "And I assure you, if your father wanted his 'goons' to secure you, I would have done so personally years ago. If it was up to me, I would have reclaimed you before your seventeenth birthday."

She couldn't accept what he was saying. Her mind was reeling, and she shook her head once, hard. Then again, to get rid of the part of her that seemed to bloom in pleasure, at the notion that he'd wanted her so badly.

"You would say anything..." she began, but she was barely speaking aloud.

He took her shoulders in his hands again, tipping her head back, making her look at him. Face to face, hiding nothing. Baring far too much.

"I will lie, cheat, steal," he said. His tone was deceptively soft—with that uncompromising edge beneath. "Whatever it takes. But you will marry me."

"I wouldn't be so sure about that!" she hissed, but it was all bravado. Inside she was awash in confusion. Full of the possibility that he, unlike her father and even unlike her mother, had wanted her after all. But unable to let herself really accept that possibility—unable to believe it.

She knew what he meant to do even as his hands tightened on her shoulders, even as his hard mouth dropped toward hers. She knew, and yet she did nothing to evade it.

In truth, she did not want to evade him.

And so he kissed her. That same fire. That same punch and roll. Even now, even here, she burned.

She did not know what that meant. She did not want to think anymore. She did not want to feel. She wanted to lock herself away somewhere—to escape.

But he raised his head, and his eyes were dark gray and

too capable of reading too much, his mouth in that grim line that called to her despite everything.

"That proves nothing," she said, because she had to say something—she had to pretend.

"Keep telling yourself that, Princess," he said in that dark, quiet voice that made her alive and bright with need. "If it helps."

CHAPTER SIX

THE day of her wedding dawned wet and cold.

Was it childish that she wanted the weather to be an omen?

A summer storm had swept in from the mountains, shrouding the ancient city in a chilly fog that perfectly suited Lara's mood. She was up before the gray dawn, staring broodingly out her windows, feeling like a princess in one of those old fairy-tales her mother had given her to read when she was a child.

It did not do much to brighten her outlook when she reflected that she was, in fact, a princess locked away in a castle and about to be married off to a suitor not of her choosing. That in her case, those old stories were real.

No matter how little it all *felt* real. No matter how much she still wanted to jolt awake and find herself back in her safe, small life in Denver. The little apartment she'd barely tolerated, and now missed. The job and the friends and the *life* that she had treasured, because it was hers. Because she had not had to run from anything anymore. She had been so proud of that. Of what she'd built when Marlena had let them stop running.

Marlena...who might not be at all who she'd claimed to be for so long. Who Lara had had no choice but to believe.

She tucked her knees up beneath her on her window seat and took in the luxury that dripped from every inch of the suite all around her—the cascade of window treatments in gold and cream, the tapered bed posts, the ornamentation of every surface, every detail. What terrified her was how, every day, the real world seemed further and further away. She spoke less English. She found her new clothes less uncomfortable. She forgot.

How soon would she forget what was truly important? How soon would she forget herself completely?

But then the door swung open, and she was no longer alone. And it was, after all, her wedding day.

She was bathed, slathered in ointments and perfumes, and dressed in a gown so beautiful, so light and airy, that it should have taken her breath away. It made her look like a dream. Like another fairy-tale princess. Her hair was curled, piled onto her head, and bedecked with fine jewels and a tiara that one of her attendants told her, with a smile, had once belonged to Cleopatra herself. There was a part of her that longed to believe such a story, that wanted to revel in the very idea of it. But when she looked at herself in the mirror, she hardly recognized herself.

If she allowed herself to disappear inside this dream, the dream she'd cherished as a girl and hardly believed could be happening now, how would she ever wake up? *Could* she ever wake up? Would she want to?

By the time they had finished with all their ministrations, the bright summer sun had burned away the morning fog, and as Lara was driven outside the palace gates it was as if she drove directly into the happily-ever-after portion of all those old fairy-tales she couldn't seem to put from her mind. The people of Alakkul crowded the streets, cheering and waving. The sun streamed down from the perfect blue sky above. She even thought she heard birds singing sweetly in the trees as she climbed the steps to the great cathedral. Everything was perfect, save for the stone inside her chest where her heart should be, and the fact that she desperately did not want to do this.

Yet...was that true?

She did not break away from her fleet of handlers. She did not pick up her heavy skirts and run. She did not even stop walking, step by measured step, toward her doom. And when she entered the cathedral and saw the figure standing so tall and proud at the altar, she knew why.

He stood at the head of the long aisle, where a few days before her father's coffin had been laid out for all to see. Where, so many years ago, she had stood with him once before, in the very same spot, and dreamed of exactly this moment. Yearned for it. Was it the echo of those long-ago dreams that kept her moving, as if it was the very blood in her veins? Or was it the way he turned and looked at her, an expression she could not read on his hard face as she drew close?

He held out his hand, his gray eyes serious and steady on hers—just as he had done in that parking lot in Denver. It seemed like a different life to her now, a different person altogether. She could not imagine who she'd been, however many days ago, before he'd reappeared in her life and altered it so profoundly. She could not reconstruct that last moment before he'd spoken, when she had been lost in whatever thoughts had consumed her then, when she had forgotten he even existed and had no idea she would ever see him again.

She could not imagine it, and maybe that was what compelled her to reach across the distance between them, and once again take his hand.

In the end, it was quick. Too quick.

The priests intoned the sacred words. Adel stood quietly beside her, yet she was so aware of him. Of his slow, deep breathing. Of his broad shoulders, his impressive height. Of the fierce, compelling strength that was so much a part of him. He was every inch the warrior, even now. Even here.

She could think of him as a warrior. As a king. It was the word *husband* that she could not seem to make sense of—it kept getting tangled up in her head.

And in the final moments, when the priest turned to her and asked her if she came to this union of her own free will, if she gave herself willingly, Lara looked into Adel's silver eyes, and knew she should say no.

She knew it.

But his gaze was so steady, so calm. So serious.

So very silver, and she felt it wrap around that stone where her heart should be, like a caress. Like a promise.

"He will make you nothing more than a puppet," Marlena had said.

But there were worse things than that, Lara thought. There were worse things than puppetry, and in any case, she could not remember what it had been like before, what it had been like without that calm silver gaze filling her, making her warm from the inside out, making her feel whole when she had not known anything was missing.

She had wanted this man forever.

"Do you come to this moment of your own free will?" the priest asked again.

And she said yes.

"Yes," she said. "I do."

She said yes.

Adel was not aware he had been so tense, so rigid and prepared for battle, until it eased from him. Her voice rang through the cathedral, and sounded deep within him. Unmistakable. Unquestionable.

It was done.

She was his.

He had fulfilled the old King's wishes, to the letter. He had staved off disaster. He had been prepared for anything today. That she might not appear. That she might try to bolt. That she might throw her defiance in his face at this crucial moment. Anything.

He had not been prepared for her beauty. For the way the white gown hugged her figure so tenderly, nor for the way the jewels that adorned her made her seem to sparkle and glow.

He had not, he realized, as he took her hands in his and recited the old words that would make them one, forever, thought much beyond this moment.

He had only thought of marrying her. But he had not spent much time thinking about the marriage itself.

They walked down the aisle, husband and wife, king and queen, and out into their kingdom, together.

She looked up at him, her eyes seeming more blue than silver in the sunlight. Her expression was grave, as if she found this marriage a serious business, requiring much thought and worry.

And he wanted her. God, how he wanted her. Not as the king she had just made him, but as the man who had wanted her since he'd been barely more than a boy. As the man who had tasted her, and touched her, when he had known he should do neither, both twelve years ago and now.

But now...now he did not have to hold back. Now, finally, he could sink into her as he'd longed to do for what felt like much too long. Now he could love her, openly and fully, as he'd always imagined he should.

"Why are you looking at me like that?" she asked, but he could tell she knew.

"Why do you think?" he asked, and smiled. He held her hand in his, and led her toward the waiting motorcade. There was the small matter of the reception to get through, and his coronation. But he was already thinking ahead. He was already imagining how she would taste, how soft her skin would feel beneath his hands. How he would make her cry out his name. How he would make her fall to pieces in his arms.

They stood for a moment, her eyes locked to his, and he felt her tremble slightly in the afternoon sun. As if she could feel it, too. As if she'd finally stopped fighting. As if she was ready, at long last, to be his.

He would make sure of it.

The High Palace clung to the side of one of the tallest mountains to the west of the capital city. In ancient times, she remembered learning as a child, it had taken many weeks of travel via sure-footed mountain goats and under the protection of guides and priests for the royal family to make it to these heights. It had been a much quicker ride by helicopter.

Standing out on the wide terrace that had been added off the King's suite sometime since her last visit here, Lara looked out across the sweep and grandeur of Alakkul and wondered how she had ever managed to forget it. So many twinkling lights in the dark, mirroring the stars above. The brighter lights of the city, the far-off glimmers of the mountain villages. The crisp, clean air, cool and sweet.

From so high, it looked magical.

Or perhaps she only felt that way, after such a long day immersed in this fairy-tale that was, somehow, her life. It had to be a fairy-tale, because it couldn't possibly be real. None of it felt real. *She* hardly felt real.

Adel moved behind her. She sensed him first—that prickle along her neck, that banked fire blazing to life within her. She let out a breath she had not known she was holding as she felt him step behind her, his warm hands smoothing along the curve of her neck, tracing down over her shoulders.

"Nothing seems real," she heard herself say, so softly she thought for a moment the night breeze stole her words away.

"I assure you, it is." His voice was a low rumble. So amused, and still, her breasts swelled against the bodice of her dress, and that insistent, intoxicating heat pooled lower—became a low ache. He turned her around to face him. "You are my wife."

"And you are now the King of Alakkul," she said, tilting her head back to study that hard, uncompromising face. Did she imagine what looked like tenderness in his eyes, so silver in the light from the candles scattered across the terrace? Or was it that she wanted to see such a thing—needed to believe she could see it?

He reached over and smoothed his hand along her cheek,

curving his palm around to cradle her face. There was some part of her that wanted to object. That should *want* to object! She did not have to give in to this heat, this need. He was no brute, no matter how calculating, how ruthless, he might be. Not about something like this. She knew so with a deep, feminine intuition.

If she wanted to stop this, she needed only to open up her mouth and tell him *no*.

But she did not speak. She only gazed at him, all of Alakkul spread out behind her, glimmering in the soft summer night and reflecting in his dark eyes as if it was a part of him. He had smiled at her outside the cathedral, his hard gaze open, and shaken her to her core—because she had seen, in that moment, how happy he was. How happy to look at her, to claim her. It had made her breath catch, her heart swell. It had made her think that he was not, after all, the enemy she wanted to believe he was. That perhaps he never had been.

She stood before him now in a dress that made her feel like the princess she supposed she always had been, technically, but had certainly never felt like before. And he was so devastatingly handsome, so strong and so dangerous, standing before her with that almost-smile on his hard mouth.

As if he knew things that she did not want to know. As if he knew far too much.

Lara gazed at him—and did not say a word.

"Tonight I am only a man," he whispered, his voice a low rasp.

Just as tonight she was finally his woman, as if all the years between them had melted away in his smile. How had she denied him this long?

He pulled her head closer, and bent down to capture her mouth. His kiss was sweet, hot, sending spirals of heat dancing through her body, making her come up on her toes to meet him. She let her hands trail up the tantalizingly hard ridge of his abdomen to his broad chest, reveling in the taut glory of his muscles.

He angled his jaw, and took the kiss deeper. Hotter. Lara felt the world fall away, spinning into nothing, and only belatedly realized he'd swept her into his arms. He kept kissing her as he moved, and she looped her arms around his neck and kissed him back. Again and again, until she found herself on her back in the center of the wide, white bed, with Adel resting snugly between her thighs.

Was she really going to do this? Pretend nothing else mattered but this fire, this need?

"Adel..." she began, but he smiled at her, even as he moved his hips against hers. Lara gasped, and forgot.

She forgot she'd ever wanted to deny him, and instead opened to his every touch. He stripped them both naked with surprising finesse and long, drugging kisses, feasting on every inch of flesh he uncovered. He trailed fire from one breast to the other, then tasted his way down the soft skin of her belly to claim the heat between her legs.

And then he licked his way into the molten core of her, and she forgot her own name.

She shattered around him, caught in a wave of pleasure so intense, so perfect, she was not sure what would be left of her. She was not sure she could survive it.

When she came back to herself, he was poised above her, his hard face sharpened, somehow, with passion.

And she realized it was just beginning.

"You are mine," he said hoarsely, and then he thrust within her.

CHAPTER SEVEN

THE summer wore on as the country settled into its new era, with its new rulers fully ensconced upon the throne, and Adel could not understand why—having finally achieved all he'd ever wanted—the only thing he seemed to think about was his wife.

Not the warring factions that forever threatened to sink the government. Not the leftover yet ever-thorny issues from the various world powers that had tried to take the strategically located Alakkulian Valley in their time. Not the need to protect and support the economy, nor the tendency of some citizens to live as if it were still the tenth century. It was not that he did not care about all of these things. It was just that his focus was Lara. Always Lara.

The way her skin felt against his, naked and soft, hot and delicious. The way her head tipped back in ecstasy, showing the long, elegant line of her neck as she cried out his name. The way her toned, athletic legs wrapped so tightly around his hips. The way she would smile at him, so dreamily, in those stolen moments after they had both reached heaven, her eyes that silver-blue that made his chest expand and ache.

He was enchanted by her, this woman he had loved for so much of his life, and the reality of her far exceeded his fantasies.

It wasn't just the perfection of her body. He even enjoyed her when she argued with him—which was, he reflected as he took in the cross expression she wore as he entered their private breakfast room in the palace—most of the time.

"I don't see the point of being called a queen when all I do is sit around the palace, staring out of windows and boring myself to death," she threw at him with no preamble, her fingers picking at the pastry before her.

"Good morning to you, too," he murmured, settling himself in his usual place opposite her while the servants bustled around him, pouring out his morning coffee and presenting him with a stack of papers for his review.

She ignored him. "I am used to working," she said. "*Doing* something, not sitting around like an ornament attached to your lapel!"

"Then do something," he suggested, picking up his coffee and eyeing her. She made his heart swell with what he could only describe as gladness. Most women cowered before him, or fell all over themselves in an attempt to please him. Never this one. She was bold. Brash. Unafraid. "You are the Queen. You can do as you like."

"Perhaps I wish to rule, as you do," she said, with a sideways glance at him, and he had a sudden image of what it might be like with this woman at his side forever, on the throne and in his bed—this warrior queen he had never expected would grow to be so strong. And yet he loved it. Her.

He shrugged. "You have an affinity for tedious meetings,

day after day, with puffed-up, pompous men?" he asked mildly. Not his Lara, he thought. She would shred them with her sharp tongue, and he would laugh in admiration, and whole decades of careful diplomacy would go up in smoke. "Men who will insult you and berate you, who you cannot treat as you would like to do? This calls to you?"

She let out a sigh. "No," she said after a long moment. "Not really."

"Because, Princess, though your charms are many indeed, I do not count among them a particular gift for the diplomatic arts." He smiled when her gaze sharpened on his. "This is not a flaw. You are too honest for politics. One of us should be."

He could feel the tension rise between them then, that tautening of the air, that narrowing of focus until he knew nothing but her face. The swell of her lips. The shine of temper in her gaze. The sweep and fall of her black curls.

He knew her so well now. He could see the way the color washed across her face, and knew it would be the same all over her body. She would pinken as her body readied itself for him. Were he to reach for her under the table, he would find her hot and wet beneath his hands. He felt himself harden. He could not seem to get enough of her, no matter how often they sated each other. No matter how easily she came apart in his hands.

"I am no longer a princess," she said, her voice husky, a gleam of awareness in her magnificent eyes. "And you never use my name."

"I use your name," he contradicted her, smiling slightly, "in certain circumstances." He did not have to spell those circumstances out. Her flush deepened, as they both re-membered the last time he'd called out her name, sometime before the dawn, when he'd been so deep inside of her he would have been happy to die there. She made him feel like a man, he realized. Not the soldier he had been, not the King he was now, but a man.

"There is more to life than sex," she said, and he saw a darkness pass through her eyes—some kind of shadow. But she blinked, and it was gone.

"Apparently not for you," he said lazily. "Apparently, you are bored with everything that happens outside our bed. One solution would be to make sure you never leave it."

"Promises, promises," she chided him, a gleam in her eyes. "Who would run the country if we spent all our time in bed?"

The man was insatiable, Lara thought.

And what was so astonishing was that she, who had always enjoyed the company of men but had certainly never felt *compelled* by them, was too.

He had her in the suites of hotels where they stayed while on royal engagements, her back up against the wall, his hand and mouth busy beneath her skirts. He seduced her on a speedboat as they made their way to one of the more remote clans, only accessible across a system of mountain lakes. There was no place he did not look at her with that dark passion, that promise, alive in his gray eyes. And no place where she did not immediately respond, no matter how inappropriate it might be.

It was lust, she told herself. And unexpected chemistry.

And she was no better.

She climbed astride him in the backseat of the plush limousine as the motorcade wove through the twisting streets of the capital city, rocking them both into bliss before a command appearance at the city opera. She had taken it upon herself to explore him in every room she could discover in the old castle—behind doors, on ancient chairs, under the fierce and disapproving glares of her ancestors high above in their glowering state portraits.

It was only lust, she thought. And lust was fine. Lust was allowed. Lust would fade. Though she could not help but note, every now and again as the summer wore on, that the more she touched him, the more she tasted him, the less she worried about the ways in which she might have lost herself in this strange little fairy-tale.

She was not an idiot. She did not, in truth, wish to govern, and doubted she would be any good at it, anyway. She would have no idea how one even went about it. Lara had no particular interest in politics, but she could, she realized, use the position she found herself in for good. There was no excuse for lying about a *castle*, of all places, feeling bored and put upon. How she would have slapped herself for even thinking such a thing, once upon a time, when her paycheck had had to last far too long and cover books and tuition as well as pay her rent! Appalled at herself, Lara began to involve herself in charity work—to get a sense of what her people, her subjects, her countrymen really needed.

And what she needed, too, if she was to stay here. If she was really to do this long-term. She pretended it was a lifestyle decision she was mulling over, like when she'd decided to stay in Colorado after college and make her life in Denver. She pretended it was a decision about a *location*, and about a *job*.

After all, fairy-tales weren't real. Not even this one.

"You are just like your father, may he rest in peace," an old woman told her as Lara toured one of the local hospitals, visiting the helpless and the needy, talking to the overworked staff. *I can help these people,* she had been thinking just moments before, as she'd tried to smile at a little girl gone bald from the cancer treatments, clearly the old woman's grandchild. *Maybe that's why I'm here.*

"I beg your pardon?" she asked, fighting to keep her smile in place as the old woman held on to her hands. It was not the physical contact she minded, she realized, but that wild intensity in the woman's eyes.

"He was a good man," the woman said, in the dialect of the upper mountains. "And a great king. I give thanks every day that you have returned to us, to bless us and help us prosper as your family has done for generations, no thanks to that evil woman who stole you away in the first place!"

And what could Lara say? It was hardly the place to argue—particularly with the grandmother of a sick child. And why did it seem as if the part of her that had defended Marlena for so long was simply...tired?

"Thank you," she said, fighting to keep her expression serene. "I hope I can live up to his memory."

Later that night, Lara met Adel at the start of a great ball to honor a dignitary whose name she had yet to commit to memory as she knew she should. The palace was alive with lights and Alakkul's most glamorous people were decked out in their finest clothes, all of it shining and sparkling. The palace gardens had been converted to a kind of wonderland for the evening, complete with a dance floor and little tables clustered in and around the flowering trees and geometrically shaped shrubberies. It was the end of August already. The twilight brought with it hints of the coming fall, the air was cool, and Lara felt a restlessness shiver through her, making her feel as if her skin was two sizes too small.

"You are fidgeting," Adel told her without altering his calm expression as they stood side by side to receive their guests. She did not have to look at him to know that he looked as he always did—so strong, so capable, his mouthwateringly male form displayed to perfection in the dark suit that clung to his every muscle and made his chest look like some kind of hard, male sculpture. He was mesmerizing. Still.

"It is just as well that you were raised since you were young to rule this place," she said, not thinking, letting the wildness that rolled inside of her have its way. "I would have made a terrible ruler. Perhaps you knew that. Perhaps my father did, too. Perhaps it is not sexism but practicality that governs you."

He did not reply. He shot her one of those dark, far-too-calm glances that made her breath catch, and something thick and heavy turn over into a knot in her gut. Then he returned to his duties, the endless greeting and acknowledging of guests, as if she had not spoken at all.

Later, he pulled her out on to the dance floor, and smiled slightly as he gazed down at her. His mouth was softer than usual, that hard line almost welcoming. The band swelled into a waltz as he held her in his arms, his hand in the small of her back seeming to beam heat and comfort directly into her skin through the silk of her gown, the hand holding hers so warm, so strong.

She did not know why she wanted, suddenly, to weep.

"What is the matter?" he asked in that quiet way of his, and she knew he was continuing the discussion from earlier, that nothing ever truly distracted a man of his focus.

"I do not know," she said, surprised to hear that she was whispering. She blinked, and tilted her head back to study his face. He only watched her, that boundless patience in his gray eyes—that calm readiness for whatever she might say, whenever she might say it to him.

"There is nothing you can tell me that will tarnish you in my eyes," he said in a low voice, sweeping her around the dance floor, his eyes on her as if nothing else existed. As if there was only the music, the palace, the low murmurs of the well-heeled guests, like a bubble around them. As if there was only this perfect, tiny jewel of a country, hidden away in remote mountains, beautiful in ways that hurt her soul. In the same way that he did.

And she understood, then, how easy it would be. To simply let go. To let him lead, as he did now, waltzing with the grace and mastery she had come to expect of him no matter what he did, his mouth in that enigmatic near-curve as he gazed down at her. It would be so easy to simply accept this life he'd given her. A country. A crown. And the endless delight of their explosive, uncontainable chemistry.

She need only forget herself. What she knew, who she was. She need only accept that her father was never the villain, but instead the misunderstood hero. She need only learn to think of her selfish, childish mother the way the Alakkulians obviously did—as the evil witch who had so destroyed their king with her string of lovers. The woman who had stolen away their princess. She need only erase all she'd believed to be true about her life, her world, *herself.*

And then she could have him, and all those dreams she'd longed for as a teenager would finally come true.

It would be as easy as breathing. As easy as letting him move her about the dance floor with all of his skill and grace. It would be so very, very easy—and she had done most of it already. She had become so concerned with turning herself into a proper queen—because she wanted his approval. She wanted that slow curve of his mouth that was only hers. She wanted the shine in his eyes that meant he was proud of her.

When had that happened? When had his opinion of her become more important to her than her own?

And why didn't that realization horrify her as she knew it ought to do?

"You look as if you have seen a ghost," Adel said softly, his lips so close to her ear that she shivered, feeling that low murmur in every part of her.

"Sometimes you make me feel as if I am one," she said, before she knew she meant to speak.

His head reared back slightly, and his eyes narrowed, but the song ended—and their ever-present aides interrupted them, prepared to usher the King to one table and the Queen to another.

"Duty calls," he murmured, holding on to her hand for a beat, then another, after the music had ended. Calling attention to the fact he had not let her go. "But we will return to this topic, Princess."

She had no doubt that they would.

And what did it say about her that anticipation was like honey in her veins, warming her, sweetening her, turning her into fire and need?

He stepped into her dressing room, and startled her as she reached to take down her hair, letting the heavy curls fall from the elaborate twist at the back of her head. She froze, meeting his gray gaze in the great mirror she stood before, its heavy gold and jeweled accents seeming to fade next to the raw power of the man who filled the doorway behind her.

Her heart began to speed up in her chest. Adel did not

speak. He only held her gaze with his as he moved toward her, prowling across the thick carpet, all of that restrained power and force seeming to hum from his very skin. She did not look away, even when he came to a stop behind her, and traced a pattern along the sensitive skin at the nape of her neck. She did not look away when he bent his head and used his mouth instead of his hand, kissing and tasting a molten path from the tender place below her ear to the bared skin of her shoulder.

"You do not taste like a ghost," he said, a raw sort of urgency in his voice. She did not understand the darkness in his eyes then, but her body responded to it, as it always did.

"Neither do you," she said, turning her head and pressing her lips to his hard jaw.

"You do not feel like a ghost," he continued. She turned in his arms and pressed her breasts against his chest, then tested the shape of his arms beneath her hands.

His mouth claimed hers, insistent and demanding, and she gave herself over to this wicked sorcery, this dark delight, that only he could call forth in her. She slid the suit jacket from his wide shoulders, then busied herself with the buttons of his stiff dress shirt.

He growled with impatience, and shifted forward, lifting her up by her bottom and settling her back against the small table behind her—paying no heed to the small bottles and tubes he knocked out of his way. He reached down and pulled up the hem of her long gown, baring her to his sight. He let out something that sounded like a cross between a sigh and a groan, and then he reached down to hold her softness in his hand, feeling her molten heat, making her moan and move against him.

He made short work of the scrap of lace that concealed her femininity, and then, with a few quick jerks at the fly of his own trousers, he was thrusting into her. Lara shuddered as he entered her, shattering around him, and coming back to find him watching her, those gray eyes intense. As if he could see deep into her, as if he knew the things she was afraid to face herself.

"Please…" she murmured, not knowing what she asked for, but he began to move.

He pulled her legs up, hooking them over his hips, as he thrust inside of her again and again. She felt the fire catch and then burn anew, bright and hot. He leaned down and took her mouth, possessing her, claiming her, making her nothing more than these sensations, these feelings. She burned for him, and he knew it, and she could not even bring herself to mind.

She could only fall apart once more, and hear his hoarse cry as he followed right behind her.

When she woke in the morning, wrapped around him in the great bed, she felt the seduction of this impossible fairy-tale pull at her yet again. She need only let go, and how hard could that be, she asked herself? Why did she fight it?

The slight chill in the morning air, blowing in through the open windows, reminded her that it was coming up hard on September already. She still felt as if it was June—or ought to be. She let her eyes drift closed again, inhaling Adel's intoxicating male scent, feeling his strength and heat beneath her. Where did the time go?

A thought occurred to her then, washing over her like a cold sweat. Her eyes snapped open. She counted back— tried to remember… But no, it was true. She had not had her monthly courses since she'd been in Denver. And she had not even thought about it.

But she thought about it now, sitting up straight in the bed, her heart in her throat and what remained of the fairy-tale shattering all around her like glass.

CHAPTER EIGHT

THREE days later, it was definitely September, Lara was most assuredly and unhappily pregnant, and more important, she'd finally woken up from the spell she'd been under ever since Adel Qaderi had appeared in that supermarket parking lot back in Denver. She was so wide awake it actually hurt.

She buckled herself into the plush seat in the private jet, willing herself to keep her emotions under control. She did not look out the window as the plane began to taxi down the runway. She did not glance back as the plane soared into the air, clearing the spires and parapets. She knew the country was spread out before her like a canvas, and she refused to indulge in one last look. She reached over and pulled the shade closed, as if she could block out the last few months as easily.

It was one thing to fall under Adel's sensual spell. She wasn't sure how she could have resisted him, once he'd looked at her with that passion simmering in his dark eyes. But it was something else entirely to bring another child into another loveless marriage. Hadn't she spent the whole of her life paying for her parents' marriage? Wasn't she still? Her hand crept over her still-flat belly. She could not do that to a child. *She would not do it.*

Her time in Alakkul might have felt like a dream, *her* dream, but it had also served to open up her eyes to the uncomfortable truth about her childhood—and her parents. She shut her eyes against another rush of emotion that threatened to suck her under. The truth was that her mother had stolen her away from her father, and had deliberately made Lara believe the worst of him. Another truth was that her father had not come to claim her, nor tell his side of the story before he died—not in twelve long years. Her mother had poisoned her against King Azat, all the while hiding the truth about the funds she'd taken and her own infidelities. The King, meanwhile, had sold his only child into a convenient marriage, to serve his own ends.

It didn't matter which parent she looked at, because the truth was blindingly clear to her either way. She had never been anything more than a pawn to either one of them. She certainly wouldn't inflict that same kind of life on her child. She'd die first.

Because as much as she'd claimed to hate King Azat to please her mother, and in many ways she had, the truth was that she'd yearned for a normal family like any other girl. She'd wanted a father *and* a mother.

And she'd missed Alakkul, too. And Adel, her first love. She did not know how she would manage to shove all those memories aside as she'd done before—but she knew she'd have to do it, somehow. The precious life she carried inside of her could never know the deep pangs of longing she felt for that cool, bright valley, tucked away in a forgotten corner of the world. Or the deeper yearning for a hard-faced man with eyes like rain and gentle hands. It would fade, she told herself. Someday, it would fade.

She let her head fall back against the cushioned headrest, and pretended she was unaware of the tears slipping from her eyes to trail across her cheeks. She would forget him. Again. The truth was that their chemistry had been so unexpected that she'd allowed it to confuse her for the whole long summer. It had only served to conceal the truth. Adel did not want *her*. He wanted King Azat's daughter. He wanted the throne of Alakkul. She could have been anyone, as long as he had gotten both of those things.

She was still nothing but a pawn. A strategy. A convenience he happened to be attracted to. And she knew with a deep certainty that her child deserved more. Much more.

Her heart might seem to break into more and more pieces with every mile she flew away from him, but she would lock that up with all her memories and put it away. She would do it, somehow. For her child, if not for herself.

Lara came awake slowly, confused. It took a moment or two to realize that the plane was on the ground, instead of in the air, and was rolling along the tarmac. Frowning, she pulled up the window shade nearest to her, but all she could see were streaks of rain against the window, and splotches of light in the dark. A terminal, perhaps—but where?

"Excuse me?" she called, twisting in her seat to seek out the hovering air hostess. "Where are we? What's going on?"

"It is nothing, Your Majesty," the woman said, her voice soothing, her smile calm. "The plane has been diverted to deal with a slight mechanical issue. A hotel suite has been secured for your use, and you should be on your way again in the morning."

Lara was still half-asleep, perhaps—or just confused in general, so she almost forgot to ask, again, where they'd landed. The nervous tension she'd felt disappeared when the woman named a small Baltic country far to the north and west of Alakkul, and she realized that she'd suspected the plane had simply returned her to Alakkul while she'd slept. She told herself she was delighted to be wrong.

There was not much to see of the country so late at night. She was escorted into a waiting car, and whisked away to an elegant hotel in a city center not twenty minutes away from the air field. Lara felt suspended—at loose ends—and knew it was because she had to stop here and *think* about what she was doing. That had not been her plan. She'd wanted to be firmly back on American soil, deeply ensconced in her old, comfortable little life again before she had to think about the ramifications of her abrupt departure from the new life she'd been living all summer.

She had not even spoken to Adel. She had not given him any warning. She had simply seen the royal physician, confirmed what she'd known must be true, and had plotted her immediate escape.

But as the elevator took her toward the penthouse suite, one more luxury she would forgo the moment she returned to the real world, she could not help but ask herself if what she was doing right now was any different from what Marlena had done so many years before. Was it different because the child she carried was not yet born? Wouldn't the child be the heir to the throne just as Lara had been? Wouldn't this same cycle play itself out all over again? Could she really be responsible for inflicting this much pain on her own baby?

She had no answers. And, as she stepped into the suite, she took a deep breath, noted the expensive displays of flowers and the subtly elegant furnishings, and realized—with a start and a leap of something like anticipation in her belly—that she was out of time.

Because a man stood there, half concealed by the shadows deep in the room, watching her approach as if he'd summoned her.

Adel.

He could not remember being so angry before. Ever. Because he could not recall ever caring this much—about anything.

His gaze tracked her as she walked toward him, then stopped. She flinched as she recognized that she was not alone. She looked tired—dark smudges beneath her eyes and her skin too pale in the warm glow of the lamps that lit the large room. He was so furious it was all he could do to keep it locked inside of him. To keep from shouting at her. To keep from demanding she tell him that this was not really happening—that she would not leave him like this, taking so much with her. Surely she could not really do this. Surely it was a mistake—a misunderstanding.

"Be easy," he said quietly, but even he could hear the lash in his voice. "I will not put my hands on you when I am this angry."

Her gaze flared into a bright blue blaze, as if he'd deeply offended her. But how could he have done?

"I take it this is all some complicated charade," she bit out. "There is nothing wrong with the plane, is there? There is no mechanical failure!"

"That rather depends on your definition," he replied icily.

"I would categorize an abdicating queen as a failure of the highest degree."

She let out a small noise, too rough to be a sigh, and turned her head away. She sank down on one of the butter-soft leather couches, but did not seem to see it. She wrapped her arms around her torso, and still, did not look at him. Something hard and heavy, like a stone, fell through him.

She was really doing this. She had done it, and he had only managed to engineer this stop at the last moment. She was leaving him, and taking his child with him. *His child.*

He was a man of action, of deeds and solutions, and he could only stand there, frozen. What had she done to him? How had he been reduced to this? Why could he think of nothing save how to comfort her?

"I cannot do this," she said in a low voice. "I gave you your throne. What else can you possibly want?"

"I want you," he said, the words torn from him. Painful. "My queen. My *wife*."

"Your pawn," she countered, her head whipping back around so that her gaze could meet his. He was shocked by the pain he saw there, the darkness. "Do you know something, Adel? I have been the pawn of one king or another since the day I was born. I am sick of it."

"You are not a pawn," he began.

"How can you say that with a straight face?" she demanded. She surged back to her feet. "Did you chase me across the world because you liked my personality? Because you thought about *me* at all? No—you wanted what only my particular parentage could give you. My special genetic make-up. If that does not make me a pawn, then I do not know the meaning of the word."

"You do not understand," he said, gritting out the words,

because he did not like the picture she painted—and yet, given the option, he would do it all over again in exactly the same way. If he knew that, why should it eat at him? "I had no choice in these things, but that has nothing to do with what is between us now. What was always between us, even when we were young."

"There is nothing between us." Her voice was flat, her eyes unreadable. Like a stranger's. "It was the madness of summer, nothing more. I gave you what you wanted. Now it's your turn to return the favor."

"What is it you want?" he asked, although he knew what she would say, and she did not disappoint him. She was so cold, and yet that dark anger shone in her silver-blue eyes and hinted at the turmoil beneath, the fire he knew burned within her.

"My freedom," she cried at him.

"Perhaps that can be arranged," he said, then prowled closer to her, noting the way her pulse jumped in her throat, and she swallowed—nervously, he thought. He moved even closer, making her tilt her head back to keep looking him in the eye. "But I have one question about this freedom of yours."

"What?" It was as close to a growl as he'd heard come from her lips, and under other circumstances he might have found it amusing. But not tonight. Not here. Not when his whole life hung in the balance.

"What of the child?" he asked.

Lara felt herself pale, and thought she might have swayed on her feet—but then temper took over. She shook off the urge to collapse into some kind of decorative swoon, and glared at him.

"That doctor had no business telling you something private!" she hissed. "So much for confidentiality!"

"He is the royal physician," Adel snapped. "Last I checked, he serves at *my* pleasure. Of course he told me—especially after I tore the palace apart trying to find out where and why you'd gone. How could you think to keep your condition from me?"

"How could you think I would tell you?" she threw at him, hearing the wildness in her own voice. The years of baggage. "So you could have one more bargaining chip to hold over my head?"

A muscle worked in his jaw. His gray eyes seemed to chill, and then turned to some kind of steel. Lara shivered, but she could not understand herself. Why should some reckless part of her want to comfort him? Even now? What was the matter with her?

"So this, then, is what you think of me," he said in that low voice, and she realized, perhaps for the first time, that he was not as in control as he appeared. That the clenched jaw and deliberately controlled voice were smoke screens. That he was as furious as she'd ever seen him.

"It is nothing more than the truth," she said, bravely, because the understanding that he was not the cold, controlled creature she'd imagined made her tremble deep inside. It changed everything, she thought—and yet, could change nothing. She could not let it.

"This is who I am to you," he continued. "After all that has passed between us."

"You mean sex," she threw at him, heedless of the danger. Her temper—fused tightly to a growing feeling of despair— threatened to swamp her completely. "Threats and compulsion and sex—that is all that has ever passed between us!"

"I love you." The words were like a slap—thrown down, harsh and abrupt, to lie between them. There was an expression she did not understand in his dark eyes, and a rush of joy she refused to acknowledge in her own heart.

"That is a lie." Her throat hurt, as if too much lodged there that she could not bear to say.

"I have loved you from the start," he said with a certain dignity, a quiet insistence. "From the first moment I saw you, when you were little more than a girl. I have loved you my whole life. Nothing has changed that. Nothing could."

Oh, how her treacherous heart yearned to believe him! But she knew him—more than she wanted to, and better than she should. She knew his ruthlessness, his focus. In bed and in his pursuit of whatever else he wanted. Look at how quickly he had turned her from defiance to purring contentment in his arms! Look at the way her body warmed for him even now!

"You will say anything," she said, appalled to hear the catch in her voice, but unable to stop it, much less the hot tears that followed. "*Do* anything. Do you think I don't know that? You told me so yourself. This is who you are. The man who cannot compromise. The man who is not modern."

"Lara—"

"I cannot do this again!" she cried, and there was nothing held back anymore, nothing hidden. She looked at him and she saw all the betrayals and disappointments of her youth. All the times she'd known, somehow, that Marlena was not telling her the truth. All the lonely days and nights spent waiting for Azat to come and claim her, to let her know she was worth something to him. Worth fighting for.

"There is no *again*," Adel said fiercely. "There is only

you. Me. This child. I cannot change the circumstances that have brought us here, Lara, but how can you doubt—"

"I won't do it," she threw at him. "I won't subject my own child to this endless tug of war, this game with no end. I will not have this baby grow up wondering what she's worth, and why, and have her squabbled over like a piece of meat in the market. Not this child!"

"This child will be loved," he said, in that wild voice, low and throbbing. Uncontrolled. "Celebrated and adored."

"Yes, far away from thrones and politics. And you."

The silence seemed to hum between them. Lara was aware, suddenly, of the rain beating against the windows, and her own tears wet on her cheeks. She dashed at them with her fists, her breathing too fast, too hard. And all the while, Adel gazed at her, his beautiful, hard face open in a way it had never been before—*shattered*, a small voice inside of her whispered.

As if she'd destroyed him. As if she—or anyone—could have that power.

She wanted to turn away, but she could not make herself do it. She wanted to go to him, to press her lips against the uncompromising lines of his jaw, his brow. She did not do that, either. Could not let herself.

"I told you I loved you," he said, as if from a great distance. "I have never loved anyone else in my life. Only you. Always you."

"Prove it," she heard herself say—harsh and fast. Before she could think better of it, or change her mind. "Let me go."

She thought the bleakness in his eyes might have killed her right there, on the spot. She felt it pierce her heart, and shoot like fire through her veins, making her stomach lurch. She gasped for breath.

But Adel merely bowed his head slightly, as if the anguish she could see in his face was nothing at all.

"If that is what you want," he said, his voice the barest thread of sound, and yet it still seemed like a lash against her flesh. "Then it is yours."

And then Lara watched him turn and walk out of the hotel door, leaving her, just as she'd claimed she'd wanted.

So why, when the door closed behind him and the room was empty of everything save the rain against the windows, did she feel as if part of her had just died?

CHAPTER NINE

SHE walked back into the palace like a warrior, proud and strong, and Adel felt his heart stop in his chest.

Then begin to beat, hard. Something inside of him, granite and cold, began to ease as she stalked across the great marble floor of what had once been the throne room and was now the antechamber to his office.

"I did not expect to see you again," he said, standing in the doorway between the two rooms, his arms folded across his chest. It had been two days. He knew, intellectually, that those forty-eight hours had been no longer than any other set of forty-eight hours, but it had not felt that way.

He had believed she was lost to him. Forever.

"I did not expect you to give up and slink away like a whipped puppy," she threw at him as she closed the distance between them, going immediately for the jugular. He should not admire that as he did. She should not arouse him, with her temper and her daring. He should be furious that she had turned on him, run from him—and on some level he was.

But more than that, he wanted her. He wanted her, and she was here, and she was glorious.

And his.

"You told me to set you free, Princess," he drawled. Surely she had come back in all ways, or why would she have come back at all? "I was only following your orders."

She came to a stop before him, her remarkable eyes a mix of bravado and something else, something that made him long to touch her. It took all he had to keep from doing so.

Not yet, he thought. Not just yet.

"Since when do you listen to what I want?" she asked, a slight frown between her eyes. "I cannot recall a single instance of you ever doing so, in all the time I've known you."

"I cannot follow this conversation," he replied, his tone silky, his attention on her lush mouth. "I am a bully if I do not listen to you, and a whipped puppy if I do?"

She did not answer him. She only gazed at him for a long moment, her full mouth soft, her eyes big. Adel could feel the tension between them, the kick and the spark. He could see the truth of it reflected in the way she caught her breath, the way her body swayed toward his as if of its own volition.

Mine, he thought, deep inside. Like a perfect note played on a traditional *balalaika*, low and true.

"You said you loved me." She said it so matter-of-factly, yet he could still hear the question. The uncertainty.

"I do." And then he could not help but touch her, reaching across the space he did not want between them to hold her soft cheek in his hand. She shivered slightly, and then leaned into it, like a cat. "And I suspect you must feel the same, or you would not be here. You would have gone on to America. You would not have returned."

"It seems I cannot stay away," she said softly.

"Nor should you," he said. "You are the Queen, Lara. You are my wife. This is your home."

Lara blew out a breath, as a shadow moved over her face. "I do not want what my parents had," she said, her silver-blue eyes so serious it made Adel ache. "I refuse to do to this child what was done to me. Or to you. I refuse."

"Stay with me, Princess," he said softly, raising his other hand to hold her face between them, looking deep into her eyes, into their future. "We will make the world whatever we wish it to be, together."

Once again, Lara stood out on the terrace high in the mountains and looked out over the Alakkulian Valley. It sparkled in the bright morning light, the chill of the coming autumn already moving in from the higher elevations, bringing a sharper kind of light and a certain crispness to the air. She pulled her thick robe tighter over her torso and snuggled into it, flexing her toes against the cold stones beneath her.

She felt...alive. More alive than she had ever felt before.

Because she had chosen, finally. For the first time since Adel had appeared before her in that far-off parking lot, as if conjured out of the June afternoon, *she* had decided.

She had sat in that anonymous hotel room for what seemed like weeks, unable to process both what had happened and her own reaction to it. She'd wanted to die. She'd felt as if part of her had, as every moment stretched out and seemed to last forever, all of them resoundingly, painfully empty of Adel. She had not understood how she could yearn for him so much, *hunger* for him. How his absence could feel like a missing limb. How she could want him near her as much for the calm, quiet steadiness of his presence as for the desire he could stir in her with a single glance.

But then she'd realized that this time, it was up to her. He had let her go. His doing so had shocked her, but it had also freed her, as she'd wanted.

And once she was free, and could choose to be anywhere, Lara had realized that there was only once place on earth that called to her. Only one place on earth she could feel like herself anymore.

How had that happened? When had it happened? How had she put all of her past aside without even noticing it? Because while every word she'd thrown at him in that hotel room had been true, the truth was, there was no point being free, or strong, or *alive*, without him. None of that held any appeal.

She heard the French doors open behind her. She smiled slightly. They had hardly slept—reaching for each other again and again in the night. Re-learning each other. Revelling in her return, and renouncing their separation in the most intimate way possible. She leaned back into the warm, solid wall of his chest as he moved behind her, marveling at the way her body readied itself for his touch. Her knees felt weak. Her core melted. She even felt heat behind her eyes.

He was hers. He loved her.

Standing in his arms, looking out at the beautiful country of her birth, Lara realized that finally, *finally*, she'd found the home she'd been looking for all of her life.

She turned to look at him. That hard face. That uncompromising mouth. That tough, warrior's body. And all of it hers, forever.

Because she'd been given the choice—a real choice this time—and she'd chosen him.

"I love you," she whispered, though it felt like a shout, a howl, that could be heard from mountain to mountain across the great valley. His mouth curved.

"So you have showed me," he said quietly. He let his hand trace a path down her body, slipping it inside her robe to her abdomen, where he placed it over the child they'd made. The child they would raise together, in this country they would rule.

And maybe, just maybe, just for them, if they worked hard enough to make it happen, the fairy tales would come true. Exactly as they'd dreamed together, so many years ago.

* * * * *

The Ordinary King

NINA HARRINGTON

Nina Harrington grew up in rural Northumberland, England, and decided at the age of eleven that she was going to be a librarian – because then she could read all of the books in the public library whenever she wanted! Since then she has been a shop assistant, community pharmacist, technical writer, university lecturer, volcano walker and industrial scientist, before taking a career break to realise her dream of being a fiction writer. When she is not creating stories which make her readers smile, her hobbies are cooking, eating, enjoying good wine—and talking, for which she has had specialist training.

Look for Nina Harrington's new novel,
Her Moment in the Spotlight.

Dear Reader,

I am often asked if the ideas for my stories are based on real life events or situations which I have experienced in person and I hate to disappoint them.

But for this novella I did find my inspiration in the many eco technology projects which are staffed by volunteers in developing countries around the world. Their goal is simple—to give these communities the opportunity to develop a digital future for themselves and their children.

But it did make me wonder about the sacrifices these volunteers make in order to give their time and energy so selflessly and the reasons behind their decision to leave their ordinary lives behind.

How wonderful it would be if one of these volunteers was recognised by the tribal kingdom in Africa they call home, and asked to become a village chief? A king? That is exactly what happens to IT graduate Simon Reynolds. But the only person he truly wants to impress is Kate O'Neill. The girl he left behind in England.

I do hope that you enjoy travelling with Kate and Simon on their journey to discover what and who they truly want in life in the beautiful setting of Ghana in Africa.

I love to hear from my readers so please feel free to contact me through www.ninaharrington.com.

Very best regards,

Nina

**Praise for
Nina Harrington:**

Tipping The Waitress with Diamonds
"Witty, warm-hearted and wonderfully emotional,
with this novel Nina Harrington once again
balances pathos and humour so deftly that readers
will be laughing and crying in equal measures as
they get swept away by this tender, believable
and heartwarming story."
—Cataromance.com

Always the Bridesmaid
"Complex characters with terrific chemistry enhance
Harrington's simple plot. It's a delightful effort
from a new author to watch."
—*RT Book Reviews*

CHAPTER ONE

'I AM so sorry, Kate, but there is still no sign of your luggage. They are chasing up the airline, but you may have to do some emergency shopping. Not, perhaps, the finest welcome to Ghana you could have had.'

Kate O'Neill smiled across at the company's PR agent for West Africa, who had already gone beyond the call of duty to try and track down her precious suitcase. 'I blame it on that five-hour delay leaving Mexico. I only just made the connecting flight out of London with minutes to spare. It was a bit optimistic to expect my bag to have done the same, but thank you for trying, Molly. I really appreciate it.'

Molly Evans sighed heavily and took a sip of her coffee. 'Fingers crossed it will turn up soon. You do know that Andy will never forgive me if I don't look after you on your first field trip to Ghana, don't you? He feels bad enough leaving you in the lurch like this at zero notice.'

'I'll be fine,' Kate answered. 'Have you heard from Andy

yet? His wife was still in labour when I spoke to him yesterday from Mexico.'

Molly lowered her cup and grinned across at Kate. 'There was a text message waiting for me this morning. His twin boys are healthy, hungry and tired, just like their parents. I am so pleased for him. He has a lot of sleepless nights to look forward to, and wouldn't have it any other way. Andy has waited a long time to have the family he wanted, even if the boys did decide to make their appearance three weeks early. Good luck to him.'

Kate lifted up her coffee cup and clinked it against Molly's. 'I'll drink to that. I only hope that the delegates don't expect me to know as much about the country as Andy does. He has been here—what?—fifteen or twenty years?'

Molly nodded. 'At least. And don't worry; the organisers know that you had to step in at the very last minute.' Then Molly paused and looked at Kate over the top of her spectacles. 'Unless, of course, I can persuade you to take over from Andy on a more permanent basis?' Molly added in a casual, innocent voice, her eyebrows raised.

Kate hesitated for a moment, her mind reeling with the impact of Molly's innocent question.

Take over? Take over a job so totally engrossing and demanding that you could forget any kind of family life? Oh, no! She had seen for herself what had happened to Simon's father, and the impact his total dedication had had on his wife and son. She would not be making that same mistake.

'Ah. That would be no,' Kate replied with a warm smile. 'I am only working on the project for the next few weeks or so, while Andy is on paternity leave.'

'Your work in Mexico has been very impressive, Kate,'

Molly said with a slight nod. 'We could really use someone with your experience to support the team here in Ghana, and I know that Andy has been looking for a long-term replacement for months. Why not think about it over the next few days?'

Luckily for Kate, at that moment there was a rush of chatter from the hotel reception desk as the airport shuttle bus dropped off more new delegates for the technology conference and Molly immediately started bustling together her paperwork and slurping down the last of her coffee.

'Sorry, Kate. Duty calls. Catch up with you at the welcome session. And…Kate?'

Only Kate was not listening. Her attention was totally focused on the tall, rugged-looking man in very dusty clothing who was standing in the elegant lobby, and her jaw dropped in that fraction of a second when she recognised who it was—who had just walked back into her life after three years.

A bolt of energy hit her hard in the stomach, and sucked the air from her lungs so powerfully that she had to clutch onto the edge of the table with both hands to stop herself sliding off the chair and onto the floor.

She could not believe that this was happening.

It had to be some sort of crazy nightmare, brought on by lack of sleep from two long-haul flights after a busy week and way too much caffeine to compensate.

There was nothing else that could explain this giddiness.

She did not do giddy. She never did giddy.

Except that six feet two of broad-shouldered, brown-haired hunk of a man-boy from a distant country she called the past was blocking her view of the hotel entrance and the light from the halogens above his head. Even at this distance, with only a side view of his head, there was no doubt at all about who she was looking at.

It was a face she'd used to know by heart. A face she had kept in that safe locked room in her memory alongside the fading images of the people she had once loved.

But there was no mistaking him.

Simon Richard Reynolds. *Her Simon.*

The last person on the planet she had expected to see at that moment, in this hotel, and still in Ghana after three years, took a couple of steps closer—and the sight of him sent her brain into a complete spin.

This must be what it feels like to have a heart attack.

Her hands moved instinctively to smooth down the fabric of her skirt, and she had to force herself not to check her hair and her shoes to make sure that she was clean and neat and *almost* good enough for the smartest, richest boy in her university class. It seemed that old habits were hard to break.

'Oh, there's Simon,' Molly said with a smile. 'Have you two already met?'

Met? Kate did not know whether to laugh or to cry. Her brain was racing with memories of Simon laughing, Simon racing along the beach holding her hand, Simon kissing her so hard that she thought she would die from the pleasure of it… *Her Simon.*

'Yes. We were on the same course at university back in England. But that was years ago,' she added quickly. 'I haven't seen him since. I certainly had no idea he was still in Africa.'

'He most certainly is,' Molly said with a certain lilt in her voice, 'and likely to stay in Ghana for quite some time. We're all very excited about what Simon has achieved here.'

'Really? Is he working on one of your field projects?' Kate asked as casually as she could; only it came out squeaky and a lot wobblier than she wanted.

Molly looked up at her in surprise. 'Oh, no. Simon was working with Andy. I am looking forward to his presentation this afternoon—so far it sounds like one of the company's most successful initiatives. Lucky girl—he's all yours. Now, if you will excuse me, I promise I'll catch up with you later. And welcome to Ghana, Kate. *Akwaaba*.'

Breathing was starting to become difficult.

Simon had been working with Andy? *He was all hers?*

That could not be right. She had read through the files on the three projects Andy was supervising during the long flight from Mexico, and she certainly hadn't seen Simon's name come up. Tired she might be, but she would not have missed the name which was engraved on her heart.

And then Kate sighed out loud.

Of course. *Stupid girl.*

All of the proposals for company sponsorship had to go through the most senior member of that particular small tribal kingdom in Ghana. Royal protocol demanded that only the king for the area made those sorts of decisions. Volunteers like Simon would not be listed on any of those high-level reports.

Kate's cup rattled on the saucer as the terrible reality of her situation hit home.

Suddenly it was all a bit too much. She was on a new continent, for goodness' sake, in a new country, without her luggage after a long nightmare journey from Mexico. Her body clock had no idea what time of day it was, and she was eating breakfast when she should probably be sleeping.

And now she was going to have to work with Simon Reynolds if she was going to make a go of her temporary promotion and impress her boss, just when she *needed* promotion so very badly.

Kate sucked in a lungful of air and watched Molly meet and greet the other conference delegates, dressed in bright African robes or western dress, and felt even more guilt. The company she worked for was one of the main sponsors for this conference. She should be on her feet, smiling and shaking hands like Molly and Simon were doing now. Networking. Explaining why Andy was not there to meet them as usual. Making the delegates feel welcome.

But that would mean talking to Simon. And she was not ready for that. Not yet.

How did you start a conversation when what you really wanted to say was along the lines of, *Hi, Simon—isn't the weather nice for this time of year? Oh, by the way, do you still blame me for destroying your parents' marriage and generally ruining your life? Because I would really like to know why you abandoned me just when I needed you the most and broke my heart in the process. If it is not too much trouble?*

Suddenly her confidence faltered and shuddered to a grinding halt.

Kate swallowed down the huge lump of emotion and regret in her throat that was threatening to overwhelm her. She had sworn three years ago, during that terrible summer after he left, that she would not waste one more tear or sleepless night on Simon Reynolds while her stepdad and her sister needed her to be strong for them.

She could do this. The company needed her to be a total professional and do her job. Simon was just another volunteer working on the company-sponsored rural IT project. That was all.

She was going to show him that she had changed in the past three years. Kate O'Neill was not the push-over he had known at university, who had relied on her extrovert boyfriend to make all the big decisions for them both. The tables had turned. *She* was the one making the decisions now.

Forcing her head up, she stood up from the table, smiled across to the delegates and lifted her chin, back straight.

Only at that same moment Molly said something to Simon, and they both turned their heads in her direction.

Simon's gaze met hers, locked and held.

She had always been able to read Simon from those remarkable grey eyes, but at this distance it was not possible— except for a flicker of… What? What was it she saw in that instant? Hurt? Need? Confusion? Surprise and amazement? Remorse?

Kate's stomach clenched and tied into a tight painful knot under the cold, analytical focus of his stare. Then Simon gave one hard blink and the moment was lost.

With one brief smile and half-bow to the group around him Simon turned towards her and strolled in slow, deliberate steps across the room, as though he owned the hotel, the resort and most of the world around it.

Confident. Strong. Impressive.

Simon Reynolds had been brought up to be a leader amongst men, and it showed in every step that he took—no matter where he was or what he was wearing.

In fact she might have been intimidated by him if it had not been for a few tiny aspects of his new look. The super-smart, casual but expensive preppy clothes his mother had used to buy him in London when he was a student had been replaced by a loose short-sleeved shirt made from the same type of striped fabric she had seen being worn at the airport the previous evening. The faded and darned fabric hung over the scruffiest trousers she had ever seen in her life. The knees were patched with several irregular pieces of fabric in various patterns, which seemed to have been cut out with the same nail scissors he had used to trim his hair. A brown cowhide shoulder bag was slung casually across his chest.

He was unshaven, he was trailing a line of red dust along the floor as he walked, and he looked tastier than hot bread straight from the oven.

Mouth-watering. Hot. Bread.

Perhaps he was more country Sourdough than buttery brioche, but Simon Reynolds still looked just as delicious, and her treacherous heart yearned for a taste.

Her whole body prickled to attention, aware of every move that he made.

Kate sucked in a breath, dropped her gaze, and pretended to gather together her papers on the table, trying to ignore the hot pulsing of the blood in her head as her fingers fumbled and trembled.

Then Simon took another step forward, pausing to greet a delegate on the way, and the air seemed to catch in her lungs in the form of her old nervous cough. The one she had thought she had got rid of.

She couldn't do it.

She couldn't talk to him like this in front of the other people in the room. Her emotions were too open and exposed. And her failure to control herself had hit so hard that she knew she would have to escape until she could steady herself.

A minute. That was it. She needed a minute to get her head straight before she went back to work. This time she would be the one running away from him.

Simon watched from the other side of the room as Kate quickly gathered together her paperwork and strolled out onto the hotel terrace, her back straight and her shoulders high with tension.

Kate O'Neill!

Of all the technology conferences in the entire world she had to walk into this one.

He could hardly believe it! But there could only be one tall, curvaceous, elegant blonde-haired woman called Kate O'Neill, and it had taken a single brief glance to confirm it. Katie was back in his life.

He had not even realised that she was working for the same international IT company that was sponsoring his project until an hour ago, when he had finally managed to get through to Andy and her name had echoed down the line like a bolt from above.

Andy Parsons was his contact, his friend, and his long-standing connection to the outside world from the remote rural village in the Volta area of Eastern Ghana where Simon had made his home. Andy had been a keen supporter of his work right from the first time he had met him with his dad all those years ago. Only now Andy was back in England with his new babies, and judging from the telephone conversation they'd had that morning he was so thrilled and stunned that Simon could not begrudge him one single moment of that happiness. Andy had earned it with years of dedication and hard work serving the same people Simon was trying to help now.

Of course Andy had wished him well for his presentation on the pilot study they had worked so hard together to make reality. He believed that Kate O'Neill would be an ideal replacement for him at the conference, and well able to back Simon up in the technical questions.

What Andy did not know—and what he could never know because Simon had not told him—was that Simon and Kate had a history together. Andy had been replaced by the only woman who had every reason to hate his guts. The same woman he needed to be his most avid supporter.

Just fantastic!

Simon ran one hand through his hair, which was freshly coated with a layer of dry red dust from the long road trip from the village. They were late—he was late—and the village of several hundred people had placed its economic future in his hands. He could not let them down—he *would* not let them down.

He needed a shower and to change, and most of all he needed to persuade Kate O'Neill to take him seriously before the media circus arrived and the pressure really started.

Of course this was only about the work.

The lump in his throat and the thumping of blood in his head had nothing at all to do with the fact that in three years his Katie had grown into the beautiful woman he had always known she would become. Only this time he needed her to be the best friend he had in this world.

That meant she would have to put aside the fact that after three years at university together, where they had shared their lives, dreams and hopes and every waking moment, he had dumped her only days after they'd graduated.

Apart from that...

Time to get to work. He could only pray that she was ready to do the same.

Simon sighed out loud and sniffed.

He was doomed.

Kate stood on the terrace looking out towards the ocean, with her fingers clasped hard around the smooth wooden rail, willing herself to be steady, resolute and professional and failing on every count.

She had never expected the sight of Simon Reynolds to destroy her composure like this, but it had—in every way possible. And it had nothing to do with the past few exhausting days and everything to do with how much she still felt about this man.

Which made her so angry she clenched her nails even harder into the wooden railing.

He had been the one who had walked out on her.

He had been the one who had been full of promises and not kept one of them.

He had been… He had been the love of her life, who had left her behind just like all the other men in her life who had abandoned her when the going got tough. If it had not been for her stepfather, Tom, she would have given up on the whole sorry lot of them a long time ago. Now Simon was here, in this stunning country, and she was going to have to deal with him.

A peal of happy children's laughter rang out from the beach below, interrupting her thoughts, and Kate blinked hard in the dazzling bright morning light to focus on the stunning view before her.

The hotel terrace faced the ocean, and the beautifully kept lawns stretched out to a wide strip of glowing white sand, where her view of the lapping waves was broken only by the thin trunks of tall palm trees.

It was like a poster of a dream beach from the cover of a holiday brochure, complete with a long wooden canoe on the shore and umbrellas made from palm fronds to protect the professional sunbathers from the heat of the African sun in January.

Palm trees. She was looking at real African coconut palm trees. The sky was a cloudless bright blue, and the warm breeze was luxuriously dry and scented with the salty tang from the sea blended with spice and a tropical sweet floral scent.

A great garland of bougainvillea with stunning bright purple and hot pink flowers wound its way around the handrail, intertwined with a wonderful frangipani which spilled out from a blue ceramic pot, attracting nectar-seeking insects to the intensely fragrant blossoms.

Kate spent most of her life in small air-conditioned computer rooms surrounded by office equipment and machinery. It was only natural that she should bend down to appreciate the frangipani flowers close up. Only the biggest insect she had ever seen in her life was inside one of the flowers at the time, and decided to leave just as she bent her head to sniff the blossom. Insect and cheek collided, and the insect was just as unhappy about that fact as she was.

Ouch! 'Oh, no, you don't,' Kate mumbled as she stood up and wafted the offending creature away. 'No wasp stings. Not on my first morning in Africa.'

'Hello, Katie,' came a voice as familiar as her own. 'Talking to yourself again?'

CHAPTER TWO

'WELL, this is quite a surprise,' Simon said, in that educated formal voice which could only come from a lifetime of privilege and expensive private schools. And it was still as amazingly, jaw-droppingly able to light a match under her fire more than any other voice she had ever known.

Her heart and body leapt to attention at the sound of his voice, so fast and so loudly she was surprised that he had not heard it. Speech was impossible, and it maddened her more than she could say that he still had the power to unsettle her so badly.

But she was determined not to let him see that he had got to her. Those days were long gone.

'Hi, Simon,' she said through a dry throat, in as casual and controlled a voice as she could imagine. 'Likewise. I had no idea that you were still in Ghana.'

'Oh, yes,' he answered. 'Still here, still working, still unpaid and still a volunteer. I'm even in the same village. Unlike some people I could mention. It seems like *you* have come up in the world, Katie.' He tilted his head to one side and grinned. 'Congratulations. The company must have a lot of faith in you to suggest you take over from Andy at such short notice. That is quite an achievement.'

Simon pushed one hand deep into his trouser pocket as he leant his other elbow on the railing and towered over her, blocking the blazing sunlight from blinding her, but also shading her with his shadow.

To her unending shame Kate felt her neck flame red in embarrassment and delight that Simon should take pleasure in her promotion—or was it just the impact of that killer grin of white teeth against his unshaven deeply tanned skin?

'Thank you,' she whispered, 'although I certainly hadn't planned to be here. Yesterday morning I was in Mexico, expecting to fly home to a grey London for the weekend. Instead of which...' Kate waved her right hand in the air towards the rolling waves under the azure blue sky. 'Andy Parsons' little boys arrived ahead of schedule, so the company asked me to take his place for a few weeks.'

And then she paused, lifted her head, and looked deep into Simon's face. They were standing so close together that none of the other delegates who had ambled onto the wide long terrace around them could possibly hear what they were saying.

But that did not change the fact that their history together was real, and as far as she was concerned not as much in the past as she had imagined. The only way was to go forward and face the consequences.

'I hope my being here is not going to be a problem for you?'

Simon paused for a second, before turning slightly away from the rail so that his whole body was facing towards her. It was just the two of them on that part of the terrace.

And in those few seconds of silence every one of her senses was attuned to every tiny movement he made.

The way his once soft hands and arms had filled out to become sinewy, strong and powerful. The way the hairs on the back of his hands had been bleached almost blond by the sun, which made them stand out pale and golden against the deep brown tan. And the way his pale grey eyes widened and then narrowed as he looked away from the ocean and back to her. The crease marks at the corners of his eyes were paler than the rest of the tan that if anything made him even more handsome than before—if that was possible.

He had always been able to mesmerise her with just a look.

And then his gaze hardened, and with one look straight into her eyes Simon answered her question without having to say a word.

The surface might have changed, but on the inside he was exactly the same man who had walked away from her and the chaos he'd left behind on that hot July morning three years ago—and he had not forgiven her for choosing to stay with her family instead of coming out to Africa with him, just as she had not forgiven him for leaving. One. Little. Bit.

'It's wonderful news about Andy. But does that mean you're taking his place just for the conference or as project manager for all the local IT initiatives?' Simon asked in a low, calm, steady voice—his serious voice, with a tiny lift of concern at the end.

'Both,' she replied with a slight nod. 'I'll be covering the conference, then shadowing Molly on a field visit to Andy's two new projects along the coast. In the meantime I need to catch up with the progress reports. According to Molly, Andy was supervising the project you are working on. I suppose that means that I'll be your acting project supervisor for the next few weeks.'

She gulped down her apprehension and disquiet.

'I need to know whether we can work together, Simon,' she said quickly, but Simon was already ahead of her, and he shook his head slowly as his grey eyes bored into hers.

'Don't worry about me, Katie. I can work with you any time. The real question is are you willing to work with me? I need to know that I can rely on you completely over the next few days. Especially during the press conferences and TV interviews.'

Kate felt her blood rise, and her fingers clutched even tighter into the handrail until she feared that she would have no nails left.

'What do you mean, TV interviews? That wasn't on the agenda I saw,' she replied, bristling with indignation at his implied accusation that she was not capable of doing the job as well as Andy could.

Simon raised both hands in the air in submission. 'I don't mean to criticise. It is just that there is a lot at stake here, and I really need to bring you up to date with my project as Andy's replacement. Whatever happens, we are going to have to work together as a team.'

'Then I suggest you start talking.' Kate picked up her dossier and waved it at Simon, still bristling at his implied concern. 'Which areas of the report do you expect to be asked questions on?'

Simon nodded. 'I have known Andy so long he probably didn't record the details, but the local tribal leaders in my village have invited me to do something pretty special, and Andy was going to use it as part of the PR plan to help with extra fundraising for the project.'

Kate looked from the report back to Simon in confusion, her throat dry.

'Okay,' she replied in a quivering voice, trying to sound confident and not in the least upset that all the plans she had carefully sketched out for her day had probably just been blown away. 'Can you tell me about it now?'

Before Simon could answer there was a great cacophony of loud car horns mixed with angry shouting and lively chatter coming from the road leading up to the hotel. Both Simon and Kate leant out over the terrace railing just in time to see a huge white TV camera van drive across the pristine lawns to overtake two large off-road estate cars which had tried to squeeze through the narrow road at the same time. They had crashed into one another and were now blocking the entrance to the hotel

'Too late. Sorry, Katie, I'll have to tell you all about it later. I need to find a shower and get changed before the media frenzy gets underway.'

Kate threw up her hands and pointed to his chest, blocking him from running back inside.

'Frenzy! Simon Reynolds, you are not moving from this terrace until I know what is going on. What is it that you are not telling me?'

'Oh. Right. Yes. A few weeks ago the principal King of my village invited me to become their Chief of Development—the Ngoryi-Fia—which means that I am now officially a royal prince of the tribal kingdom I call home. It is an amazing honour.' Simon took one glance at Kate's shocked face and smiled. 'My coronation is next Saturday, if you're still around. It could be your only chance to see a geek being crowned as King.'

'Prince? Royal? King?' Kate squawked, and Simon

grinned at her and shrugged his shoulders as she pressed one hand to her chest in shock.

'I know that it is hard to take in. I'm still getting used to the idea myself. We only have one royal family in Britain, while in Ghana…?' He raised his hands in the air. 'It is a *very* different story.'

'But…how? I mean, when did all this happen?' Kate spluttered, her head still spinning.

'A few weeks ago. I only hope the press pick up the real story, about how much the community suffered when the cocoa business failed. The whole region needs as much sponsorship as we can get. Your company has done a brilliant job with the pilot scheme I am running, but there are a dozen villages where they need the same support.'

'Sponsors, story, prince,' Kate murmured, and shook her head. 'Any more shocks you would like to spring on me? Just to get them all out of the way at once, as it were?'

Simon frowned and pretended to think. 'No, I don't think there is anything else at the moment. But I wasn't joking about having to put on a united front for the media. Andy wanted to make sure that the press knew that your company were still going to fund the next phase of the pilot study. Sort of a win/win for both of us. That was the plan. If you are up for it?'

She scowled at him. 'Oh, I am up for it. If we need to create a united front for the media then I'll see it through.'

Then she smiled and waved at a group of hotel guests who had wandered onto the terrace. 'Just as long as you don't expect me to bow and scrape and call you Prince Simon!' she hissed under her breath.

'Not at all. We are old friends, after all,' he replied without a hint of sarcasm. 'And you know the sacrifices we made to make this happen.'

Kate lifted her chin. At last he had said something she could relate to.

'Oh, I never had any doubt that you would get the job done. You made it abundantly clear that was the only thing that you were interested in when you left.'

Simon turned and focused his laser-sharp gaze on her face as she continued to smile at the other people behind his back. His voice was just low enough to make sure that his calm words were for her alone.

'You know that my father made commitments and promises to the people and the villages. He promised that he would not let them down, and I wasn't prepared to let all that work go to waste. It was my job to continue the work he had started and make good those promises. And that is what I've been doing this last three years, Katie. Building on what he started.'

'Terrific. Then I look forward to hearing your presentation this afternoon.'

The air was fierce between them, crackling with energy and emotion, and the feeling was so intense that Kate was almost grateful when the new arrival of delegates burst through onto the terrace, filling the space with lively chatter and energy and bringing her down to earth with a smash.

She glanced at her watch, then peeked inside the lounge, which was starting to fill up.

'You'll have to excuse me. I need to go through the project timelines before the conference presentation starts.'

A shadow of a smile flashed across Simon's mouth so fast that anyone else would have missed it. Strange how she remembered that little twitch at the side of his mouth so well. It was like an old friend saying hello.

'Of course. I was hoping to report back to the tribal elders tonight about how the press events went, so it would be nice to make a start—*Miss O'Neill.*'

It was the first time he had used her surname. And the way he threw it down to her like a gauntlet across the face shocked her more than she wanted to admit. Three years ago she had been forced to choose between keeping her own promises and helping Simon keep the promises his dead father had made. Now he was getting his own back. And she was going to have to take it because, like it or not, it looked as if Simon Reynolds was her project leader, and her promotion depended on her ability to work with him. One to one.

'Then I suggest we get started, *Mr Reynolds.* Shall we say thirty minutes in the main conference room?'

'Looking forward to it,' he said, his eyes sparkling with something close to wicked humour. 'See you in thirty minutes. *Partner.*'

CHAPTER THREE

WITH a low groan, Kate propped her elbows on the table, dropped her head into her hands and pressed her fingers onto her throbbing temples.

She was pathetic.

'Are you feeling okay, Kate?' Molly asked, her gentle voice full of concern as she softly touched Kate's arm.

I am surrounded by kind people who are here to help me do a great job, Kate thought. *I am an idiot.*

Kate immediately sat back and smiled. Time to snap out of this and get the work done. Molly had a conference to keep on track.

'Touch of a headache. Nothing to worry about,' she replied, and watched Molly's frown relax. 'I'm fine. Do you need me to help you with anything?

Molly shook her head. 'The other way round. I've tracked down this fine young man, who has been working with Simon on one of the projects you have just taken over. He has a few minutes to spare, so this is a good time to get to know each other before the presentations start.'

Molly turned to one side and gestured towards a tall, gangly teenager who had been lurking behind her. 'Paul, this is Kate O'Neill, who I was telling you about. I'm sure she would love to hear about the programme in your village. Why don't you sit down and join her?'

Kate grinned and held out her hand towards Paul, who reached out his long arm and gave her fingers a brief shake before sitting down awkwardly opposite her. Before Molly could join them the reception desk filled up again, and Molly excused herself and took off.

'Lovely to meet you, Paul,' Kate said, as she took in Paul's immaculately pressed white long-sleeved shirt, smart black trousers with a sharp crease, and black briefcase.

He was tall, and his shoulders and chest were just filling out, so she was guessing that he was probably around sixteen or seventeen years old, yet there was a certain air of confidence about him which blended with a certain touch of childlike wonder that was absolutely charming. This one was going to break hearts one day.

Paul, on the other hand, seemed totally uninterested in her, and was staring, apparently mesmerised, at the laptop computer she had in front of her, at her palm-top organiser on the table next to it, and her smartphone. All the latest models from top suppliers.

Men. Kate chuckled to herself.

Once the way to a man's heart had been through his stomach. Now it was through whatever the latest gadget or gizmo the world had created—especially at technology conferences.

'I would love to catch up with some of Andy's projects, Paul. I did not have time to go through the field reports before flying out here, so anything you can tell me would be a great help.'

Paul dragged his gaze away from the technology and gave her a dazzling smile. Oh, yes, the girls would be queuing for miles to have that smile turned on them. No doubt at all. Heartbreaker in the making.

'Of course, Miss O'Neill. I would be very pleased to answer any of your questions,' Paul replied, in English so perfect that she could cut it with a knife. Which totally stunned her for a second. Either Paul had been in expensive formal education in Britain, or somewhere in Ghana there was an impressive coaching service for spoken English.

Kate swallowed down her personal prejudices. She had worked hard to learn how to speak correctly and cover up the strong regional dialect and poor speech patterns from her early years. She had no right at all to judge someone whose parents had probably worked just as hard to afford an education for their son. Even if it did rattle her a little.

After all, wasn't his voice one of the many things which had attracted her to Simon Reynolds on that first day at university? She'd yearned to be around people who had been brought up to speak that way from the day they were born. Be part of that crowd. Overcome what she had left behind in her old life and reinvent herself as a new person.

That was why she had agreed to move with Tom and Gemma to the historic university town, with its ancient stone walls and centuries of history. So that she could start all over again.

She had taken her adopted father's surname instead of her real name, and matched it to a new voice, new haircut and clothes. New hopes and aspirations. New dreams.

Kate swallowed hard and pushed down the instinctive urge

to copy Paul's speech patterns. He might think that she was mocking him, the way she'd used to copy Simon and make him laugh so hard he fell off his chair. And that would not be fair to Paul.

Especially when all he was here for was the conference, which must look like Santa's grotto to any teenager not used to being surrounded by the latest technology.

'Here's an idea. Why don't you start by describing the communication systems you are using at the moment? Do you have a satellite phone and laptops? And what comms software are you running?'

Paul's bright eyes widened, and a cheeky grin picked up the corners of his mouth when he answered. 'It would help if I could take a look at *your* computer. Just to compare.'

'Really?' Kate nodded, and pretended to consider. 'Well, in that case, please feel free to fiddle as much as you like.'

With that she gave a short laugh, and turned the notebook computer around so that Paul could see it. Kate looked on in delight as Paul wiggled his shoulders and fingers a little, as though preparing to present some amazing magic trick. He had just lifted the lid and powered it up when Simon stepped out of the elevator, tugged once on the cuff of each jacket sleeve, and lifted his chin with a smile. She was smitten. Seriously, jelly legs smitten.

He had changed into a charcoal-grey business suit with a pale blue shirt and a striped blue and pink-banded narrow tie. The crisp shirt collar contrasted with the deep tan of his face and neck, and the sun-bleached tips of his clean, swept-back hair. Shiny black shoes. Smart watch.

Despite the business suit, the preppy version of the Simon she'd used to know was gone. Now there was a shocking air of wildness about him which seemed to call out to her.

His dark curly hair was cropped short to match his sharply chiselled features, and he had lost weight but gained muscle. Under the smart clothing Simon Reynolds looked like a man who worked outdoors every day instead of running a computer server.

And there was something else. The way he held his head, his stance, his body language and even the low pitch of his voice screamed out confidence and power. He had done well here. Two of the other men even gave him a gentle bow of respect as they came up to him and bent their heads over the agenda for the day.

Suddenly she was a student again, on her first day at university. Terrified. Exhilarated. Excited and totally, totally intimidated by the clever rich people who surrounded her.

Looking back, she felt sorry for that girl who had been so crippled by her own feelings of insecurity and her lack of self-worth, and the deep-held belief that she did not even deserve to be there, at that prestigious university where really clever and important people went to learn.

Only there'd been this boy at the back of the class, talking about computers and technology, and his voice had been so confident and rich and embracing that she hadn't been able to stop herself being drawn across the threshold and into the new and incredible world she had longed to be part of.

Simon had been holding court as though he was the lecturer, and as he'd lifted his head he had winked at her. Her world had shifted and she'd known that she was doomed. One simple gesture was all it took. She'd been eighteen going on nineteen on the surface, but about fourteen on the inside, just melting with the heat and boiling turmoil that one look created.

He'd made her feel as though she was starting out fresh all over again.

Simon Reynolds had been the golden boy of the class. His father had been a famous IT guru who was about to launch another company after selling his dotcom start-up for millions. There had even been a profile of him in the Sunday newspapers.

Simon had been so far out of her league he'd been playing in a different game where she'd had no idea of the rules. When he'd asked her out the first time she had actually thought it was some sort of cruel joke, and laughed it off as just that. When he'd asked her the second time she'd started to get interested.

He must have asked her out several times each month before she'd finally relented over coffee and a seminar they were both taking, when one of the lecturers had thought it would be interesting to pair them up on a project.

Dynamite. Explosive, competitive and intellectual dynamite.

She'd had no idea how much fun it could be to spar with someone who was just as clever as she was and just as quick—but Simon had been funny with it. She'd been geek girl, only interested in being top of her class and the pot of gold at the end of the rainbow in the form of a top-paying job. He'd been the golden boy who could do no wrong, who didn't need the money but who loved the challenge.

How could she not have fallen for him? How could she not have been totally in awe of the great Simon Reynolds? And when she'd got to know him better... Ah, that was when she'd slipped into love without even realising it.

But that had been long years ago, and they were both different people now.

Nevertheless it was a struggle to smile gently as Simon strolled over to them and dropped his arm onto Paul's shoulder just long enough to give him a reassuring shake.

'I see you two have met. Excellent. I can always rely on Paul to seek out the latest technology and the prettiest girls.'

Kate's lips curled. She was not going to be drawn into that one, even if Paul *was* looking up at Simon with nothing less than adulation. There was a genuine friendship here, and she envied them that. But she could not dwell on missed opportunities. It was time to clear the air so that they could move forward—and if Simon could look at it that way then so could she, no matter how much it hurt.

'Hi, Simon,' she said with a smile. 'Nice suit. But you really shouldn't have gone to all that trouble just for me.'

Her reward was a lopsided hidden smile. The left side of his mouth twisted up and his eyes crinkled to match, just enough to show that he knew exactly what she was up to.

'Oh, this old thing,' he replied, and pretended to straighten his tie. 'Had it for years. Thought I would give it a bit of an outing. Don't want to let the village or the company down.'

Then he paused, and she could feel the intensity of his eyes as they flicked down her body from head to toe, making her squirm and blush—which was clearly his intention. 'Good to know that you still choose grey too. That must be very reassuring. To know that you always have the same colour hanging in your wardrobe.'

The silence stretched out between them, his grey eyes burning into hers. And they both knew that he was not talking about clothing.

He was thinking of people like his dad, who spent their

entire working lives in offices wearing the same kind of suit as every other man in the office. Even his dad had traded in his jeans and T-shirts for the corporate look, but he had laughed it off with talk about putting on a costume so that he could play a part, like some actor in a movie where *he* had written the script. It had been a game, an act. At least for a while.

Perhaps Simon had changed? If he was prepared to put on a business suit for the sake of the people he was helping, then he might just be someone she could learn to trust. Again.

'Actually, this is the *only* suit hanging in my wardrobe. My luggage did not catch the same flight,' she replied with a rueful smile. 'So you might be seeing this suit for a few more days to come.'

Simon laughed out loud, and then quickly scanned the foyer before closing the gap between them, holding his paperwork as though they were talking business. Only Kate noticed the tell-tale way that he licked his bottom lip and paused for a fraction of a second before he looked into her face and said, 'Best of luck with that. But…um…do you have a few minutes to spare? There are a couple of things we need to go through before the sessions open. I'm sure Paul will look after your laptop while you are away.'

Simon held open the door and watched Kate stroll in her high heels across the sunlit foyer into one of the small boardrooms. Everything told him to call after her with some vague excuse when her steps slowed and she half turned and looked back at him over one shoulder. He fell into her blue eyes and was a teenager again, lost and bewildered around this girl he had never been truly able to fathom but who challenged him and attracted him like no other girl before or since.

If she had been an enigma to him then, the elegant and professional grown-up version of Kate he was looking at now was a miracle sent back into his life at just the worst time possible. Or was it the best?

The fact that she was here for the company who were sponsoring his eco-technology project was a matter of fact, too hard to be avoided.

'What is it, Simon?' she asked quietly across the space and the years that separated them, and he could hear the strain in her soft voice. Her cheeks were flushed despite the air-conditioning, her blue eyes wide and sad and imploring.

And he was right back to seeing her for the first time all over again.

How did she do it?

He had spent the last three years fighting to get over her and convince himself that he had made the right decision to come to Ghana and leave her behind!

He had a job he was obsessed about, responsibilities for people who were relying on him for their future, and enough worries to last him a lifetime—and here she was, waltzing into his life out of the blue and destroying any hope he had of getting through this next week with something like control.

She knew him. There had been a time when she'd known him better than his parents ever could. Shared his dreams and hopes and fears. Until fate stepped in and ripped them apart.

No. He had to get it together for the people who needed him now. *Today.*

It was time to prove to his village that they had made the

right decision when they'd made him Prince and asked him
to be their King.

Katie was here from the company who made his work
possible. He needed her to be on his side all the way. The
rest of the day was going to be a blur of business and media
events. If he was going to do it at all, then he had to do it
now.

He could only hope that she was willing to accept an
apology from the man who had hurt her.

'This isn't about work, Katie,' he said with his arms
crossed, and then he uncrossed them. 'Well, it is—but not
directly. I've been thinking about what you said this morning, and we really do need to sort things out if we are going
to be working together.'

'Oh? I thought you said everything that needed to be said
the last time we met. You were certainly clear enough then
that you never wanted to see me again, unless I was prepared
to leave my dad and Gemma behind and come out here with
you,' Katie said, and turned away from him with a sigh that
pierced his heart.

'I know,' he whispered. A lump the size of Wales had
formed in Simon's throat, and he did not dare to speak. He
leant his hands on the back of the nearest chair instead, and
watched her pause and turn back to face him, confusion
creasing her brow.

'You know?' Kate bit her lower lip the way she'd used to
when she was nervous.

In a way that simple gesture reassured him that the old
Katie was still in there, beneath the professional grey skirt
suit and the discreet jewellery and straight long blonde hair.
He had never seen hair that colour anywhere. Ash blonde
mixed with something. It had always fallen long and straight

and he had never understood why she hated it. She had no idea how stunning she looked. To her it was a dumb blonde look that was going to ruin her chances of being taken seriously in business. He had even stopped her from dying it dark brown once. How could he ever tire of running his fingers through that long silky blonde hair, smoothing it down over and over again?

He cursed himself for missing out on the time that they could have spent together.

'I still cringe when I think about how cruel I was. I am so sorry for leaving you when your dad was sick. I should have been strong enough to stay and work it out, but I just couldn't. And I am so very sorry. I regret leaving you like that more than I can say.'

CHAPTER FOUR

'You're sorry?' Kate looked at him with amazement and something close to bewilderment in the depths of her wide, sad blue eyes.

'After my father died…we were all such a mess that it was hard to think straight…'

Kate dropped her head for a moment, and Simon's heart sank to the pit of his stomach at the thought that he was hurting her.

Her head lifted, but she paused just long enough to tell him that this time she was not going to avoid the massive elephant in the room. 'You didn't want to talk about what happened between my dad and your mum, and I understood that because neither did I. But running away with you would have meant leaving my dad and Gemma behind just when they needed me most.'

'What happened between them? Let's be honest, Katie. They had been sleeping together for months. I would call that an affair. Wouldn't you? Because that was certainly how my dad described it. Oh—about two hours before he drove his car into a tree and killed himself.'

'You don't think I remember that? We were together when the police knocked on the door. I went with you to where the accident happened and saw what was left of the car. The investigators said he just lost control, Simon. Why can't you accept that?'

The words swirled around inside Simon's head and he squeezed his eyes tight shut against the blinding heat of the sun as it broke through the window.

Just lost control.

Kate moved closer but clenched her right hand, steadying herself for what was coming next.

He knew that he did not have to explain those images to Kate. He did not have to because she had shared every one of them.

It was Kate who had taken his hand and stood by his side every step on that day, until she was too exhausted to go on.

Kate who had slept on the sofa so that she could be with him.

Kate who had tried to balance out the overwhelming despair which had turned to anger over the next few horrific days.

Kate who had tried to make him understand that his mother needed him.

Kate who had taken the brunt of all of his rage against the mother he loved so much but who in his eyes had betrayed his father and caused his death, who he could not bring himself to speak to face to face.

Kate who had held him when he cried.

Kate who told him that he could get through this.

And Kate who had had the power to destroy him when she'd refused to go with him. She had been his only friend, his best friend. And more.

'You made me choose between staying with my family and being with you. It was hard, Simon. So very hard. And you need to know that if it hadn't been for Gemma I would have packed my rucksack, taken your hand and walked away from all that chaos. And, believe me, I wanted to do that just as much as you did.'

Her voice quivered with the intensity of her feelings, and it was all there in her eyes for him to see.

She was telling him the truth. After all these years. And, whether it was absolution or regret that he was feeling, Simon felt as though a spring that had been held tight inside his heart had suddenly uncoiled.

'You wanted to go with me?'

She nodded. 'I followed you to the end of the road,' she whispered. 'And hid in the neighbour's garden until you turned the corner and were out of sight. It would have been so easy to run after you and just go. My passport was in my pocket. I had saved a little money in the bank. Yes. Of course I wanted to go with you. But…'

There was a deep sadness in those blue eyes which reached out and touched him at the very spot where a big black hole called Katie had used to live, and the tiny pilot light he had persuaded himself had been put out burst into action. A gentle orange flame flickered into life, warm and welcome and as unsettling as a forest fire.

So he had not imagined it after all. Their relationship *had* meant as much to her as it had to him.

Simon shuffled two steps closer to her, his eyes fixed on

the table where they were standing. Anywhere but on her face. Her face would be too much.

'Were you scared?' he asked, in a low voice.

Her answer was a whisper. 'Not for myself. I had survived a lot more than you knew to earn that place at university. I would have got by. But you hadn't lived that life, Simon. You had grown up with more than enough money to do whatever and go wherever you wanted, and your parents were always there for you. Then suddenly your father was gone and you wouldn't even talk to your mother. I was scared for you and what you were going to have to face alone out here. I was frightened for you. But I knew that I had to let you go. And that was so hard.'

'Is that why you told me that you loved me?' he asked. 'To try and persuade me to change my mind about going? Or did you mean it?'

Kate's fingers pressed against the back of his hand for a fleeting second, and she opened her mouth to answer—but before she could say the words there was a bustle of activity and lively chatter at the door to the boardroom, and Molly popped her head around the door with a broad grin.

'Ah. There you are, Simon. The TV crew will be ready for you in a few minutes. Sorry to interrupt, Kate, but the star of the conference needs to make his first royal speech. See you in a few minutes.' And with a small finger-wave she pulled the door closed.

Simon and Kate looked at each other for a few seconds before she took the initiative, reached out and straightened his tie.

'Looks like it's time to get out there and meet your public, Your Majesty. Your subjects await.' With one final shake of the head Kate smiled warmly at him and said in a low, soft voice which thrilled him beyond belief, 'Let's go and tell them what you've been up to these last three years. *Partner.*'

Two hours later Kate collapsed down onto a hard chair in the huge ballroom which served as the main conference area and slipped off her shoes, rubbing her poor crushed toes back to life.

Frenzy had been just about right. As soon as Simon appeared he had practically been mobbed by three teams of TV reporters, all clamouring for interviews and the inside story on what it felt like to be the very first western Prince, soon to be King, of a tribal kingdom in rural Africa.

He had handled every one of the often daft questions about protocol and the best way to wear a toga with courtesy and style, while she and Molly had run themselves ragged handing out press releases and project reports on the company's IT products and the current sponsorship programme in this part of Africa. It had almost been a relief that most of the questions had been aimed at the star of the day—all she'd had to do was stand next to Simon with Molly for the compulsory photo call.

When his arm had snaked behind her back, pressing her close to his side, her smile had become even more fixed and professional. No speaking part required, thank goodness.

Now the media crews had drifted into the dining room like locusts, for the free buffet lunch the company had provided, giving her a precious few moments to catch her breath before the official conference welcome session.

Shame that she was already exhausted and the real work had not even started. *Whimper.*

What made it even worse was that Simon seemed as fresh

as ever. She could only watch in awe as he ran through his talk with Paul.

'You are going to be just fine,' Simon said, and pointed at the projection screen behind Paul's head. 'The presentation looks great. One more run-through and we're done. Okay? Okay.' With one final nod Simon strolled to the back of the room, sat down next to her, and stretched out his long legs before pointing towards the podium where Paul was fiddling with the laptop.

'I hope you don't mind but I've asked Paul to give the presentation on the pilot study. I think it will mean a lot more if it comes from one of the pupils instead of the project worker who started it.'

'Actually, I think that's a great idea—especially when Paul is so eloquent. Is he your star pupil?'

The smile on Simon's face widened into grin of delight and pleasure, which startled Kate. The affection and delight he obviously felt for this boy was genuine.

'Paul is the son of the paramount King of our area, and probably the greatest natural talent I've ever seen. You would never believe that he only touched his first personal computer at the age of twelve. He is already head boy of the local school, and I think he's a genius. The only thing holding that boy back is the lack of opportunity and equipment. This is where we come in.'

Katie tilted her head slightly to one side. 'I think there is more to it than that. Do you want to tell me about it?'

Simon shook his head before replying. 'You could always see right through me, couldn't you? And you're right. Paul's father gave me a home when I needed one, took me in, and then listened to my crazy schemes to introduce solar power and digital technology to a village which at that time had only the most basic school building. And by basic I mean no educational materials at all. No books and certainly no money to pay for teachers. They were doing the best they could, but it was tough.'

Kate nodded then pursed her lips. 'Sorry to question your ability, Your Royal Highness, but I can't see you as a junior school teacher.'

Simon chuckled. 'I tried, but there are people better qualified to teach the basics these children need before they can even use a computer. I learned pretty fast that food and clean water and a safe place to sleep are higher up the priority list than a reliable internet connection.'

Kate sighed out loud. 'Do you remember the first time you dragged me to that talk on graduate volunteer projects in Africa? I blame you entirely for my whole career.'

He snorted out a reply. 'You used to call it my middle class obsession. I certainly didn't expect that we would both be working in the same field all these years later. Perhaps it is just as well that we can never truly know how things are going to turn out? Although…'

'Although?' Kate asked, half turning in her chair so that she could face him.

'Don't hit me, but I was surprised when Andy told me that you had already worked on projects in India and Mexico. After what happened with Dad, I did wonder…' Simon raised both eyebrows and gave her a gentle closed-mouth smile.

'You thought I might stay clear of volunteer work?' Kate said with a lilt in her voice. 'That's a fair question, and the truth is, yes, I *did* think very long and hard about working overseas. But at the end of the day this is the fastest way to step up the promotion ladder to head office.'

Simon nodded. 'Which means you could live at home?

Right. That makes sense.' He turned away from her, as though disappointed.

'Wait a minute, Simon. Don't get me wrong. I wouldn't be doing this unless I believed that the work was important. And it *is* important. That is what this conference is all about—and I never, ever confused the work you were doing with why you left.'

She leant forward and locked onto his grey eyes.

'Perhaps it's time to show me what you have been up to these past three years before I read it in Andy's report? Let's get this conference started.'

CHAPTER FIVE

KATE stood sideways to check her profile in the mirror and immediately pulled in her stomach, vowing that, no matter where she went, from this minute onwards she would always pack a jersey dress or something—*anything*—that would fold up small and not crease in her hand luggage instead of her suitcase.

It was no good. Whatever she did there was no way that the dress she had borrowed from Molly Evans was going to hide the bulges that came from several years' worth of snatched meals and sitting hunched over a computer terminal for twelve hours every day of the week.

Molly was a lovely lady, and had been very generous to offer her the use of a dress for the conference dinner. The grey business suit was fine for daywear, but people were bound to notice if she was to wear it again for the dinner that evening, and then all the next day—even longer if her missing suitcase did not turn up.

She turned quickly from side to side with her arms outstretched, and watched in relief as the silky fabric of the maxi-dress slid loosely over her hips.

That only left one problem area.

Kate tugged at the side of the dress and tried to hitch it up a little further, but her generous bosom had already filled all the spare fabric. Worse, an enormous shell-pink passion flower now covered her left breast, creating a very different type of eye-catching design.

Options... *Come on, Kate,* she told herself. *Time to get creative! That's what they pay you for.*

Kate flung open the wardrobe door and gazed at the meagre contents of the rails. She blinked several times at the pathetic range of lingerie she always carried in her hand luggage, right to left and back again, pulled each item out and held it against the dress—and instantly noticed how the shell-pink of her fitted pyjama top matched the shade of pink in the dress almost exactly.

The pyjama jacket might just work as a make-do bolero top. *It just might.*

Even if she was going to be in the presence of dignitaries and royalty. Including several princes. And one in particular.

Kate's left hand pressed hard against the wardrobe to support her weight.

Simon was Prince of a Ghanaian village and was going to be crowned King in a few days.

Her Simon. A king. A king!

That afternoon she had sat in the front row of the conference room as Paul talked through slide after slide of stunning colour pictures of the village where he had been born and had spent his life, and the amazing countryside which surrounded it. Dazzling photographs of wide tranquil lakes covered with water lilies had been followed by shots of thick jungle forest land, backed up by cliffs with spectacular cascading waterfalls.

It looked a magical and awe-inspiring place, made real by the people Paul and Simon shared their lives with.

To her eyes Simon had dominated every scene, whether he was carrying bricks for the half-built tiny schoolroom, or balancing on a couple of rusty oil drums to repair a leaking roof in the middle of a tropical downpour. It was Simon who had leapt out at her from the photos of tribal leaders in their ceremonial robes, coming together to celebrate the opening of the first solar energy unit. His pride of being part of their community had shone out.

The presentation had been a revelation, and had earned both Paul and Simon a standing ovation from the entire conference.

Wow. Something that felt an awful lot like pride welled up inside her, and she blinked away the prick of tears in the corner of her eyes. Allergies. *Must be her allergies.*

Of course he had always been the golden boy, expected to take over his father's company when he left university. Shame that his family had had no idea that the business had serious financial problems—how could they? His father had not told them about the trouble he was in—not even when he was flying all over Africa investigating alternative technology initiatives.

Sometimes she'd used to wonder how things would have turned out for them if Simon's father had not become so obsessed with this amazing country. But she had played the 'what-if' game too many times and the result was always the same—his father was dead and it was too late to turn back the clock. She and Simon had been student lovers, that was all—happened all the time. You met someone at college and then you had to grow up and go out and live your life.

But with Simon it was different.

This time Simon was going to be a king—not because of some inheritance, but because he had earned that honour through his own investment and hard work. His father might have sparked the original idea for a digital communication centre, but it was Simon who had made that dream a reality by his own sweat and his constant drive to find sponsorship and support from any organisation or charity with the resources he needed.

There was no point in denying it. She *was* proud of him.

Kate pushed her arms into the sleeves of her pyjama top, took one final glance in the full-length mirror and twirled from side to side, then lifted her hair up into a loose twist.

Much better! In fact it was positively regal.

Time to shout about Simon's good news from the rooftops. Starting with one very special little lady. Her sister Gemma—who would want to know everything!

Simon pulled on a faded T-shirt bearing the name of a pop group nobody here would know, and peeked through the blind of his hotel room window. The sun was already low on the horizon, but this was the first time he had felt able to escape the bustling crowds and constant banter from reporters and other volunteers which had followed him all day. The conference had become a hotspot for anyone looking for a human interest story to fill a gap in a news report or magazine around the world—and today it was his turn to be in the spotlight.

He had been hijacked—and he had to put up with it. No

matter how much he squirmed inside when the cameras were pointing at him. He was prepared to act out his part and do his bit. His village community and the project were all that mattered. Not him.

Molly had dug out an old photograph from the tribal meeting when he had first worn a toga and added it to the press release at the very last minute. Embarrassed did not come close!

Simon cringed at the mental picture of poor, unsuspecting readers opening their newspapers at breakfast tables and on tube trains on the way to work back in England and finding *that* horrific image staring back at them.

Of course Molly Evans had done a wonderful job in the PR department—that was her job—and Kate had backed him up every step of the way. But by the end of the formal presentations he had felt as though the village chiefs who had recognised his commitment to building their future and offered him this amazing honour had become lost in the rush to focus on him and *his* unique story instead of theirs.

He didn't blame the press for being interested—he would be too. But there were only so many times he could tell his personal story without making himself out to be some sort of hero. Which was so very far from the truth it was ridiculous.

If they only knew that he was the last person in the world he would have called a hero.

If they wanted to know what sacrifices he had made to be here then all they had to do was ask Kate O'Neill. The only person who truly knew every one of his many faults.

He had spent most of the day looking out of the corner of his eye for a glimpse of a blonde-haired girl in a grey suit.

And she had been everywhere—working, doing her job with elegance and panache!

Katie handing out conference goodie bags and notes from the four presentations that had followed the welcome session. Katie standing alongside Molly as they chatted to local government health department officials about the projects her company sponsored in Ghana. Katie introducing Paul to other charity organisations who had the resources they needed so desperately, giving him moral support when he faltered.

Katie. The girl who had been *his* Katie. Setting up meetings and printing out press releases and project proposals for the decision-makers. She probably hadn't realised that he was watching her, professional IT person in action, just as he had always imagined she would be. Intelligent, quick, dedicated and charming in her high-heeled executive shoes and smart grey suit. The company should be proud of what she'd achieved today.

He certainly was.

Simon closed his eyes and raked his fingers back through his hair.

Oh, Katie. As if his life was not in enough turmoil. The last thing he needed right now was Katie O'Neill turning up, just in time to stir up the past and take him back to a place where he had been so lost.

One thing was clear—he needed fresh air and to feel the wind on his face before he could brave a tight shirt collar, the stuffy conference dinner that evening, and all the extra media attention that would come with it.

The sun was an orange ball of stunning flame in a sky of the deepest azure blue with apricot streaks by the time

Simon slipped down the stairs and out through a side door to the path leading to the shoreline.

He had always loved the sea. And so had Katie. The day after their second-year exams had finally been over he had shared a magical week away with Katie at a beach cottage in Dorset that his mother had rented from a friend for the whole of the summer. They had spent their days swimming and sunbathing, followed by barbecues and moonlit walks along the beach. And their nights…?

Simon stopped and closed his eyes for a second, reliving those heady nights of young love and the simple joy of waking up with Katie in his arms and a smile on his face. The sex and the intimacy had been so mind-bogglingly amazing they had changed his life.

He had never been happier.

Shaking his head with a contented grin, Simon waved at the few hotel staff who were clearing away the debris left by their guests, and in the fading light stepped onto the white sand and strolled down the shore, away from the brightly lit hotel. Here the beach angled more sharply into the Atlantic, and the palms clung tightly to a narrow strip of shallow soil.

With every step he took further from the hotel Simon could feel the tension ease from his shoulders. Strange. He'd used to love the idea of working in high-tech offices surrounded by the buzz of electrical equipment and busy office chatter, the constant cacophony of telephones and fax machines and printers.

No longer. *This* was his idea of heaven.

The sound of waves from the Atlantic Ocean rolling pebbles onto the sandy beach only a few feet away. Sand beneath his feet. The trill and chirp of birdsong and the wind in the palm trees—all to the background noise of insect wings and frog calls. Somewhere a dog was barking and seagulls called. This was the soundtrack to his life and he loved it.

Simon dropped back his head, eyes closed, and just listened. Savouring the moment and trying to clear his head of the clutter and noise of the day.

That was probably why he felt like screaming out loud when the ring-tone from a cell phone destroyed his precious moment of calm. His eyes snapped open and he stomped across the beach for a few minutes to the shoreline, to where the sound had come from, intent on giving the owner his opinion.

But he didn't. *He couldn't.*

Because sitting on the shore, with her back pressed against a tree, was his Katie. She was alone and crying. And she seemed to be wearing a long, silky flowery nightdress and a pink pyjama top.

All his bluster and anger vanished in the breeze.

Her eyes were closed, but as he took a step closer his foot crunched down on a piece of driftwood and her eyelashes flicked several times as she reacted in alarm. Then they slowed and blinked away the trace of tears. One escaped and ran on to her cheek. She sniffed and quickly brushed it away with the back of her forefinger.

She tried to smile up at him, but her mouth didn't make it. Instead the fingers of both hands cupped tightly around the cell phone in her lap and she brought it up to her face in the fading light so that she could key in a few words of text.

He knelt down on the shoreline in front of her, with his back to the sun, and watched her read the message that came in reply to her text. A small smile creased her mouth before a single tear rolled down her cheek—only she had pressed her hand to her mouth so tightly that she could not wipe the tear away.

So Simon stretched out and moved the rough pad of his thumb across her soft cheek to do the job for her. Her delicate pale skin was illuminated against the ridges of his working hands. Her response was a sharp intake of breath and a wider smile—for him.

Neither of them spoke, but her eyes were locked on his now, and even when she dropped her phone onto her lap she did not look away.

What Simon saw in those eyes was something more than the look of a girl who had taken an upsetting phone call. It was a cry for help from someone who was not able or willing to say the words to ask for it.

And that look destroyed him.

He couldn't handle this as Prince Simon. For Katie he needed to go back to that first day at university, when he had managed to build up enough courage to actually speak to the prettiest girl in his year group instead of just winking at her and playing the idiot.

'Hi there, pretty girl. You new around here?'

And instantly, without hesitation or delay, she shot back with the same answer she had given him all those years ago—only this time in a croaky rather than jokey voice, 'Yes, but don't tell anyone. I'm supposed to be giving the lecture.'

And *then* the cool, collected, sophisticated businesswoman burst into tears.

CHAPTER SIX

IT SEEMED only right and natural for Simon to shuffle forward and take Kate into his arms, as he had done a hundred times before, and just like a familiar warm glove she slipped into the shape of his body as though she had never left. Her head fell onto his shoulder as she clung to him, her chest pressed against his, soaking in the strength and heat of his love and his support as he held her close.

As her sobs ebbed away Simon's hand moved in gentle wide circles around her lower back, just the way she'd used to like. He felt her chest heave with emotion, then slow to a more regular movement as her breathing calmed under his caresses.

His head pressed against her silky hair, but there was something sharp and hard under his chin and in the fading light he realised that she put her hair up. With two fingers he slowly pulled out the comb and two hair grips, and dropped them onto the beach towel she was sitting on. With exquisite pleasure the fingers of his right hand smoothed back the hair back from her forehead and gently, gently teased out the strands of her hair until it was falling in a waterfall of silken tresses over the back of his hand.

Kate shuffled slightly against him and he held his breath, in fear that she was going to break this tenuous, remarkable connection. But to his delight and wonder she was not moving away—she was snuggling closer. And his heart sang. He had never, ever expected to feel so powerfully like this again.

She felt so right. It was as though she was the last piece in the complex jigsaw puzzle that was his life, which he had not even realised was missing until he had found it hidden in the most unlikely of places.

His mouth was pressed into her hair now, kissing the top of her head, breathing in the essence of who she was, and as Kate turned within the circle of his arms she closed her eyes so that he could hold her and brush his lips across her forehead and temples.

'I am so sorry,' she choked out, and looked up into his face. 'You must think that I am totally pathetic, but the call was about Gemma. Oh, no,' she added quickly, when Simon gasped in alarm. 'She's fine. Or at least as fine as she ever will be.'

Kate shook her head and pressed her palm against his chest, sending delicious shivers through him. 'Tom has been called in to repeat some tests after his yearly check-up. He has a cold that won't go away, and she is terrified that his cancer has come back.'

'Oh, I am so sorry,' he murmured as gently as he could. 'Are you worried?'

Her answer was a short shrug. 'Not yet. I know that there is nothing I can do until the test results come back tomorrow, and all his other tests are fine, but I can't get that through to Gemma.' Kate gave a long sigh and waved her cell phone at him. 'A boy she likes at her special needs school made some jokey comment and she didn't know how to take it. She got upset. Then he got upset. Then the rest of the class got upset and before long the teacher had to call my dad.'

Kate closed her eyes and rested her head against the crook of Simon's shoulder.

'He didn't say anything insulting or unkind. Nothing like that at all! But she just didn't understand that he meant it as the kind of banter that we used to have. And it breaks my heart. Every. Single. Time. There are so many things that she will never love like we did. I just want her to be happy. And it's so hard.'

Simon groaned out loud. 'I am the one who should apologise. I have seen you all day and not once asked how Gemma is getting on. How old is she now? Twelve?'

Kate smiled as though the sun had come out again, and Simon's heart leapt at the intensity of joy in Kate's face. 'She'll be thirteen in three weeks' time, but she is already a teenager at heart—right down to the nail polish and fashion. I shall be working extra shifts at head office at this rate, to pay for all the designer labels that she will need to look cool in the next few years.'

Simon paused for a moment, before lowering his voice and asking, 'Is that why you agreed to take this assignment? So you could work sooner at headquarters and be closer to home?'

Kate laughed out loud and shifted back slightly, so that she could stroke his cheek with one finger.

'You always were too clever for your own good, Reynolds. Do you know that?' But then her laughter eased away. 'You're right. I sold my flat in London six months ago and moved back to live with dad and Gemma. It wasn't… Well, it wasn't working out very well for me.'

'Ah,' Simon replied with a knowing nod. 'Was that not working out because of some uncaring boyfriend? Or was it—' and at this he flashed his teeth in a pretend grimace '—a lazy husband who did not polish the silver to your exacting standards?'

Kate reared back, wide-eyed, and stared at him. 'Has all this African sun gone to your head? No, Simon. No husband, boyfriend, or, in case you were wondering, illegitimate children.' And then she smiled and shot him a cheeky glance. 'I would have told you if you had asked. And of course I don't need to ask *you* about children. What did you used to say?'

She lifted her chin, and to Simon's horror gave a very good impression of his normal speaking voice.

'The first five years are crucial to career development, darling. Family life must wait until there is a firm financial footing.'

Simon dropped his head onto his chest and groaned. 'Oh, no. Did I really sound so arrogant and pompous back then? I don't know how you put up with me.'

'Oh, it wasn't so bad. You did call me darling now and again, and of course it wouldn't have been half as much fun without you to keep me on my toes.'

He looked down at her and pursed his lips. 'Fun? What *can* you mean?'

'We made a good team. Having you around meant that I had to work that little bit harder to get top marks in every class. You would claw your way to the top, then I would knock you back into second again. Just to keep you busy, you understand. I knew how you hated to be bored.'

'Hah!' he snorted. 'So that was the reason! You need not have worried. It was never boring when you were around. Darling.'

He smiled into her eyes, and she into his, and as the sun set behind Simon's back the only sound was the soundtrack of nature which was playing in the background.

It was as though they had never been apart. She made him feel young, and so full of enthusiasm and fire and life and energy for what was to come. So innocent, in many ways. She was the only girl he had ever felt so easy and comfortable with. The only girl he had allowed to peek below his outside layer of confident bravado so that they could share their goals and dreams.

Kate had taken hold of his hands and was splaying out his fingers on the skirt of her dress, which was now only just visible in the fading sunset.

Her face was lit by the rays of the setting sun, and seemed to glow in the orange and pink-tinged light. Her blonde hair was a halo of gold, her skin like sheets of the finest softest silk. He took in every tiny detail of how she looked and what she was wearing, the beach and the tree…and at that moment he fell in love with Katie O'Neill all over again. If he had ever fallen out of love with her in the first place—which, if he was being honest, he knew was highly doubtful.

He never wanted this moment to end.

'Are you happy here, Simon?' she asked in a soft and tender voice. 'I have no idea what being a king means, but the people must respect you very much. You should be proud of that.'

'Grateful rather than proud. It's a real honour.' He could hardly see her hand now, but meshed his fingers between hers before answering. 'I *am* happy in so many ways, but it's the usual story. The more I do, the more I see what could be done. I will have the chance to give my ideas on how to build a better future for young men like Paul. But it's not going to be easy.'

'Do you have a…a wife or a girlfriend to support you?'

He shook his head with a grin. 'No one will put up with me like you did.'

'I'm sorry to hear that. Of course now you are going to be a tribal king of the village I expect the girls will come flooding around to take a look at you. Girls *and* their mothers! Speaking of which—and don't bite my head off—have you told your mother your news? I know that she would be very proud of you and what you have achieved.'

Simon inhaled slowly before answering in as calm a voice as he could manage. 'Actually, I *have* told her. We've met up a couple of times over these past few years, on my rare trips back to London, but only for coffee…maybe dinner. But this is different. The King has asked me to invite my family to the official coronation ceremony next weekend and, seeing as she is the only family I have left outside Africa, I asked her if she'd like to come and take her place as—well, sort of a village Queen Mother.'

He looked up and grinned into Kate's shocked face. 'I'm not sure that the village is ready for the Parisian couture hats, but she will be staying with me for a couple of weeks out in the wilds.'

'Your mother? Queen of the couture boutiques? Alone with you in the jungle? Oh, I would pay to see that.'

'Then why don't you stay, Katie? It would be great having the two of you in the village. They won't know which way to look first. A lovely blue-eyed blonde or a haughty aristocratic brunette. It could be great fun.'

'Fun?' Kate snorted with a harsh laugh. 'Oh, Simon. You have to be kidding. I won't be coming to your coronation, and I certainly don't want to meet your mother again any time soon.'

'Wait a minute,' Simon replied in a tight voice. 'I thought you got on well with my mother?'

'Oh, I did,' Kate said in an exasperated voice, and shook her head. 'Until she decided to have an affair with my widower dad while still being married to yours. I know…' She held up her hands in response to Simon's harsh cough. 'I know my dad was equally to blame. But have you any idea what it was like for him? He had been alone for so long, and then he met your mother. She was married, she was lonely, and he fell in love with her out of the blue. He didn't ask your mother to come into his life—she just did. And I know that neither of them could have predicted what happened. It just did. And then he had the cancer diagnosis and she dumped him.'

Kate shook her head from side to side, eyes closed, and her voice dropped into her shoes. 'She dumped him when he needed her, and he let her go without saying a word because he cared too much to make her stay and watch him suffer. I still can't forgive her for that. If you need someone to blame for me not coming with you, you can start there.'

Simon paused and gave a short chuckle.

'No, Katie, that's not fair. Tom is an adult. He could have dealt with his life and let you be free to live yours the way you wanted.'

'Oh, Simon. Don't you get it? It wasn't Tom I stayed for. I stayed behind for Gemma.'

'Gemma? I don't understand. She has a wonderful school for the deaf, and people to help her.'

'Yes, she does, but I was the only person in Gemma's life who stayed when the going got tough. Gemma really loved having you around, and then you were gone. She kept asking me where you were. Tom was having chemotherapy, and she was so terrified that he was going to die and leave us, like Mum had. Do you know that she still has panic attacks every time we pass the hospital where he was being treated? She couldn't go to school. I couldn't go to work. It was a nightmare!'

Simon sat back on the beach towel with a resigned thump. 'And Gemma asked you to help her get through this? Is that right?'

Kate nodded. 'She begged me to stay. She was so terrified that I was going to leave her that she had to sleep in my bed for the next six months, so that she could wake up and realise that I was still alive and not going to walk out on her or die. On the day our mum died I promised Gemma that I would always be there for her. And that came before anything. Even you, Simon. Which was why I needed you so very badly.'

Kate clutched at Simon's arm, almost scrabbling at it with the intensity of making him understand what she was saying. 'I was so lonely. Tom and Gemma were depending on me, but who was there for *me*? That's why I needed you, Simon. I needed you more than I had ever needed anyone in my life before. And you weren't there. Not a message, a phone call, a postcard. Nothing. You cut us off as though we didn't exist any more. Have you any idea how painful that was? To be rejected—again! It doesn't get any easier, you know. Being rejected and abandoned isn't something you get used to.'

'Oh, you don't need to tell *me* about that. Don't you remember what it was like when my father left for yet another trip to Africa? We'd spent two years together before I even started uni, putting together the technology the villagers could use with help from volunteers, but that was never enough. He kept going back, and back, then back again. It was an obsession, and every single time he left he gave me the same speech about how I was wasting my time at university when I should be out here with him to make the project work. He might have sacrificed his business, but in the end it was his family he truly left behind.'

Kate knelt in front of Simon on the towel, so that she was looking up into his strong and loving face which was cracked with grief and confusion.

'I remember that you cared about him, and wanted him to be safe in Africa. That was why you were so angry at your mother and Tom for letting him down, when he was doing such amazing work here,' she whispered, taking his hands in hers and hoping that he would listen. 'I wasn't too happy about it myself. But you blamed *me* for bringing them together, and that wasn't fair, Simon. I was there when they tried to explain that neither of them expected to fall for each other. Do you remember? Tom certainly never saw it coming. I know that.'

Simon gave a brief nod and blinked before answering with a sigh, 'I know. You told me that my father was a coward for taking the easy way out, and that if I left I would be doing the same thing. Running away from the hard decisions.'

Kate winced. 'That was cruel of me. I am sorry for being so hard on you.'

Simon slipped a hand out of her grasp and reached up and stroked her face. Her eyelids fluttered half closed at the delicious sensation.

'Don't be sorry,' he said, in a low, tender voice. 'You were telling me the truth but I wasn't ready to hear it. I idolised my father and he was never there for me. Never. Do you know the real reason I went into maths and computing? It was so that he would be proud of me and we would have something to talk about when he came home. I think you were the only person who knew just how hard I worked to get his seal of approval.'

Simon choked on his words and slipped back on the towel, found something fascinating to look at on the beach stretched out in front of him.

'I think it was a case of facing up to the truth that my dad was not the perfect man I had built up in my mind over the years. Far from it. He loved his work here, and he devoted so much of his life and time to it he never once counted the cost for the family he left behind. Mum was lonely and Tom's a fine man. I don't blame her, and I am sorry that I blamed you for making it happen.'

Kate opened her eyes and stared Simon in the face. 'It's not the same. Call me hard and callous, but your mother abandoned Tom when he needed her.'

Then her voice changed, and when she spoke again there was a chill in her tone.

'And then you did the same to me. How could you do it? How could you walk out on me like that at the precise time when I needed you most? And then blame me for not going with you?'

CHAPTER SEVEN

KATE sat back on her heels and waited, hardly daring to breathe but desperate to finally hear Simon's reply. The silence stretched out between them, so that when he did speak his words seemed to echo around the cool night air and vibrate with the tension in his voice.

'The day of his funeral, I looked into that grave and I saw that all my efforts had been a worthless joke. I had lived my life striving to be the best in class so that he would pay me some attention, and there I was. A first-class honours degree. Graduating joint top of the class. And it meant absolutely nothing. The man I had worked so hard to please was gone. My mother had fallen for your dad and my family was gone for ever. I felt as though everything I had built my life on had been swept away by some giant landslide.'

The anguish in his words hit her like a physical blow. 'I wanted to be there for *you* when he died,' Kate said, desperate not to break the connection between them. 'That's why I decided to wait until a better time, when we could both think straight about how we should build a future together. I didn't have a second of doubt that we could do it. As a team. Me and you. Only you left before we could talk. And that's what hurt the most. The fact that you cut me off.'

His head dropped forward onto his chest and his fingers clutched onto Kate's, drawing her next to him. 'I didn't know who I was any more. And then I turned and looked at you,' he said, in a sweet voice with a gentle smile. 'You were standing next to me at the graveside. You *were* there for me. And I saw someone who put her family first, before herself—and still got the grades by working twice as hard as anyone else in the class. You wanted to work to give yourself a future. And it blew me away. That's when I knew that I had lost the sense of what I truly wanted in life. The old me was in that grave with my dad, and I had no clue what to do any more.'

Kate started to speak, but Simon's forefinger pressed against her lips to silence her. 'You're right. I did run away. I ran way to find myself. It was a selfish thing to do, but I knew that if I stayed I had nothing to give you or offer you. *Nothing.* No home, no money, and not even the job we had both worked so hard for. It was all gone. I can't even guess at how tough it must have been, but you had always been a fighter. Until that moment I don't think I fully realised just how much I had come to rely on you for my strength. I loved you, Katie. I loved you and I had not once told you that out loud.'

His eyes scanned her face as his fingertips brushed gently across her forehead and into her hair. 'So, you see, you were right to call me a coward. Telling you how I felt would have been a sign of weakness, and the Reynolds family did not *do* weakness.'

His laugh was hollow and bitter, and Kate shook her head in gentle agreement. 'Oh, Simon. I wish you had talked to me about what you wanted.'

'And said what? My dad had promised the village that he would finish the work he had started—they were relying on him! But I knew that was never going to happen. He was gone, and so was the finance. All I could offer the people was my time and my commitment to keeping the promises he had made.'

He dropped his head back and pressed both hands palm flat against the top of his head as he closed his eyes. 'I know you, Kate O'Neill. I knew that you would never leave Gemma—especially when your dad had cancer. And I had been to Ghana before. I *knew* there was no way you could have brought a child out here. Life was tough enough for a single man on his own. I just about coped with finding clean water and food to get by. A little girl like Gemma would have been…impossible to care for. And I was certainly in no state to be a father figure. No. You had to put her first. And that meant you had to stay. And I had to leave on my own. No matter how much it hurt.'

'Were you lonely?' she asked, after what was probably only a few seconds of silence which had seemed to stretch for hours.

He nodded. 'Missed you all like crazy. But somehow being in Ghana helped me mourn my father. This was the one place where my dad and I had been happy working together. The village gave me a home and a purpose in life. A lifeline, if you like, when I needed it. Everything I have done since then has been to repay that debt. They are my family, and now they are going to be my people.'

'You kept the promises your dad made. You should be proud of that.'

Simon smiled a couple of times. 'I suppose I did. Just

as you kept your promises to Gemma. And *you* should be proud of *that*.'

The light had faded now to a dim glow from the white sand, and as he smiled in reassurance Simon noticed the dark shadows that were growing all around them as the final rays of the sun dropped below the horizon, taking the glorious sunset with it.

Suddenly Kate rolled to one side, away from Simon, and in one movement started gathering together her things and tugging the dress she had borrowed from Molly back into position.

'What is it, Katie? Are you cold?' Simon asked.

'No. Not cold,' she replied, with a smile he could hear in her voice. 'Just sad.'

He reached out and caught her hand, forcing her to be still for a moment.

'Why sad? We've both come a long way these past three years so that we can sit on this beach together in this beautiful place. Who knows what the next three years will bring?'

'Oh, Simon. Don't do this. You are a prince, soon to be a king, with responsibilities and people who need you. Right here in Ghana. While I still have a sister back in England who needs me, and a dad who is sick. So not much seems to have changed on that front, does it? If anything, I would say that our lives are even further apart than ever.'

Simon gasped and choked out a question. 'You don't mean that? We have only just…'

'Just what? Remembered old times? Yes, it has been wonderful, and just for the record I never stopped missing you. But unless one of us is prepared to move to another continent this is one long-distance relationship that is not going to work. We both know what this kind of job does to couples.'

Simon took an even tighter grip on both of her hands.

'Don't give up on us quite just yet, Katie. You were always the creative one. Won't you even try to come up with a few ideas? Andy doesn't work here all year—far from it. And there are webcams and video links we could bring in, so that you could see your family and talk to them any time you wanted.'

She paused for a moment, then nodded. 'That's true. But it would have to work both ways, so that you could talk to the other tribal leaders from the UK. Here is an idea for you. From what I saw today you are proud of being a one-man band, taking all the responsibilities onto your own shoulders.' Kate slid closer to him along the beach towel. 'It doesn't have to be that way. Most of the other presentations today came from teams of volunteers, where the company has provided the equipment and there's more than one project leader.'

She reached out and touched his face with one finger before smiling at him. 'Maybe it is time for you to share the workload and forgive yourself a little. After all, you are Chief of Development. You could spend time raising funds and extra sponsorship back home and still...' Then she stopped and sighed. 'But you don't want that. Do you?'

He slowly shook his head from side to side. 'I am going to be the new king, with all the responsibilities that come with that honour. I can't leave my people without the support they need.'

'Then we are stuck, aren't we?' she answered, and slowly slid her fingers from his grasp, breaking their connection. 'Perhaps we ought to get back in time for dinner, Simon?' Kate said, trying to keep her voice calm and light. 'Molly will be wondering where we have got to.'

And with that she turned away from Simon to gather up her shoulder bag, and waited for his reply—which never came.

The final touches of sunset were throwing deep shadows along the beach now, the red and scarlet bands adding texture and colour to a sky which seemed to go on for ever across the horizon. But under the trees the light was fading fast. The hotel lights shone ahead as a beacon, and lanterns had been hung in the palm frond pagodas along the edge of the shore, but Kate was struggling to see Simon's face.

Something had changed in the air between them, as though the light under their easy camaraderie had just been extinguished.

'Can you find your own way back?' Simon finally asked, in a low voice full of concern but distant and cold as the night air.

Simon was still sitting with his arms resting on his knees, staring out towards the horizon. She could not see his eyes at all now, but she knew. She had made a mistake. And this one was not going to go away.

Her own way back? No, she did not want to find her own way back.

She wanted to dance along the moonlit shore, with Simon holding her hand like he used to. She wanted to skip in and out of the waves and laugh so hard that her stomach ached.

She wanted him to want to be with her. But that was impossible.

'Don't worry about me,' she replied. 'I've made it on my own this far. I don't need anyone to show me the way.'

And with that she set off back down the beach alone, grateful for the cover of darkness so that nobody would see her fresh tears.

CHAPTER EIGHT

'HEY—guess what the airport shuttle just delivered?'

Molly Evans strolled into the sunlit hotel breakfast room, dragging behind her a battered-looking trolley suitcase, that was looking very sorry for itself.

Kate dropped her coffee cup with a clatter and knelt down to fling her arms around the dirty bag. 'You made it with only hours to spare! Oh, I am so glad to see you, old pal.'

She gave a contented sigh before sliding it closer and grabbing the handle. 'The bliss of having working clothes for the field trips! I don't think these girls would last long out there. Do you?'

Molly and Kate both looked down at Kate's shoes as she sat down and stretched out her legs. Her very high platform court shoes might have come from a famous French show-maker, but they both burst out laughing at the horror of what Kate would probably be wading through during her project trials.

'Good point,' Molly replied with a grin. 'But they certainly worked their magic. These last few days have been terrific—thanks, Kate.'

And then Molly stepped forward and gave Kate a warm hug. 'You were fantastic, and I know that Andy will be thrilled at the feedback. I confess Prince Simon did help with the media coverage of the event, but you will be pleased to know that four new corporate sponsors are interested in his pilot study. So, job done.'

'Thank *you*, Molly,' Kate replied, and blew out a sigh of relief. 'It has certainly been an eventful few days.'

Then Molly looked from side to side, to check that nobody was close enough to hear what they were saying, rubbed her hands together, and sat down opposite Kate at the breakfast table, propping her elbows next to the juice and toast.

'Now,' she whispered, and leant across the table, 'onto far more important things. How are you and Simon getting on?'

Kate opened her mouth, then closed it again. 'Oh, Simon. He did give an excellent presentation, and the solar energy…'

Molly waved her fingers across the table and hissed, 'I don't mean about work—although he was totally brilliant— I meant *you* and Simon.' And Molly raised her eyebrows several times.

Kate took one look at Molly's face, groaned, and dropped her head into her hands. 'Oh, no. Was it that obvious?'

'Totally. I know Simon, and the fact that you couldn't keep your eyes off each other sort of gave the game away.'

'We couldn't?' Kate whimpered.

Molly shuffled in her chair like a schoolgirl anxious for gossip. 'So tell me everything. When are you coming back? Or is it Simon's turn to visit you? I am dying to know. You do make a very handsome couple.'

Kate swallowed down a gulp of coffee and looked over her cup at Molly. 'Sorry. Not going to happen. We both have too many other people to think about.'

Her voice broke as she said the words, and she sniffed away the burning in her throat as she reached out for more toast. Only Molly beat her to it, and laid her hand on top of Kate's.

'The last thing I need are two lovestruck people on my watch. Let's order more coffee. I want to know the whole story. Right from the start.'

Two hours later Kate stopped outside Simon's hotel room door, raised her hand, then lowered it again.

She was leaving this lovely conference hotel and heading out to see the two new projects that Andy had started. Which meant that it was time to say goodbye to Simon. There was no need to visit his village—the work there was well under way and all her questions had been answered. If she did go it would only be a feeble excuse to spend more time with Simon.

Of course she was tempted to stay. Simon was right. Modern communication technology meant that she could see and talk to Gemma every day if she wanted, even from rural Ghana, but there were so many other things to consider. And her head and heart were not co-operating very well. Perhaps these next few days on the road would help to clear her thoughts. She certainly hoped so.

Come on, Kate told herself. *You need to do this. You are a professional. It is a common courtesy to say goodbye to your client. Even if it is Simon.*

Every part of her heart was screaming *stay*, while her head was running through all the perfectly sensible and logical reasons why that was such a crazy idea, and she should run as far and as fast away from Simon as her legs and a fast plane could carry her.

She had held it together through a nightmare dinner, where they had only been seated three chairs apart, and then days of official presentations and speeches and reports. The conference had been a constant buzz of frenetic activity and deliberate business, designed to make certain that there was no time when she could be left alone with Simon to express a simple *Nice to see you again. Goodbye. Have a nice life, Your Majesty.*

As far as the other delegates were concerned she and Simon were simply work colleagues supporting an important local initiative.

This was how she wanted it. *Wasn't it?*

Shame that Molly and goodness knew who else had seen through her little charade.

But all she had to do was survive the next few minutes and then she could walk away and get on with her life. From now on their relationship would be totally professional, and conducted through the safety of an internet connection. If he could do that, then so could she.

So, before she could change her mind, Kate pressed the doorbell on Simon's room and instantly heard footsteps on the other side of the door.

He was wearing his old cargo trousers and T-shirt and looked about seventeen, but it was the expression on his face that took her breath away.

He was looking at her with such love, and with a smile so honest and open and real, that just being so close to him, so near and yet so far, was overwhelming.

'Hey. Everything all right?' he asked, scanning her face

in concern. 'Sorry that things were so busy that we haven't had a chance to talk.'

He doesn't know. He doesn't know that I am leaving.

'Absolutely, but the conference has been a huge success.' She smiled politely, and then said what she had to say before he had a chance to answer or her nerve failed. 'Molly's waiting for me downstairs, but I wanted you to know that I heard back from Tom this morning.' She paused for a second, then smiled to reassure him. 'The last results came back as negative. It was a false alarm—he just has a bad head cold.'

She watched Simon's shoulders slump and relax, and then without hesitation he simply stepped forward and wrapped his arms around her in a delicious welcoming embrace of such love and warmth that it disarmed her. Every good intention she'd had of simply walking away from him fled out of the window.

'I'm so pleased for you… But did you say Molly was waiting? Does that mean you are heading out on your field trips?'

She nodded, incapable of speech.

His hand came up and pressed her head closer into his embrace. He drew her into the room and out of the empty corridor.

'Oh, Katie,' he whispered as his cheek moved against hers, filling her with the smell of him and hotel shower gel.

Kate rested her head on his shoulder. If she was ever going to say it, then this was the time to do it. 'The other night,' she whispered into his shirt, 'at the beach. When I told you that I had made my own way so far and didn't need anyone. That wasn't even close to being true.'

He turned his head just enough so that she could see the dust on his eyelashes and the huge dark pupils at the centre of the grey eyes which had entranced her from the first moment she had seen them all those years ago in the lecture theatre at university. The words she was about to say froze on her lips.

'I know. This is hard on both of us,' he said, his voice intense, almost a harsh whisper. 'Can I at least talk you into staying until my coronation?'

Kate slowly shook her head, and braved a closed-mouth smile before replying. 'Promotion will mean that I can work full-time from home. I will be there to make Gemma's breakfast and spend every evening and weekend with her. Tom has done an amazing job over these last few years when I have been travelling, and he has never once complained, but he is due to retire next year and is ready for a rest. It's my turn, and I want to be there—no matter what his test results say.'

'I understand. You have to be there for Gemma and your dad. But the last few days have shown me that we have something amazing here, Katie—and don't even try to deny it. We could be happy together, and that usually does not come around twice.'

His fingers were on her forehead now, stroking her hair back from her face, and the pleasure was so heavenly that she could have died with the wonder of it. She longed for him to keep going. But she couldn't—not when she was so close to the knife-edge between leaving and staying. This time she had to be the strong one.

'You're right. I am still as crazy about you as I ever was. But things are so different now, Simon. You have your responsibilities to your people. I have my sister to think about, and we come as a two-for-the-price-of-one package deal. If I moved here so would Gemma, and we both know that would never work. It has taken years for us to find a perfect school for the deaf, and Gemma loves it there. Moving her away from her friends and studies at this stage would be way too traumatic. She needs that special help and I promised her that it was all going to be okay.'

He started to protest. 'No.' She pressed a fingertip to his lips. 'Please don't make it even worse. It is better for me to go with the knowledge that we still care about each other. That's something we can take with us wherever we go.'

His hands cupped her face as he leant in and kissed her with such gentleness and tenderness that she almost lost her nerve. It was if he was pouring every special memory of their life together into one kiss, and she sank into it with all of her heart.

It was the most wonderful kiss she had ever received, and she knew that she would never forget it.

And then her cell phone rang, and she pulled back and smiled, fighting off the tears as his fingers slid away from her skin, probably for the last time.

'That's probably Molly with my transport. She's arranged for me to spend two days doing field work out of town.' She paused and tried to form more words, but her mouth and throat were not co-operating. Instead she smiled and brushed her lips against his cheek, and fell into his arms, hugging him, embracing him, eyes pressed tight shut, desperate to capture how his touch felt so that she could remember how it felt to be loved in the cold winter days to come.

Seconds seem to last for as long as the years they had been apart, but finally Kate pushed herself away from his body and stood back on wobbly legs.

'You are going to make a wonderful King. I love you. And don't you dare forget that.'

She had done it. She had told him she loved him. And the words had been just as heavy and wooden and as awkward in her mouth as she had imagined they would be. Her pain and regret felt as exposed as if she had ripped open her chest and cut her heart out, then presented it to Simon on a platter crafted from her stubborn pride and sacrifice.

Before she could change her mind, Kate flung her bag over her shoulder, snatched the hotel room door open and ran away from the man she loved so very much. And it broke her heart all over again.

Simon stood on the balcony of his hotel suite until the Jeep carrying Kate away from him was nothing more than a hint of red dust in the air lifted by the old tyres.

Watching her load her bag into the boot and slump dejected into the passenger seat had been one of the hardest things he had done in a long time.

Molly and some of the conference delegates had come out of the hotel to see her off, and she'd waved farewell to them through the open window, smiling at their laughter, but he'd only had to catch a glimpse of her face to see that her heart was breaking as much as his.

Seeing Kate again had reminded him what it felt like to be with someone who knew you and loved you for yourself, despite your faults. And he had plenty of those. Oh, Katie. The only girlfriend he had ever truly loved.

How could he have been so selfish and blind to her needs, to the burdens that she had been carrying back then?

He had been so very, very selfish and self-centred. It was a wonder that she had stuck with him at all. And now she was gone.

He had to do something—anything—so he paced back and

forth across the room before picking up the dossier he had worked on with Kate. On the front cover was a photograph Paul had taken of the new schoolroom they had built in his village. In the picture the children were crowded around Simon, chatting and eager for his attention. Their energy and enthusiasm seeped out from the image and helped him shed a little of his pain with the memory of the touch of each small hand in his. This was his life, captured in a small photo on the page of an official report.

He paused and pushed his hands deep into his trouser pockets, finding a few teeth-rotting sweets which would be snatched up with great joy by the children when he got back to the village later that day with his mother. Those children were future entrepreneurs and leaders in this wonderful country of people filled with big hearts and spirit—but it was going to take a lot of work and energy to help them get there.

His energy. His time. His work.

Simon's steps faltered. Was Kate right? Did it have to be all his own work? Was there any way he could achieve the same things with the help of other volunteers? Could he work smarter? He had trained gap-year students, college drop-outs and environmental scientists for years. Many of them came back to work on individual projects, but up until now it had been one sponsor and one project at a time.

In a few days he would be crowned King—perhaps it was time to show the village that they had been right to put their faith in him.

'Simon? Are you okay?'

Molly Evans appeared in the open doorway to his room. She had taken off her smart jacket and was dressed in a simple cool top and trousers. She looked about twenty years younger than he felt at that moment.

'I'm...' Then he stopped. 'No. I'm not okay. I'm losing Katie all over again—only this time she is the one doing the walking away.'

'Of course she is,' Molly replied in a totally matter-of-fact voice as she strolled onto the balcony. 'You can tell me not to interfere, but from what I've seen Kate loves you. She knows that she can't make a life with you without impacting your work as the new King or her family back in England. She's scared, Simon. Scared of losing you but also scared of what staying would mean.'

Then Molly smiled and added in a low voice, 'Every King needs his Queen. It's time to put all that expensive education to good use and come up with a plan. And it had better be a good one.'

Simon smiled back with a self-dismissive snort, then paused and nodded sharply towards Molly. 'You're right. It is time to get creative. And I have an idea. It's going to take a lot of work, and I am going to need your help to see it through.' And then he hit Molly with one of his killer smiles. 'This conference is not over yet.'

CHAPTER NINE

COMPARED to the green and lush world where she had spent the last two days, visiting dedicated and under-resourced project volunteers, the hard surfaces of the airport seemed a cold and unwelcome place.

Passengers of all shapes and sizes were shoving and pushing their way forward, trying to find the correct check-in desk for their flight or meeting up with friends and family.

She had never felt so startlingly bereft and alone.

The lights were too bright, and the clattering sounds of people and equipment and aircraft seemed deafening inside her head, creating a whirlwind of crashing sound.

She perched on the very end of a hard metal mesh bench, already crowded with several families and their assorted luggage, and hugged her precious suitcase even closer while she waited for her check-in desk to open. She was late, and the gate was later. But she had left it right until the very last minute before leaving for the airport. Hoping against hope that Simon would call her on her cell phone.

But he had not called. Why should he? She had made it

clear that she did not see any future with him in Africa, and this was where his heart was now—not the rolling chalk hills of cold and green Hampshire, England.

Simon was gone. She had pushed him away with logic and common sense and practicalities. All because she had been too cowardly to fight against convention and persuade Simon and the wonderful, generous people she had met over the past few days that she and her family could have a new home here.

That had been a few short days ago—but not any more.

Ghana had worked its magic on her.

As she'd tossed and turned in the stifling hot village accommodation she had been offered so generously by the project team, her mind had constantly come back time and again to Simon's challenge.

Perhaps Simon was right and this *was* a place where she could create a new life?

The more she thought about it, the more options seemed to spring up. Molly had emailed her details of the latest communication software the company were rolling out to the field operations and it was certainly impressive. The more she considered what her life would be like in the next five years, the more she wondered if living and working with Simon in Ghana could become a reality. Could she work part-time in Ghana and England? Andy had managed it for years. But could *her* family cope with that?

A single telephone call had been all that was needed. It had lasted hours, and probably cost the company more than she wanted to think about, but at the end of it both Tom and Gemma had agreed that her happiness was all they wanted. Gemma would love her to be home now and again, but she had always adored Simon, and any chance of a trip to Africa was a brilliant bonus—especially now that he was going to be a king.

She had never loved her family more.

To say that Andy had been thrilled that she wanted to apply for his job would be the understatement of the year! In fact she'd had to rein him back and talk job-share and part-time. But that was next week's problem.

Anything to stop her heart melting at the memory of Simon's tender kisses.

Simon had always been her prince, and now he was going to be a real king, with his own people. The hard reality was that she was going to have to work hard to prove that she was up to the job of being his queen.

She had always thought of herself as Cinderella, making the fire for her stepsisters—or in her case her sister and stepdad. That was where she belonged, wasn't it? Not upstairs, sharing her life with a king.

Kate closed her eyes and tried to block out the noise. Perhaps she should risk the heat and head outside for an hour, to help relieve her headache? The check-in desk might be open by then. At least she would escape that strange drumming that was going on inside her head. Drumming and chanting and… Drumming?

Kate's eyes flew open just as the crowds of passengers seemed to part like the Red Sea before Moses, leaving a wide channel for a very strange procession which seemed to be focused on…*her*. Two drummers in bright striped skirts and bandanas jigged and jogged their way through the airport lounge towards her lowly metal bench, followed by a line of men and women in stunning togas, headdresses, and heavy golden necklaces and royal regalia.

Then she felt her eyes widen as two men in full ceremonial

Ghanaian dress walked in a stately fashion towards her. One of them even dared to give her a wink, and gestured with his head over his shoulder as they got closer.

Startled, Kate blinked several times before she recognised that the handsome young Ghanaian was Paul, looking every inch the Prince in his splendid costume.

Hardly daring to breathe, Kate lifted her head and looked over Paul's shoulder—into the pale grey eyes of Simon Reynolds.

And her heart sang.

He was wearing his tribal toga—a brightly coloured strip of woven cloth wrapped around his tall, athletic body, with the end thrown over one shoulder. A golden sash crossed his bare bronzed shoulder, and his lower arm was wrapped in a stunning amulet. To complete the picture, one of the boys she had seen on the photo of the village school was struggling to control the weight of a great fabric parasol and hold it over Simon's head.

On either side of Simon were royal attendants. The tall proud men each carried a golden ceremonial staff, topped with a large carved golden standard, and as she watched in stunned silence Simon turned slightly and whispered to one, then the other, before stepping forward so that he was right in front of her.

Kate looked into his smiling eyes and tried to express how totally confused and elated and stunned she was, but failed. It was all too much. He came to her rescue.

'I might be only a prince, not yet a king, but I come from a long line of proud people,' he said, his voice resonating around the airport, which seemed to have come to a universal halt while everyone found out what was going on and why there was a royal procession there.

He glanced to one side, and out of the corner of her eye Kate saw Molly giving him a supportive thumbs-up. 'A wise woman once said that every King needs his Queen. So I come to you today, Miss Kate O'Neill, and offer you my hand.' His eyes smiled, and she could see the edges of his mouth quiver with emotion. 'Will you do me the honour of being my future Queen? My partner? My wife? Will you share my life with me, Kate? Say yes. You have always been a princess in my eyes. Let me make you a queen I can share with the world.'

Somewhere in the airport an announcement was going out about the check-in desk for a flight to London, but Kate wasn't interested in that any longer.

All she could think about was this man in a toga, who was asking her to marry him before a crowd of strangers. All that mattered was Simon, his grey eyes fixed on her with such pleading and such love that the only thing she could do was smile and nod in reply, and keep on nodding until the doubt on his face was transformed into startling happiness and joy.

Then the drummers started banging away for all they were worth. Simon's friends from the village began dancing from side to side, their ceremonial staffs transformed into marching band batons, and the great parasol slid slowly to one side as its holder joined in the jig.

'You have always been my Prince, Simon Reynolds. I never thought you could one day be my King. We will find a way to make it work, because I don't want to spend one more miserable day away from you. That's why I applied for Andy's job yesterday.'

'You did?' he replied, his forehead so close to her. 'I've spent the last twenty-four hours convincing your company to build on what we have achieved so far and use us as a pilot study for similar initiatives all over the kingdom. They'll be sending a whole team of new graduates to make it happen. But I'll need you with me every step of the way to make it work. Say yes, Katie. My beautiful princess. My Katie. Say yes, so that I can take you home to begin our new life together.'

CHAPTER TEN

IT WAS a perfect morning in June, and the cathedral bells were ringing out across the old narrow lanes and university buildings of the ancient city which Kate now called her wet season home.

They were ringing for her, Kate O'Neill, and the man she was going to marry. When Simon had been crowned King of the village all she'd had to do was watch in wonder as the local tribal Kings and their families gathered in the huge Durbar Square. Simon and the elders had paraded around, greeting the hundreds and then the thousands of local inhabitants who had come to meet their new King.

Under the huge parasol, and again accompanied by the elders carrying tall staffs with golden standards, Simon had accepted the honour of having the crown placed onto his head with such dignity and gratitude that Kate had swallowed down tears of pride and happiness as he'd sworn allegiance to the principal King and been given his new name.

It had been a magical day. The crowning ceremony had been followed by feasts and wonderful food, then dancing late into the night—and music: music all day. Music so joyous and exuberant and full of life that just the memory of that day made her grin with pleasure.

It was memories like that which had sustained her over the winter months and the weeks they had been apart as Andy and Molly had worked to create the new project programmes.

Sometimes it had felt as though she had dreamt the whole thing.

Simon—her Simon—was a king. A *king*!

A man other people loved and respected and went to for advice and decisions and help. She was so proud of him, but the more she thought about her new role, the more she sometimes felt intimidated by the enormity of her responsibilities.

It had truly hit home when she'd returned to the village with Tom and Gemma in the Easter holiday. It had come as quite a surprise when the village matchmaker had called on her father out of the blue with his attendants, to start negotiations for her marriage to their King. Traditional gifts had been offered, which she'd had to formally accept and examine with great detail before they could finally become officially engaged in the eyes of the community.

It was only then that it had seemed real. She was engaged. To a king.

Kate smiled to herself as she looked out onto the sunlit streets, then suddenly Gemma sneezed, and Kate looked up at her across the width of the limousine and smiled as Gemma rubbed her nose and grinned back at her.

Trust Gemma to bring her back down to earth.

Gemma had loved everything about Africa. The light, the colour and the atmosphere. And the villagers had taken her into their homes and their lives. The pretty blue-eyed girl with the lovely smile had already broken the hearts of several local boys, but there was only one person Gemma had wanted to be with and spend her day with—and that was Simon. She'd followed him to school, lip-reading his answers to her non-stop questions, helping out on the computers, sitting next to him at mealtimes and holding tight onto his hand when they'd been in the crowds of well-wishers and curious people.

Kate reached out and squeezed Gemma's hand for just a few seconds, and Gemma crinkled up her nose in reply and used sign language to say, 'You look so beautiful.' She waved her hands above her ears. 'Especially the head thing.'

Kate casually patted the diadem the hairdresser had pinned onto the chignon below her veil. The tiara had been a surprise gift from her future mother-in-law, and it was a precious vintage piece which had been passed down through the family. Simon had called it a peace offering, and perhaps it was, but it was also the closest thing to a crown that Kate had ever worn, and it felt and looked amazing.

'Oh, this old thing,' she replied to Gemma, and they grinned in secret code.

'A crown for a princess.' Tom laughed on the seat next to her, and pushed against her shoulder playfully, in the jacket of his new morning suit. 'My two girls look lovely. I am proud of you both.' And with that Tom O'Neill sniffed several times and took a moment to look out of the window, trying to look casual, as though he did this every day of the week.

Kate's heart melted. 'Now, do *not* get me going,' she croaked. 'This make-up has taken hours to put on.' And then they all laughed, sharing a precious last moment in private as the car slowed and turned into the long drive that led down to the cathedral steps.

Molly had already texted her to say that the cathedral was full to bursting with dignitaries, friends, extended family, colleagues—and sixteen very special guests from a small village in Ghana, who had arrived with Simon a few days earlier for a Royal tour of the town and the local countryside and a small inspection of Kate and her home.

Television cameras were already placed to broadcast the wedding to the world.

In fact, the whole week had been a blur of things to be done and organised, with radio and TV interviews, and time with the local dignitaries and the royal party from Ghana.

Chaos had reigned in the O'Neill household. The wedding dress had come first, and then coping with the stress on Gemma and Tom, and meeting Simon's mother again. The stress had never seemed to end. She was so grateful that Simon had arrived to help.

And of course there was extra stress in that this was no ordinary wedding. This was a royal wedding! Complete with complicated rules of protocol and statesmanship and visiting diplomats and so many people that there had been times when Kate had had to remind herself that she was doing this for Simon.

It scarcely seemed possible that their great day had finally arrived.

And now the car was crawling to a stop. The sound of bells rang out louder and louder across the square, and she saw the crowds of well-wishers and the press gathered outside the cathedral entrance. Her will faltered just a little.

She did not want to let Simon down at the last minute by doing something wrong, or saying something stupid, or falling flat on her face on the steps in front of the TV cameras. Not with the world's media looking on.

'He is still Simon,' her dad said softly, and clasped hold of her hand as she gulped down her racing heart, fired by exhilaration and excitement. Kate looked into the face of the man who had given her and her sister a loving home, and wondered how he had known. 'He loves you,' Tom said. 'Always has and always will, no matter what you do or say, and that is all that matters, isn't it? Okay?'

Kate threw her arms around her dad, hugging him even tighter. 'Thanks. That's what I needed to know.'

Then the chauffeur was holding the door open. Gemma had already skipped out of the car, and was waiting patiently with Kate's bouquet of yellow roses, fragrant freesias and white frangipani, which Simon had sent over to the house the day before, after sending the local florist into raptures.

'Are you ready to tell Simon how much you care about him?' Tom asked and smiled, and Kate felt her shoulders relax a little as he hooked her arm over his. 'I think you have both waited long enough for this moment. Don't you?'

She managed a brief nod before turning to grin at Gemma, who was far too excited and impatient to wait any longer. And then Kate looked into her dad's face for a second, before straightening her back and lifting her chin.

In an instant Kate had stepped out of the car and was standing in the warm sunshine, looking up at the impressive grand old cathedral. She was surrounded by light and noise and the clamour of people cheering and bells ringing and the steady beat of African drums and hornpipes.

This ancient place must have seen some remarkable celebrations and ceremonies over the centuries—but surely none more unique than this very special wedding.

Two of the musicians from Simon's village were standing on either side of the huge carved stone entrance to the cathedral, each holding a cow horn and blowing into the end of the horn with swollen cheeks to create the most remarkable fanfare of music this cathedral had ever heard. Their necklaces and bright striped bandanas were somehow perfect in the bright June sunshine.

Suddenly a band of Ghanaian drummers and dancers emerged from inside the cathedral, and as Kate and Tom approached they started dancing and singing with such joy that Kate's heart sang.

Then the ancient doors of the cathedral swung open, and with one final squeeze of her dad's hand Kate walked slowly into the majestic church. Far above her the organ played 'The Wedding March', and somehow the combination of drums and horn-playing and organ music came together to create a magical combination of traditional English and African wedding music.

The dancers from Simon's village were first in line, followed by the drummers, all dressed in brightly striped woven fabric, and the whole group danced and moved and shuffled into the long aisle of the church which stretched between the entrance and the altar.

The music soared higher and higher into the carved stone roof of the cathedral, blending with the organ sounds and echoing back into the church.

Then the pace of the music changed, and the horn players and drummers started to sound faster and louder, and on each side of the aisle people started swaying to the music with a joyous rhythm.

Gemma walked proudly in front of Kate, carrying a smaller version of her bouquet, her body swaying to the wonderful beat of the drums.

The congregation rose as one, shuffling chairs and

benches, all attention focused on Gemma. It had taken a lot of persuasion to convince her that a white net floor-length skirt with a Ghanaian fabric belt was the perfect outfit for a teenage bridesmaid. But Kate needed only one bridesmaid, and this was Gemma's day almost as much as it was hers.

The emotion was almost too much for Kate to stand as the wave of music swelled around her.

Kate was grateful for her father's arm as she stepped slowly forward, and for the first time in her life she felt beautiful, loved, adored and admired.

She looked out through her flowing silk net veil and could see two tall, proud figures standing next to the altar in front of her.

The dancers and musicians parted to each side and there he was, the remarkable man who wanted her to be his bride, achingly resplendent in his royal robes. His toga was of the finest cloth, woven just for this occasion. The golden sash crossed his chest under the clothing, matching the rich gold amulets on his arms. The polished glittering metal reflected back coloured light from the huge stained-glass windows which brought a whole spectrum of colour and light into the stone walls.

His crown was black, with gold emblems, and standing next to him was the principal King of the village and his attendants, standing tall and proud with their golden standards, heavy necklaces and medallions. But it was Simon—her Simon—who shone brighter than anyone else.

His happy smile beamed out as Tom took the final steps towards the altar and placed her hand in Simon's, and who looked into her face with such love and happiness that it made her head spin with joy.

He claimed her as his own as the warm sun outside the

cool stone building shone through the stained glass, as the organ music blended with the drums and hornpipes. He lifted her veil and sealed their marriage with a kiss so tender and loving that she knew more than at any other time in her life that she had made the right decision.

He was the King and she was his bride and they would make a new home together in Africa. This was the life she had longed for. This was the life she had promised herself over all the years of struggle and fear and doubt and regret. It had all been worth it. She was ready to start her new life with the man she loved. Her husband and her King. It was time to begin the most exciting adventure of her life and she could hardly wait.

EPILOGUE

A SPECIAL report from the *Hampshire Times Magazine*:

A small African village welcomes its very special new Queen

Queen Kate O'Neill Reynolds might come from a small Hampshire village in England, but the computer scientist and her family now have a new home in Ghana.

In January this year her then fiancé Simon Reynolds was crowned King of a tribal kingdom after spending years building on the work started by his late father to establish a technology centre in the Volta region of Ghana.

When Kate and Simon married, in an extraordinary cathedral wedding in Hampshire in June, their very special guests included the village's paramount King and his entourage. They had been so impressed with Kate's dedication and commitment to their area that the King decided to bestow this unique honour on Mrs Reynolds.

Kate Reynolds then travelled to Ghana and was made

Queen, before Kings, chiefs and elders from across Ghana, together with her father Tom, younger sister Gemma, and hundreds of citizens, colleagues and well-wishers.

In a tradition known as the Enstoolment Ceremony Queen Kate received blessings before being presented with her official tribal clothing—golden slippers, a very special Kente woven toga and a golden crown, before feasting and dancing late into the night in one of the largest celebrations to be held in the area for many years.

It is understood that Queen Kate has already begun her royal duties by working on a new school for handicapped children in the district.

* * * * *

The Prince's
Forbidden Love

RAYE MORGAN

Raye Morgan has been a nursery school teacher, a travel agent, a clerk and a business editor, but her best job ever has been writing romances—and fostering romance in her own family at the same time. Current score: two boys married, two more to go. Raye has published over seventy romances, and claims to have many more waiting in the wings. She lives in Southern California with her husband and whichever son happens to be staying at home at the moment.

Raye Morgan's most recent novel is
Crown Prince, Pregnant Bride,
which was available in February.

Dear Reader,

Weddings are wonderful—white lace and promises. Summer and spring weddings are the best with bridesmaids in pastel colors and pictures taken on wide, sweeping lawns. What might be even better? Royal summer weddings, of course. The gowns are even more elaborate, dripping with crystals and seed pearls and antique Victorian handmade lace. The men all look so dashing, like a casting call for Cary Grants. The tiny flower girls are so adorable with their baskets full of petals. But best of all—there are princes and princesses everywhere. Magic!

Why do we love royalty? I think we catch royal fever from fairy tales we hear as children. Those princesses rarely get caught mopping floors or doing dishes— unless named Cinderella. They spend their time getting fittings for ball gowns and dreaming that someday their prince will come. And when he shows up, the adventures and romantic intrigues begin! The entire production captures the imagination and sends it into the clouds.

And then we grow up and read the tabloids and realise those royal people aren't so different from the rest of us after all. In fact, they often seem so much worse! Still, they're royal. That sets them apart, and the dream that starts in fairy tales lives on.

I hope my story captures the dream for you.

All the best!

Raye Morgan

This story is dedicated to Kirsten,
our own princess

CHAPTER ONE

CROWN PRINCE ANDRE RASTAVA of the Royal House of Diamante, rulers of Gemania, was bored, and when he got bored he tended to get restless. The noise of the crowd in the casino was giving him a headache, and he found himself shrugging away the caresses of the exotic lady who had draped herself up against his body like a sleazy silk scarf.

What was her name again? It didn't really matter. Lately the women had become as interchangeable as all the other decorative items in his life. He couldn't tell one from another.

"Your Highness?" the croupier nudged, waiting for his call.

He glanced back at the roulette wheel and shrugged, pulling his tie loose and shoving back the sleeves of his Italian suit.

"Let it ride," he said, his voice hoarse. It hardly mattered if he won or lost. He wasn't really here for the gambling. Though few around him realized it, he had a far more dangerous game to play. That usually kept his attention razor-sharp.

But for some reason not tonight. Maybe it was the early spring heat wave coming in on the winds through the high mountain pass and numbing his senses. Or maybe it was the throbbing pain from the shrapnel that still lodged in his leg from the near miss he'd had in the explosion of his car the previous year. Or maybe he was just getting tired of this lifestyle.

He looked at the snifter of cognac that no one ever seemed to notice he seldom touched. It was all part of the show—just like the two young ladies who were his guests here this evening, just like the gaming, just like the setting. Just like the onlookers who didn't know they were merely part of the audience to this play.

He looked out at them, at all the interested faces. Many of the men gazed at him with awe and a bit of envy. The women tended to smile as though hoping to catch his attention, even if for a fleeting moment. They seemed like nice enough people. Why were they watching him? For just a second he felt almost apologetic.

It's all an act, people, he wanted to say. *Don't you get it?*

But something happened that stopped that thought cold. As his gaze skittered through the crowd it met a pair of dark brown eyes that took his breath away. He knew those eyes. He knew that pretty, comical face with its sprinkling of freckles over the pert nose and its impatient pout.

But…it couldn't be.

Shaking his head, as though to clear it of a fantasy, he closed his eyes and tried to erase her. But when he looked again she was still there, her blond curls like an enchanted cloud around her pretty face, her dark eyes blazing accusingly.

One sleek eyebrow rose as he stared back, curling his

lip. He was letting her know from the start that he regretted nothing. She could take her complaints elsewhere. At least that was what he'd hoped to convey. But something in those soft dark eyes held him a beat too long. And suddenly he found himself sinking into her gaze in a way that caught at his breathing. Strange. He pulled away and blinked quickly. This wasn't like him.

His number won again. A larger crowd was gathering, which didn't help under the best of circumstances. His wide mouth twisted as he frowned and glanced at the croupier. The young man shrugged imperceptibly and appeared a bit bewildered. Prince Andre motioned to have his winnings collected and prepared to leave, ignoring the murmurings of the crowd and the entreaties of his two young female companions.

But when he rose and turned toward where he'd seen her she was gone.

Had he been dreaming? He scanned the room. No, he was still living in the real world. There she was, walking quickly toward the outer terrace that overlooked the lake, her honey-blond hair bouncing against her lovely back, the skirt of her yellow sundress swishing about her shapely knees.

He hesitated for another second or two. Was he sure it was Julienne? How could it be? His ward should be living under veritable lock and key in the mountain convent where she'd been ensconced for years now. The entire staff was under strict orders not to let her roam free. Was this merely a lookalike? A twin sister he'd never known about?

No matter. In any case, he had to check it out. He turned to leave the roulette table.

"Your Highness," the exotic beauty was saying, reaching for him. "Please…."

"May we go with you?" her Scandinavian partner was asking plaintively. "We're supposed to accompany you to—"

"Find Rolfo," he said shortly, barely glancing at them. "He will see that you are taken care of. I have something urgent I must attend to."

And he was off.

Princess Julienne was hurrying toward an exit, if only she could find one. She'd come up in an elevator, but now she was disoriented and wasn't sure where it was. This had been a bad idea. She should have known better.

This entire scene was alien to her. She'd never been in a casino before. She hadn't really been in a city before—at least, not for years. She was a convent girl. What had made her think she could come here and beard the lion in his den? She'd thought she would have the element of surprise, but she hadn't realized he would have every other advantage.

He was so darn scary. Funny how she'd forgotten about that. Strength, power, and a casual disregard for danger seemed to exude from him like she'd never seen in anyone else. There was no way she could fight him. What had she been thinking? She wasn't going to talk him into anything. She'd do better making a run for it.

A little part of her had hoped. She hadn't remembered him as an ogre, exactly, and she'd thought she might be able to spark a little tiny flare of compassion in him. If she just had a chance to talk to him, face to face, surely….

But, no. She'd seen now how the land lay. There had been a time when she'd thought he cared about her, that he wanted her to be happy as well as useful to the crown. He was out of her life as far as she was concerned. He could just stay here with his fancy ladies and gamble and—

She stopped herself, biting her tongue as her gaze darted about, searching for a way back to the parking lot.

She'd left Popov, the driver from the convent, down below with the car. Dear, sweet Popov. He was the only person she could trust. Now…could she trust him to take her to the border and help her get across? Once she told him that was what she wanted, would he still be her only friend? Or would he become just as mean as everyone else?

She made one last attempt to find an elevator, but she'd lost track of where she'd come out on the floor, and besides, she was out on a wide terrace now. There were so many people, so much noise and color, with the blue waters of the lake shimmering behind it all. But ahead she saw an opening to wide, curving steps and she hurried forward, hoping to take them down.

The question remained—was he following her?

She glanced back over her shoulder as she started down the huge sweeping staircase to street level. There was some sort of commotion back on the casino floor. That only spurred her on, and she raced down the steps, leaping from one to the next, her heart in her throat. Her only hope was to make it back to the parking area and find her driver before anyone could catch her.

She was going to get away.

Prince Andre was finding it necessary to push himself through a growing knot of people who were gathering about the table, as though just watching him play would make them rich. He cleared them just as she disappeared down the stairs, and by the time he got to the railing he could see that she was more than halfway down to the street. If she reached it before he caught her she would melt into the tourist traffic and be gone for good. He hesitated for barely a second. His impulse was to call out to her, but something told him she wouldn't obey his commands and he might as well save himself the trouble.

He glanced at the wrought-iron decorative work that led from one window to another on the outer building walls. The thought of his bad leg only deterred him for half a second, and then he was up on the railing and reaching for the ironwork. A shift in balance, a lunge for a hand-hold, a leap of faith, and he landed, upright and poised, right in front of Julienne as she made it to the last step.

That brought her up short and caught her attention, and she stared at him, her eyes wide as saucers.

"Wow," she said, thoroughly impressed.

The small crowd lining the upper railing sighed in awe as well, and a couple of them even clapped.

He managed to cover up the gasp of pain his leg gave him upon landing and glared at her.

"So it *is* you."

She nodded, still thunderstruck by his Tarzan stunt. Funny, but that pretty much fit in with the way she'd always seen him—a bit larger than life. And it did appeal to her feminine senses.

But then, he always had. She gazed at him almost hungrily, taking in all of him. It had been so long since she'd last seen him. She realized he considered her nothing but a hindrance, a ward who had been thrust upon him, a responsibility he didn't need. But she'd always thought of him as her own personal hero. Only lately he hadn't been living up to that part.

"What the hell are you doing here?" he demanded, looking fierce.

She frowned at him, lifting her chin defiantly. She wasn't a child any longer and she wasn't going to let him treat her like one. "Don't swear at me. I'm your ward. You're supposed to be a role model for me."

"And you're supposed to be at the convent, preparing for your wedding."

She made a face and looked guilty, her gaze sliding to the side. "Yes, about that…"

He groaned. Trouble. Nothing but trouble. He could see it in her eyes.

A crowd was forming on the street level as well now. Before he knew it the paparazzi would get wind of this, and then there would be hell to pay. It was time to disappear from view.

"Come along," he told her gruffly, taking her hand and beginning to lead her toward a shadowy space behind the stairs. "We need to talk."

"Exactly what I was thinking," she said pluckily, though the sense of his forceful personality was wafting over her like a tidal wave and she knew she had to resist. "We've got a lot of catching up to do."

That wasn't quite what he had in mind, but he didn't comment. Instead, he led her in through an unmarked door and then onto a private elevator that opened to his coded entry. Soon they were hurtling toward the penthouse of the ten-story building, and Prince Andre's suite.

He looked her over, glancing sideways. She'd always been pretty, but she'd developed a luminous quality since he'd last seen her—a sort of inner glow that reminded him of angels.

Angels! He gritted his teeth. Just as he'd feared, she was more appealing than ever. He had to get her back to the convent as quickly as possible. Once she was married to his cousin, Prince Alphonso, he could wash his hands of her.

The elevator doors opened right into the Prince's suite, making Julienne blink with surprise. As she stepped out she looked about, eyes wide with wonder. Everything was shiny chrome, gleaming dark cherry wood and smoky tinted glass, with sleek leather couches and huge abstract art pieces on the walls. One side of the room was a floor-to-ceiling picture window, overlooking the lake and showing off the snow-capped mountaintops in the distance.

When she'd been eight years old she'd gone on a trip to Paris with her parents and she'd stayed in places almost as elegant as this. But it had been a long time since then, and she'd become used to the simple, rough-hewn décor of the convent. This place took her breath away.

"Nice," she said casually, trying hard not to come across as the wide-eyed-in-wonder country bumpkin she felt like.

"I like it," he replied shortly. "Why don't you sit down?" he added, nodding toward one of the softer-looking couches. "I'll get you a drink."

"A drink?" she said hopefully.

"Nothing fancy," he warned her. "I think I've got some lemonade in the refrigerator."

"Oh," she said, somewhat deflated.

She'd been hoping he would serve an adult beverage, as though it were her due—a sort of sign that he understood she was of age now. No such luck. He still thought she merited lemonade. She was used to wine of a sort with meals at the convent, but it was hardly more than colored water as far as she'd ever been able to ascertain. His lemonade would probably provide more punch, even if it didn't contain a bit of alcohol.

He watched the expressions change on her face and felt as though he could read every thought that was coursing through her mind. He had to turn away to hide his grin. Despite being fundamentally annoyed that she'd popped up into his world like this without warning, he couldn't help but be charmed by her—as he always was.

What the heck—he supposed he could give her some vodka in her lemonade to make her feel as though she were doing something slightly sophisticated.

"Here you go," he said, handing her a tall frosted glass. "I added a little something, but just barely enough for you to feel it. We can't have you going back to the convent tipsy."

She smiled at him, delighted, but at the same time vowing that the convent was the last place for her tonight.

He dropped smoothly onto the arm of the couch and looked down at her. He knew he should call Mother Superior to let her know Julienne was with him, but he didn't want to. Surely they would try to contact him when they realized she was gone. And then he would have to make plans as to when he would take her back. Much as he wanted her back where she belonged, he began to realize that she wouldn't have come if there wasn't a serious problem. The goal was to get her to the church on time, with as little hassle as possible.

Still, he would have to take it easy and figure out the best way to accomplish that. Barking orders wouldn't get her to do what he wanted. Cooperation was his goal. In order to achieve that he had to find out what had motivated her into coming to find him this way.

He grimaced. Being sensitive to the needs of others wasn't

usually uppermost in his mind. He was used to being catered to. Time for him to learn to stretch himself a little.

"Okay, Julienne," he began slowly, feeling his way. "Explain to me just exactly what you're doing here."

His voice was low, but with enough command to let her know he expected a complete and coherent answer.

She took a sip, nodded approvingly, and smiled up at him again, waving one hand with a flourish.

"This is merely a courtesy call," she told him cheekily. "I thought, as my guardian, you might like to know what I plan to do with my life."

He frowned, wary, but still in control of his reactions. "As your guardian, I already know what you're going to do with your life. In fact, I planned it myself. No need for you to bother."

"Ah, but that's where you've gone wrong." She took another sip, just for bravery, and set the drink down on the glass coffee table. "You see, I'm no longer a minor, no longer in a position to be your ward." She took a deep breath and faced him squarely, her gaze simple and direct. "In fact, I quit. I'm old enough to be on my own. And that is what I choose to do."

He looked pained. "Julienne, you know very well your life was mapped out seven years ago as part of the Treaty of Salvais."

She glanced down at the drink, began to reach for it, then drew her hand back and nodded quickly. "I know. I know. But, you see, that was done without my consent, and—"

"Your consent!" He shook his head, losing control of his patience a bit. "Julienne, your wedding is in less than a week. You can't back out now. The invitations are out. The gifts are streaming in. It's too late to stop the momentum. It's going to happen, whether you like it or not."

She didn't look convinced. In fact, she looked downright resentful.

"And are you planning to show up this time?" she asked, challenging him with her dark, honest gaze. "Or do you have your usual 'business to attend to' instead?"

His head went back in reaction. She'd pushed exactly the button that was guaranteed to open the floodgates to the guilt he felt about his guardianship. Over the last few years he'd avoided seeing her, missing every Christmas, every birthday. He knew his actions had hurt her. But it couldn't be helped. As her guardian, he had to protect her from predatory men. What he'd never expected when he took on that role was that he would be his own prime target.

"Julienne, all this is beside the point. You are required by treaty to marry Prince Alphonso next week, and marry him you will."

She shook her head, lower lip thrust out rebelliously. "I never signed any treaty," she insisted. "I never gave consent."

He jerked to his feet and began to pace the floor, holding back his quick surge of exasperation. Was he going to be forced to go over the whole history with her once again? No, she was just being stubborn. She knew all about the fighting between the three royal houses that had ripped their country apart for generations.

Right now an uneasy truce prevailed, but it had only come about after a long, bloody war. Too many people had died. He thought, with a quick slice of pain, of his own mother, killed by an assassin's bullet. The factions had fought each other to a standstill, and then it had taken a long, torturous struggle of negotiation to finally settle things, and that had only happened once Julienne's parents, the King and Queen of the House of Emeraude, had agreed that she would marry Prince Alphonso when she reached twenty-one years. Their marriage would tie the houses of Emeraude and Diamante together for evermore, and help balance the struggle of power between the three houses.

It had to happen. If she didn't follow through with the treaty's promise, the country was very likely to go up in flames again. No one wanted that, and as one of the architects of the plan he couldn't let it happen. In fact, it was up to him to make sure she followed through.

"Your parents gave all the consent that was needed," he told her coolly. "The deal was sealed. There is no going back on our word."

"I know all that," she was saying, looking at him earnestly. "But I've thought it over and I think I can fight it in court."

"In court?" He stopped pacing and stared at her, not knowing whether to laugh or cry. Didn't she realize that as far as this went he was pretty much all the "court" she was going to have at her disposal? How could he explain to her? She really didn't have a choice.

"Yes," she said emphatically. "I'm sure forcing me to marry is against my civil rights."

"Really?" he said, still staring at her. "You think you have civil rights?"

She sat up straighter, looking shocked that he would even question that. "Of course. Everyone does. And making me marry someone just to hold a country together doesn't make a lot of sense. I bet there's not another girl in the world who is being expected to do that."

Poor Julienne. He regarded her with a mixture of exasperation and a certain sad bemusement. How had she managed to make it this far without learning that being royal meant you weren't like everyone else? That had its obvious advantages, but there was also a downside. She was stuck. She could twist and turn and try to think of every sort of angle, but there was no escape. She would feel a whole lot better about things once she accepted that and got on with her life. In a strange, convoluted way, her plight touched his heart. But there was nothing he could do to remedy it.

She looked so young, so innocent. The late-afternoon light shafting in through the huge picture window seemed to turn her skin a creamy gold.

"You're probably right," he told her, fighting off the impulse to reach out and cup her lovely flushed cheek in the palm of his hand. "You're the only one."

He saw the hope that flared in her eyes and he hated to douse it, but it had to be done. He knew it was asking a lot to rest all the culture and peace of one country on the shoulders of one tiny twenty-one-year-old girl. But what was right and what was fair just plain didn't matter. That was the way it was. Her situation was her situation, and if she didn't abide by the rules he'd set up a lot of people might die. It had happened before. It could happen again. They couldn't risk it.

"You're looking at this all wrong," he told her helpfully. "You should be proud of the sacrifice you are making for your country."

Her eyes clouded and she wrinkled her nose. "Sorry. Ask someone else, please."

Was she going to cry? He tensed. If she started to cry it would be impossible to keep his distance and he knew it. But she looked up and smiled at him tremulously. And that was almost as bad.

He had to turn away and begin pacing again. When she sat there looking so adorable, everything in him seemed to yearn toward her. And so he paced, gritting his teeth and searching for strength.

He thought of the first time he'd seen her, when she was only fourteen years old. He'd spent a hard few days negotiating with her parents, the King and Queen, in order to convince them that the only way peace would be achieved would be for them to lock their daughter into a marriage contract that would cement the ties and keep the jealousies in check. With Emeraude and Diamante joined as one, the renegade House of Rubiat wouldn't dare try another power-grab.

They'd invited him to share their dinner, and, though he usually didn't like to socialize with negotiating partners, he'd liked the two of them well enough, and respected them enough, to make an impulse decision to eat with them. They'd been talking pleasantly when Julienne had come into the room.

"And here she is," her father had said fondly. "The center of all our conversation these days." He'd smiled at his daughter. "Prince Andre, may I present Princess Julienne?"

He remembered rising and giving her a deep bow, while she curtsied in her charming way. He recalled smiling at her and thinking she was the cutest thing he'd seen in ages. For just a moment he'd wished he had a young sister about her age, someone he could take under his wing and mentor in the ways of royal life. And that was odd, because he'd never had a thought like that before in his life—nor had he since—and yet that was pretty much what very soon came to pass.

She'd charmed him right from the beginning. She was such a sweet, lively girl, but with a spark of humor and a quick understanding that seemed to belie her young age. He'd liked her immediately.

Only weeks later her parents had been killed when their light plane went down in the mountains. Andre became her guardian from the first, with the consent of all concerned. He'd been the architect of the treaty and it was up to him to make sure its elements were complied with.

He'd brought her to Diamante Castle and treated her like one of the family from the first. King Harold, his father, was busy with affairs of state, his life's work, which he'd thrown himself into with a vengeance once Nadine, his wife, queen and Andre's mother, had been killed by a sniper years before. They rarely conferred. Harold was the sort of man who seemed weighed down by his work. To the casual observer, he was an old grouch. But not to Andre. Andre knew the tragic sorrow he carried with him at all times and he loved him for it.

Still, his father never showed much interest in the young, lively and engagingly coltish girl who'd come to live with them, and it was up to Andre, despite the fact that they were less than ten years apart in age, to act the part of elder authority along with everything else. And the two of them had got on well together. He looked back on those days as some of the happiest of his life.

As she'd grown older, he'd known it couldn't last. And then came her eighteenth birthday and the dance—and the kiss.

That was when he knew he had to call upon some inner well of strength to get through the next few years until she married. And here they were, with six days left. Was he going to make it?

CHAPTER TWO

"ALL right, Julienne," Prince Andre said, sitting down on the couch again. "Come clean. How did you manage to escape from the convent?"

She bit her lip and gazed at him levelly. "You see, just the concept of my having to 'escape' is offensive. I'm a grown woman."

He hardly knew how to counter that, because she was right. But that didn't matter, so he ignored it.

"You must have had help."

She hesitated, then nodded. "There's a person who's always available to help me. He drove me down."

He felt a flash of anger, but he stifled it. He looked at her, his gaze veiled. "I see. Is he waiting for you outside?"

She hesitated. "I'm afraid he is. Should I…?"

Andre felt every muscle tense. "Does he have a mobile?"

She shook her head. "We don't have cell phones at the convent."

A twenty-one year old woman without a phone. How was that possible?

"Where is he?" he asked crisply. "I'll have someone tell him to go back. I'll handle your travels from here on out."

She hesitated, feeling a bit deflated. "But…"

He turned and pinned her with a penetrating look. Her reluctance to do as he asked made him suspicious. "Is he your boyfriend?"

"Oh!" She laughed at the concept. He was old enough to be her grandfather. "No, not at all. He's an old man."

Andre frowned. "Older than I am?"

"You?" She looked shocked at the concept. "You're not old."

He grinned. He couldn't help it. "Oh, Julienne, you have no idea." His gaze met hers and held for a beat too long, and then they both looked quickly away.

"And anyway," she said, reaching for her lemonade, "where in the world would I get a boyfriend?"

Yes, that had been the whole justification for sending her to be educated in the convent. Hopefully she was telling the truth, and things had worked out just as he'd planned. Lots of study, lots of peace and spirituality, and a complete lack of male companionship. Perfect. The only trouble was, she seemed to have picked up some bad ideas anyway.

Julienne looked around the room nervously, wondering how she was going to cope with this questioning. So far so good—but she was used to the convent, used to quiet. She prayed and read and recited poetry and bible verses. And she dreamed.

For the last few years she'd helped the sisters with the younger girls. She'd been old enough to go away to university, but when she wrote to her guardian about applying he didn't respond.

So she stayed at the convent and lived a simple, quiet life. Mother Superior had allowed her to enroll in some online college courses and helped her study—and in fact she was well on her way to earning a degree in European history. But lately her interest had flagged. History wasn't really where her heart lay. It lay in a very secret place where she'd been forbidden to go—many times. What she lived for was not allowed to someone of her stature. The fact was, the Princess of Emeraude loved…to cook.

Pastries, mostly. Fortunately the woman who was the convent cook—and Popov's wife—thought her ambitions were wonderful and indulged her whenever she could get away with it.

But that was then. Now she was in the real world, dealing with a real man, and she knew she had to be on her toes. And she definitely did not want him to know about the pastry business. That was her special secret.

"Okay," he said, still not clear on what her day had been like before she'd walked into the casino. "So you found someone to drive you down here to the city. But you didn't tell them at the convent that you were leaving?"

"Oh, no. They would never have let me go."

He nodded, feeling slightly reassured.

"In fact," she went on, feeling chatty now, "I put a 'do not disturb' sign on my door, saying that I was studying for an exam. Then I rigged up a dummy in my bed and tiptoed out."

He groaned and looked pained. "That is the oldest trick in the book."

She nodded. "It's old because it works. I've done it before."

"What?" He was back to visions of dangerous boyfriends and hot cars, despite what she'd said, and it was shocking how much he hated that scene as he imagined it. "Julienne..."

She shook her head at him. "Don't worry, it was just so that I could take walks in the hills without people hunting me down and telling me to be careful every step I took. The convent is a nice, quiet place, but everyone knows what you're doing at every minute of the day and it can get suffocating."

"Oh." It was embarrassing how relieved he felt. "I see."

"So when I decided I had to come find you, I used it again. It was easy."

He grimaced. "Why did you feel you had to come all this way? Why not write a letter or send an email? Or even pick up the phone and give me a call?"

She looked outraged by his suggestions. "Are you kidding? I wrote letter after letter detailing all the indignities I was forced to live under at the convent."

He was glad he'd missed those. "Itemizing your complaints, you mean?" he noted cynically.

"Of course. And I've got a few."

He grimaced. "Spare me."

"Why should I? You haven't exactly been a hands-on guardian of late. I thought I deserved a little more personal care. But you never responded." She shrugged. "If the mountain won't come to you, you've got to go to the mountain."

He raised a cynical eyebrow. "I'm a mountain now, am I?"

She favored him with an impish grin. "Kind of. You're big and scary, anyway."

He groaned, but she ignored that and went on.

"I begged you to come and see what conditions were like for yourself. Letter after letter. Didn't you read any of them?"

He shrugged. "In truth, I don't remember reading anything of the kind." He frowned, thinking that over. "Perhaps my secretary read them." He looked up and decided to go a step further. "Read them and thought them too childish to pass on to me."

"Oh!" Now she was angry. "That's just outrageous."

He bit back his grin and pretended to agree. "You're absolutely right. She should have let me know how things stood."

"Indeed," Julienne said indignantly, ready to confront the woman on the spot. "Where is she?" she added, looking around as though she thought she might be lurking in the shadows.

Andre forced back the smile that threatened. "I'll let her know you were asking after her."

"You do that," she said, looking at him suspiciously. "I think she should be reprimanded."

He shook his head. "Sorry, can't do that. She's not working for me any longer. In fact, she recently left on a round-the-world cruise." His mouth tilted at the corners as he prepared to give her the whole story. "She married an itinerant poker player she met in the casino. They plan to spend their lives aboard cruise ships, traveling from one port to the next."

She stared at him for a moment, then made a face. "That sounds crazy."

And he agreed. "Oh, it is."

She looked at him speculatively, blinking a time or two.

"But lovely at the same time. Traveling from place to place." She sighed. "I've never really travelled at all."

Ah, here was his opening, and he took it with vigor. Dropping down beside her on the couch, he leaned in.

"Once you marry Alphonso you can do as you please. Travel. Shop. Eat at fancy restaurants. No more convent. You'll have your own palace. The world will be your oyster."

She stared into his eyes for a long moment, then shook her head slowly. "No, it won't," she said perceptively. "He'll be in charge. I'll have to do what he says. It will be worse than the convent." She made a face and threw up her hands. "You see, that's just my point. The whole world gets to go off and do crazy things except for me. I don't get to do even normal things."

He sighed. It was becoming clear that this was going to take longer than he'd thought. He glanced at his watch.

"How about this?" he suggested. "We'll go down and get something to eat, talk for a while longer, and then I'll drive you back to the convent. Sound good?"

She stared at him. He just refused to get it, didn't he? She wasn't going back to the convent.

His telephone rang and he excused himself, disappearing into what she assumed must be the bedroom to answer it. She sat stiffly where she was and stared out the huge glass window. It was so disappointing. She'd been so sure—once she saw him again, once they'd had a chance to talk and she'd let him know how she felt—that he would see things her way and even understand why she couldn't do this.

She should have followed her first instincts and just made a run for the border. Now she wouldn't have as good a head start. But she would go. She had no choice, really. It was that or consign herself to a life of misery.

Why couldn't he see her point of view? She'd once thought they had a special rapport, a unique connection that held them together as friends forever. Now she wasn't so sure. He didn't want to hear her side. There was really no hope. So why was she hanging around, waiting to be driven back to the convent? She had to get out of here while she had the chance.

She glanced at the bedroom door. From the sound of it, he was still talking on the phone. Rising from the couch, she walked quickly toward the elevator she'd come up in. All she needed was a little time. She might be able to make the border yet.

Andre came out of the bedroom frowning, not pleased with the news he'd just received, but all that flew out the window as he looked around the room and realized Julienne was gone.

Well, that had been stupid. He should have known she would be a flight risk. He only hoped it wasn't too late to stop her.

The elevator had a kill switch and he used it now, then headed for the stairs. If she was still on her way down he would catch her at the bottom. If she'd already left the building he would be lucky to find her again. Ever.

Julienne had just reached the ground floor when she heard the gears grinding to a halt.

"Oh, no," she whispered in despair. She knew what that meant. He'd caught her again. She tried punching the door button but nothing moved, and she sighed, waiting for the inevitable.

It seemed forever until the doors slid noiselessly open and

Andre stood waiting, his arms crossed over his chest and a dark look on his face.

"Gotcha," was all he said.

She was chilled by the frosty look in his blue eyes, like caverns of ice, but she glared at him anyway. She expected him to join her on the elevator, but instead he reached in and took her hand and pulled her out onto the tiled pavement.

"You want to show me where your boyfriend is?" he said coldly. "I'm sure he's out here somewhere close."

"He's not my—!" She stopped herself and heaved a sigh as she rolled her eyes. She wasn't going to give him the satisfaction of answering. Raising her chin, she looked away.

"Come on," he encouraged, sweeping his arm out toward the street and the multi-level parking structure across the way. "Where is he?"

Folding her arms across her chest, she looked resolutely in the other direction. "I have no idea," she said evenly.

He waited a moment, studying her profile and hoping for more information. When she didn't say anything more, he shrugged.

"Okay," he said shortly. "If you won't talk, we might as well go eat. Come on." He tucked her hand into the crook of his arm and began to escort her out into the lower level of the casino. She tried to pull her hand away at first, but he wasn't letting it go and she decided it was just too embarrassing to start a tug-of-war. Besides, she had to admit she sort of liked the way it felt, letting him escort her this way.

He liked it, too. He only hoped no one recognized her or did a quick internet search to figure out who she was. If so, the media would know next. He glanced around at the hungry female stares following their progress through the crowd, and he winced. Sometimes it seemed as though every woman he met was measuring him for a groom's coat with her eyes. And why not? After all, he'd been considered the most eligible bachelor in the country for the last ten years. But he'd learned to guard himself from relationships of any kind.

The one close female friend he'd had was his cousin Giselle, but that had pretty much ended when she'd turned her back on royalty and thrown her lot in with the common man. That was something he could never do. He was born and bred to royalty, and when his father died he would be king. It was nothing less than his place in the world.

That was what Julienne had to learn. She had her place, too, and it would make her life much easier if she would accept it. Looking at her, he could see she was enjoying the attention. Hopefully, this would begin a reassessment on her part.

As they walked through the crowd and into the restaurant Julienne noticed the ripple of interest Andre evoked everywhere they went. Despite her anger with him, and the circumstances, she couldn't help but feel a frisson of excitement herself. He was so handsome, and it felt so good to have his arm and...

"Oh!" she said, suddenly realizing she was wearing a simple cotton sundress and every other woman in sight was dressed to the nines. She grabbed Andre's arm with her other hand and leaned close.

"I'm not dressed for dinner," she whispered, casting a worried glance at the *maître d'*.

He covered her hand with his own and looked down at her. A wave of tenderness came over him, and at the same time there was a strange feeling in his chest.

"Don't worry," he told her softly. "We're eating in a private room."

"Oh."

She seemed relieved, but still nervous, and yet he noted she had enough of the royal instinct to walk through the main dining room with her head held high and proud.

He opened the door to let her in to the private space, then closed it again and pulled her close for a moment.

"You could be naked," he said softly, touching her hair, "and there would still be no doubt that you are a princess." He smiled at her. "Bravo."

She was breathless. Though he released her quickly, and turned to pull out a chair for her, the intimacy of his touch and his words left a tingle in her blood. If only…

She wouldn't let herself think that thought through. He was her guardian, not her lover. She had to be satisfied with what she could get. Or try to, at any rate.

Andre ordered for them both—grilled salmon with a saffron curry puree, cous-cous, and a mint-green apple salad. Every bite was so delicious it was difficult to remember that they were enemies now.

But he managed to remind her.

"You see, Julienne," he told her between courses, "being royal gives you access to private rooms, exquisite meals, the best wines. Why would you want to throw that away?"

She took a sip of the wine. The only relationship it could possibly have to the liquid they poured in her glass at the convent was the rich golden color. But she wasn't going to admit that to him at this point. Instead, she turned and gave him a gimlet eye.

"I've lived twenty-one years with this little invisible paste crown on my head," she told him tartly. "It's like being in prison—and being innocent of whatever crime landed you there in the first place." She shrugged. "It's the age-old lament. I just gotta be free."

He shook his head and she knew he thought she was whining.

"You have probably been the most protected young lady on the face of the earth," he pointed out.

"I'd rather be free than protected," she told him in no uncertain terms.

He shook his head again, looking her over with a bemused smile. "You don't know what you're talking about."

Her royal chin rose again. "I think I have a bit of an inkling," she told him firmly. "I've stared matrimony in the face and I've decided it's not for me." Her glance his way was cool and flippant. "And I'll bet that's more than you've ever done. You haven't come close, have you?"

To her surprise, something flashed in his clear blue eyes—something that signaled pain and an emotion she wasn't sure she recognized. Her words had wounded him in some way.

"You shouldn't make bets on things you don't understand," he said calmly, reaching for his wine.

She blinked and didn't answer back. She'd brought up something that had upset him and she wished she hadn't.

She had assumed he was a playboy and that was what he had always been. Was there something else? Had someone broken his heart in the past? She swallowed hard and looked down at her plate, wishing she could learn to keep quiet when on unfamiliar ground. To think she'd hurt him was like a knife in her chest, but she couldn't think of a thing she could do to undo it.

The waiter brought dessert—a gorgeous creation of three

types of chocolate intertwined and topped off with a heavenly puff of whipped cream. Andre wasn't hungry any longer, and he set it aside after two small bites, but Julienne devoured the entire thing, commenting on flavors and techniques as though she were an expert in this sort of thing.

He sat back, entertained by her commentary, entertained by her obvious relish of the sweet, and generally enjoying watching her, unable to stop. He liked the look of her so much he was like an addict. He couldn't stay away. Everything about her was fresh and free and beautiful. He felt faded and old hat. She was new. He didn't want to sully what she was. She was too special.

Still, he couldn't sit here watching her forever. They both knew very well that she shouldn't have come down to find him in the first place, but now that she was here he supposed he was going to have to do something with her.

But what?

He'd already realized he was not going to be taking her back to the convent tonight. He needed space and time to work on her reluctance to marry Alphonso. She had to come to an understanding of what her responsibilities were and why she had no choice but to fulfill them. If only he could think of a good way to do it.

Lecturing was doing no good at all. Bullying wouldn't make any more headway. It would just put her back up and make her more defiant.

Bottom line: she had to go back and she had to marry Alphonso. His job would be to convince her of that without real blood being spilled.

But how?

A few different scenarios flitted through his mind and he rejected them in turn. He glanced across the table at where she was sitting, looking like a teenager, with her bargain basement clothes and her legs stuck out in front of her. As he studied her, he wondered what it was about her that appealed to him so strongly—and made her so dangerous. She was certainly pretty, but so were most of the women he knew.

She caught at his emotions rather in the way a passionate aria could transport him into feelings he didn't know he had. She did something mysterious and magical to his soul. And that was why he had to get away from her as soon as possible.

But first he would deal with her concerns and convince her that being a princess was better than the alternative. What could he do to make it appeal to her more?

One thought that came to mind was introducing her to city night-life and what it was like to cruise the clubs as royalty. In one night he could show her what it was like to be a star. After all, she had never been out in public, and had no idea what a princess was actually treated like in her own country. Once she had a bite of the apple...

Might that change her mind? He looked at her sweet face and mentally shook his head. No, that wouldn't really work. Something told him that swelling around the nightclubs with a bunch of substance-impaired groupies lurching after her wasn't going to do the trick, no matter how much her subjects would adore her.

And they *would* fall in love with her at first sight, of that he had no doubt. She was imminently lovable. Even a crusty older man like himself was not immune.

At any rate, he didn't want to be the one to open her world to *la dolce vita* with all its glamourous disguises and ugly underbelly. This merry-go-round he'd been on for the last ten years was a sad and poisonous way to live, and he was heartily sick of it himself.

How had he let this happen to his life? He'd once had high hopes of all the good things he would do for his people and his country—how he would bring in industry, improve education, raise the standard of living for all. Somehow he'd become bogged down in trying to keep the alliance together in order to avoid another war, and he spent his days playing this soul-deadening role in order to do his part.

Funny how it had taken the arrival of this fresh, free spirit to show him the truth in that. The times needed to change. But right now he had a mission to accomplish. He had to convince her to marry Alphonso. That was going to take some time. And if she was going to stay with him for a day or two she would obviously need some clothes.

"What size are you?" he asked her.

She looked startled. "Why?"

"I think I'll have my man, Rolfo, pick up some things for you in the hotel shop. He'll bring them up and you can try them on and decide which ones you want to keep."

Her face was transformed. "Clothes?" she whispered, as though she were receiving a wonderful present, something she could only dream of in the past. "New clothes?"

He couldn't help but laugh at her funny face. If he'd known this was all it took to bring her such joy he'd have been sending her packages from department stores for the last three years.

"We'll see how sophisticated Rolfo's taste is." He pulled out his phone. "I'll get him right on it."

CHAPTER THREE

PRINCE ANDRE escorted Princess Julienne back to his penthouse suite as soon as their meal had run its course. She went willingly enough, though she did have a qualm or two. Had he tempted her with the promise of new clothes just to make sure she didn't try again to make a run for it? Or was she getting a little too suspicious for her own good?

Since her parents had died when she was fourteen, she'd known almost nothing but life in the Diamante Castle—a stark, forbidding structure manned mostly by servants. She'd studied with a governess, and the daughters of local noble families had been brought in to be her friends, but the days when Andre was home were what she'd lived for. Andre was her hero and her best friend. When he showed up, her drab life had suddenly lit up.

But once she'd turned eighteen it had been mostly life in the convent. She was allowed to go back to the castle at Christmas for three days, and for two weeks in the summer she was sent off to stay at the lake house. On her birthday someone would come to visit her bringing presents. Until two years before that someone had been Prince Andre. But without explanation he had stopped coming.

Dear Prince Andre, she mused sarcastically, glancing at him sideways. Her guardian. The man who was in control of her life. And he wouldn't even come to visit her. They'd told her that he was too busy. They'd said he was an important man and couldn't be bothered. And he hadn't answered her letters.

So she'd finally come to see for herself.

He was busy, all right. Busy living like a playboy. As she thought of it now, she was more furious with him than ever—and that only confirmed her determination to fight him. House of Diamante, House of Emeraude, House of Rubiat—who cared? They could take this royal life, this relic of the past, and they could keep it for themselves. She would have no part of it.

"Did you enjoy the dinner?" he asked her, pulling off his tie and opening his shirt a few more buttons' worth.

She nodded, going back and forth between thinking he was the most handsome man on earth to resenting how he'd treated her over the years.

"It was wonderful," she admitted.

"I'm glad you liked it." His eyes were deep and sultry. "I want you to be happy."

But still he expected her to marry Prince Alphonso.

He left the room and she turned away and looked at the moonlight over the lake. She really didn't know Alphie well, but she'd met him a time or two, and this last summer he'd come to the lake to see her for four days—the longest, dreariest four days of her life.

If only he were more like Andre maybe she could stomach the thought of it. But he wasn't like Andre. Nobody was like Andre. She put her hands against the cool glass and sighed.

He came back into the room, poured himself a drink and got her a lemonade—this time without enhancement. She sat on the long couch and stared at it. He was treating her like a child again, she supposed, but there were so many things she was trying to fight him on, she decided to take a pass on this one.

She was defying him and she was going to go on defying him. What was he going to do about it? Actually, the answer to that terrified her. He was the scariest man she knew. And yet her soul was filled with a pure, crystal-clear, female anger—the anger of a woman who felt she deserved a little more attention than she had been getting. If he thought he was going to start shooting orders at her and having people confined to their quarters and things like that, he could think again. Those tactics weren't going to make her change her mind. This wasn't the old dark ages of the royal world any longer. He couldn't get away with the Anne Boleyn treatment these days. She had a few rights of her own, and he was going to have to listen to her point of view.

She looked down the couch at where he was sitting. He hadn't spoken for a long time and he was staring moodily out the darkened window. Dark curls had fallen over his forehead in a very sexy way. He was so handsome. Her anger began to melt away. She knew he was thinking over the situation and that he was trying to decide what to do with her, how to fix this dilemma. She had a sudden surge of sympathy for him.

"Do you remember how we used to play chess?" she asked him.

He looked up and met her gaze. Reluctantly, he gave her a half-smile. "Certainly."

"And how I used to let you win?" she added mischievously.

"Let me win?" A look of outrage flashed over his face, and then he laughed. It was the first genuine laugh she'd seen from him, and a bubble of happiness burst in her chest. This was the Prince Andre she remembered.

Rising, she moved down and sat very close to him.

"I understand that I'm making waves. I understand that this is a problem that you feel you have to solve. But you know what? You don't really have to solve it."

"No?" He searched her eyes as though looking for a hopeful sign.

"No. I'm sure one of my cousins from my uncle's second marriage would be glad to marry him. And that should fulfill…"

He rose, making a sound of disgust. "Julienne, stop it. Your name is on the treaty. You are the only bride Alphonso will accept. And a marriage between the highest-ranked in our two houses is the only thing the Rubiat will accept. If they don't see that happen, they'll feel justified in attacking again."

"I don't understand. Why do they care that much?"

"Tradition. You can't fight it. It's in their blood."

She shook her head. "But why do they care so much about Alphonso and me? What do we mean to their lives?"

"The two of you are nothing. It's the Houses you represent. The royal families. The myths. And their need for power."

She sat very still, thinking that over, wishing she could pull it apart and find a flaw so that she would attack it properly. But very soon she forgot all about that. She was sitting very close to him, her thigh touching his, and little by little that became the whole focus of her mind, her senses, her emotions. She wanted to turn and touch him with her hand. She wanted to press herself to him. She wanted to taste his mouth, breathe his breath, feel his heartbeat against her skin. Her own heart began to pound so loudly she was sure that he must hear it. Her breathing began to pulse with the beat, faster and faster, and she wanted…she wanted…

He rose, suddenly, and left the room, not saying a word. She turned beet-red where she sat, sure that she'd driven him away with her relentless need for him. It was embarrassing. But it was such a deep part of her she couldn't really regret it.

She knew she loved him. She always had. The fact that she could never have him was her own private tragedy. Tears welled in her eyes.

And then the elevator dinged and she whirled, watching the doors open. In came an enormous rack full of clothes. Her jaw dropped as she watched it arrive.

"Is this for me?" she asked, stunned.

The older man who was pushing the rack stopped and leaned around to smile at her. "I don't know if you remember me, Princess. I'm Rolfo, Prince Andre's assistant. I want you to call on me if you need anything."

"Oh, thank you," she said, though she couldn't take her eyes off the clothes. She went closer, touching one fabric, then another. "What am I to do with all these? I can't possibly wear them all."

"No." He laughed. "You're to go through them and pick out the ones that appeal to you. Try them on. And then make a few choices."

She looked at him, her eyes wide. This was the most delicious moment she'd had in ages.

"How many am I to take?" she asked breathlessly.

"As many as you like, Your Highness."

She shook her head. "But I don't know…"

Her voice trailed off.

"Take your time, Princess," Rolfo said in his kindly manner. "The answers will come to you."

As she turned to begin sorting through the treasure trove she was overwhelmed. It was really too much. For a moment she couldn't speak. She'd spent most of the last seven years wearing a crisp white blouse with a plaid skirt. She had no idea where to begin. Reaching out, she touched a white lace blouse, a red velvet skirt, a sky-blue fitted silk sheath, and she sighed.

Rolfo watched her for a moment with a smile, then he left so discreetly she forgot he'd ever been there.

Prince Andre reappeared, raising his eyebrows as he surveyed the scene.

"I see Rolfo has brought you quite a stack of clothes," he said. "Go ahead and have some fun choosing some things to wear for the next few days. I've got a couple more calls to make."

He realized that this was only fair. After all, he should have taken care that she'd gotten suitable clothes long ago. She was a princess. It was way past time to put away her schoolgirl clothes.

From the look on her face, he could see this was something she wasn't used to. But that didn't make sense. Why wasn't she amassing some sort of massive trousseau? She was supposed to be preparing for a wedding. Why wasn't someone making sure she was going to her groom properly attired?

With chagrin, he realized *he* was the one who should have been taking care of making sure that happened. Some guardian he was.

And yet he knew why he'd been neglecting his duties. The more he thought about her, the more he wanted to think about her—and that was something he had to avoid. He'd stayed away for a reason, and it appeared others had not jumped in to take up the slack as he would have hoped. For a few seconds he indulged in a flash of anger toward his aunt, the Duchess of Fersuit, who lived with them at the castle off and on. Why hadn't *she* taken over this task? Just how lonely had Julienne been these last few years? And all because he couldn't trust himself to be near her.

But those days were over. He was going to take over this project and get her married, come hell or high water. And once he got through with her she would understand the sort of life she could lead as a princess, as opposed to what it would be like for her if she chose to turn her back on her destiny.

He watched her look happily through the clothes and only half listened to her chatter as she reacted to each piece, holding one up in front of herself in the mirror, then laughing at the effect. There was no denying it. She was enchanting, and he was tempting fate just having her here.

But that was just how it had to be. He was strong enough to handle it. Not easy, but possible. He'd been through danger before. He grinned suddenly, laughing at himself and his preposterous comparison of this danger to those more immediate and physically damaging incidents, like being shot at by a sniper and having his car blow up in his face. He could handle one little twenty-one-year-old girl—couldn't he?

"Shot through the heart," he muttered to himself, shaking his head.

"I am so in love with all these clothes," she said, holding up one outfit, and then another. Suddenly her smile dimmed as she had a thought. "Do you always do this?" she asked curiously.

He looked up, surprised and not sure what she meant. "Do what?" he asked her.

She took a deep breath. "Do you always have Rolfo run down and buy clothes for your girlfriends?" she asked, her eyes dark and luminous. And then she said something kind of mean, though it came out of the flash of pain she was feeling. "I suppose you probably have him buy them nightgowns."

"My girlfriends don't wear nightgowns," he said without thinking, then regretted it as she turned bright red.

"Oh, Julienne." He started toward her, ready to take her hands in his, then stopped himself. "That was just a joke. I didn't mean it. I couldn't resist when you gave me such a perfect opening."

"Okay," she said, trying hard not to sound a bit shaky.

He shook his head, looking at her with pure affection. "Julienne, you are just too…too…"

"Young? Naive? Silly?"

Actually, he'd been thinking more along the lines of adorable, charming, refreshing, delectable…. And now he had to stop, before he said something he would really wish he hadn't—even in his own head.

"Never mind," she said, waving him away. "Go make your phone calls. I'll be here, having fun."

He hesitated. "You won't make another run for it?" he asked softly.

She flashed him a quick smile. "Not right now. I've got too much to do right here."

He grinned and retreated to the bedroom, though he left the door open so that he could keep an eye on her. And when he came back out ten minutes later he found the mood had changed drastically.

No longer sorting through the rack, she was sitting on the couch, arms folded across her chest.

"What's the matter?" he said, startled by the transformation.

She looked up at him, her gaze cloudy. "I can't take any of these clothes."

"What are you talking about?"

She shrugged—all tragedy, all the time. "For one thing, you're trying to bribe me with them."

He stopped in his tracks, looking outraged. "Bribe you? What are you talking about?"

She looked at him accusingly. "That's what this has all been about, hasn't it? The meal, the dessert, the clothes."

She seemed to have a unique gift of finding the exact wording that would make him the angriest. He had to work hard at keeping his fury at bay. Bribe her, indeed!

"How much of a clothing allowance have I given you over the years?" he asked her carefully.

"Clothing allowance?" She looked blank. "I never saw any clothing allowance. I just took what you had Mathilda, the housekeeper, get for me. She would go on shopping trips and come back with the ugliest clothes you've ever seen."

He stared at her, feeling a well of regret growing in the pit of his stomach. She really did have a point, didn't she?

"Julienne," he said softly, "I'm so sorry. I never paid enough attention…."

"No, no, it was fine." She shook her head so hard her hair slapped her cheeks. "I had plenty of clothes. And the few times I really needed something special Mathilda found something for me at the Saturday market. Like for Christmas or my birthday."

That wasn't really good enough. She should have had the best. What kind of a jerk was he, anyway?

"You've been the perfect ward," he said, really angry with himself. "And I've been the worst as a guardian. Why didn't you tell me?"

She shrugged. "Remember those emails I sent you?" she pointed out. "And the letters?"

He shook his head. "You deserve some clothes. I owe you."

She began to put things back on hangers. "No thank you," she said softly.

He watched her, frustrated and annoyed—but mostly at himself, not at her. And he wanted her to take some of the clothes. Actually, he wanted a lot of things, but at least *that* was doable.

"Are you going to wear your sundress to bed?" he asked archly.

She looked up at him and made a face. "No."

"Then you're going to have to take something, aren't you?"

"No," she said stoutly, though she was beginning to see his point.

He was about to make a response, but his mobile rang and he flipped it open impatiently. "Yes?" he said.

She went on putting the clothes away.

"Good," he said to his phone companion. "Okay, I'll tell her."

She stopped, looking at him questioningly as he closed the phone and turned her way.

He looked at her with a faint, hopeful smile. "I take it you understand you're going to have to stay here tonight? But don't worry. In the morning I'll take you back."

She frowned and faced him bravely. "No. I won't go."

His smile faded. "You will go."

She shook her head. He searched her eyes.

"I can read the thoughts whirring in your clever little mind, Julienne. You have plans. But I'm afraid I'm still a step ahead of you."

"Oh?"

"Yes. Rolfo found your driver. I've sent him back to the convent." He was smiling again. "So I'm afraid any run for the border you might have had in mind will have to be postponed."

She looked away, biting her lip. He was right. Without Popov, her plans were down the drain. Now what was she going to do?

"Sorry about that," he added, and she felt a shiver of outrage at his attitude. He could at least try to understand her point of view. But she had to admit his taunting tone put a different light on things. And now she *was* going to need some clothes, just to survive.

But only a few. Looking back at the rack, she began to pick through all the things she'd loved at first sight, rejecting one after another and reaching for some simpler items—a pair of jeans, a jersey pullover, and of course a basic nightgown. It was time to have a more honest romance with fashion.

Andre showed her the room she could use for the night. It

was fairly plain, but the queen-sized bed looked like luxury to a young woman who was used to the thin, firm sleeping arrangements at the convent.

He looked at her thoughtfully as she stowed her new clothes away in a drawer in the bureau.

"We really should have a chaperone," he noted, almost to himself.

She thought he was nuts. "Of course," she responded with a hint of sarcasm. She looked up at him, her eyes wide with mock innocence. "Maybe you can call one of your lady-friends from the casino? I'm sure either one would be happy to come and be my pal for the evening."

He knew she was needling him, but he grinned. "Don't be ridiculous."

"I see. Perfect companions for you, but not for me."

"Exactly."

She shook her head. "Don't you have staff with you?"

"No. I prefer to be alone."

"But…"

"I have Rolfo, my valet, and a couple of bodyguards available at a moment's notice. But they are very discreet. You won't even know it when you see them." He hesitated over the term *valet*. After all, Rolfo was a lot more than that to him. Still, that wasn't something he could explain to her right now.

"They tell me you spend a lot of time gracing the pages of the tabloids. But, since I'm not allowed to read the papers until they're censored, I don't know that first-hand."

His mouth twisted. What could he say? He was perfectly happy that someone was keeping his lurid image and all the make-believe stories away from her. It was all garbage anyway.

"Let's talk about your wedding," Andre said suddenly.

"It's *your* wedding," she responded crisply, rising and going to the expanse of glass overlooking the lake. The lights of the city were reflected in the inky black water. "You're the one who planned it."

"Most women love to talk about weddings," he said, slightly exasperated. "Why don't you want to talk about yours?"

Turning to face him, she put her hands on her hips. "I'm not having a wedding, Andre. I don't want to marry Alphonso."

"*Prince* Alphonso," he corrected sharply.

"Prince Alphonso," she repeated dutifully. "Or, as I prefer to call him, Prince Dweeb."

He frowned. "Enough of that. He's a perfectly decent and respectable young man."

"That may be, but I don't love him."

"Love?"

He had to bite back his original response. She was still so young. She had no idea how naive she sounded. Love had nothing to do with this. He searched her wide, innocent eyes, wondering how to explain that to her.

"No one is asking you to love him," he said carefully at last. "But you have to marry him. Everyone expects it. The two of you were betrothed years ago. It's too late to change your mind. If you two don't marry, all hell will break loose." He shook his head impatiently. "The wedding will go forward as planned."

He waited for anger, or at least tears. That was the way most of the women of his acquaintance usually fought their battles. But Julienne was gazing at him levelly, as though searching for the chink in his armor, the weak spot she could use in her attack. Walking over to the couch, she flounced down not far from him.

"Just how well do you know Alphonso?" she asked him at last.

He blinked at her, nonplussed. "I know his mother."

"There you go. You don't know him at all, do you?"

"I've seen him. I've met him." He avoided her gaze. Actually, now that he thought about it, he knew where she was coming from. The young man had been no paragon of manliness the last time they'd been together. But he was young. He would grow into his role quickly enough. He turned back and looked at her.

"But, Julienne, that isn't the point. It doesn't matter what Alphonso is like. He's a symbol."

"I'm supposed to be satisfied marrying a symbol?" She threw out both hands. "That's it? That's my life?"

"You think I don't understand what you're going through? Am I not royal?"

"Yes, but you…you…"

"I have to abide by the rules and the responsibilities just like you do."

She shook her head, looking at him rebelliously. "But it seems like you *like* it."

His head jerked back as though she'd slapped him. "No, Julienne," he said coldly. "I've had to deal with my own disappointments. Being royal gives us some incredible benefits. At the same time it means we aren't allowed to live like others do." He sighed and looked out at the midnight lake. "Sometimes it doesn't seem fair. Sometimes it isn't. But it remains our reality."

She stared at him, wondering what had happened. From

the haunted look in his deep blue eyes, she knew something had.

"Tell me," she whispered. She reached out but she couldn't quite touch him. "Tell me what happened to you."

He gave her a scathing look and turned away. "Nothing happened to me."

She didn't believe that, but she could see he wasn't going to tell her anything. "The thing about Alphonso is—"

He rose abruptly. "Enough. I don't need to hear all these complaints about Alphonso. It's your duty to marry him."

Walking to the desk along the far wall, he sank into the chair and pulled out a stack of papers, beginning to sort through them. She watched for a moment, then rose herself and began to stroll around the room, looking at various pieces of art on the bookshelves, and at some of the books stacked there, too.

But, inevitably, she was drawn to the desk where he was working.

"So you're missing a secretary?" she noted, looking over his shoulder at the letter he was reading.

"That I am," he acknowledged, giving her a quick smile.

She bit her lip. A new idea suddenly occurred to her. At first thought it seemed a real winner, though she had a feeling he wasn't going to agree. Still—nothing ventured, nothing gained. She might as well throw it out there and see what his reaction might be.

"Hey, *I* could be your secretary."

He looked up in surprise, then a look of distaste swept over his handsome face. "No, you couldn't."

But the more she thought about it, the more she liked the idea. "Yes. Don't you see? It would be perfect."

He shook his head, dismissing it out of hand. "You're a princess."

She blinked at him. "Princesses can't be secretaries?"

"No." As far as he was concerned he'd said the final word on the subject, and he went back to sorting through his papers.

She knew it was probably a lost cause, but she wasn't ready to abandon it just because he hated the idea. There were lots of things about it that appealed to her pretty strongly. And, anyway, anything was better than marrying Alphie.

"Wouldn't it be fun, though?" she said, walking toward the window. "I mean, I'd be there all the time, and you could keep track of me and be sure I wasn't getting into mischief. When you went to meetings I would be there with my laptop, typing away. Then we could go to lunch, maybe at a five star restaurant, and…"

"No." He was watching her. How could he help it? And it was hard to keep the affectionate amusement he felt toward her transparent act from showing in his face.

She frowned at him, tapping her foot in frustration. "I think I'd make a much better secretary than I do a princess," she pointed out. "You should want to encourage me to follow where my talents lie."

"Your secretarial talents seem to tend toward early lunch in nice restaurants," he noted wryly.

"I mentioned typing, didn't I?"

"You mentioned it. But I've never seen any evidence of skill in that direction."

"Maybe you should have read some of my letters," she pointed out triumphantly.

He had to laugh. She had him there. But he sobered quickly, looking at her and shaking his head. "You don't even know what is involved in being a princess," he said. "You don't have a clue. I'm just beginning to realize that no one has ever shown you what being royal is all about."

She looked at him archly. "Wasn't that *your* job?"

He sat back and stared at her, realizing the truth of her accusation. "Maybe. Yes, maybe so."

She resumed walking about the room, though she was aware of his gaze following her everywhere she went.

"So far I haven't seen a lot of advantage to being a princess," she said over her shoulder. "There are a lot of rules to follow. Everyone seems to have an opinion on how you should behave at any given moment, and I never seem to be doing it right."

"So what's the plan, Julienne?" he asked her. "If you do manage to escape my evil clutches and get across the border, where will you go? What will you do?"

She turned to look at him. "I'm hoping it won't come to that," she said earnestly. "It would be so much better if you would just understand and take my side and…and maybe we could fix things so I wouldn't have to run."

She stared into his eyes and he stared back.

"It won't work," he said at last. "Everything we've fought for these last ten years would be destroyed. It just won't work."

She stood before him with her hands out, palms up, as though offering him something from her soul but not sure how to give it to him. She didn't speak, but her eyes were pleading with him to find a way. Some way out.

CHAPTER FOUR

PRINCE ANDRE heard something at his door. He'd only been asleep for ten minutes or so and he was wide awake again in an instant. He went up on one elbow.

"Andre?"

It was Julienne, who should be asleep in the next room and not here, waking him. His first impulse was to tell her to go back to bed. Midnight meetings were way too dangerous to play around with. But maybe something was wrong. He had to find out.

"What is it?" he asked.

"Can I come in?"

He sighed. He should turn her down. He should tell her they would talk about whatever was going on with her in the morning. But he knew he wasn't going to do that. He couldn't.

"Yes, come on in. It's not locked."

The door opened and there she stood, her lovely form silhouetted by the living room light that made her nightgown disappear and left only a perfect view of her soft curves. His mouth went dry. Closing his eyes, he muttered an oath, and when that didn't help he added a small, intense prayer.

But she came in anyway.

"Andre, I can't sleep. This may be the last time we're together like this. And I have to know something."

"Okay," he said, his voice strained and grainy. "Shoot."

He was sitting up in the bed, his bare torso gleaming in the moonlight. She slid down to sit on the edge of the bed—so close—too close. He bit his lower lip, hard. Maybe pure pain would save him.

"We used to be friends," she was saying softly. "I used to count on you for…a lot of things. Including emotional support."

"I…yes," he said lamely.

"You were so important to me. After my parents died it seemed like you were all I had in the world."

He could hear the emotion in her voice and knew he had to do something to comfort her. He took her hand in his and held it tightly. "I know," he said softly. "Julienne, I know."

She drew in a shaky breath. "So why did you desert me?" she asked, her voice breaking. "Why didn't you come to visit me these last two years and more?"

He brought her hand to his lips and kissed it, closing his eyes and wishing he could take her in his arms. She was so lovely and so close and he could feel her unhappiness. "I…I couldn't come," he told her lamely. "I had to stay away."

She frowned, uncomprehending. "But why?"

He cupped her cheek with his free hand. Her hair was silver in the moonlight. "Do I really have to explain it to you?" he said, his voice rough as sandpaper.

"Yes." She came closer. "I'm just not sure…"

He took her shoulders in his hands and faced her. "I wanted to come. Julienne, you know I wanted to."

"Then why?" She searched the darkness of his eyes. "Did I do something to make you angry?"

"Angry?" He groaned. "Never."

"Then why? Do you know how heartbroken I was when you stopped coming to see me?"

"Julienne…"

"Why?"

He drew air deep into his lungs and tried to explain. "Don't you see? I had to stay away…because…because of this." He took her chin in his hand and pulled her close, touching his lips to hers. Her lips parted right away and his tongue didn't hesitate. He'd only meant to kiss her softly, but the invitation she presented was asking for more, and his body was so ready to bring it. She pressed herself to him and he pulled her even closer, so that he could feel her full breasts against his chest. The nipples were so high and hard he felt them through the light cloth of her nightgown, making him gasp. Every part of him ached for her, and it took every bit of his will and strength to pull away.

For a moment, struggling for breath, he couldn't speak. He had to get her out of here.

"Now, get back to bed before we both do something we'll regret," he told her roughly, hoping she didn't hear the thinly veiled panic in his voice.

"I wouldn't regret anything I ever did with you," she said with a sigh of yearning. Reaching out in the gloom, she flattened her hand against his naked chest.

"Julienne…" Her name sounded as though it had been ripped from his throat. He took her hand and pulled it away. "Go back where you belong."

"Okay," she said, rising reluctantly. She started away, then looked back. "That was lovely," she said breathlessly. "Alphonso kisses like a baby seal."

She left, closing the door, and Andre put his pillow over his head and tried to muffle the groan.

"Julienne." He shook her shoulder gently, then, when she didn't respond, a bit more firmly. "Wake up."

She stretched and smiled at him sleepily, only half awake.

"Andre?" she whispered, and then she reached for him.

Looking down at her beautiful sleepy face, he suddenly felt as though he'd just leapt off a tall cliff and was plunging through space. Everything in him wanted to reach for her and hold her close, wrapping himself in her body. Turning away abruptly, he fought it and won—one more time.

"Wake up," he said again, roughly this time. "We've got to get out of here."

Her eyes opened widely and she sat up, holding her covers to her chest. "What's happened?" she asked, fully awake now and thinking clearly.

"I just had a call from Security. Someone has either realized who you are or made a lucky guess. Rumors are flying. It's known that you've left the convent. That makes people wonder what is going on, as your wedding is only days away. Some of the young hot-heads from the Rubiat family are said to be coming this way to find out. Meanwhile the paparazzi are gathering like the vultures they are."

"Uh-oh." She knew exactly what that meant. This was the very unruly bunch that all the plans and schemes revolved around. If you couldn't keep the Rubiats happy, bad things happened.

"Exactly. We need to slip away before they get here." He looked at her candidly. "Are you game for making a run for it with me?"

"Am I?" Her eyes gleamed. Didn't he understand anything about her at all? "Of course. It's what I've been living for."

He wasn't sure he got that, but there wasn't time to quibble. "We've got a couple of hours before sunrise. Let's make the most of them."

He gave her a simple canvas bag to use for packing some of her new clothes and warned her to limit herself to three items.

"We won't have room for much," he said. "We'll be traveling on a big old Harley Davidson."

"A motorcycle?" she said in surprise.

He nodded. "They won't be expecting that. We'll be able to sail right past them." He looked her over quickly. "Tie your hair back with something that covers the color," he advised. "And wear jeans."

She did as he had suggested, feeling oddly excited. He went into his room to change, and when he came back she gasped. She hardly recognized this tough-looking man with a swagger and a leather jacket. He had on a pair of large aviator sunglasses and had slicked his hair back.

"Wow," she said, feeling a bit shy and tongue-tied.

"That's your favorite word, isn't it?" he mentioned, teasing her. He found a smaller, more stylish leather jacket among the clothes on her rack and handed it to her. "Here. You'll need it. We're going up into the mountains."

"Into the mountains?" On the back of a motorcycle, holding on to Prince Andre for dear life. This went beyond anything she'd ever dreamed of.

They were ready in moments, and in the elevator, heading

down. But before they reached ground level Prince Andre pushed a button, and suddenly they were emerging into a stairway down to a tunnel that seemed to wind its way through the inner workings of the building. After walking for what seemed like miles, they reached a parking garage Julienne knew must be far from their starting point. He led her through a series of small rooms, and finally there was the Harley.

All black paint and chrome, it gleamed like something alive and aware, and she shivered a little, looking at it. But before long she was riding that same scary machine, and just as she'd supposed she had her arms wrapped around Andre. It was purely heaven.

Andre was feeling the spirit as well. It was amazing how free one could feel, flying across the pavement on a huge motorcycle. And with Julienne hanging on, her hands making themselves noticed around his torso—what could be better?

By now the driver at the convent would have told them she was missing. Mother Superior was probably terrified of telling him. He ought to put her out of her misery. But he would let Rolfo deal with all of that.

Dawn was just breaking as they left the city, climbing higher and higher into the surrounding mountains. They found a small roadside store and stopped to ask if there was a place to get breakfast. The storekeeper had a small kitchen in the back, and he whipped them up eggs and country sausage served in a flatbread wrap.

"Delicious," Julienne declared, and then she pestered the storekeeper until he finally divulged the secret seasonings he had used.

She made Andre laugh. A princess who cared about

cooking. Unique. Watching her, he thought of what had happened the night before, how her tremulous visit had turned into a kiss that had shown his hand like nothing else could. Did she remember? Did she think of it? Or was it just another passing experience in her young life, something of a stepping stone to her full adulthood? He wasn't sure. If only things were different he would take her right now and hold her in his arms and never let her go. But things were what they were, and that was more than impossible. It would be treason.

"Where is it that we're going?" she asked him as they prepared to take off again.

"Ultimately the lake house," he said, glancing around the parking area to make sure no one could overhear him. "But first we're going to visit my cousin Giselle. You may not remember her."

She shook her head, trying to think but not coming up with anyone. "The name sounds a bit familiar, but…"

"She's Alphonso's half-sister."

"What? I didn't know Alphie had a sister."

"Different mothers," he said shortly. "Twelve years ago she was the most famous princess in the Western world. The papers were full of stories about her. She had suitors from all over—royalty, movie stars, rich industrialists. She was so beautiful, so accomplished." He smiled, remembering how stunning she'd been. Those had been happy days. But happy days never lasted long in Gemania.

"And," he added, "she was one of my best friends."

That got her attention. "What happened to her?"

He held her gaze steadily with his own. "She threw it all away. Just the way you want to. She married a starving artist, a nobody, a man who never did become successful."

He shrugged. "Her father disowned her. She gave up being a princess. And now she knows what it is like to be a commoner, with no money, no connections. No help from the people who loved her."

Julienne felt the tragedy of poor Giselle's situation deeply. She could identify with it in every way.

"But she has love," she said hopefully.

"You can't eat love," he told her cynically. "It won't pay the rent." He shrugged again. "The last time I saw her the man she'd married was gone. He left her with three little children to take care of on her own." He let that sink in, watching as her eyes clouded, and then he added, "She's had it pretty rough."

Julienne thought about that for a long moment and frowned at him. "Haven't you tried to help her? You said she was your friend."

"Of course I've tried to help her. She's too proud to accept anything from me. She knows she turned her back on all of us when she made her choice, and she's living with the consequences." He watched her steadily. He was piling it on a bit thick, but it had to be done. If Giselle's story could help turn Julienne around, it would all be for a good cause.

Yeah, what a cause. He was heartsick when he thought of it. He had to make her marry another man in order to save his beloved country from war. Great. And what did that leave him? Not a hell of a lot.

But it had to be done. The country had to be his highest priority.

Thinking about Giselle, Julienne was developing a lump in her throat. "I would help her anyway!" she insisted. "In fact, I'm an adult now. It's time for me to have a living of my own. *I'll* help her. I will!"

"Really?" He felt almost cruel doing this, but it had to be done. "How can you help her if you aren't a princess anymore?"

She drew her breath in, knowing he thought he'd trapped her. Well, let him think so. She would find a way.

"I haven't been to see her for a few years, but Rolfo got word to her that we were coming. She'll be expecting us."

"And why, exactly, are you taking me to see her?"

He turned to look at her, hoping she understood his basic motive was to make things easier for her, every time. "I think you've figured that out for yourself. I want you to see her and the conditions she's living under since she gave up being a princess."

"A cautionary tale, is it?"

"Pretty much."

She was quiet as they rode through the villages, going higher and higher into the mountains. Of course she knew what he was doing. He planned to show her that choosing poverty over royal life was fraught with peril and ugliness and heartbreak. And he was probably right. But what choice did she have? Life with Alphonso promised to be much the same.

They pulled off the main road about an hour later, so that Andre could show her a meadow back in the interior—a place where he'd camped as a boy. Red and yellow wildflowers littered the valley floor, leading up to a waterfall with a huge drop, making for a magical view. They stood beside the parked bike and took it all in.

"Gorgeous," Julienne said. "I've never seen anything more special."

He smiled and looked at her, thinking she was pretty special herself. It was amazing how happy it made him just to have her appreciate something that he loved. But then, it was amazing how happy it made him just to be with her.

But any chance of that would soon be over. In just a few days she would be married to Alphonso—come hell or high water. It had to be.

The meadow was so beautiful they found they didn't want to leave it, and they walked down the path until they found a small stream. Sitting beside it, each on their own flat rock, they talked and teased each other, and just generally made the day last a little longer than they had planned.

And finally Andre got down to business.

"All right, Julienne, since you have all this worked out, tell me what you think you're going to do with your life. If you get your wish and don't have to marry Alphonso, what will your life be like?"

Suddenly she was nervous. She hadn't told him her plans and she knew he wouldn't approve. "Well, I'd rather not go back to the convent," she said, stalling for time. "I think I'm ready to move beyond that."

"Agreed." He looked at her levelly. "But you are rejecting life as a princess, rejecting poor old Alphonso, and I want to know what you see for yourself instead. What is it that you have your heart set on? What is it that you would most like to do?"

Could she tell him? She glanced his way and decided against it. He would never understand.

"For a start, I want to learn how to drive," she said, avoiding the issue altogether.

"Didn't anyone teach you that?" No mobile phone, no driver's license—what sort of modern woman was this?

"No. You know very well there are no cars at the convent. Except Popov's, of course. And even if there were, they wouldn't teach me. They were too afraid I'd run off as soon as I had a way to do it."

He waved that away. He really didn't want to delve into it. "Okay, you want to learn to drive. That's easy enough. I could teach you in an afternoon." His look was penetrating. "Then what?"

She avoided his gaze. "What do you mean?" she said evasively.

"I mean, what is it that you want to do, Julienne? What passion calls to you?"

Should she tell him? She looked at him sideways and scrunched up her face, ready to do the dirty deed. She knew he would never look at her the same way again once she'd admitted her passion to him.

"Okay. Here it is." She took a deep breath. "I...I want to go to pastry school."

He blinked, not sure he'd heard her correctly. He leaned closer. "What kind of school?"

She looked up at him, baleful. "Pastry."

He shook his head, still at sea. "I don't understand."

Now he was starting to annoy her. Didn't understand! *Hah!*

"Peach tarts. Napoleons. Eclairs." She was facing him now, her passion expressed clearly in her face. "I want to learn to make them. I want to create new forms. I want to—"

"Enough," he said shortly, holding up his hand. He was finally getting the picture, and the picture filled him with horror. "You're trying to tell me you would rather slave away in a hot kitchen all day than be a princess? You actually expect me to believe that?"

Her shoulders sagged. "Believe what you want," she said

sadly. "You asked me to tell you my passion, and I told you." She turned away. "Let's change the subject."

He knew he'd hurt her feelings, but he still couldn't believe it. They sat in silence for a few minutes, then he tried again. This time he told himself he would remain calm.

"Tell me how all this came about. What made you fall in love with the idea of being a pastry chef?"

"I love good pastry. Who doesn't?"

"Yes. Well, I love a good steak, too, but I don't plan to be a cowboy."

She rose and turned away. "Let's just go."

"No." He rose as well, taking her by the shoulders, stopping her and gazing down into her pretty face. "I want to know how it all began. Please tell me."

She searched his eyes. Could she trust him? But how could she not?

"Okay," she said slowly. They began to walk along the stream, back toward where the motorcycle was parked. "I guess it all began when Nooma, the cook at the castle, began to let me help her in the kitchen."

He frowned, wondering if the woman should be fired. "Did she do this often?" he asked.

"Often? Yes, it was often. But it was my doing, not hers." Her quick humor was back and she laughed at him. "What do you think I was doing all those long winter days, waiting for you to show up?"

He didn't laugh back. "I expected you to be improving your mind with worthy reading, learning to play the piano, practicing your French...."

"Well, I wasn't doing much of that. I was in the kitchen, baking pies."

He frowned. "Where was my aunt, the Duchess, during

all this? I thought she was keeping a firm hand in your development."

She shook her head. She was going to have to rat on the lady, but she guessed it didn't matter. She'd long ago moved to the coast of France. "Your aunt, the Duchess, was usually confined to her room with a headache and a bottle of vermouth most days until teatime."

He stared at her, aghast. "Are you serious? Why didn't you tell me about that?"

"Because I wanted to be in the kitchen, not reciting lessons to the Duchess. It worked out better for both of us. She had her thing. I had mine."

He groaned. Guilt was piling up all around him. If he'd thought about it he would have realized the Duchess wasn't living up to her agreements. But he was as bad as Julienne. When he came to the castle, he'd wanted to be with her, not quizzing the Duchess to see if she had been a hard enough taskmaster.

"Oh, don't worry. I had my lessons with the governess in the morning. I got plenty done."

"Well, I guess that's a relief."

"And then I went to the convent. At first they wouldn't let me into the kitchen at all. But about six months into my stay the convent cook came down with hives and someone had to take over the cooking. The next thing you know I was in there, baking away." She smiled, remembering. Happy memories. "When I volunteered they were all relieved, and even after she got over the hives and came back she was glad to have my help in the kitchen. She taught me a lot."

He was shaking his head. "No one ever told me."

"No? Why should they?" She threw him a scathing look. "By that time you'd decided to wash your hands of me."

"Don't be ridiculous."

"I'm only taking off the rose-colored glasses and facing reality. You stayed away. You left me to my own devices. What did you expect? You're just lucky I didn't decide to become a bomb-throwing Marxist. Plenty of royals are into that these days."

That made him smile, and that was a relief. Life was better when the Prince was smiling.

She remembered how it had been when she'd first come to the Diamante castle to live after her parents had died. At first she'd been afraid of him. He'd seemed so tall, so strong—so unsmiling. But then she'd become more comfortable around him and their relationship had blossomed into something close to friendship.

He'd made it a point to eat at least one meal with her a day when he was at home in the castle—just the two of them. Those were the times she really treasured. She'd had to sit through a hundred stern lectures about how she should behave, but it was worth it. When the lecture was over, his hard, handsome face would soften with affection and he would ask her how her day had gone, or what she'd learned from her governess, or they would take the horses out and ride over the hills. He was wonderful. He was her life.

That all changed when she turned eighteen. He authorized a big party for her birthday. Her aunt invited a hundred young people from royal and noble families. There were afternoon games and then a sumptuous feast in the great hall, and finally a ball that lived up to all her fantasies. Even now, when she closed her eyes, it all came back to her—the swirling lights, the throbbing music, the excitement, the colors. The young men had all wanted to dance with her and the young women wanted to be her friend. For the first time in her life she was the center of it all. It was intoxicating—a magical night.

But best of all was the last dance at midnight. And that dance, of course, was with the Prince.

She still remembered the song that had been playing—"The Look of Love". They had swayed together without either of them saying a word, and she'd felt as though she'd entered a dream. They were out on the terrace, away from all the others. There was moonlight, shadows and music—and a gorgeous man in her arms. The song began to fade away and she looked up, yearning toward him. His mouth was there, and then the kiss. Slow and deep and delicious, it awakened senses in her body she hadn't known she had. And then he pulled away, and others surged out onto the terrace, and it was over.

But everything changed after that.

She had to admit she'd had her daydreams, even though she knew there was no reason for it. Thinking of that now, she sighed and sank against the back of his leather jacket, holding on to him as though she could hold on to the dream as well.

They entered the peaceful valley that led to Giselle's home about an hour later. Andre was looking forward to seeing her. She'd always been his favorite cousin.

He remembered when she'd come to him for advice. What had he told her? He tried to think of his words at the time. Something about not being foolish, not to count on anyone else in this world. Love didn't last. She was going to throw away everything for the chance to reach for something that would melt away like a snowflake once she'd grasped it.

She'd laughed at him, called him cynical. Was she laughing

now? They would see the answer to that one soon enough. He only hoped Giselle would be ready to tell the truth to them both.

Julienne could sense his moodiness. Was she really as attuned to his emotions as it felt like she was—or was she fooling herself? She thought of all those long, lonely nights when she'd stared at the ceiling of her small cell in the convent and thought about the Prince. And all the waiting she'd done. That really was the hardest part, as hope slowly faded.

And now here she was, holding on to him with both hands. It was glorious, and she meant to savor every second of it.

CHAPTER FIVE

THE big Harley made a lot of noise driving into the valley—an excessive amount of noise for people trying to hide from too much attention, in Julienne's mind. She had a feeling Andre had been looking for an excuse to ride it out into the countryside. But she had to admit she was enjoying the trip as well.

As they neared the cottage where Giselle lived they stopped at a corner, and a young girl suddenly swung down, hanging off a branch on a tree before them.

About nine years old, she was wearing ragged jeans and a yellow pullover with a faded picture of a monkey on the chest. She stared at them from under a curly mop of light brown hair and they stared back. Andre cut the engine and swung off the bike, ready to catch her in case she should fall, but not wanting to be too obvious about it.

She let go just before he got into place, and landed on her bare feet all on her own. He grinned at her.

"Are you one of Giselle's girls?" he asked at last.

The child nodded solemnly.

He grinned at her again. "What do you know? For a moment there I thought you might be Tom Sawyer."

"Andre!" Julienne remonstrated.

"I'm Lily," she said. "Are you the Prince?"

"Yes, I am." He bowed low to her. "At your service."

Her dark eyes took him in and seemed to approve. "Mother says I can be a princess if I want to be."

"Do you want to?"

She made a face. "Heck, no. They have to sit on silk pillows and eat yucky food and wear frilly pink dresses that stick out."

He exchanged a quick look with Julienne and both of them tried not to laugh.

"Is that what your mother told you?" he asked her.

"Uh-uh." She shook her head. "I read it in a book."

"Well, I'm here to tell you right now your mother didn't spend a lot of time sitting around on silk pillows when she was your age. And, while it lasted, your mother made a wonderful princess."

Lily seemed pleased with that. "But she didn't like it. She told me she didn't ever want to be one. And I don't either."

"No frilly dresses for you, huh?"

She shook her head emphatically. "I like my clothes just fine," she said, kicking the dirt with her bare foot.

Andre gave Julienne a significant look that she knew was meant to convey how sad this was for Giselle, who must be regretting what she'd given up every day. And he might be right. But that didn't mean Julienne would regret giving up the royalty business. She wasn't Giselle.

"Hey, Your Highness," Lily was saying, looking over the chrome and black beast before her. "I sure would like a ride on that motorcycle."

"Uh…" Andre looked at Julienne and she waved her permission, jumping down herself.

"Go ahead. Give her a ride. Take her on in. I can walk. In fact, I'd like to. It's so pretty in this valley. Let me take some time to enjoy it." She handed over her helmet to the little girl and started off.

The snow pack had been a good one this year, and the wild flowers were taking advantage of all the extra runoff water. The entire valley was a riot of color.

She laughed as she watched Andre take Lily for a tour through the village, giving her a thrill with a couple of little wheelies while he was at it. Those elicited shrieks of happy excitement from Lily.

Before she arrived at the cottage at the bottom of the hill a woman emerged from inside and waved at her. Probably in her mid-thirties, she had a full, sensual beauty that looked a bit careworn but must have been something spectacular when she was younger.

"Hello," she called out. "You must be Princess Julienne. Welcome! We're so glad to see you."

Andre arrived with Lily in tow, and two other little girls gathered around, begging for a ride as well.

"After lunch," Giselle told them. "We've got salad and finger sandwiches. The girls made the sandwiches themselves."

Going into the cottage, they all sat down around a large table. The sandwiches were free-form, as you would expect when such young ones did the cutting. But everything was great—in a homespun way.

But as Julienne began to look around the room she began to notice something. Everything was very simple, but there was a spare elegance to it that bespoke something other than poverty. As she studied her surroundings she noted more and more items that were first-quality and looked very expensive. One way or another, this family was doing quite well for itself.

But Andre didn't seem to have noticed.

"Whatever happened to…what was his name? Tavist?" he asked his cousin.

"Tavert?" Giselle looked at him, bemused. "You mean my husband?"

Andre looked surprised. "Was that his name?"

"It was, and it still is." Giselle grinned at him.

"Oh. I thought he was gone?"

"He is gone, but he'll be back. He's in Paris right now, negotiating with a major distributor."

Andre was looking more and more confused. "A major distributor? Of what?"

"Garden decor. Mainly statuary. You didn't notice on your way in?"

She led them to the window and pointed out the many fantasy creatures inhabiting the yard, from unicorns to geese to garden gnomes.

"We started experimenting with cement forms and casting from our own designs. We sold a few in our little shop, but things didn't really take off until we started selling on the internet. Now we have customers from all over the world."

They chatted a while longer, and Julienne hoped that Andre was coming to terms with the fact that his cousin's life hadn't been completely ruined after all.

"So you're still happy with the choice you made?" Julienne asked Giselle when she got a chance to talk to her privately. Andre was giving the girls turns at riding around the block on the motorcycle.

"Absolutely. The best thing I ever did."

"You ought to let Andre know. He thinks you made a big mistake."

Very quickly she explained about Alphonso, and how Andre was trying to convince her to marry him willingly. Giselle listened to the whole story, asked a few questions about the background and the treaty, then shook her head.

"Julienne, you do understand that the only reason you were paired with Alphonso was that Andre was already betrothed to that Italian princess?" she said, bringing up something Julienne had never heard a hint of before. She wondered if she'd heard what she thought she had.

"Wh...what?"

"You didn't know that?"

"Italian princess?"

"Yes. And, believe me, he wasn't ready to get married at the time. This was almost eight years ago. He fought it hard, but his father, King Harold, insisted he had to do it for the good of the country. And I have to admit Andre is all about duty and the country. He's the essence of the patriot. He finally agreed to do it."

"No! No one ever told me." Julienne shook her head, stunned. "But he never did get married, did he? What happened to her?"

"She died. It was very sad."

And Andre was back, so their conversation ended. But the revelation was shocking to Julienne and she couldn't stop thinking about it. Was it true? Giselle had intimated that she might have been paired with Andre instead of Alphonso if the timing had been right. The very concept took her breath away.

"We'd better get going," Andre was saying. "We want to make it to the lake house before dark."

"Ah, you're going to the lake house?" Giselle shook her head with a bemused smile. "So many happy summer memories, so many years ago."

Looking at her, he realized the current practices his family engaged in needed updating. Why not invite Giselle and her girls to the lake house? Why not let a new generation start building those happy memories for themselves? It wasn't as though she was the enemy, just because she'd reached for something else out of life.

But he couldn't make policy on his own. He would need the King's approval. That was something he was going to have to look into once this wedding situation had settled down. Still, he couldn't help mentioning it and suggesting he was going to talk to his father. Seeing his cousin with her girls, he knew they were exactly what the lake house was meant to host.

"We do need a vacation," Giselle admitted. "We are working much too hard. We're going to have to figure out some way to take some time off. But at least we're here and we're together and we have our girls with us all the time. I couldn't ask for a better life."

Andre looked skeptical, but he didn't challenge her on it.

As they were preparing to leave, Giselle came up to give Julienne a personal farewell.

"Julienne, you're so beautiful. Your decision must involve both your heart and your head. The heart shows us the path to joy; the head shows us the way to wisdom. You need both to find happiness."

"Thank you so much." The two women shared a warm hug. "And I hope to see you and your family again soon."

A moment later they were back roaring across the

countryside, but they hadn't gone far before Andre called back a message.

"We're going to take a short detour," he told her, pulling to a stop at a crossroad intersection.

"What kind of detour?"

"I want you to see the mining district. The fountain of our country's wealth."

"Oh."

They rode over dirt and rutted roads, breathing dust and bouncing painfully. And finally they reached a lookout point where they could gaze down at the mining activity below. Huge gashes in the earth made way for big trucks and men with handcarts. It was a beehive of activity.

"There you see it," Andre told her. "The backbone of our economy, the foundation of our royal houses, the reason we've gone to war with each other through the centuries. It all comes down to wealth and power, as always."

"But there is peace right now," she said.

"And that peace is based on a balance of power between the Royal Houses that depends on you marrying Alphonso. If the Rubiats sense a weakness in our commitment to getting that done, they'll attack again. It's just what they do."

She sighed. It always came back to that. "Why don't I have to marry someone in the Rubiat family?" she asked out of curiosity.

"They don't have anyone who is right for you to marry. They haven't been able to produce a successful new generation in a long time. That's why they have to pick fights to get their way."

She looked down at all the miners, working so busily. "Is it all gemstones?" she asked him.

"Not at all. Much of the mineral material is actually used

in technological and industrial ways. The gems are only the flashy, public relations side of the industry."

"The fun stuff?"

"Exactly." He turned to look at where she sat behind him on the bike. "And this is a big part of your legacy."

Her legacy. What a tiresome phrase that was getting to be. Right along with "her destiny." But she didn't talk back, and soon they were on their way again. She was growing more and more excited. She'd always loved the lake house, but for the last few years it had been so disappointing to go during the summer, be told Andre would surely come this time, and wait and wait, only to be forgotten again.

And then, finally, it was just ahead, a huge old brooding house, filled with comfortable rooms and memories, the place where everyone came eventually, every summer. It was late. The light was fading. She hugged Andre tightly as they rode up to the door. At last they were home.

CHAPTER SIX

THE morning dawned like Christmas, with a gift in every scene. There was the sunlight on the lake, the sound of birds flying by, the scent of spring flowers in the air, the prospect of a ride out on the water in a rowboat, just the two of them.

It was early in the season and there were no servants yet, no other inhabitants to spoil the fun. In just a week or two the place would be crawling with royals and their staffs. But for now they had the place to themselves.

Julienne cooked a nice breakfast of Belgian waffles and cinnamon syrup—totally delicious, if she did say herself, but Andre didn't comment. That either meant he hadn't noticed, or that he didn't want to encourage her interest by letting her know how good she was. She couldn't quite decide which it might be.

They took a walk through the orchard, with its peach trees just setting fruit, then down along the water, skipping stones and laughing at each other. Andre went out to survey some broken fenceposts he'd noticed as they rode in, and Julienne went exploring in the house.

Every room seemed to have a treasure trove of mementoes from past summers. She found amazing things everywhere, and then she pulled a beautifully bound copy of *The Highwayman* from the shelf. The Alfred Noyes poem about the tragic love between a robber and a landlord's black-eyed daughter had always been a favorite of hers, and she opened the book, prepared for a treat. But the first thing she saw was that the flyleaf had been torn out, as though someone wanted to either preserve or destroy whatever was written there. She frowned, then noticed there were indentations on the next page. A note had been written, and with enough pressure to leave a pretty good impression. Searching a nearby desk, she found a pencil and proceeded to shade it lightly across the pertinent area. The missing note sprang into view.

"Hah!" She couldn't help but give a little crow of victory. Then she put down her pencil and attempted to read the note.

"My darling A," it began.

She bit her lip, wondering if it had been written to Andre.

You are my Highwayman, and, like Bess, I'll be waiting by moonlight. Your first love, your true love, Denise.

She stared at the note. Now she was certain it was meant for Andre. Her teeth began to chatter, and it was a moment before she realized she was trembling. She shook her head, trying to shake it off. How silly of her. Of course he'd had women who'd adored him. Who knew how old this was? What did she expect?

And yet somehow it just got into her heart and twisted it. Pure pain. Jealousy? Maybe. Why not? Of course it hurt to think of him with another woman, no matter how silly that was.

Clasping the book to her chest, she went in search of him and found him, just back from his trip around the estate.

"Who's Denise?" she asked bluntly, not waiting on niceties.

"Denise?" He frowned, then his brow cleared. "Oh, Denise." He glanced at her quickly, his eyes sharpening. "What do you know about Denise?"

"I found this book." She held it out to him. "It looks like she dedicated it to you."

"Ah." He smiled, then quickly erased it.

"Did you love her?"

He rose slowly, turning away and looking out into the sky. "I thought I loved her. She was very beautiful. I was very young." Turning back, he met her gaze candidly. "We were both young, and we were thrown together, and we did what young people do." He hesitated, then shook his head ruefully. "Okay, here's what happened. Her father was the lake house butler. A summer romance. It was over by the time the leaves turned."

She stared at him, but what she saw was the entire story playing out in her head.

Summer magic.

"Did you want to marry her?"

"Marry her? Why would I want to marry her?"

"Ah, yes. She was the butler's daughter." Julienne made a significant face.

But he laughed at her. "Julienne, you're too old to live in a dream world. Face facts. We didn't make the world the way it is and we can't do much to change it. We are royal. We have to follow a certain path in life. Live with it."

She felt her lower lip coming out in rebellion. "No."

He shook his head, not sure what she meant. "What do you mean, no?"

She flashed him a look. "I think you know what I mean. I won't do it."

So she was talking about the Alphonso thing again. He gritted his teeth in annoyance. "The hell you won't."

She glared at him, then flounced off to sulk in the kitchen. And while she was there she whipped up a pan of delectable pastries such as he had never had before. He ate a few, then ate a few more, and had to admit she had the knack. But he still wouldn't give her the satisfaction of hearing it aloud.

"Tell me what happened with the butler's daughter," she coaxed, once he was full of pastry and groaning with pleasure.

He looked at her and shook his head. "Okay, Julienne. Here goes. I was crazy about her that summer. She was gorgeous, with thick red hair and a wide red mouth that just begged to be kissed."

Julienne turned away, biting her lip and hating this. Too much information. But she had to know.

"We pledged to meet in the fall in Cairns," he said. "I was going to university there. She was going to dental assistant school. I got to town early and raced over to find her apartment, hoping to surprise her. And there she was, in bed with some skinny grad student." He shrugged. "The end. She betrayed me and I never saw her again."

"She betrayed you?" She had a flash of intuition. Was this one of the seeds of his cynicism about love, about marriage? Could be.

He grimaced. "Well, it was hardly fair to even call it that. Looking back, I saw that she realized sooner than I did that it was never going to work. Only pain and unhappiness could result. It was time to move on, and she did just that."

Suddenly he realized that she'd come up next to him and was lacing her fingers with his.

"I'm sorry," she said, her eyes huge and dark with sadness. "I'm so sorry your heart was broken."

He meant to laugh at her, to tell her how naive she was being, but something in those big brown eyes wouldn't let him. Instead, he just smiled and let her comfort him.

Looking at her, he was reminded of the feeling he sometimes had as his work-weary gaze settled on a rolling green lawn. A calm serenity seemed to gather around her like a haze, and then her face would turn his way, her eyes sparkling with mischief, and he would think of her as a spray of colorful wild flowers dancing in a spring breeze instead. It just made him happy to look at her.

What a contrast she was to the life he'd been living, with all its boredom, cynicism, and backbiting treachery—the sort of thing he had to deal with every day. It had been exciting at first. He'd reached an important level of power early in his life and he'd used it. Now he didn't feel so powerful anymore. The excitement was gone. All that was left was the endless responsibility.

And she thought *she* was caught in a trap.

A half an hour later, they were out on the lake in the rowboat, drifting happily in the noonday sun.

"So, were you ever engaged?" she asked him out of the blue.

He thought about it for a moment.

"I guess I was. At one point, a long time ago, I was supposed to marry an Italian princess from an old royal family."

She looked at him earnestly. "But you didn't?"

"No. She died."

She nodded. "Giselle told me about it." She looked up at him. "She also said that they would have made the betrothal between you and me instead of Alphonso if it hadn't been for your engagement to the Italian princess."

He frowned. "She shouldn't have said that. I'm not sure it's true."

She stared at him. He was so darn obstinate. "So what exactly happened to the Italian princess?"

"I only met her once, fleetingly." He frowned again, re-membering things best forgotten, things he hadn't thought of for years. "She seemed very frightened," he said softly. "I always wondered…"

There was a shiver in the air between them.

"How did she die?" Julienne asked, tensing for the answer.

He looked at her, hollow-eyed. "She drowned. In the estate swimming pool. She went swimming alone late at night."

He stared into Julienne's eyes and knew they were both thinking the same thing. Did she drown on purpose? Did she love someone else? Did she hate the idea of marrying Andre so much that she would rather die than submit?

"We'll never know," he said, so softly she blinked, won-dering if he'd really said it aloud or if they had both thought it. It made her catch her breath, the way they seemed to be able to invade each other's thoughts at times. Like some kind of magic. Could he really read her mind? Could he see how she really felt about him? And could he stand it?

"Will you ever marry?" she asked him.

He shook his head emphatically. "No."

His easy acceptance of that outraged her. "Why not?"

He looked at her, his eyes haunted. "The only thing that would make me marry would be if I needed to do it for the good of my country."

She winced. "Like I'm expected to do, you mean?"

"Yes. Like you."

She shook her head, laughing softly. "So you're willing to throw yourself on that grenade if it gets tossed your way? But you won't go looking for it on your own?"

He shrugged. "Something like that."

They were silent for a long moment, listening to the splash of the water lapping against the sides of the boat, and then she said, "I think you should marry. And right away, too."

He looked up at her, bemused. "Really?"

"Yes. I think you should marry for love."

He stared at her, his blue eyes hooded. "What if I don't ever love anyone?"

Did he really think she was going to buy that at this point?

"Well, that's your misfortune," she snapped. "*Try* loving someone, why don't you?"

He shook his head, half smiling at her response. "What do you know about love? You don't love anyone. Or do you?"

She threw out her hands, palms up. "Only you, my liege."

Closing his eyes, he threw back his head and sighed deeply. "I never know for sure when you're being serious," he said softly. "Tell me the truth."

"I'm being as honest as I know how," she countered quickly, wishing she dared reach for him. "Ever since my parents died you have been the one person in the world whom I adored. I clung to you, needed you...loved you."

He looked at her as though that wasn't what he'd wanted

to hear. "That's a different kind of love," he said gruffly, looking away.

"Is it? I don't know. You were the center of my universe." She watched him avoid her gaze, and then went on. "And then you stopped coming to see me. You stopped answering my letters. And it was as if everything in my world died."

"Julienne!"

He stared at her, transfixed. What could he say? It was for her own good that he'd done that. He hadn't meant to hurt her. In fact he'd only meant to save her from what might happen if he saw her too much. He should have been more open about his motives. He should have explained why they were necessary. She was so young—how was she to know the dangers that could lurk in the male heart?

But he should have been more careful. He should have made sure she had someone to turn to. Looking at her now, he ached with regret.

Taking her hand in his, he looked into her eyes. "Julienne, I'm sorry," he said simply. "I didn't realize you would be so hurt by my neglect. You are so...so charming and lovely, and everyone loves you. I thought you would hardly notice if I just faded into the background and left you alone. Everyone was so enchanted by you."

She stared into his eyes, sank into their depths. "I didn't want everyone. I wanted you."

Those were the words that stuck with him as the day began to fade. She'd said it starkly. There could be no doubt as to her meaning. And yet there was nothing he could do about it. The future was set in stone.

When they were back in the house he tried to talk to her about Alphonso, about giving him a chance, about trying to like him.

"You do know he collects insects, don't you?" she told him, when she'd had about enough of his goading.

"He collects what?" He leaned closer to try to hear what she'd said.

"Insects," she said, as clearly as she could. "Those things with too many legs."

He sat back, nonplussed but interested. "Well, good. He has a scientific turn of mind."

"No." She shook her head. "It's not like that. He has them in little bottles. All over his room. With little name tags."

He shrugged. "Latin names?"

She sighed. "Andre, try to focus. There are no scientific notations on these bottles. There are names. Nicknames. Like Fred—and Cindy. Those are two beetles he introduced me to. These little bugs aren't part of an experiment. They're pets."

His face began to mirror distaste at last. "Oh, my God."

She nodded, glad he finally got it. "Well might you say so." She flipped her hair back and flashed him a look. "And you want me to marry this man."

He couldn't help it. He laughed aloud. And after a moment she laughed along with him.

"You see how impossible it is?" she challenged him.

He shook his head. "I'll talk to him," he promised. "He's young. He'll change."

"Really? Can I get that in writing?"

He didn't answer, but he didn't have to. She knew in his mind she was already as good as married to Alphie. She was going to have to begin making plans again.

She looked at him, and it was suddenly as though the sun had broken through the clouds. She understood something about him she hadn't realized before. His first allegiance was to his country. He could never be like her, ready to throw it all away and dash for the border. He loved his country, he lived for his country, and he would never do anything to harm it. To him, royalty was the life's blood of this land. Though on the surface one would think of him as a philandering playboy, the Andre inside wasn't that way at all. He was good, responsible and true—a man you could depend on. And she loved him all the more for it.

She didn't want to marry Alphonso. She hated the thought of it. But how was she going to be able to convince a man like this to let her out of her commitment? It wasn't going to happen.

The day blended seamlessly into evening. There was a cold snap in the air, and Andre built a fire in the fireplace while she prepared dinner out of canned supplies she found in the kitchen. After eating, they sat on the couch in front of the fire, each with a glass of wine, and talked softly.

"Okay, Julienne," he said grudgingly. "I have to admit it. You are a very good cook. Everything you make has some sort of special quality that raises it above normal cooking. You've got talent."

She smiled. She already knew that, but to have him notice made it so much more important.

"But as a princess of the realm," he said, "I don't know how you ever thought you could get away with going to pastry school somewhere."

She nodded. "I've thought about it long and hard," she told him. "And looked into resources. And from what I've managed to learn, I think the best thing would be to start a national culinary institute right here in Gemania." She shrugged. "If I actually had the power, I would bring the instructors to me."

He nodded. "Have you spoken to Alphonso about it?" he asked.

She stared at him, color draining from her face. Didn't he understand? Alphonso was not going to be a part of her life. It just couldn't happen. What he thought had nothing to do with her future. But there was no point in arguing about that. She didn't want to ruin their last evening together.

A bit later she watched him staring moodily into the flame and knew she was the source of his problems. She had a strong impulse to go over and take his hand, smile up at him and tell him, *It's all right. I'll do it. Anything that will make you smile again.*

But she would be lying, because it was something that she really couldn't do.

She realized now she'd had a dream in her head when she'd come looking for him. She'd thought he would look up and see her and electricity would zap between them and he would realize she really was the only one for him. She'd even gone so far as to fantasize him saying, *If I can't have you, no one can*, and then they would come together for a passionate kiss, then run off to the South Seas to live on a tropical island under assumed names. It sounded good to her. Obviously he didn't agree.

Turning toward him, she pulled her legs up under her and leaned back against the pillows.

"Do you remember when you kissed me?" she asked him.

He raised one dark eyebrow. "Do you mean last night?"

"No, not that time. At my eighteenth birthday party. The last dance."

She held her breath, watching his reaction. Did he re-member? Or was it so normal for him to kiss a woman he was dancing with that the kiss she held as so special was just one of many in his mind.

He turned toward her slowly, and then he nodded, his eyes dark in the firelight. "I remember," he said softly.

She laughed with relief. "I've lived off of that kiss for three years."

Frowning, he turned away and stared into the fire. "Well, you shouldn't have. That was the catalyst, the reason I had to stay away from you."

"Because of a kiss?"

He glanced back at her. "Because of an emotion. I knew if I was near you…." He turned away and shook his head. "Well, I think you know what would have happened."

"Do I?" she said softly. "What was it? Tell me."

He raked a hand through his thick hair, making it stand on end, and looked at her from under lowered brows.

"I don't know why you want to know all this. I don't know what it helps. But I'll be honest. I was falling in love with you. And I couldn't let that happen."

She was trembling, but not in fear. In sweet anticipa-tion.

"Why not?"

"The treaty." He set down his wine glass and stared into her eyes. "The treaty is fundamental to peace in this country. We can't let anything ruin that."

The country. Yes, of course that was important. But for once couldn't he just look at her and let the feelings between them work? Did he always have to let the country get in the way?

"So…do you love me now?" she asked him.

He took a long time to answer. "It's not fair to ask me that."

She drew her breath in. "I take that as an affirmative."

"Take it any way you like. It doesn't change anything."

"Oh, yes it does." Reaching out, she took his hands in hers and gazed up earnestly into his eyes. "Andre, tell me true. Would you marry me if you could?"

She expected him to react badly, to pull away, to claim such a thing had never entered his mind, but to her surprise he didn't do any of those things. Instead, he looked back at her and said quietly, "I don't know. I never expect to marry anyone."

Her hands gripped his tightly. "Find a way," she begged him. "Oh, please, Andre. Find a way."

He didn't promise to do that, but he did lean toward her. This time his kiss was sweet and simple. She closed her eyes and delighted in it, until he finally pulled away. And then she sighed and snuggled down into the pillows.

"I love you, Andre," she said softly, not even looking at him. "I love you with all my heart."

He didn't answer, and when she finally looked up he was gone. Tears filled her eyes, but she smiled through them. He did love her and she knew it. Now what on earth were they going to do about it?

CHAPTER SEVEN

"ANDRE, look!" Julienne cried as they turned up the long, sloping driveway to the castle. "It looks like just about everyone is here already."

The extended parking lot was filled with limousines, and servants were trundling trunks and clothing racks to and fro.

Andre pulled the Harley up to the entry colonnade. "It's not surprising," he said. "The wedding is only a few days away. And royals like to party at things like this for days at a time."

She sighed. "I was hoping we'd have some time…" Her voice trailed off and she bit her lip. Time for what? She still couldn't put it into words. "I don't know. I can't face all these people. What am I going to say to them?"

"You'll be fine, Princess," he told her, chucking her under her chin. "You'll think of something."

A sort of despair surged over her. She wasn't supposed to be here. She was supposed to be in Paris by now, checking out pastry schools.

"Andre, I only came back with you because you said…"
She shook her head. Had he really said anything she could
cling to? "What I mean is, I'm counting on you to come
through for me this time. Don't leave me waiting at the door
with no hope. Don't do that to me again."

He looked at her. A part of him was astonished. What
did she expect of him? What could he do to change things?
He'd never promised to release her from the treaty. He didn't
have the power to do that.

And yet, looking deep into her eyes, he knew exactly what
she expected. Would he be able to come through for her?

They went into the castle and the bustle was even worse
inside. As they walked through the courtyard toward the
dining room, where a late brunch was being served, she
saw Alphonso at the other side of the fountain. She stuck
her elbow in Prince Andre's ribs.

"There he is," she whispered loudly. "It's Alphie."

Andre craned his neck and shook his head. "I really don't
see the resemblance myself," he told her.

She frowned. "What resemblance?"

He met her gaze sideways. "To a baby seal."

She laughed. "You haven't kissed him," she murmured
as they entered the dining room.

"And I don't think I ever will."

She smiled. "Lucky you."

He smiled back and knew, suddenly, that he had to find a
way to have her for his own. She seemed to be having similar
thoughts.

"Andre, listen to me," she said, grabbing his arm and pulling him into a private area off the courtyard. "I'm not sure
why I came back with you, because I won't marry Alphie.
Don't think you'll talk me into it. I say no. I understand that

you're prepared to do anything for your country. That's who you are. And I'm prepared to do a lot. But I won't do that. There has to be another way to satisfy the country—and especially the Rubiats."

She stared up at him with huge eyes.

"It's up to you to figure out what can be done," she warned him.

He covered her hand with his own. "And you're not involved?" he asked, a smile twisting his wide mouth.

"I don't have the experience and I don't know the ways of diplomacy. You've been doing it for years. Teach me, and I'll join in. I'm willing to do anything you tell me to do, short of marrying Alphie."

He stroked her lips with his forefinger and turned away. "Believe me, Julienne, I'm working on it. Just give me some time. I'll think of something."

In fact, an idea was beginning to take form in his head that might have even more advantages than appeared at first glance. He'd wanted to get out of the pretend-playboy business for quite some time. Though he'd actually left it long ago in spirit, the image remained strong. He was ready to lose that, too. Could this be a blessing in disguise?

He worked on his idea for the rest of the day. He met with Alphonso, getting to know him a bit better, and made Julienne be friendly to him. Strangely enough, the feeling he got from the younger man was out of step with what he would expect from a happy groom. He didn't seem much happier about the prospect of marrying Julienne than she did about marrying him.

"Alphonso seems out of sorts, doesn't he?" he mentioned to her that evening.

"Well, yes. Understandable, under the circumstances."

He nodded. "Perhaps he needs a little distraction. I think I'll take him down to the casino and put him up in my suite for a day or two. Would you mind?"

"Mind?" She made a face. "How about a slow boat to China? Or a trip to the moon? Or…"

He grinned at her. "I get the picture. You have no objection."

Of course she had an objection. If he took Alphonso off somewhere, that meant *he* would be gone as well. And right now she wanted to savor every moment with him she could muster. But she could see that he had a purpose in mind, and she only hoped it would develop into something that would help their situation.

So the two men left for the casino and she stayed where she was, enduring rehearsals and dress fittings and meetings with older royals who needed to be shown respect. And before she knew it the wedding day was dawning, bright and clear.

And she was in a panic. She hadn't heard from Andre. She'd expected to see him back before now. And Alphonso… where was he? What were the two of them up to? She had no way of knowing, and the hour of the ceremony was drawing closer all the time.

What was she to do? She was on a conveyor belt toward matrimony and she wasn't sure if she would be able to jump off in time to save herself. Her only hope was that Alphonso would have cold feet. If he didn't show up she would have a chance at stopping everything in its tracks and making her escape.

She went through all the preparations, feeling like a robot. Cousins and aunts and nieces all gathered round, chattering happily and helping her get ready for the biggest day of

her life. She listened and answered and laughed along with
them, but her mind was with Andre.

Where are you? was the refrain that kept screaming in
her head. *What are you doing? What have you done with
Alphonso?*

She didn't understand why no one thought it strange that
the groom—and the Crown Prince—were missing.

"Oh, they'll show up," people kept telling her. "You know
Prince Andre. He always has something unusual up his
sleeve."

That was all well and good, but she would feel much better
about it if she had some idea of what his unusual trick was
going to be this time. Here she was, watching the driveway
for Andre again, just as she'd been doing for the last three
years every time there was a gathering of the clan. It gave
her a very sick feeling in the pit of her stomach.

"It's time, Your Highness."

It was time. She was standing in the prep room in a beautiful satin and lace gown, with flowers and seed pearls and
everything else one would expect—and the groom hadn't
shown up. But it was time.

A wedding march began to swell through the ancient
halls. She walked out into the foyer where King Harold was
waiting, stepping very carefully. The King smiled at her and
said, "Quite a situation, quite a day. I'm sure you'll both be
very happy." She smiled back at him, assuming he was just
talking pleasantries.

Meanwhile, she was shaking like a leaf and afraid she
might faint. Her only hope was that there would be no one
waiting for her at the end of the aisle. Then she could turn
to the crowd and shrug and say, *Oh, well! I guess we can't
have a wedding today.*

But what would she do if Alphonso was waiting there? She needed an escape plan and she needed it fast.

There were too many people standing and waving and *oohing* as they passed. She couldn't see clearly toward the altar. If he was there, she would run for it. What would all these people think when they saw the bride racing for the exit? Would anyone try to stop her?

She had Popov waiting at the side entrance, just in case. He didn't know that she would be asking him to drive her all the way to the border. He no doubt thought it would be back to the convent. Would he rebel when she told him? She would have to deal with that when she came to it. Right now, her only goal was to make sure she and Alphonso never actually exchanged vows.

The crowd seemed awfully noisy. Weddings were usually quieter affairs, with the music and the minister making all the noise that needed to be made. But right now people were laughing and calling out to each other as though it were a sports event. She looked around, puzzled. What was going on?

There was someone waiting at the bottom of the long walk, waiting to marry her, but she couldn't see clearly. Was it Alphonso? Or someone who was going to call the whole thing off? Her mind was abuzz with too much sound and color. She couldn't think straight.

And then she came around the last bend and there was her groom, standing there for all the world to see. And now she saw why the room was in chaos and commotion.

She gasped, broke away from King Harold, and dashed forward, reaching out and throwing her arms around her husband to be—Prince Andre.

"What—? How—?" she babbled as she held him close, half laughing, half crying with relief.

He leaned down, smiling with all the love in the world in his eyes. The crowd was laughing and applauding, giving him cover to whisper in her ear.

"I've fixed everything," he told her. "I've announced that your engagement to Alphonso was a ruse to pave the way for your wedding to me. Alphonso is happily ensconced at the casino, taking my place there. My father and all the other princes have signed off on the changes. We're free to have a life together."

Free.

That was all she'd ever wanted.

Well, that and the most handsome prince in the land. Just those two things.

Electric with happiness, she joined him at the altar and waited for the ceremony to begin.

"I do," she said at the appropriate time, loud and clear. "Oh, yes, I do!"

* * * * *